DEATH WISH

"Did you hear all the screaming at their house tonight around dinner time?"

Judith stiffened. "I did, as a matter of fact. But I didn't know where it was coming from."

"Goodriches', that's where. It sounded to Ted and me as if they were having a world-class brawl. Honestly, wouldn't you think that when people get older they'd want to live in peace?"

Wearily, Judith leaned against the door frame. "Not really. Fighting and arguing may prove that they're still alive."

Jeanne snorted. "It might be better if Mrs. Goodrich wasn't. Alive, that is. Everybody would be better off if Enid would drop dead."

Everybody, including Judith, was about to find out if Jeanne Ericson was right.

MARY DAHEIM

Nutty As a Fruitcake

A BED-AND-BREAKFAST MYSTERY

AVON BOOKS NEW YORK

AVON BOOKS, INC.
1350 Avenue of the Americas
New York, New York 10019

Copyright © 1996 by Mary Daheim
Inside cover author photo by Images by Edy
Published by arrangement with the author
Visit our website at **http://www.AvonBooks.com**
Library of Congress Catalog Card Number: 96-96422
ISBN: 0-380-77879-3

First Avon Books Printing: November 1996

AVON TRADEMARK REG. U.S. PAT. OFF. AND IN OTHER COUNTRIES, MARCA REGISTRADA, HECHO EN U.S.A.

Printed in the U.S.A.

WCD 10 9 8 7 6 5

ONE

JUDITH GROVER MCMONIGLE Flynn grabbed at the pine branch, felt the ladder fall from under her, and held on with all her might. Her booted feet kicked at the damp air while her gloved hands tightened on the tree limb. Judith hoped that the branch was as sturdy as she was.

A glance at the frosty ground told her it was a good eight-foot drop. In her youth, Judith might have risked it. But at fifty-plus, she wasn't as agile as she used to be. The Christmas season was upon her; she had a bed-and-breakfast to run. There was no point in taking unnecessary chances. Instead, she screamed. Someone would hear her—the Rankerses next door or the Dooleys in back or the Ericsons on the other side. On this first Sunday of Advent, they should all be home.

Judith screamed again. Her husband had gone to Earnest Hardware to buy a new tree stand; her mother was deaf. Or so she pretended. Maybe the Rankerses were having one of their famous family feuds to kick off the yuletide season. The Dooleys might be Christmas shopping. The Ericsons could be jogging. Judith's arms were beginning to ache. The cold air hurt in her lungs as she cried for help a third time.

"Hey, coz," called a voice from below, "how come you're hanging in the tree like that? You make kind of a big ornament. Ha-ha."

Out of the corner of her eye, Judith saw Cousin Renie at the edge of the driveway. She was muffled to her short chin, gazing upward. "Move that ladder, you idiot!" shouted Judith. "Hurry!"

Renie shuffled a bit. "I wish I had my camera. This is good."

Judith's hands were turning numb. "Get me down! If I fall and break my neck, you'll inherit my mother!"

The threat worked. Renie righted the ladder, then angled it under Judith's feet. "It's too soon to make a swag. This is still November. The boughs will dry out by Christmas."

Somewhat shakily, Judith descended the ladder. "I know that, but when you run a B&B, your guests expect you to be decorated right after Thanksgiving. If I have to put up a new swag the week before Christmas, so be it. But I'll buy one. I'm too old to swing from tree branches."

Renie helped Judith collect the clipped boughs as they headed for the house. "Is that one of your guests?" Renie nodded toward the cul-de-sac.

"Where?" Judith asked. "I don't see any strange cars except that pickup parked across the way on the through street."

"That's what I meant," Renie replied. "It's got Oregon plates. I figured it was one of your visitors."

Judith peered the sixty yards to the far side of the street. The pickup was old, shabby, and a mottled orange, with what looked like tools in the back. "I don't have anybody due in from Oregon tonight," she said, setting her collection of boughs down on the porch.

Renie did the same, rubbing pitch from her hands. "Maybe it's some leftover Thanksgiving company for the people who live on the other side of the cul-de-sac."

"Could be." Judith opened the back door. The kitchen, with its old-fashioned high ceiling and modern appliances, smelled of ginger and nutmeg and cinnamon. Renie made a dive for the sheep-shaped cookie jar.

"Yum!" she exclaimed. "Ginger cookies! A great favorite of mine!"

"What isn't?" Judith poured water into a coffee can, then

inserted the freshly cut branches she'd brought inside along with several sprigs of holly. "Speaking of neighbors, I'm proceeding with my plan. The meeting is here, tonight at seven. That's why I made cookies."

Renie had seated herself at the kitchen table and was now devouring her second cookie. She knew that Judith intended to ask the neighbors to join forces in decorating their homes' exteriors for Christmas. Hillside Manor was nestled among six other houses in a cul-de-sac on the side of Heraldsgate Hill. Judith readily acknowledged that the holiday concept was self-serving.

"Sure," she admitted, expanding on the thought as she poured milk for herself and Renie, "I know a festive atmosphere enhances the B&B. But it's a chance for us to do something neighborly. We lead such busy lives that sometimes it feels like we're strangers. The only people I see much of are the Rankerses and the Dooleys, and part of that is because we're all SOTS."

Renie nodded faintly. Although she lived on the other side of the Hill, she was also a SOT, as the parishioners of Our Lady, Star of the Sea Catholic Church were familiarly known. "I know. I've never actually met some of our newer neighbors. I hole up with my graphic design business in the basement den and all I can see out the window are the local cats and an occasional squirrel."

"It's a shame," Judith said, her strong features softening in a commiserating expression. "We live in the city, cheek by jowl, and we hardly recognize each other. We're just too isolated and self-absorbed. To tell the truth, I always feel guilty about expecting our neighbors to put up with the comings and goings of my guests."

Renie snatched another cookie. "It helped some when Bill organized our block watch a few years ago. But not everybody comes to the meetings. Even when they do, some of them move away a few months later. We've got three rentals along our street."

"Carl Rankers is our block watch captain," Judith said, as her cat, Sweetums, meandered into the kitchen. "We haven't met in over a year. I think it's because I married a cop. Everybody has a false sense of security.''

Renie was glaring at Sweetums, who was glaring right back. "Joe should give Carl a nudge. Bill and I try to schedule a meeting every eight or nine months." Sweetums took a swipe at Renie's Nubuck loafers; Renie pretended to claw Sweetums; Sweetums, in fact, clawed Renie—on the ankle. "Damn!" Renie cried. "Your cat is awful! Have you thought about having him put to sleep?''

"Put to sleep?" Joe Flynn poked his head into the kitchen. "Are you talking about my mother-in-law?'' His voice was hopeful.

Judith scowled at her husband. "We're talking about Sweetums. Or, rather, Renie was." Judith reached down to stroke the animal's long orange-and-gray fur. "She's just jealous because her kids are allergic to cats, so she's deprived. Did you get a tree stand?''

Joe grimaced. "I sure did. Industrial strength, fifty bucks. We could put a telephone pole in it. In fact," he continued, shrugging out of his khaki field coat, "why don't we do just that? A ten-foot Douglas fir is going to cost us another eighty bucks. On the way home, I priced the ones they're unloading at Nottingham Florists.''

Judith made a face at her husband. His first wife hadn't cared much about holiday decor, except when it came to lining the garbage cans with empty Jack Daniels' bottles. Judith's first husband had preferred lining his stomach with almost everything, including the year he'd eaten a cluster of blue plastic grapes off the tree.

"We've always had a big tree," Judith declared, "even when I was a kid." One hand gestured in the direction of the long paneled living room. In her mind's eye, Judith saw a succession of trees—or were they years, with the tree always the same? She smiled, then glanced at Renie, who was fixated on the cookie jar. "Grandma and Grandpa Grover used to decorate it the day before Christmas, and no one else saw it until Christmas Eve. Do you remember how we used to try to peek under the curtain they put up in the middle of the room?''

Renie also smiled as she reached for another cookie. "I sure do."

Judith slapped Renie's hand. "Stop that, you hog. I have to save those for tonight."

Almost fifty years of love and memories prevented Renie from reacting with more than a twitch of her eyebrows. "Everybody would congregate at the far end of the room and we'd wait for Santa," she said, now looking at Joe, who had settled in at the table with a glass of beer. "There'd be—what?—thirty of us, with all the aunts and uncles and cousins. Then we'd hear the jingle of a bell outside. The part of the room that was curtained off would be dark. We'd all gasp and everybody would stop talking and Santa would come in through the French doors. He'd start to talk to us from behind the curtain and ask each of us kids if we'd been good and what we wanted for Christmas. We'd be absolutely agog. Then he'd say some things to the grown-ups that we didn't understand—like asking Auntie Vance if she was getting anything and asking Uncle Corky if he was getting *any*. My mother would ask if Mrs. Santa was putting out cookies and Santa would say that Mrs. Santa wasn't putting out, period. The grown-ups would laugh some more. And us kids could hardly stand it, waiting for Santa to turn on the tree lights. Finally, he would, and we could see them through the curtain—and then he was gone. Uncle Corky and Uncle Al would take the curtain down because they were so tall, and there would be that great big shining tree with those beautiful presents spread out all over the floor." Renie's brown eyes had grown very bright.

Judith's lower lip quivered with emotion. Her first Christmas memory was when she was four, in 1945. The uncles—and Aunt Ellen—had come home from the war. They were battle-scarred and forever changed, but she had been too young to realize that. What she remembered most was the adults' restraint, which gradually changed into unbridled hilarity. The Grover clan had always been noisy, full of laughter, choking back tears. But the year that Judith turned four and began to take in the world around her, she saw her parents, her grandparents, her aunts and uncles, and the usual shirttail hangers-on in a strange, raucous outpouring of what she later realized was relief.

"Christmas meant war," Joe was saying, and Judith was caught short, aware that her reminiscences had caused her to lose the conversational thread. "My dad always got drunk. More drunk, I should say. My mother would lock herself in the bedroom and cry for about four days, usually right through Christmas. My brothers and I would unwrap our presents by ourselves, then get into a fight over who got the best stuff. That was pretty pointless—there wasn't any 'best stuff.' My family couldn't afford nice gifts. We got socks and underwear and maybe a shirt. One year, my holiday highlight was a football, autographed by Sammy Baugh. That was really special, until I found out my dad had won it in a poker game at the local tavern. Then my brother Paul borrowed it and some punk beat the crap out of him and stole the ball. That's what I remember about Christmas."

Renie, who'd never heard the story before, gaped at Joe. Judith, however, hung her head. "I shouldn't brag about what wonderful times we had. Renie and I were lucky."

Joe's laugh was forced. "Or dumb. You two sound like a pair of Alices, walking in a winter wonderland."

"What's wrong with that?" Renie retorted. "Selective memory is a great asset. Why dwell on the bad stuff?"

Joe's eyes snapped at Renie. "What if that's all you've got? Do you want to hear about my grown-up holidays, with a wife crooning carols into a bottle of bourbon? How about having your daughter and your stepkids ask why Mom won't wake up for Christmas dinner? Then, for a really jolly-holly time, you get called out to somebody else's unhappy home where Mom just sank the carving knife in Dad's chest. The only sparkle you see is the glint off the handcuffs you're putting on whichever member of the family is going down for Murder One. Christmas memories!" Joe passed his hands over his face and shook himself. "Sleigh bells? How about sirens and screams and the sound of your spouse falling face first into the cranberry sauce?"

"Not here," Judith said, more sharply than she intended. "We've spent three Christmases together, and they've been fun. Or so it seemed to me."

Joe's expression grew sheepish. "Yeah, right, they've been . . . fine. It's going to take me a couple of decades to get over the first fifty years, okay?"

Judith averted her eyes. While she knew of Joe's unhappy childhood and his miserable first marriage, she hadn't realized that her husband wasn't as full of holiday enthusiasm as she was. He had *seemed* to enjoy the previous Christmases. But maybe he'd been pretending.

Joe saw the melancholy in Judith's face; he reached across the table to ruffle her silver-streaked hair. "Forget it, Jude-girl. I'm doing my best to be a merry elf. But while you're still calling me Scrooge in your mind, I'd better give you another piece of negative news—the Goodriches aren't coming tonight. I saw George when I pulled into the cul-de-sac. His grandsons had just arrived."

"Paying homage to Grandma?" Judith sounded caustic. "Those kids hardly ever visit their grandparents."

"They aren't kids exactly," Joe noted, sipping his beer. "They both look close to thirty. Anyway, you'll have to count Enid and George out for this evening."

Judith frowned. "How come? Is it because they don't want to decorate, or is Mrs. Goodrich sick again?"

Longingly, Joe gazed at the cookie jar. Judith rolled her black eyes and held up one finger. Joe removed a cookie. Renie growled at him. Sweetums, who had curled up at Judith's feet, stretched, scratched, and growled at Renie.

"I'm gone," Renie announced, getting out of the chair. She paused to delve into her purse. "Here's Auntie Vance's coffee cake recipe you asked for. I've got to stop off at my mother's with her fruitcake mix. She says if she doesn't make it today it won't have time to set before Christmas."

Joe winced. "I hate fruitcake. It's always gooey and full of nuts."

"Not my mother's," Renie countered. "She makes the dark kind and doesn't put in nuts because I'm allergic. It's soaked

in whiskey and not only does it taste terrific, but you can get
a buzz on if you eat enough. See you.'' Renie sailed through
the kitchen and the back hallway, and out of the house.

Judith sighed into her empty milk glass. ''So what's going
on with the Goodriches? I'd hoped they wouldn't spoil a unan-
imous vote.''

''Enid's arthritis is bothering her,'' Joe said with a trace of
asperity. ''She doesn't want to come out at night. And poor
old George doesn't like leaving her alone.''

''Enid's a pain in the butt,'' Judith said bluntly. ''She's
always been a hypochondriac. Even when I was a kid, Mrs.
Goodrich was always ailing. I felt sorry for her children. And
for George.''

Shrugging, Joe got up from the table. ''You've known them
forever. I haven't. Maybe you can talk them into stringing
some lights on their rhododendron bushes. The bottom line is
that they're not coming to the meeting.'' He paused, opening
the refrigerator door. ''I'm doing dinner tonight. How about
chicken kiev?''

Judith brightened. ''Sounds good. Make two for Mother.''

Joe shot his wife an ironic glance. ''If I make it, will she
eat it?''

''We won't tell her. We never do.''

''Okay.'' Joe rummaged in the freezer section.

Judith put the milk glasses in the dishwasher. She was accustomed to the hostility between her husband and her mother.
Gertrude Grover had never forgiven Joe Flynn for dumping
her daughter more than a quarter of a century earlier. Judith
and Joe had been engaged, but another woman had intervened.
Never mind that Joe had been drunk at the time and that the
other woman had taken advantage of his state to whisk him
off to Las Vegas. Never mind, either, that Joe's inebriation
had been caused by his first encounter with teenaged drug-
related deaths: Others might forgive a rookie policeman's re-
vulsion, but not Gertrude. Nor, for many years, did Judith
understand what had happened to her erstwhile fiancé. She had
been left almost literally at the altar. Retaliation had come
in the four-hundred-pound shape of Dan McMonigle. Never

had revenge proved so sour. Judith had lived as Dan's wife for eighteen years, until he had—as she so unscientifically but aptly put it—blown up at the age of forty-nine. It had only been by chance that Judith and Joe had met again, when a fortune teller had been poisoned at Hillside Manor's dinner table. Joe Flynn had shown up as the homicide detective of record. Judith had tried to hide her shock, her dismay—and her feelings. Joe was still married to Vivian Flynn. But Vivian—or Herself, as Judith called her archrival—had long since buried the marriage under a pile of bourbon-on-the-rocks.

Now, almost five years later, Judith and Joe were together. They had been married for three and a half years, while Herself had gone into voluntary exile in Florida. Though the Flynns had spent the past three Christmases together, this would be the first year that Joe's daughter, Caitlin, would join them. Caitlin lived and worked in Switzerland. Judith was excited at the prospect of spending some time with her stepdaughter. The two women had met only once before, at Joe and Judith's wedding.

But Caitlin Flynn wouldn't arrive until two days before Christmas. Judith's son, Mike, and his girlfriend, Kristin, would get into town a day earlier. Judith's black eyes danced.

"You look pretty happy for somebody who's about to be sabotaged," Joe remarked as he put four chicken breasts in the microwave and poked the defroster command. "I take it you figure you can use your legendary charm to coax the Goodriches to go along with your little plan?"

Judith wrenched her mind away from the family holiday gathering. "Well—maybe." Judith's greatest asset in running the B&B was her ability to get along with virtually every type of personality. Her compassion and openness not only established rapport but also invited confidences. Perhaps she could work her wiles on the Goodriches. "I think I'll wander down the street before I make that coffee cake."

Putting on her heavy green jacket, Judith exited through the front door. Usually, the main entrance was reserved for guests. At present, Hillside Manor had only two rooms occupied. The

B&B had been full since before Thanksgiving, but the visitors who had come to spend the holiday with relatives or get a jump start on Christmas shopping had all headed home by Sunday morning. The two new sets of guests were both married couples who were passing through on their way to California and Arizona. Neither couple had yet checked in.

It was not quite four o'clock, but the pale globe of sun that fought its way through the gray cloud cover was already sinking over the mountains to the west. Standing halfway down Heraldsgate Hill, Judith could also see the concrete, steel, and glass high-rises that formed the downtown skyline. She never tired of the view, which juxtaposed modern civilization with the natural wonders of sea, forest, and mountains. Judith knew she was blessed with not only the powers of observation but of appreciation. The holidays always heightened her senses. Maybe it was the colorful decorations or the sounds of familiar carols or the aroma of seasonal delicacies. She hoped it was all of those things, and more. Amid the frenzy of Christmas preparations, Advent still brought Judith a sense of inner peace.

Awash with communal feeling, Judith strolled along the cul-de-sac. Idly, she noticed that the old pick-up truck was gone from across the street. She passed the Ericsons' ultramodern makeover, then the first of two modest brick Tudors. The Goodriches lived between the Ericsons and Mrs. Swanson at the corner. Jeanne and Ted Ericson were in their thirties, so far childless, and held responsible jobs downtown. Ted was an architect who had redesigned the original 1920s nondescript bungalow. Jeanne was a stockbroker with a large investment firm. Mrs. Swanson had been a Japanese war bride whose husband, Andrew, had died shortly after Judith moved back to the family home. While Miko Swanson was of another culture and a different generation, she and Judith had found common ground in the loss of their husbands within the same six-month period. The greatest difference had been that Mrs. Swanson had been overcome by her loss. Judith, in all honesty, was not: Her initial reaction had been relief. Sorrow had come later, and even then, it was more for Dan than for herself.

The Swanson and the Goodrich houses were mirror images of each other. While the Goodrich home faced the cul-de-sac, the Swanson residence looked out onto the cross street. Judith started along the stepping stones that led through a carefully tended, if now fallow, garden. There was no sign of visitors, so Judith assumed that the grandsons had left. It was only when she reached the front porch that she remembered the Goodriches' preference for using the back door. Sighing, Judith retraced her steps and followed the driveway that the Goodriches shared with the Ericsons.

A wooden gate led onto the Goodrich property. The latch opened easily. Even in late autumn, the small backyard was immaculately tended. Judith knew that George did all of the work himself, either out of love for gardening, or as an excuse to escape Enid.

Passing the garbage can and recycling bins, Judith noticed a neatly stacked woodpile and a chopping block. Sheltered under the porch were several empty clay pots of varying sizes, a couple of trowels, a shovel, a rake, and an edger. Just beyond the wooden fence stood the Goodriches' single garage. Its doors were closed, but Judith knew that George's aging but well-maintained Dodge sedan sat protected from the elements.

She stepped onto the lattice-enclosed porch. The single chime of the doorbell finally summoned George Goodrich. Judith hadn't seen George up close for some time, and was surprised at how wrinkled his long face had grown. But of course he must be close to eighty, Judith realized. The two Goodrich children were a few years older than Judith.

"Judith," George said in mild surprise as he adjusted his glasses on his thin nose. "What can we do for you?"

Judith shuffled a bit on the doormat. "I have to ask a favor." She smiled. "May I come in?"

George Goodrich's expression was uncertain. He pushed his glasses up on his thin nose, then turned to call over his shoulder: "Enid—it's Judith Grover. She wants to ask us something. Is it all right for her to come in?"

Judith was used to still being called by her maiden name
among the oldsters on Heraldsgate Hill. But George's defer-
ence to his wife was jarring. Nor did Enid Goodrich reply
immediately. When she did, her voice was petulant.

"Very well. But she must know I'm in poor health. I can't
be putting myself out for much of anything these days."

With a diffident smile, George stepped aside. Judith entered
the immaculate kitchen. It had been a long time since she'd
actually stood inside the Goodrich house. Strangely, nothing
seemed changed. The white counter tiles probably had come
with the house some seventy years earlier. They were faintly
yellowed and cracked, but scrubbed to perfection. The For-
mica was of a later vintage, but it, too, shone in the late afternoon light. Crocheted pot holders hung pristinely from
magnets on the unblemished refrigerator. There wasn't a sign
of anyone ever having consumed so much as a crumb in the
Goodrich kitchen.

George led Judith through a small hallway off the equally
tidy dining room. Mrs. Goodrich was in the master bedroom,
reclining on one of the twin beds. She had been watching a
big color TV console, but condescended to have George turn
the program off. The furniture was old and solid but unre-
markable in design except for the fluted mirror on the dressing
table. A medicinal smell hung over the room, which wasn't
surprising, given the collection of bottles and jars and drinking
glasses that crowded Enid's nightstand. Its mate, which Judith
assumed belonged to George, held a single etched glass, a
bottle of liquid antacid, a clock-radio, and a spectacles case.
A brass reading lamp hung over Enid's bed; the space above
George's headboard was bare. The bureau and dressing table
held cosmetics and cologne and jewelry cases and a set of
quilted satin organizers. Even the clothes that Judith could see
in the half-opened closet all appeared to belong to Mrs. Goodrich.

"Judith," Enid said in a musing voice that conveyed faint
disapproval. "Do you want to borrow something? If you do,
you promise to bring it back. That Swanson woman has had
our lawn edger for over a month."

"Now, dear," George began in a soothing tone, "we've borrowed a few things from her. I still haven't returned her hatchet after we got that load of wood for the fireplace."

"Wood!" Enid spoke scornfully. "Now that was plain foolishness! Wasteful, too. When have we built a fire in the fireplace? All it does is get ash on my nice beige carpet. Besides, no one's allowed in the living room except special company." With a long-suffering expression, Enid turned to Judith. "Naturally, I haven't been able to entertain for a long time. I'm much too ill. George seems to forget that. Among other things." She shot her husband a malevolent glance, then resumed speaking to her visitor. "Now exactly what is it you wanted to borrow from me?"

"No, it's not that," Judith began, wondering if she should sit on the cedar chest at the end of Enid's bed. There were no chairs, and she doubted if Enid would tolerate anyone sharing space on the mattress. "As you know, I've asked the neighbors to . . ."

"Neighbors!" Enid sneered. She was a small woman who, as Judith recalled, had once been almost pretty. Time had not treated her kindly. The strawberry-blond hair had been dyed until it had lost not only its luster but its fullness, too. Despite her thin frame, the once firm jawline sagged into jowls, and the skin under the eyes was puffy. Her aquiline nose had sharpened, and the mouth, which Judith remembered being carefully outlined in bright pink, was clamped into a tight line that would have rebelled at any hint of a smile.

"Neighbors!" Enid repeated, this time almost wistfully. "What kind of neighbors have we got these days? Those Ericsons are never home, Mrs. Swanson isn't what I'd call friendly, the Porters always have a bunch of cars they're supposedly fixing, and the Steins are just plain snooty. I remember a time when everybody was pleasant. Except for that bunch of rowdies with their outdoor picnics and gallons of beer and ukeleles and singing half into the night! Now *there* was a noisy nuisance! We had to call the police at least four times."

"That was *my* family." Judith realized that her eyes had narrowed and her jaw had set. "I believe you're referring to the wedding reception for Auntie Vance and Uncle Vince in 1951.''

Enid glared at Judith. ''Did they get married *four* times? What about your uncle? The one who put the cherry bomb in the barbecue on Independence Day? Every year, I cringe when July rolls around. His antics are completely unnerving.''

Judith had stopped wondering about sitting down. Now she only wanted to figure out how she could leave without harsh words. ''That was Uncle Cliff,'' she said stiffly, recalling the puckishness of Renie's father. ''He's been dead for twenty years.''

Enid was obviously startled but quickly regained her aplomb. ''I should think so!''

Judith sighed. ''Look, I know you don't feel up to coming to our meeting tonight. We're going to discuss outdoor Christmas decorations. I thought it would be nice for all of us in the cul-de-sac to put up some lights or something this year. Would you like to join in?''

A contemptuous look crossed Enid's face. ''Christmas? What about the Steins? They're Jewish. Mrs. Swanson is Japanese. I've never known the Ericsons to attend any church. And the Porters are Negroes! What does Christmas mean to any of those people?''

Having forgotten that Enid Goodrich was impossible, Judith surrendered. ''Okay, forget it. I won't impose any longer. Good-bye, Mrs. Goodrich.'' Judith gave George an apologetic little smile. ''Sorry I bothered you.''

George's long face had fallen so far that it looked as if his chin could touch the top button on his worn cardigan. ''Yes, well, it's no bother. Except that . . .''

''George!'' Enid's sharp voice cut through the slightly stale air. ''Get my pain medicine! It's after four! And put ice in the water this time. It was lukewarm at noon.''

''Yes, dear.'' George wore his air of resignation like an albatross. Back in the kitchen, he headed straight for the cupboard. Judith glimpsed a vast array of pharmaceutical bottles. ''Enid suffers so from her arthritis,'' George explained as he peered at the various labels. ''Headaches, too. And her stomach gives her fits. It's so hard to fix food that won't upset her.''

"That's too bad," Judith said, her usual sympathy at a low ebb. "Thanks, George. I'll see you later." She reached for the doorknob.

"Uh . . ." George was running the tap water. "Last year you . . . ah . . . brought over some really wonderful little cookies. And candy. I was . . . um . . . wondering if . . . well, Enid can't eat sweets as a rule, but . . . er . . ."

Taking in the pitiful old face, Judith smiled. "Of course. I usually make spritz cookies and fudge about two weeks before Christmas. My mother does her divinity and penuche about that time, too. We'll be sure to see that you get some, okay?"

George returned the smile, his tired gray eyes lighting up behind the thick glasses. "That's very kind of you, Judith. And your mother, too. Thank you. At year's end, I still help with the meat packing company's books. They get so busy, you see. It's nice to have a little something to nibble on when you're working into the wee hours. It's not just an indulgence—it's good for me, when my ulcers act up." George glanced away, as if embarrassed by his frailty as well as his industriousness. He probably was unsettled, Judith thought, no doubt because Enid resented any attention being expended on anyone but her. "And . . . uh . . ." he went on, nervously looking at Judith once more, "I'm sorry we couldn't be more . . . helpful."

So am I, Judith thought, but she bit back the words. George had enough problems without hearing a neighbor's sarcasm. "That's okay. Take care." She closed the door quietly.

Coming out of the driveway, she noticed the pickup truck on the other side of the through street. It hadn't been parked there over the Thanksgiving holiday. Judith had never seen it until that afternoon, when Renie had pointed it out. Mentally, she shrugged. It wasn't her problem, as long as whoever owned it didn't park in the already crowded cul-de-sac.

Instead of going directly into her house, Judith stopped off at the converted toolshed behind the garage. It took eight knocks before her mother appeared. Gertrude Grover leaned on her walker and exhaled a cloud of blue smoke.

"When's supper?" she demanded.

For once, Judith ignored the question. "Mother, have you ever wanted to kill Enid Goodrich?"

"Sure," Gertrude replied cheerfully, puffing away at her cigarette. "A couple of years ago, after she threw a bucket of water on Sweetums, I had it out with the old bat. I warned her that if she ever did that again I'd stick her big fat head in a pot of sauerkraut and wienies and hold her down until she yelled '*Heil*, Gertrude.' How come you ask?"

Having managed to sidestep both Gertrude and her walker, Judith flopped onto the sofa. "She's probably the most disagreeable woman I've ever met. How has poor George put up with her all these years?"

"George!" Gertrude's raspy voice was full of derision. Shaking her head, she clumped over to sit beside her daughter. "Now there's a poor excuse for a man. No spine. The worst thing that ever happened to him—besides marrying Enid, I mean—was retirement. George Goodrich worked for over forty years as a bookkeeper at that meat packing place out past the railroad depot. He didn't quit until he was forced to, when he turned seventy. Then he had to stick around the house, waiting on that wife of his hand and foot. What a sap."

Briefly, Judith reflected on the Life and Times of George Goodrich. It was easy for her mother to criticize a much put-upon spouse. Judith's father, Donald Grover, had been a soft-spoken intellectual who had rarely raised his voice in anger. He had been a loving husband and a doting father. Gertrude had had it all, which was what made it so difficult for her to go on without Donald for over thirty years. It was also, Judith knew, what made Gertrude so difficult.

But Judith had lived with Dan McMonigle for eighteen years. She understood how one partner could be forced to endure the relentless unpleasantness of the other. There was the basic commitment, which she—and apparently George— did not take lightly. There was also love, or something like it, that no one else could possibly comprehend. Then there were children and habit and ultimately, fear: fear of change, fear of the future, fear of how the rejected spouse might retaliate. Judith recognized all those emotions, though now, almost eight years after Dan's death, musing on them was like unwrapping ugly, little-used Christmas decorations that had been shoved to the back of the cupboard.

"You never know," Gertrude was saying as she stubbed out her cigarette in an ashtray someone had swiped for her from Harold's Club in Reno, "what really goes on with other folks. Most of 'em are just plain nuts. Or dumb as a bag of dirt."

"I don't think George is dumb," Judith replied a bit vaguely. "Enid, maybe." But her mother was right. You could never be sure about other people's needs and desires. Years ago, Uncle Cliff had given Judith and Renie some sage advice: When the neighbors shut the door, remember what side you're standing on. Nobody can see through wood or into the human heart. Judith wondered if Uncle Cliff had been talking about the Goodriches even then.

"Their kids come by often," Judith pointed out. "At least Art does. I see his car parked out in front of the house a couple of times a week."

Gertrude pulled at the sleeve of her baggy cardigan. "Say, kiddo, have you put a meter on the heat in this dump I call home? I'm freezing my nummies off in this place. We had frost as thick as your husband's head last night."

Since Judith felt as if she were in a sauna, she started to protest. It would do no good, however. It never did. Even in the summer, Gertrude complained of being cold.

"Maybe we could get you a space heater," Judith suggested. "If you promise not to set the place on fire."

Gertrude turned to glare at her daughter. "What do you think I am? Daffy?" Before Judith could offer a denial—or agreement—Gertrude continued speaking: "Art Goodrich is a fine boy. He takes care of his parents. Why, he even dropped in to see this poor old coot a couple of weeks ago. Or did I tell you that already?" Gertrude's small, wizened face puckered with genuine puzzlement. Of late, her memory sometimes failed her.

"I think you mentioned it," Judith answered tactfully. "He'd lost his job at the Boring Airplane Company."

"Right." Gertrude brightened, obviously relieved to have recalled the incident. "He'd worked there for almost twenty years, but the company's had a lot of those whatdoyacallits—cutbacks or something. He's only fifty-seven, so he figures he'd better get another job until he can collect Social Security."

"Poor Art." Judith's voice was full of sympathy. She remembered him as a blond, good-natured kid who was just enough older to be the natural leader of the other children in the cul-de-sac. But Art had deferred the honor to Louis "Knuckles" Nordhoff, who was a year younger, but much tougher, and who had grown up in the house now occupied by the Rankerses. Art, as Judith recalled, had never been ambitious. He and his wife, JoAnne, were the parents of the grandsons Joe had seen visiting Enid and George.

Rising from the couch, Judith patted her mother's shoulder. "I'd better check on dinner. I'll bring it over in a bit."

"A bit?" Gertrude bristled. "It's almost five now. Why do you and lardhead have to eat supper so late? Last night it was almost six-thirty!"

There was no point in arguing. Not about "supper," not about the temperature of the converted toolshed, not about Joe, not about *anything*. Nor did Judith want to quarrel with her mother. There were worse things than being set in one's ways. That came not only out of habit but from a desire to retain what little independence was left at Gertrude's advanced age. Judith gave her mother a feeble, if fond, smile. There were worse things than Gertrude.

Such as Enid Goodrich.

TWO

JOE'S CIGAR DIDN'T quite quench the aroma of coffee cake, fresh from the oven. Judith watched with pleasure as her guests wolfed down the warm streusel-topped slices and, in between, munched on ginger cookies. As ever, she felt a sense of satisfaction in making other people happy. The years with Dan had been an exercise in futility: She could cook and bake and roast and fry until she was exhausted, but Dan was never satiated. The hole inside her first husband had been of his own making, and nothing could fill it.

"Okay," said Naomi Stein, brushing a few crumbs off her chic charcoal slacks, "we'll pretend we've got Hannukah lights."

Hamish Stein, who owned two picture-framing shops, was known as "Ham" to friends and neighbors. "Why not?" he chuckled. "We've always pretended to have a Hannukah bush. Any color preference for the lights?"

Judith smiled at the Steins. "To each his—or her—own. I just want the cul-de-sac to look festive."

Miko Swanson sat very straight in one of the beige-and-blue side chairs. She was a tiny woman of about seventy whose beautiful skin was virtually unlined. Judith suspected, however, that the black hair was courtesy of Chez Steve's salon.

"I think I'd like those very small white lights. What are they called?" Her carefully tended eyebrows arched. "Fairy lights?"

"That's right," Jeanne Ericson said, her dark blond page boy flipping on her shoulders as she turned to look at Mrs. Swanson. "Maybe we can do something with music. You know, Christmas tapes." She gazed questioningly at her husband.

Ted Ericson looked thoughtful. "Sure," he said at last in his usual careful manner. "We could get some of those choir-boy statues that light up."

"Dickens carolers," his wife put in. "I like them better. The choirboys always look sort of dim."

Everyone laughed. Judith got up to pour more coffee and tea. Joe passed the cookie plate around. The mood was congenial, though it was clear from the start that some of the neighbors hadn't exchanged more than casual greetings in quite a while.

The thought was expressed aloud by Rochelle Porter, a big, hearty woman with closely cropped gray hair. "You know, it's just a crime the way we all hole up in our houses and never really visit with each other. What's the matter with us these days? Are we afraid? Has city life turned us into people-haters?"

"Yes." It was Mrs. Swanson, nodding sadly. "We watch TV and read the newspapers and fear leaving our own property. Even behind locked doors, we are afraid. No one is safe. Every day, you hear about a new violation."

The group grew suddenly solemn. Mrs. Swanson lowered her eyes, seemingly embarrassed by her candor. Arlene Rankers broke the uneasy silence.

"Underwear," she said in a clear, firm voice. The others turned to stare. "Don't you remember? The Underwear Thief. That's where it all started in this neighborhood. It was 1973. He was deranged."

Among the guests, only Mrs. Swanson and the Rankerses had resided in the cul-de-sac twenty years ago. Judith, Dan, and Mike were living in one of a series of dilapidated rentals south of the city. But Gertrude had complained loudly about the so-called underwear thief, even though she had not been a victim.

"So he doesn't want my bloomers," Gertrude had said two decades earlier. "What if I sew some lace on 'em? Talk about a fancy pants!"

The miscreant had never been caught, though it was rumored to be the somewhat fey teenaged son of the family who lived on the property now occupied by the Ericsons. Vaguely, Judith recalled that the young man eventually had become headmaster of an all-boys prep school in the East. With women's underwear hard to find in such surroundings, Judith paled at the former neighbor lad's possible derelictions in later years.

"It was terrible," Arlene went on, one hand at her breast. "We lived in constant fear. We put dead bolts on the doors. We got a watchdog, Farky. We were afraid to go to sleep at night. All I could think of was, *What if some crazy pervert wants my underpants?*"

"You left them out on the back porch." Carl Rankers's expression was droll. "We always had a dead bolt on the front door, but you never remember to lock the back at all. And the only stranger Farky ever chased was my brother from North Dakota."

"Exactly!" Arlene nodded her red-gold curls with zest. "That's what I was saying, it was a tempest in a teapot. We worry about so many things that never happen. You have to trust in the good Lord to keep you safe and let him worry about your underpants."

The statement was vintage Arlene, exhibiting both her good heart and her contradictory nature. Judith suppressed a smile but noted that the mood had once again lightened. Sitting on two of the dining room chairs, Rochelle and Gabe Porter had their heads together, conferring about their participation in the neighborhood decorations.

"We'd like to go with something on the roof," Gabe said, turning to the rest of the gathering. He was a big, dark-skinned man with glasses and a slim, trim mustache who worked as a manager for a produce wholesaler. "How about cutouts of

Santa and his reindeer? My folks used to do that, and they gave us the stuff when they moved into the retirement home. I think it's in the garage.''

"Probably," Arlene said with her customary candor. "Your cars certainly aren't parked there. You've got them all over the street. Why don't you decorate the hoods?''

Fortunately, everyone laughed, especially Gabe Porter. The family owned four vehicles, including two beaters that consumed Gabe's attention on weekends. When the Porters' college-age daughter was home and their two married children visited, it was difficult for Judith's guests to find parking places in the cul-de-sac. The five younger Rankerses also owned their share of rolling stock. But of course Judith would never complain: Hillside Manor's clientele was also an imposition on the neighbors.

"I may have to scrub and paint the figures," Gabe was saying, in reference to Santa and his reindeer. "We'll string some lights on the house, too.''

Rochelle nodded. "All the colors. For Santa.''

Naomi Stein snapped her fingers. "I've got it! We'll do blue and white. That suits Hannukah better than green and red and orange.''

Carl was watching Arlene expectantly. She sat deep in thought, with a hand under her chin. "I'd like to put the Holy Family in the front yard. We'll get one of those sets with everybody—the shepherds, the angels, the Wise Men, the carpet cleaners.''

Mrs. Swanson's fine eyebrows arched again. "Excuse me—perhaps I don't understand all the Christmas customs even after so many years in America. But who are these carpet cleaners?''

Carl, however, didn't hear Mrs. Swanson. He was now looking at his wife with a mulish expression. "We don't have room for more than Jesus, Mary, and Joseph. Where do you think we'll put a bunch of shepherds and camels and the rest of them?''

"We can line up some of them on the front walk," Arlene declared. "People can come in the back door.''

Carl narrowed his blue eyes. "Why not? It's always open. How about hanging the angels from the cedar tree?"

"That's wonderful!" Arlene beamed at her husband. "The camels could be coming out of the garage."

Seeing one of the infamous Rankers debates brewing, Judith hastily intervened: "All of you have wonderful ideas. I'm really thrilled that we're going to do this together. Joe and I talked it over at dinner tonight, and we want to put up a miniature lighted New England village. I checked with my cousin who's a designer, and she says we can get the pieces at a local display shop."

Naomi Stein and Rochelle Porter chorused their approval. Arlene cocked her head to one side. "That's sweet, but what about the lobsters?"

Bewildered, Judith stared. "The lobsters?"

"You could serve them, of course. To your guests." Arlene's pretty face was very serious. "And the Dooleys— they shouldn't be left out."

Arlene finally had a point. "They aren't actually in the cul-de-sac," Judith said. "I thought of asking them, but they face the other street, to the west. If we asked the Dooleys, we'd have to include the rest of the block."

Hamish Stein gestured with his coffee mug. "I agree. Let's keep it among ourselves. Frankly, we don't know the Dooleys, except by sight."

The large white Cape Cod inhabited by Corinne and Darren Dooley and their passel of offspring sat behind Hillside Manor and the Rankers' house. The Dooleys were not only over-the-fence neighbors to Judith but fellow SOTS as well. Judith knew her rationale for leaving them out of the decorating scheme was logical, but she didn't want to hurt the family's feelings.

"Never mind the Dooleys," said Jeanne Ericson, who could see their Cape Cod as well as a corner of Judith's property from her deck. "What about the Goodriches? They *are* part of the cul-de-sac. Is Mrs. G. too ornery to string a few lights outside?"

"Well, no," Judith began.

"Hell, yes," said Joe. "The old bat practically threw my wife out the door this afternoon."

Judith frowned at Joe. "That's an exaggeration. Sort of. But she doesn't seem inclined to take part."

Jeanne Ericson tossed her head, this time with disdain. "To heck with her. No wonder the kids in this neighborhood call her Mrs. Badbitch. She's always carping about the driveway we share with them. Or else our trees are growing over into her yard. But the point is," Jeanne went on with her usual ability to keep a discussion on course, "there are only seven houses in the cul-de-sac. It's going to look odd if one of them is dark. I say we volunteer to decorate for the Goodriches. It doesn't have to be anything fancy—maybe some of those Mexican lights—you know, paper bags with candles and sand inside."

Judith was looking dubious. "Well—George wouldn't mind, but Enid . . ."

"Jeanne's right," Ham interjected. "The Goodrich house will stand out like a sore thumb. People who come to see the decorations will wonder what's going on in the neighborhood. We could get something unobtrusive, like a star or a snow-man."

"What about a sign?" Ted Ericson suggested in his quiet manner. "A hand-lettered banner with a happy holidays wish or some similar greeting. I could ask one of our draftsmen at work to do it." Ted's narrow, intelligent face regarded Judith questioningly. "Would the Goodriches object to that? It wouldn't require any work or expense on their part. We could use a simple spotlight."

"George wouldn't object," Judith answered slowly. "But Enid—well, she's kind of crabby."

Arlene threw up her hands. "Kind of! When our five kids were little, there was no end to her complaints. 'Your children tore up my tulips!' 'Your children threw a ball through my window!' 'Your children set fire to my garage!' 'Your children put one of the Dooleys down my chimney!' So what, I'd tell her—at least we know where they are." Arlene's entire body shuddered with rekindled indignation.

Rochelle Porter rocked back and forth on the dining room chair. "Oh, tell me about it! She was always yelling at our three kids, sometimes just for walking by her house. The woman's a bigot. She actually called our Martin a *pickaninny*! Luckily, he didn't know what she was talking about."

"Neither did Mrs. Goodrich," Naomi Stein snapped. "You should hear what she called our son, Ben. He was only six the first time, and he came home crying his eyes out. Ben had never realized before that being Jewish meant being different."

"Mrs. Goodrich has never liked me," Mrs. Swanson said simply. "But Mr. Goodrich, he is very kind. It must be difficult for him to live all these years with such a sour woman."

There was a pause, as if the entire group were paying homage to George Goodrich's patience. Judith's dark eyes flitted from guest to guest. Which was the most likely delegate? Enid Goodrich had criticized them all at one time or another. Her gaze finally rested on Joe. He had the shortest history in the cul-de-sac. He was a cop. He commanded respect. He was, as far as Judith was concerned, irresistible.

"Joe, could you talk to the Goodriches tomorrow after work?"

Clenching what was left of the cigar between his teeth, Joe grimaced at his wife. "Sure, right after I face off with a serial killer, a sex maniac, and a couple of sociopaths. Mrs. Goodrich might come as a relief. Then again, she might not."

Judith gave Joe an uncertain smile. He'd grumble, but he'd do it. Surely even Enid Goodrich couldn't resist Joe's charm. Nobody could.

Except Gertrude.

Judith had never driven a truck until that last day of November. Her attempt at reversing into the driveway wasn't helped by Renie's confused sense of direction.

"A little more to the left . . . I mean, right . . . no, maybe you should come forward first . . . Look out for the mailman; he's crossing from your place to the Ericsons' . . . Okay, straight back now . . . Ooops!"

Judith felt the bumper hit something that she hoped wasn't the mailman. Seeing him approach the Ericsons' wooden gate, she let out a sigh of relief. "What did I hit?" she asked wearily.

"Your mother," Renie replied, rolling down the window and leaning out. "Hi, Aunt Gertrude. Are you okay?"

"Good God almighty," Gertrude rasped, reeling behind her walker. "Is that my idiot daughter *driving a truck*? What kind of a niece are you, Serena, to let that moron get behind the wheel of something bigger than my so-called apartment?"

"It belongs to the Rankerses' son, Kevin," Renie shouted. "We borrowed it to pick up the New England village. He's driving his Beamer today." Her hand flapped at the white BMW that was parked in front of the Goodrich house. "Are you sure you're okay?"

Gertrude snorted. "I'm fine, but my walker's got the bends. Tell Loonyville to get out of that damned thing before she kills me."

Judith's heart was racing. She couldn't believe that she hadn't seen her mother in the rearview mirror. Shutting off the ignition, she threw the door open and jumped down from the cab.

"Mother! I'm sorry! I'm not used to driving a pickup and the mirror must be adjusted for . . ."

"Oh, shut up!" Gertrude was scowling at her daughter. "What's all that junk you've got in the back of this thing? It looks like your next guests are a bunch of pygmies."

Ignoring Gertrude's protests, Judith hugged her mother. "It's the New England village. There's a church, a general store, an inn, an old mill, three houses, and six people. Oh, and a bridge with a fake stream and a stone fence and a horse and buggy."

"You should have driven the buggy instead of that stupid truck," Gertrude huffed. "Where are you going to put this claptrap?"

"In the front yard," Judith replied, feeling her nerves settle down a bit. "It'll be wonderful. Everything lights up at night."

"So does your Uncle Al," Gertrude muttered. "Who cares?"

Judith ignored her mother's comment. Renie had also gotten out of the pickup and was wrestling with the coach inn. Arlene and Carl Rankers were hurrying across the lawn, taking a respite from setting up their Holy Family.

"Isn't this fun?" Arlene enthused. "Carl has only hurt himself twice since he put the camels up."

Carl, in fact, wore Band-Aids on both hands and forehead. "The camels didn't attack me," he said dolefully. "But Arlene did. She wanted the Wise Men emerging from the hedge."

Arlene shot her husband a nasty look. "Oooh! Carl's such a tease! Everybody knows the Wise Men didn't show up at the stable until later. I thought we could put their figures in the hedge and then move them closer every day after Christmas."

Judith started to chime in on Carl's behalf, but Renie was nodding sagely. "That's true. The Wise Men didn't arrive until the Epiphany. I like it." She turned to Judith. "Do you remember when we were kids, and Donner & Blitzen Department Store had the big Christmas window with a series of curtains where first you saw the shepherds and then the angels and then the . . ."

"It wasn't Donner & Blitzen," Judith interrupted. "It was The Belle Epoch, and the first thing you saw were twinkling stars and then . . ."

A white Toyota Camry pulled up in the cul-de-sac, distracting Judith, who watched as it parked in front of the Ericson house. Judith recognized the car as belonging to Art Goodrich. He glanced in the direction of Hillside Manor; Judith waved. Art ambled over to the Flynns' driveway.

"That's quite a rig you've got there," he said, taking off his sweat-stained baseball cap. "It looks like everybody's decorating around here this Christmas."

Judith's gaze took in the entire cul-de-sac: The Steins had already put up their blue-and-white lights; they had also volunteered to purchase Mrs. Swanson's tiny golden fairy bulbs.

Gabe Porter had rescued the Santa set from the garage and cleaned off the grime. The figures reposed in the Porter driveway, awaiting a few touch-ups. According to Jeanne Ericson, she would pick up their carolers after work in the next couple of days. Meanwhile, Ted had commissioned the sign that would stand in the Goodriches' yard. The only hitch was that Joe hadn't yet talked to George and Enid. Maybe, Judith thought, she should broach the subject with their son.

"Say, Art," Judith said, watching Renie haul one of the village houses onto the grass while Gertrude clumped along behind her niece, "we don't want your folks to feel left out. I mean, we asked them to come to our neighborhood meeting Sunday night, but your mom wasn't feeling well. You don't think they'd mind if we put a little sign in their yard, do you?"

Art, who always looked a bit careworn, grew wary. "Well . . . I don't know. What kind of sign?"

"A 'For Sale' sign," yelled Gertrude. "Isn't it about time you put those two old farts out to pasture, Arthur? That's what my daughter here did with me."

Judith spun around to face Gertrude. "Mother, you're supposed to be deaf. How did you hear that?"

But Gertrude had turned her back on Judith. She pretended she hadn't heard the question. Judith noticed that her mother's shoulders were shaking with mirth under the plaid lumber jacket she'd inherited from Uncle Cliff.

Once again, Judith looked at Art. "Mother thinks she's funny. Sometimes she is. *Sometimes.*" Judith gave Art an apologetic smile. "Actually, I haven't seen the sign. Ted Ericson is having it made. Since he's an architect, it'll be professional. We just want to let passers-by know this is kind of a holiday showplace. Neighborhood pride and all that." Judith smiled again.

"Have you asked Mama?" Art's pudgy face exhibited concern. Instead of a chunky, graying middle-aged man, Judith suddenly glimpsed the timid, awkward boy who was always reluctant to join in the other children's more boisterous games.

"Not about the sign," Judith answered, trying to keep as close to the truth as possible. "I gathered she didn't want to put up lights or figures or that sort of thing. But she didn't say no to a sign.'' Inwardly, Judith winced at the small fib. ''My husband plans to talk to your parents tonight, but I thought if you said something first . . .'' She let the words trail away. It wouldn't do to mention Enid's predictable, arbitrary resistance.

Glancing every which way, as if he expected his mother to pop out of the shrubbery, Art fingered his stubby chin. ''Well . . . gee, I don't know . . . I hate to bother her when she isn't feeling good . . . And I've had so much on my mind, what with losing my job and all, especially just before Christmas . . .''

Judith took pity on Art. She had forgotten that he'd been laid off by the Boring Company. ''I understand. How's it going? Is JoAnne still working as a checker at Falstaff's Market? I haven't seen her lately.''

''She's on the night shift,'' Art replied, relief showing in his hazel eyes. ''It pays better. Look, I've got to get going. I told Mama I'd come by at three to wrap the pipes for winter. It's two minutes to the hour. I don't want to keep Mama waiting. See you, Judith.'' Art Goodrich hurried down the cul-de-sac in his faintly bowlegged manner.

Shaking her head, Judith started hoisting the rest of the village pieces out of the truck. Renie was arranging them under the maple tree between the driveway and the front walk.

''Most of the town should be grouped to the left,'' Renie said, wearing what Judith called her cousin's boardroom face. ''Even with the hedge dividing your property from the Rankers', you don't want to overwhelm the visitor's eye. Your two houses are at the end of the cul-de-sac, and therefore, they form a visual anchor.''

Deferring to Renie's artistic talent, Judith nodded. At that moment, shouts erupted on the other side of the hedge.

''You put that Virgin Mary down or I'll brain you with this sheep,'' Arlene commanded in an angry voice.

''I don't know why we bought a jackass,'' Carl yelled back. ''I could have stuck you out here until New Year's!''

''That does it!'' his wife screamed. ''You've chipped Cas-

par's crown! Now he looks like he was in a barroom brawl
with Melchior and Balthazar!''

"Maybe they were," Carl snapped. "They traveled from
afar."

"Afar, not a bar!" But Arlene had lowered her voice. So
had Carl. Judith turned her attention back to the New England
village.

"I should have gotten some fake snow," she said, not entirely satisfied with the natural grass background. "Or a white
papier-mâché base. Which would be cheaper?"

"God's cheaper," Gertrude asserted as Sweetums wandered
through the village, sniffing and poking his head inside the
doors. "It's going to rain; then it'll clear off and get colder.
And before Christmas—bingo! We'll have snow."

Judith and Renie regarded Gertrude with skepticism. "We
haven't had much snow the last few years," Judith pointed
out. "In fact, this fall we've had only a couple of hard frosts
so far. It's over fifty degrees this afternoon."

But Gertrude stuck by her guns. "There's snow coming. I
can feel it in these old bones. Wait and see—two days before
it hits, I'll be able to smell it."

Judith started to smile, but saw that her mother was serious.
Shrugging, she looked up at the gray clouds. Like many native
Pacific Northwesters, she, too, could sense snow, but only a
day or two before the first flakes fell. Judith wondered if her
mother's advanced age had brought her closer to nature. A
drop of rain struck Judith's cheek. "You're right about one
thing—it's going to rain. Come on, coz," she said to Renie.
"Let's hustle."

For a few moments, Gertrude leaned on her walker, watching the other two women work. An occasional raised voice
filtered through the hedge. Apparently, Carl had dropped the
cow; Arlene demanded to know why she'd found a pack of
her husband's cigarettes stuck to one of the shepherds. Sweetums sat down in front of the New England parson, as if listening to a sermon. Gertrude uttered a sigh, shivered inside
the lumber jacket, and began to clump off down the driveway.

"Are you cold, Mother?" Judith called as she lifted the last pieces of fencing from the truck.

Gertrude turned to look over her shoulder. "Of course I'm cold, you nitwit. It's almost December." She hesitated, leaning heavily on the walker. "But that's not it. I feel queerlike."

Hastily, Judith set the fencing on the ground, then raced to Gertrude's side. "It's delayed shock, from me backing into you. Oh, dear heaven, I feel terrible! Let's take you to the emergency room!"

Gertrude, however, brushed off her daughter's solicitous hands. "Stick it, noodlehead. I don't mean I'm sick or sore. I mean . . ." Gertrude sucked in her breath. "I don't know what I mean. It's like somebody walked over my grave. Except I'm not in it." Confusion was written all over the small wrinkled face that was raised to Judith. "Somebody else is buried there. Who is it?"

THREE

JOE ARRIVED HOME just as Renie was about to leave. He pulled his aged red MG into the garage, then came back down the drive to admire the cousins' handiwork.

"Cute," Joe declared, taking in the artful arrangement of villagers and their surroundings. "More than cute. Are the lights hooked up?"

"We left that for you," Judith said, offering Joe a welcoming kiss. "It's getting dark. Do you want to have a drink first?"

Giving Renie a friendly hug, Joe shook his head. "I'll get at it as soon as I change. I can use what little light is . . ."

Another crash resounded from the other side of the hedge. By reflex, Joe went for his gun, then froze. The color in his slightly florid face deepened.

"Damn," he laughed. "I thought it was a shot."

A face appeared among the hedge's glossy laurel leaves. "Yoo-hoo," Arlene called. "There's no room at the inn. The roof just fell down. On Carl."

Judith gave her neighbor a half smile. "Tell them to call Hillside Manor. I may have an opening for the twenty-fourth."

Arlene disappeared again. Renie gave herself a good shake. "I don't think I could get used to living next door to the Rankers,'' she said. "As for that other couple, I never could figure out why they didn't call ahead for reservations.''

"What other couple?" Judith asked as Renie started towards her big blue Chevrolet.

"The ones who got stuck with the cowshed," Renie replied, still walking. "Mary and Joseph. Bye."

"It could have been worse," Joe said, squeezing Judith's shoulders. Noting his wife's puzzled look, he grinned and the gold flecks danced in his green eyes. "It could have been a toolshed. I don't think even the Holy Family could have put up with your mother."

"So isn't that kind of weird?" Judith asked as she finished arranging crackers, cheese, and crab dip on a tray for her guests' hors d'oeuvres. "Mother isn't usually fanciful."

Joe yawned, took a sip of scotch, and put the evening paper aside. "Fanciful, no. But let's face it, Jude-girl—your mother's pretty old and it's Christmastime. People get strange during the holidays. They look to Christmas in the same way they did as children—it'll bring happiness, solve all their problems. But it doesn't, so they get depressed. Suicide, homicide— every imaginable disaster. For a lot of people, the holiday season is the ugliest time of year. Too many expectations, too much disappointment when they aren't met." Joe shook his head sadly, then took another pull on his drink.

"I know that," Judith said, vaguely disturbed by the thought that Joe might be talking about himself. "I've heard Bill Jones say the same thing for years. But that's not Mother. She's a realist. And for all her faults, she's got her spiritual side. This afternoon was different—as if she'd had a premonition. Mother was all shivery and squirmy. She even tried to forecast the weather."

"Great," Joe sighed. "The Lizard of Oz. Just what I need in a mother-in-law. Did one of your guests swipe the sports page?"

Since Joe obviously wasn't going to take Gertrude's omens seriously, Judith dropped the subject. Carrying the appetizer tray into the living room, she set it on the gateleg table. All of her preregistered guests had checked in for the night, but none had shown up yet for the hors d'oeuvres hour. It wasn't quite six o'clock, and Judith hadn't ladled out the punch. She was headed back to the kitchen when the front doorbell chimed. Since guests had their own keys, and family and friends usually came round to the back, Judith was faintly puzzled.

Glenda Goodrich stood on the front porch, looking harassed. Judith tried to remember Glenda's married name, recalled that she'd been divorced for several years, and simply greeted her guest with a friendly smile.

"Judith," Glenda said, nervously pushing damp tendrils of auburn hair off her high forehead, "I'm upset." Not waiting to be asked, Glenda scurried into the entry hall.

"What's wrong?" Judith inquired.

"It's Mama," Glenda replied, her wide, pale face looking pinched. "Art came by earlier and said you planned to put up a billboard in Mama's front yard. Naturally, she's frantic. Has this something to do with your hotel advertising?"

For reasons that eluded Judith, there were some people who didn't understand the concept of a bed-and-breakfast establishment. Glenda Goodrich was one of them. Judith's smile grew thin.

"No," she answered, almost truthfully. "It's not a billboard. It's a joint project with the other neighbors. Everybody thought it was a wonderful idea—except your mother." Judith's smile disappeared completely.

Remorse now mingled with the distress on Glenda's face. She had never been pretty, Judith recalled, but in her younger years, Glenda had possessed a vivaciousness that had been very attractive. Middle age had done many things to Judith's onetime playmate, adding extra pounds, etching deep lines, and, most of all, lending Glenda Goodrich a patina of despair.

"Please, Judith," Glenda said in a tired voice, "I realize Mama can be stubborn. But isn't this kind of sneaky? It seems to me that everybody in the cul-de-sac is going behind her back, forcing her to do something she doesn't want to do. That isn't fair to gang up on her when she's old and ill."

"Look," Judith said, trying to be patient, "my husband plans on coming over tonight to talk to your folks. He would have done that sooner, but he was working late Monday. This evening, he had to wire our New England village as soon as he got home from headquarters. The minute he has a chance Joe will explain everything to your mother and father."

The lines in Glenda's forehead deepened. "Mama's not going to like it. I wish you people wouldn't ask special favors of her. It only upsets Mama, and then she . . ." On the verge of tears, Glenda chewed her lower lip.

Judith could guess what Glenda was going to say. "She takes it out on everybody else, right? Especially you and Art."

Glenda's pained expression contained a hint of gratitude for Judith's insight. "It's not only my brother and me," she said in a rush. "Mama picks at everybody in the family—Art's wife, JoAnne, and their boys, Greg and Dave. Usually, she spares my daughter. But last night Mama and Leigh had a big row. I don't know what it was all about, but the fact that she got mad at Leigh shows how sick Mama really is."

As far as Judith was concerned, the incident showed that Mrs. Goodrich was making up for lost time. Indeed, Judith marveled that Enid had ever treated any of her kinfolk kindly. As for Leigh, Judith vaguely recalled Glenda's daughter as a sulky, overweight teenager.

"Adolescence is hard," Judith said in a voice distracted by the sound of footsteps overhead. "Along with everything else, kids at that age lose all respect for their elders."

Glenda frowned at Judith. "Leigh's twenty-two. She's a model. Didn't you see her last month on the cover of *Vogue*?"

Judith hadn't. Or if she had, she certainly hadn't recognized the superpuss staring out at her from the checkout stand at Falstaff's Market.

"That's wonderful," Judith gulped. "Does she live in New York?"

"Part of the time," Glenda replied, her pinched features relaxing slightly as the conversation switched to a more pleasant topic. "But she came home for Thanksgiving and plans to stay until after New Year's. Leigh has a lull in her schedule, and she doesn't really like New York or Paris or Milan that much.''

Clearly, Leigh had changed quite a bit since Judith had last seen her. She would have inquired further into the young woman's career, but the first of her guests were descending the stairs.

"I'm sorry," Judith apologized. "I must get the punch ready." Noting Glenda's abrupt return into gloom, Judith hastily invited her to stay for a drink.

"I can't," Glenda said with a faint nod at Judith's guests. "Mama will wonder where I am. I promised to give her a massage. Please don't pester her anymore. It's so hard on . . . everybody." With slumped shoulders, Glenda departed.

To Judith's relief, Joe had filled the punch bowl. She whisked it off to the living room, chatted briefly with the retired couple from Idaho, greeted the German professors from Bonn, and scooted back into the kitchen before the young lovers from Redding arrived.

"Maybe we should shelve the plan to coerce the Goodriches into putting up that sign," Judith said as Joe poured them each a scotch. She explained about the visit from Glenda. "Enid refuses to cooperate. Why borrow trouble?"

Joe opened the oven to check the steaks under the broiler. "It's not healthy to let people always get their own way."

Setting her drink on the counter, Judith got out the table settings, including one for Gertrude. "You're right, Joe. But Enid's too old to change. She's got George and her kids and the grandchildren under her thumb."

"Not us." Joe tested the potatoes that were boiling on top of the stove. "Hey, Jude-girl—you know me. I can't let people get away with stuff. It's my job, remember?"

Observing the sudden steeliness in her husband's eyes, Judith realized she was up against a war of wills: Joe versus Enid. The phone rang before Judith could say anything.

It was Ted Ericson, who announced that he had brought home the sign for the Goodriches' yard. Judith groaned inwardly. "We still haven't cleared it with Mrs. Goodrich," she said into the phone. "I guess Joe's going over there after din-

ner.'' A glance at her husband caught him nodding his head.
"We'll get back to you. Thanks, Ted.''

"You see?'' said Joe, draining the cauliflower. "Ted's done
his bit. It probably cost his firm a few bucks, too. We can't
back down just because some cranky old bitch hates Christmas. She probably hates herself, too.'' Abruptly, Joe set the
colander in the sink and stared out the kitchen window. "It's
still raining,'' he remarked in an oddly detached voice.

Sweetums, who had been taking a nap under the kitchen
table, ambled over to the stove. He sniffed, presumably at the
meat. Joe gave the cat a nudge with his foot. Sweetums let
out a low growl, then wandered away.

"I'll take him over to Mother's when I bring her dinner,''
Judith said, trying to forget the Goodrich dilemma for the time
being. "She can feed him.''

"Our steaks are ready,'' Joe said, "but your mother's isn't
done to her usual bootlike standard. She's probably out in the
toolshed cussing her head off because it's after six.''

Judith found a steak knife for her mother's use; given Gertrude's penchant for overcooked food, a saw would have been
appropriate. "I wanted to show Mother the village with the
lights on, but it's too wet. Did you flip the switch?''

Mildly, Joe swore. "No. I forgot after I tested the bulbs.''

"I'll do it,'' Judith volunteered. She headed out through the
swinging door to the dining room. A scream erupted from the
living room just as Judith set foot in the entry hall. A shout
followed, and then a clattering noise. Judith reversed her step
and raced into the living room. Sweetums was sitting in the
middle of the hors d'oeuvres tray, licking crab dip off his
whiskers.

All six of Judith's guests wore varying expressions of horror. Mortified, Judith grabbed the cat, fending off its outraged
protests and slashing claws.

"I'm so sorry! He's never done that before! Really!''
Sweetums wriggled free and streaked into the dining room.

"I'm going to be sick!'' cried the retired wife from Idaho.

"That cat's rabid!'' exclaimed the young man from Redding.

"*Das katz ist ein* rabbit?" goggled one of the German professors. "It looks like *ein katz* to me!"

Judith had gathered up the appetizer tray, as well as the punch cup that Sweetums had knocked off the gateleg table. "I'll prepare some more," she promised in a shaking voice. "Really, I feel just awful. The cat usually doesn't stay in the house, but it's raining, so he . . ."

Having recovered from the initial shock, the Idaho husband guffawed. "Never mind. I had a golden retriever once that ate our entire Thanksgiving turkey before we could sit down."

His wife glared at him. "Susie was a wretched dog. She also ate two of my purses."

The other German chuckled heartily. "*Ja, ja*, dogs have the craziness. *Mein Weimaraner*, name *ist Scheisskopf*, in English means . . ." At a loss for words, he turned to his colleague, a spare, bald man who apparently was still trying to figure out Sweetums's species.

Judith fled. Courtesy of her German grandmother, she knew what *Scheisskopf* meant in English. It wasn't suitable for mixed company, and Judith had suffered enough embarrassment for one evening. Back in the kitchen, she hurriedly got out another tray, piled on more crackers, added a garlic cheese spread, and opened a can of smoked oysters.

Joe was sitting at the table, sipping his drink and finishing the newspaper. "Problems?" His round face was bland.

"Oh, shut up!" Judith raced off with the fresh set of appetizers.

The guests, who seemed to be into their second round of rum punch, were now quite jovial. The young woman from Redding smiled widely at Judith, then spoke in a whisper: "I have a cat. His name is Swill."

Judith arched her dark brows. "Really?"

The young woman nodded. "His full name is Stephen William the Fourth. It's a family name. My parents had three daughters but no sons. So I named my cat after the brother I never had. It got shortened to Swill." She nodded again.

"That's . . . swell." Judith's smile was strained. Minor crises at Hillside Manor were hardly unusual. But her nerves were already frayed by Enid Goodrich's mean streak. Judith was apprehensive about Joe's visit. She was beginning to think that even her husband's patented Irish charm couldn't sway the cantankerous old woman.

On the way back to the kitchen, Judith remembered her original errand. She flipped the switch in the entry hall, then couldn't resist going outside to admire the lights in the New England village.

The rain was steady, but not daunting to a native Pacific Northwesterner. Judith stood on the parking strip, smiling with pleasure. The white clapboard church, the mill with its water-wheel, the quaint old inn, the snug little houses, and the cluster of cheerful shops looked delightful. The half-dozen residents seemed bursting with high spirits as they were caught in the middle of their holiday bustle. Judith couldn't stop smiling.

Until she heard another scream.

Galloping back into the living room, Judith was astonished when she found her guests laughing and gobbling up the latest hors d'oeuvres. Only the couple from Idaho seemed to notice their hostess's puzzled expression. Somewhat sheepishly, Judith skulked off to the kitchen.

"It was probably Arlene," Joe said calmly after Judith told him about the scream. "Your mother's steak is done. If I cooked it any longer, we could make it into a pair of boxing mitts."

After Judith returned from the toolshed, where she had listened to her mother's diatribe about supper being late, the Flynns sat down to dinner. Joe had kept their steaks on a warming plate. Judith, however, ate without her usual appetite.

"Stop fussing," Joe urged. "You're kind of nervy tonight. Forget the Goodriches. Think about the sable coat I'm giving you for Christmas."

Judith gasped. Then she saw the gold flecks in the magic green eyes. "You're kidding, right?"

"Of course." Joe added more pepper to his mashed potatoes and pan gravy. "In fact, I'm stumped. Choosing gifts is another holiday hassle. What do you want?"

Ignoring Joe's carping, Judith grew dreamy-eyed. Out in the living room, the guests began to drift away, getting ready for their own dinner engagements. Silence filled the kitchen, warm and comfortable, heightened by the aroma of hearty food.

"I don't know," Judith said at last. She reached across the table and took Joe's hand. "I've got everything I want."

Joe's smile was sheepish. "Scratch the sable coat." With his free hand, he put down his fork. "Your guests have departed. Shall we?"

Judith giggled. "Why not?" Then she remembered. "Oh! You're going to see the Goodriches."

Joe stroked her hand. "So? Aren't warriors heading into battle allowed one last moment of erotic delight?"

Judith started to protest, considered Enid Goodrich, and squeezed Joe's fingers. Visions of Enid in armor, chain mail, war paint, and fatigues marched through Judith's mind. Attila, Genghis Khan, Charlemagne, Napoleon—all paled beside Enid Goodrich. Judith got to her feet.

"Come, soldier mine. Sheath your weapon."

With surprising grace, Joe jumped out of his chair. "Oh, no, sweet concubine. Quite the contrary." He wrapped an arm around Judith, pulling her close. "I intend to unsheath my weapon whilst you shed your inhibitions. Thus shall we find earthly pleasures ere I face the dreaded enemy."

Laughing softly, they went up the back stairs. Neither one noticed Sweetums, swishing his tail and eating the last of the smoked oysters off the kitchen floor.

Joe returned from the wars battle-scarred. He was still swearing when he came in through the back door, dripping rain and red of face.

"And I thought your mother was contrary!" Angrily, he took off his wet jacket and gave it a good shake. "The old bat wouldn't even see me! George said she was worn out from the visit with her children! Bull, they come around all the time! Enid Goodrich is stubborn, selfish, and just plain mean!"

Judith let out a big sigh. "That's it, then. We'll have to tell Ted to forget the sign. Or," she went on, trying to find a bright spot in the dark scenario, "we could put it at this end of the cul-de-sac. If visitors think it's odd that the Goodrich house is dark, that's not our fault. Should anyone ask, I'm going to tell them what a pill Enid is."

"Merry Christmas," Joe muttered as he poured out the last cup of coffee. "Jeez, with people like her around, no wonder the rest of us lose the holiday spirit."

Judith was at the phone, dialing the Ericson house. "You can't have that attitude. Think about the decent people we know, instead of wishing she'd drop dead."

Jeanne Ericson answered on the second ring. "Drop dead? Who is this?"

Embarrassed, Judith laughed lamely. "It's me, Jeanne. Judith. I was talking about Enid Goodrich."

"Oh." Jeanne's voice tightened. "That's understandable. She might as well drop dead. She seems to make everybody's life miserable. Did you hear all that screaming at their house tonight around dinnertime?"

Judith stiffened. "I did, as a matter of fact. But I didn't know where it was coming from."

"Goodriches', that's where. It sounded to Ted and me as if they were having a world-class brawl. The next thing we knew, Glenda ran out of the house and drove away. She tore out of the cul-de-sac so fast that she almost hit a truck that was parked on the other side of the street." Jeanne made a disapproving noise. "Honestly, wouldn't you think that when people get older they'd want to live in peace?"

Wearily, Judith leaned against the door frame. "Not really. Fighting and arguing may prove that they're still alive."

Jeanne snorted. "It might be better if Mrs. Goodrich wasn't. Alive, that is. You were right the first time. Everybody would be better off if Enid would drop dead."

Everybody, including Judith, was about to find out if Jeanne Ericson was right.

FOUR

PHYLISS RACKLEY WAS singing a hymn at the top of her lungs, but the vacuum cleaner mercifully muffled the noise. Judith had just finished spotting the living room rug, and left her cleaning woman to her tasks. Phyliss had arrived promptly at eight-thirty, filled with Christian zeal, the Protestant work ethic, and a lot of phlegm.

Or so she claimed. But inasmuch as Phyliss enjoyed poor health to the hilt, Judith dismissed the latest in a long line of complaints. An hour after her arrival, Phyliss had changed the guest beds, started a load of laundry, cleaned the second-floor bathrooms, and was now attacking the living room. Judith sat down at the kitchen table to drink a fourth cup of coffee and pay bills. She always wrote checks on the first of the month, and this December was no exception.

Judith was trying to ignore both Phyliss's singing and the vacuum's roar when she heard a knock at the back door. The sound was loud and persistent. Judith had the feeling she might not have heard it the first time.

Arlene Rankers's pretty face was flushed with excitement. "What's going on?" she asked, her voice unusually high-pitched. "Such a commotion! I'm dying of curiosity!"

Judith stepped aside to let Arlene into the narrow hallway. "It's just Phyliss. She's singing. Sort of."

Arlene gaped at Judith. "Not that! I mean in the cul-de-sac! Firemen, medics, police! I think they're at the Goodriches'. Do you suppose George had a heart attack?"

"Goodness!" At a near run, Judith led the way into the kitchen, through the dining room and the entry hall, and out onto the front porch. Sure enough, the emergency vehicles filled the cul-de-sac, their red-and-blue lights flashing in the morning drizzle. The two women slowed their step as they started around the curving sidewalk. Three firemen came out of the Goodrich house and headed for their truck. Judith could hear a voice coming over a radio band but couldn't make out the words.

"Look," Judith said, lowering her voice for no apparent reason other than the sense of tragedy that the scene conveyed, "there's Art's Toyota parked in front of the Ericsons'."

Arlene gave a brief nod, but her attention was elsewhere. "Oh, my! This must be something really terrible! The front door is open!"

Judith grimaced. "You're right. Enid doesn't let people come in that way." She moved closer to the police car, noting its number. Judith knew the officers who came on duty after eleven A.M. But the vehicle that was parked in the middle of the cul-de-sac didn't belong to Corazón Pérez and Ted Doyle who were assigned to the afternoon beat on the south side of Heraldsgate Hill. This was the morning shift, and while Joe knew the pair by sight, Judith did not.

With some tricky steering, the fire truck pulled out into the intersection. Judith frowned. "It's serious if the firefighters weren't needed. When did you notice all this?"

Arlene glanced at her watch. "About fifteen minutes ago. The firemen came first, then the medics. The police were just pulling up when I ran over to your house. I can't believe you didn't hear the sirens."

Judith started to explain about Phyliss and the vacuum, but at that moment, the medics exited the Goodrich house. Somewhat to her dismay, she recognized one of them. Ray Kinsella had come to Hillside Manor some five years earlier, when Madame Gushenka was poisoned.

"Ray!" Judith called, waving her arms. She trotted past the Ericson gate with Arlene at her heels. The medic stopped in the middle of the sidewalk, peering at Judith through the rain.

"Do I know you?" he inquired, as his partner opened the van's back doors.

Judith gestured over her shoulder at Hillside Manor. "Yes, certainly. The fortune-teller? January of . . ."

Kinsella nodded abruptly. "Mrs. McSomething, right?" He shook his head. "This is a hard-luck neighborhood, I'm afraid." Moving quickly, he helped his partner roll a gurney into the Goodrich house.

"I'm Mrs. Flynn now," Judith shouted. "Mrs. *Joe* Flynn." But Ray Kinsella and the other medic had disappeared inside the house. "Rats," breathed Judith.

Arlene regarded Judith with disillusionment. "I thought you were going to find out what happened. Should we bar their way when they come out?"

Judith looked askance. "Hardly. Whoever they're hauling off must be in bad shape." Aimlessly, Judith began pacing the sidewalk. Despite the holiday decor, the cul-de-sac wore a mournful look. Bare branches of maple, hawthorn, horse chestnut, and plane trees reached up into the dead, gray sky. The air smelled damp, decay mingling with the rain and a hint of the salt water in the nearby bay. Judith felt depressed and helpless. Or maybe, she reasoned, she felt depressed because she was helpless. It wasn't her style to stand aside and let others take charge. Life had demanded much of her, and she had been forced to meet the challenges in order to survive.

Kinsella and the other medic emerged from the house with the gurney. One of the policemen, a young man with blunt features and almost no neck, ordered Judith and Arlene to step back. They obeyed, though Arlene shot the policeman a disgruntled look.

It was impossible to tell who was on the gurney. The body was covered with blankets, and there was an oxygen mask over the face. Judith peered through the rain as the victim was placed in the back of the van. Kinsella disappeared inside. Judith shook her head as his partner closed the doors and rushed to the passenger side.

"Ridiculous," grumbled Arlene. "The least they could do is tell us who they're taking away. How else will we know who to pray for?"

"Try everybody," Judith retorted, then gave Arlene a rueful look. "Sorry. I guess I'm upset."

"Who isn't?" Arlene demanded with a toss of her red-gold curls. "To have something like this happen right in front of us and not know what's going on is an absolute outrage!"

The siren's wail had almost faded when Glenda Goodrich parked her Ford Taurus in the spot vacated by the medics. Judith grabbed Arlene by the wrist. "Let's calm ourselves. Glenda will know."

Glenda, however, wore a stunned expression. She didn't bother to close the car door behind her but stumbled towards her parents' house as if in a trance.

"What's happened?" Judith asked, hurrying to Glenda's side.

Glenda's mouth was open, her breath coming in small gasps. By reflex, she started down the driveway, to the back door. "I can't believe it," she said in a stricken voice. "I can't believe it!"

"Believe what?" Arlene had sidestepped Judith to confront Glenda. She grabbed the dazed woman by the lapels of her raincoat and gave her a sharp shake. "Talk, Glenda! This is me, Arlene Rankers! There are no secrets—do you understand?"

With difficulty, Glenda's eyes focused. "Arlene! Oh! Please . . . I must go inside." She swallowed hard as she tried to free herself from Arlene's firm grasp. "It's Mama. There's been an . . . accident."

Arlene refused to let go. "What kind of accident?"

"Please!" Glenda wrenched free, then flew down the drive, clumsily sidestepping a freshly cut Christmas tree that lay between the houses.

Arlene was fuming. "She's impossible! The first time I met

her, she wouldn't tell me how much she weighed! Can you imagine being so secretive?''

Judith scarcely heard Arlene. Her mind was racing, trying to figure out what kind of accident had befallen Mrs. Goodrich. Just as Judith turned to head back to the front of the house, Ted Ericson pulled up in his black BMW.

"What's all this?" he inquired, looking perplexed but keeping his usual calm. "Did somebody have a wreck? We really should have at least a 'Yield' sign at the head of the cul-de-sac.''

"It wasn't a wreck," Judith replied as she and Ted and Arlene reached the sidewalk. Now only the squad car remained parked in front of the Goodrich house. "Something's happened to Enid, but we don't know what."

Ted's almost white eyebrows lifted. "Really? I was home until just before eight. Then I went to get our tree. Jeanne had spotted a perfect noble fir at Falstaff's. After I brought it home, I realized we didn't have a bucket or any tools, so I went to the hardware store. They don't open until nine-thirty. I stopped for coffee at Moonbeam's."

So wrapped up in his meticulous explanation was Ted that he seemed to have forgotten his point. Judith gave him an encouraging look, but it was Arlene who pounced:

"So what did you see at the Goodriches'? Or hear? Were there cries for help or loud noises? What was it? Well?"

Ted, however, looked bewildered. "I didn't see or hear anything. That's what I meant. Everything seemed peaceful this morning."

An uneasy quiet now engulfed the neighborhood. Judith considered going back inside to get a jacket. The morning was cool and her sweats were growing damp. She was still mulling when another police car turned into the cul-de-sac, followed by an ambulance. Neither vehicle flashed its lights or sounded its siren.

"Good God," Judith gasped. She knew from harsh experience what the unheralded arrival meant.

Arlene and Ted stared at her. Judith clamped her lips shut, gazing stonily at the Goodrich house. She was afraid to explain the significance of the muted vehicles. If she kept silent, an improbable miracle might prove her wrong.

Two plainclothes police officers got out of the car. Detectives, Judith guessed, sinking deeper into the gloom. The woman was young, striking, and raven-haired. The man was older, tall and broad, with a luxuriant mustache and a black patch over his left eye. Judith thought she recognized him from one of the department functions she'd attended with Joe.

The pair paid no attention to the onlookers but marched swiftly up to the Goodrich front door. The ambulance attendants remained in their vehicle.

"I can't stand this!" Arlene declared, verging on an explosion. "I have to know! I need to know! I *always* know!"

It was true. Arlene Rankers had an incredible nose for news. On Heraldsgate Hill, she was famous for hearing everything first. Accuracy was another matter. But when called by Judith on some of her erroneous reporting, Arlene defended herself by insisting that she had a right to interpret what she heard, just like any network analyst.

But on this damp December morning, Judith agreed wholeheartedly with Arlene. Her own curiosity was about to burst. She was contemplating an assault on the front door when Art Goodrich staggered across the threshold. He clung to the brick porch pillar like a man holding onto the mast of a sinking ship. Judith and Arlene charged up the walk.

Art stared at them as if they were strangers. Ted approached cautiously, and out of the corner of her eye, Judith saw Mrs. Swanson virtually tiptoeing out of her yard. At that moment, Naomi Stein turned the corner in her Dodge station wagon.

"Mama's dead." Art's voice was high and thin. He was gazing above his audience's head, with empty eyes lost in the curtain of rain. "Mama's dead," he repeated. "She was hacked to death and Pappy did it."

The awful silence that followed was broken when Art began to laugh. "Isn't that something? I can't believe it!" His head swiveled in all directions; then he tapped his feet on the front porch, like a song-and-dance-man. "Wild! It's just wild! Mama's dead and I used the front door! Is that crazy or what?''

Strangely, it was Mrs. Swanson who reached Art first. She went up to the porch with a careful, steady tread, her small figure exuding courage. Judith couldn't hear what she said to the distraught man, but a moment later, Mrs. Swanson and Art went into the house.

Arlene was uncharacteristically speechless. Ted Ericson was walking in circles, holding his head. Naomi Stein had crossed the street and was standing next to Judith.

''Is it true?'' she asked in a shocked voice. ''Is Enid really dead?''

Judith ran a trembling hand through her wet hair. ''I guess so. But the medics hauled somebody off in a hurry. I assumed it was Enid, and that she must still be alive.''

Mrs. Swanson was coming back out of the house. Now her step faltered as she made her way to the sidewalk. ''The police, they want no outsiders,'' she said quietly. ''So I must leave. Oh, oh, this is a terrible day!''

Arlene almost controlled her rampant curiosity, putting only the gentlest of hammerlocks on Mrs. Swanson. ''Is Enid really dead?''

Sadly, Mrs. Swanson nodded.

''Then why,'' Judith asked, ''did the medics race out of here?''

Free of Arlene's grasp, Mrs. Swanson fingered the silk scarf that was tucked inside her herringbone coat. ''Mrs. Goodrich is still inside. The medical men took Mr. Goodrich away.'' The black eyes filled with tears. ''Poor man, he must have been overcome with remorse. He took pills to kill himself.'' The tears overflowed, but Mrs. Swanson's voice didn't waver. ''Wouldn't you think he'd want to live without her? I would.''

As a rule, Renie tried to keep her distance from Hillside Manor when Phyliss Rackley was around. The cleaning woman's chronic hypochondria and persistent evangelizing drove Judith's cousin absolutely nuts. Renie wasn't a morning person anyway, so she used the time until noon to run errands and do household tasks. Afternoons were usually devoted to her graphic design business, which, except for occasional and much detested meetings, she did at home.

But Enid Goodrich's death brought Renie to Hillside Manor shortly before eleven. Fortunately, Phyliss was finishing the laundry and the ironing in the basement. A reluctant Arlene had gone to pick up Carl, who had left one of their cars at the repair shop. Thus, Judith was alone in the kitchen when Renie arrived.

"Have you told your mother?" Renie asked, accepting a mug of fresh coffee from Judith.

"Yes. She was horrified—for about twenty seconds." Judith sank into one of the four captain's chairs. "Then she said it served the old bat right, she'd driven poor George to it, who could blame him, blah-blah-blah. But she insisted she hadn't had a premonition. Maybe she did forget, and won't admit it."

"Maybe," Renie said, looking unusually grim, "she doesn't want to admit she sensed death. At her age, that could be scary."

"It's scary at any age," Judith noted, taking comfort from the warmth of her coffee mug. "But she's definitely being herself otherwise. Mother decided to torment *your* mother by calling her and *not* telling her what happened."

Renie gave a shake of her chestnut curls. "Oh, jeez. I don't know what's more appalling—your mother using the telephone or being so perverse."

"Using the telephone," Judith replied calmly. Gertrude despised the phone, and since Judith had bought her a cordless style, the older woman persisted in losing it. As recently as the previous Saturday, Judith had found it in the birdbath on the patio.

"So that's all you know?" Renie asked, removing the lid of the sheep-shaped cookie jar.

"I'm afraid so. There isn't much else to find out, except if George pulls through. I'll try to call the house after the police leave."

The ambulance had departed while Judith was coming back from visiting her mother in the toolshed. She had seen it slowly pull out of the cul-de-sac, moving at a hearselike speed.

"Art and Glenda are still there with the police," Judith went on, ignoring the face Renie made after discovering that the cookie jar was empty. "Gosh, coz, I feel awful. I can't spare a tear for Enid, but I could weep buckets over George. Mother's right—she drove him to it. A man can only take so much. The really terrible thing is that I'm afraid this Christmas decorating project may have driven him over the edge."

Renie tried to look sympathetic. The expression somehow seemed foreign to her, even though the emotion was real. "After almost sixty years of marriage, it's a miracle George didn't kill her sooner. Don't blame yourself. Whatever set him off must have been an accumulation of abuse and misery. He finally snapped. It happens."

While Judith appreciated her cousin's commiseration, she remained glum. "This certainly puts a damper on the holidays."

"Why?" Renie asked in her typically pragmatic style. "Enid hated Christmas. Look at it this way—with her gone from the neighborhood, there's nobody around to snipe at the season. If they let George out of the funny farm, he'll probably give you permission to put up your sign."

Judith was aghast. "Coz—you're callous."

"No, I'm not. I'm realistic. Lots of people will croak before New Year's. As long as I'm not one of them, I'll try not to let that fact spoil my holidays."

Phyliss Rackley dropped a wicker clothes basket onto the floor with a loud thud. "Blasphemy, Mrs. Jones! How can you say such things? Besides, the Good Lord wanted Mrs. Goodrich to come home for Christmas. He'll see that she has a good time in spite of herself."

"The good Lord had nothing to do with it," Renie said flatly. "That was all up to George and his . . ." She paused, gazing inquisitively at Judith. "His what? An ax?"

But Judith could only shrug. "I don't know. The term Art used was . . . 'hacked.' " Judith gulped on the word.

Phyliss shrieked. " '*Hacked*'? You mean he didn't just up and shoot her like husbands usually do? Why didn't you say so?"

"I guess I forgot." Judith was sounding even more dismal.

Renie was on her feet, heading for the front door. Judith assumed she was trying to escape from Phyliss. But even as the cleaning woman began a homily on the afterlife featuring joy-filled codgers in flowing white robes welcoming Enid to her mansion in the sky, Renie returned.

"The cops are gone," she announced just as Phyliss got to the part about Enid's brow being adorned with a pearly crown, "but Art and Glenda's cars are still there." She arched her eyebrows questioningly at Judith.

Judith stood up, her energy renewed by the call to action. "I should go over and see if we can do anything for the family," she said, avoiding Renie's fixed gaze. "Maybe I could make them some lunch."

"Hold on," Phyliss said crossly. "I didn't get to the angels playing tunes of glory on their harps."

"Praise the Lord," murmured Renie.

"What did that heathen say?" Phyliss demanded.

Judith gave her cleaning woman a weak smile. "Ah—raise the Ford. Glenda Goodrich drives a Ford, and my cousin wants to . . . er . . . um . . ." Judith was still searching for words as she followed Renie through the entry hall.

"I'm not a heathen," Renie declared. "I'm a Catholic."

"Same thing to Phyliss," Judith retorted, then came to a dead halt in front of the Ericson house. "Shoot—they've put up crime scene tape. Do we dare jump over it?"

"At our age, can we?" But the cousins were still sufficiently nimble to try. They chose to invade the Goodrich property through the shared driveway. Judith noticed that Ted Ericson had finally left for work. The handsome noble fir was now behind the split-rail fence, reposing in a shiny new galvanized bucket.

"We'll defer to the deceased's wishes and use the back door," Judith said, leading the way to the rear of the house.

Renie wrinkled her pug nose. "What's so big about that? We usually use the back door at your place."

"That's different. It's easier, for one thing. Our garage is in back. If you pull into the drive to leave on-street parking for guests, the back door is closer. Plus, I try to reserve the front for the paying customers. It adds tone.''

The latter remark evoked a dubious expression from Renie. ''But Mrs. Goodrich didn't run a B&B. What was her excuse?''

''She didn't want to get her living room dirty,'' Judith answered as she started up the four steps that led to the back porch. Her foot struck something hard that crunched beneath her weight. Judith looked down at the cement walkway. ''Glass,'' she said. ''Be careful.'' Gingerly, she picked up the offending shard and put it in the garbage can that stood next to the walk. ''Somebody broke a glass. The rest of it's in the can, but be careful. They must have dropped some of the pieces.''

On the porch, the cousins listened for footsteps inside the house. After almost a full minute, they heard them, ponderous and dragging.

Warily, Glenda opened the door. She was still looking stunned. ''Oh!'' The presence of the cousins seemed to dismay her. ''Art and I were just leaving. We want to be with Pappy when he comes to—*if* he comes to.''

Judith quickly introduced Renie, though the women had met years ago, in their youth. Renie and Glenda were the same age, and had gone to high school together. However, neither seemed to recognize the other. Judith knew that Renie had a poor memory for faces. As for Glenda, shock and grief probably had hampered her powers of recollection.

Judith shifted awkwardly on the small back porch. ''We won't keep you, then. Is there anything we can do while you're gone?''

Glenda started to shake her head, but her brother appeared behind her. Art seemed to have gotten himself under control, though he was pale and drawn.

''There is,'' he said, his voice startling Glenda who hadn't heard him approach. ''JoAnne and maybe the boys are coming by in a little while. It might be easier if someone were here to let them in.''

Judith brightened. ''Sure, we'd be glad to. Unless,'' she

added, growing uncertain, "the police would object. I mean, they've put up that tape. . . ."

But Art dismissed the crime scene tape with a throwaway gesture. "I take it that's routine. Besides, you're married to a detective. I'm sure Morgan and Rael won't mind. They probably know Mr. Flynn."

Judith quickly sorted through her memory for Morgan and Rael. Rael meant nothing, but Morgan rang a bell. He was the male detective, and, she recalled, was known as Patches. Recalling the eyepatch, Judith realized the reason for the nickname.

Once the cousins were inside the house, Art and Glenda seemed anxious to leave. Not three minutes passed before the pair drove off in their separate cars. Judith and Renie were left in the kitchen, staring at each other.

"This place gives me the creeps," Renie declared. "I've never been inside before."

Judith's gaze traveled to the table, which was bare except for a pair of salt and pepper shakers cast in the images of Fred Astaire and Ginger Rogers, and a plastic holder containing paper napkins. The only evidence of a breakfast meal was two coffee mugs, sitting empty in the sink.

"I wonder if Joe knows about this," Judith said, leading Renie into the living room. The drapes were closed and the furnishings were protected by heavy plastic. Only the lamps, a couple of end tables and a Queen Anne breakfront with a built-in desk were exposed to the elements. Judith felt a sense of oppression; even the air smelled slightly stale. "I suppose it depends on what Joe's working on," she commented with a sudden longing for the constant chaos and motion of Hillside Manor. "As of yesterday, he and Woody were still investigating the Shazri murders."

Renie was frowning at the beige rug which was partially covered by a plastic runner. "Execution style, right? I read about it in the paper. How's Woody?"

Judith smiled at the mention of her husband's long time partner, Woodrow Wilson Price. "Great. He and Sondra have the two kids now, and they're all thriving. Ever since Woody got promoted, Joe swears he'll make chief someday. We're having them to dinner Saturday after next. Do you and Bill want to come?''

''I'll have to check the calendar,'' Renie replied, obviously wondering if she dared sit down on the cloistered furniture. ''It's such a busy time of year, but I'd love to. Bill's never met Woody and Sondra.''

Judith was also wondering, but not about sitting down. Her eyes had strayed to the carpet, where she noticed a track of evergreen needles. They zigzagged across the living room, going almost to the front door. Judith got down on her knees for a closer examination.

''Coz—do these look like a Noble to you?''

Renie bent over, peering at the floor. ''Sure. They're blue and stiff. What else could they be?''

Judith stood up and walked back out to the kitchen. Sure enough, there were more needles, all the way to the door. Cautiously, she started for the short hallway that led to the bath and bedrooms.

''Look, coz. These needles go this way, too. In fact,'' she said, focusing on the sporadic trail, ''they lead right into . . . the master bedroom.''

Judith stood up and gazed into the room where she had been an unwelcome guest the previous Sunday. The bed, the floor, and the wall were splattered with blood. Judith groaned; Renie shrieked. At that moment, they both realized the enormity of what had happened in the Goodrich house.

Enid had indeed been hacked to death. In life, she had possessed an ugly streak; her death had not been pretty, either.

FIVE

JoANNE GOODRICH GAVE the impression of never having been young. Yet Judith knew better, because she had been a year behind Art's future wife at Heraldsgate High School. A redhead who relied on artificial means to stay that way, JoAnne was too thin, too nervous, and too lacking in self-esteem.

Or so Judith appraised her former schoolmate as JoAnne hovered on the back porch with two hulking young men below her on the steps. Anxiously, she introduced her sons, Greg and Dave.

"I'm sick to my stomach," JoAnne asserted, apprehensively entering the kitchen. "Can you believe this?"

"Yeah," said the taller of the two young men.

"No kidding," said the other, who was already beginning to bald.

The trio fell silent, their eyes furtively scanning the kitchen as if they expected the appliances to attack them. It was obvious that neither JoAnne nor her sons felt at home in the Goodrich house.

"What should we do?" JoAnne asked in a hushed voice.

Judith wasn't certain what JoAnne meant. "About your father-in-law? Or the . . . house?"

Trembling, JoAnne sat on the edge of a kitchen chair.

"That's it—I don't know. Maybe we should call a lawyer."

"Do you have one?" Renie inquired, brazenly sitting on the kitchen table.

"No." JoAnne eyed Renie with minor horror. "My in-laws did, though. It's a woman in the BABU Tower. Glenda used her for the divorce."

Judith knew the Bank of Burma's location downtown in the financial district. It was a handsome structure, some fifty stories high. Judith guessed that office space must command exorbitant rents. She was surprised that any of the Goodriches could afford such a high-priced attorney. Judith started to say something to that effect, thought better of it, and merely nodded.

"You'll need someone for probate, no matter what happens," put in Renie, whose mother had been a legal secretary. "If criminal charges are filed, you'll need a lawyer who specializes in that type of defense."

JoAnne shuddered. "That's awful! You don't mean that Gramps would be treated like a . . . *murderer*?"

Renie grimaced. "The law doesn't always make sense. But he probably wouldn't go to jail. They'll send him to a . . . hospital of some sort."

"Weird," breathed the taller Goodrich grandson.

"No kidding," murmured his balding brother.

"But he may die, too," JoAnne said, almost brightening at the thought. "Then it would be okay. I mean," she went on, flushing slightly, "he wouldn't have to go through a trial and all that."

Renie, who was still sitting on the table, managed to knock over the salt and pepper shakers. "It'd be a hearing, not a trial," she explained, righting the shakers and tossing salt from Ginger Rogers over her shoulder in an unconscious superstitious gesture. Judith was reminded of Fred Astaire, flipping his partner in a graceful arc. Renie wasn't nearly as agile.

"They'd determine if George is fit to stand trial," Renie continued, brushing salt from her sleeve, "which is probably dubious, given his age and apparent unstable mental condition.

Media coverage would be minimal, so the family wouldn't suffer much embarrassment.''

Cautiously, JoAnne edged farther back on the chair. She seemed visibly relieved and glanced from one son to the other. "Maybe we should go to the hospital to see how Gramps is doing. Then . . . whatever happens, we could swing downtown and find that lawyer. Glenda will know her name."

"Right," said the taller son.

"No kidding," said the balding Goodrich.

With obvious relief, the trio headed for the back door. JoAnne hesitated on the threshold, giving the cousins a tremulous smile. "Are you sure you don't mind staying here? I mean, it's kind of . . . gruesome."

"We do gruesome real well," Renie replied with a sly glance at Judith. "Don't fuss over us."

JoAnne sighed with relief. "Gee, thanks! I appreciate it. I'm so glad we don't have to sit around in this pathetic old house. It was bad enough to visit when Enid was alive, but now . . ." JoAnne lifted her thin hands in an expressive gesture.

"Bummer," said the tall son.

"No kidding," said the bald son.

The three Goodriches beat a hasty retreat.

"You're going to have a sign on this property after all," Renie predicted as the cousins wandered back into the living room. "It'll be put up by a real estate company. The heirs can't wait to unload this place, and I don't blame them."

Judith nodded as she dared to leave the carpet runner and inspect the Queen Anne breakfront. "I doubt that it's ever felt like home to any of them, George included." She sighed. "Poor George. I wonder if he's pulled through?"

"We could call the hospital," Renie suggested. Her eyes had strayed to one of the end tables. Its only adornments were a brass lamp and a framed photograph of Enid. The picture had been taken a long time ago, when she was still young and pretty. "Her eyes don't smile," Renie remarked, studying the curiously unappealing face. "And why is she wearing a pie on her head?"

Judith was momentarily diverted from studying the breakfront desk. "That's a hat, dopey. The style always looked more like upside-down soup bowls to me. Our mothers wore them in the Depression."

"No wonder they were depressed," Renie remarked, setting the photograph back on the end table. "But it's kind of nice the way young women dressed up in those days. Enid couldn't be more than sixteen in this picture. Yet there's still something hard in that face. I wonder what George saw in her?"

"Who knows? What did I see in Dan?" Judith couldn't refrain from trying to open the desk. At first she thought it was locked, but after jiggling the front panel a bit, it fell forward on its hinges. "That's odd," she said, staring at the lock itself. "It looks as if it's been forced. Look, there are a bunch of scratches in the wood."

Renie had joined Judith at the breakfront. "Those scratches look fresh. Enid wouldn't like having her furniture defaced."

The cousins were exchanging curious glances when someone pounded at the front door. They could see only a blur through the amber bottle-glass panes. Cautiously, Judith turned the knob.

"Yo-ho-ho," exclaimed the man Judith knew as Patches Morgan. The black raincoat was lined in crimson, and the suit under it was a flamboyant shade of green. "Who have we here?" The brown eye that wasn't covered by the patch held a hint of menace.

Swiftly, Judith put out her hand. "I'm Judith Flynn, Joe's wife. We met last spring at a department retirement party."

Morgan's bushy black brows rose. "Ah! And what might you be doing here, Ms. Flynn?"

Judith explained that she was a neighbor who had come with her cousin to help the bereaved family. "We were just leaving," Judith fibbed.

"A good thing," Morgan replied, his right eye twinkling. "This *is* a crime scene. Detective Rael and I have work to do. Then we'll put someone on site to keep trespassers out. We're a bit short-handed this morning." The eye still twinkled, but the deep voice conveyed a warning.

"I guess we'll be going then," Judith said, her smile frozen in place. "Is it true that the weapon was . . . an ax?"

The mouth under Morgan's mustache turned stern. "Now, Ms. Flynn, you know we can't make statements like that until we've checked everything through our forensics people."

"A knife?" Judith hazarded.

Morgan was trying to conceal his impatience. "Not a knife," he said. "Now run along, so we can do our job, eh?"

Docilely, Judith and Renie trooped through the front door, down the three steps, and along the walk.

Detective Rael was just getting out of the city car. The rain was coming down harder, and she brushed back her raven hair with a graceful hand.

"Excuse me?" she called. "Are you witnesses?"

Renie pretended not to hear, but Judith dutifully turned around. Once again, she went through her connection, both to Joe Flynn and the Goodriches.

Detective Rael's startlingly blue eyes widened. "So you're Joe's wife," she said, almost in awe. "He's a terrific cop. I'd love to work under him someday." Her perfect oval face betrayed just the slightest leer. Or so Judith thought.

"Joe's very . . . conscientious," Judith allowed, wishing Detective Rael weren't so young, so beautiful, and so insinuating. "I don't think I caught your first name."

"It's Sancha," the other woman replied with a toss of her raven hair. "It means 'sacred.' "

"It means trouble," Renie muttered after the cousins had completed the exchange of pleasantries and were heading back to Hillside Manor. "Has Joe ever mentioned her?"

"I don't think so," Judith replied, somewhat distractedly. "She must be new."

"New but used," Renie said as she paused to admire the New England village. "No, I shouldn't say that. I'm sure she's a perfectly nice young woman."

"Right." But Judith's voice held a note of doubt. "Shall I switch on the lights so you can see how the village looks in its full splendor?"

"No. I'll come by after dark," Renie responded. "Let's go inside. It's really coming down."

So it was, a pelting rain that seemed to contain a trace of snow. But as Judith and Renie stepped onto the back porch, the outdoor thermometer registered forty-two. The threat of colder weather seemed remote.

Judith immediately headed for the telephone directory. "I forgot to ask where George is being treated. I'll try Bayview Hospital first," she said. "That's where they usually take emergencies."

Judith was correct. The brisk voice on the other end of the line refused to give out any information except that a George Henry Goodrich had been admitted. Judith asked if his son or daughter might be available. The voice didn't know and seemingly didn't care. Judith hung up.

"Blast," she sighed, going to the window over the sink that looked out onto the Rankerses' property. "Maybe Arlene can ferret out his condition. She and Carl aren't back yet."

Renie was leaning against the refrigerator. "Are you going to feed me lunch, or do I have to go pick up fish and chips?"

Judith glanced at the old-fashioned schoolhouse clock. It was almost noon. "We'll both go. But let me fix a sandwich first for Mother. She hates fish and chips."

Fifteen minutes later, the cousins were sitting on worn vinyl seats in an old but semi-respectable restaurant at the bottom of Heraldsgate Hill. The Christmas decor at Buster's Cafe featured red paper bells and strands of silver tinsel that had long ago lost their luster. But the food was good, and Renie had managed to find a parking place by using her big Chev and harsh language to outmaneuver a smaller imported compact.

"I'm worn out already," Judith confessed. "Thank God Phyliss is putting in a full day. I should go Christmas shopping this afternoon. I still have to get gifts for Mike and Kristin and a little something extra for Mother."

"How about a muzzle?" Renie suggested, digging into her cole slaw. "I'm almost done shopping, except for the kids. If they don't have twenty-five gifts apiece under the tree, they whine until Groundhog Day."

Judith knew that Renie was exaggerating—but not by much. The three Jones offspring were spoiled, even more spoiled than Mike. Maybe. Judith was about to comment on the annual devastating expenditure of Christmas when she recognized a bearded man who was just entering the restaurant.

"That's Gary," Judith whispered. "Glenda's boyfriend. I've seen him with her at the Goodrich house."

Renie tried to stare discreetly over her shoulder. "Are you sure? He looks too young."

"It's him. I recognize the jacket. He works with Glenda at Cascade Beer. I think he drives a truck."

Swiftly, Renie checked out the emblazoned jacket and the man who wore it. "I still say he's too young. Forty, maybe? Glenda's my age."

Judith shrugged. "Ten, fifteen years' difference isn't that much these days. Older women, younger men. I'm not sure, but I think Glenda and Gary have been going together for a couple of years."

At the moment, Gary was going to the counter. Judith chewed on her thumb, shot Renie a conspiratorial look, and jumped out of the booth. Sidling up to the unsuspecting Gary, she filled her voice with sympathy: "I'm so sorry about the family's loss. How is Glenda doing?"

Gary practically fell off the stool. "What? Glenda? Who are you?"

Briefly, Judith thought she'd made a mistake. But she persevered. "Glenda Goodrich. Her mother was killed this morning, and her father's very ill. Surely you've heard?"

It appeared that Gary hadn't. He reeled from the stool, walking back and forth in a daze between the counter and the booths. Several customers and a waitress stared. Judith waited patiently. To her surprise, Gary came to a sudden halt and frowned at her.

"Rough luck," he said, looking embarrassed as well as nervous. "I mean, it's too bad about Glenda's folks. But count me out. We broke up last night."

"Oh!" Briefly, Judith was taken aback. Putting a hand on Gary's arm, she gestured at the booth where Renie was blissfully devouring chunks of fish. "I'm Judith Flynn, a neighbor.

Why don't you join my cousin and me so that we can fill you in?''

Gary seemed bewildered. The neatly trimmed beard was straw-colored, as was his curly hair. At a shade under six feet, Gary was broad-shouldered but carried an extra twenty pounds. The hooded hazel eyes were wary as he considered Judith's invitation.

"I've only got half an hour for lunch,'' he began, then apparently was overcome by curiosity. He turned back to the counter, calling to a weary-looking waitress. "Hey, Angie— make that the usual. I'll be in the booth.''

Judith introduced Gary to Renie. In the process, the cousins learned that Gary's last name was Meyers. "I know we've never met,'' Judith explained as Angie brought coffee refills. "But I've seen you with Glenda. I've known her and Art since we were little kids. Renie knows the family, too.''

The cousins' credentials didn't seem to impress Gary. "So what happened to the old lady and what's-his-name?''

Judith tried to be tactful as well as cautious in relating the grisly events at the Goodrich house. Gary reacted with appropriate horror. A nerve next to his right eye twitched, and he rubbed at it in agitation.

"Mrs. G. was a bitch on wheels, always on somebody's case,'' he said as his order was delivered. "The usual'' was a cheeseburger with fries and several slices of raw onion. "I tried to steer clear of the old girl. My ex-wife was a nag. That's why she's my ex. Why can't women learn to shut up?''

"Because men don't learn to listen,'' Renie put in. "Not all women nag. And sometimes men do listen. Now take my husband, Bill . . .''

Judith didn't want Renie to get launched on the topic of Bill. Renie would go on forever, even—especially—if she intended to heap praise upon her mate. Judith managed to distract her cousin by attempting to steal her tartar sauce.

The ruse worked. Judith turned back to Gary, who was sitting next to her in the booth. "Mrs. Goodrich wasn't a pleasant woman. I hate to say that, but it's true. I hope you and Glenda didn't break up because of her mother.''

For just a brief instant, Gary's fleshy features hardened. Then he laughed in a forced manner. "Let's just say there was too much family, okay?"

The table grew silent. Judith munched on the last of her fries, trying to think of an appropriate comment. None came to mind. Gary and Glenda were kaput. There was no reason, other than ordinary human curiosity, why he should care what happened to the Goodriches. Nor did Judith have any reason to press questions upon Gary Meyers. Giving herself a little shake, she glanced at Renie.

"We'd better go if you're Christmas shopping this afternoon." Judith picked up her bill, then waited for Gary to get up so she could exit the booth. "It was nice meeting you, Gary. Have a merry Christmas."

Judith thought Gary looked relieved. His mouth was full of cheeseburger. He nodded, waved, and turned his full attention to his meal. The cousins stopped at the register, then went outside into the rain.

"I'll take you home," Renie said. "Then I'm heading downtown."

Judith paused in the middle of fastening her seat belt. "We're halfway to town already. I'll go with you. I can call Phyliss and Mother from there to let them know where I am."

Renie gestured at the restaurant they'd just left. "Call from here. There's a phone by the entrance to the bar."

Judith went back inside. Phyliss answered almost immediately. "What did you spill on the kitchen floor?" she demanded. "It's so greasy. I'll bet you let that awful cat eat off of it."

Naturally, Judith denied the accusation. But she wondered. She always did when it came to Sweetums.

"In the kingdom to come, there won't be any cats," Phyliss declared. "They're wild things, worshipped by those Egyptians, who didn't know any better. Have you ever seen Moses petting a cat?"

"I've never seen Moses," Judith replied. "If I run into him downtown, I'll ask."

"Now see here," Phyliss huffed, "don't you start blaspheming! I won't put up with such ungodly talk! That's one of the reasons I quit working for Enid Goodrich. She was always contradicting me about religion.''

Judith felt a passing pang of sympathy for Enid. Humbling herself, Judith tried to make amends. She didn't want to anger Phyliss, especially not now, with the holiday season upon her.

The call to Gertrude was mercifully brief. Gertrude was watching a talk show. "Freaks of nature," she said. "People who are completely abnormal. You know, like your husband." Gertrude hung up.

Coming out of the darkened entrance to the bar, Judith all but bumped into Gary Meyers, who was leaving the dining area. Gary reacted as if he'd been attacked by aliens. Judith apologized.

"I had to make a couple of phone calls," she said, wondering why she felt an explanation was necessary. "There's so much to do this time of year." Judith winced at her own meaningless chatter. "The morning just flew by, with all the trouble at the Goodriches'.''

Gary had opened the door for Judith and was now standing on the sidewalk, his hands stuffed inside the pockets of his Cascade Beer jacket. His expression was still nervous, even wary. "Trouble is right. That family was born for trouble. Maybe Glenda's okay, but the rest of them . . ." He shook his head in a hapless manner. "Women! They're the real trouble-makers!''

Renie was honking the horn. Judith gave Gary a feeble smile and hurried to the car. Oblivious to the rain, Gary remained on the sidewalk, staring vacantly down the street.

"The meter ran out while you were on the phone," Renie said as they pulled into traffic. "The parking violation goons watch this area like vultures. I got a ticket last month for parking in front of a fire hydrant.''

"I should think so," Judith said reasonably. "It's illegal.''

"Which is stupid," Renie countered, taking up two lanes at once. "Nothing was on fire. Why should a parking space go to waste on the off chance that the store I'm shopping in is going to ignite? How often have you been anywhere and had the place go up in flames before you'd paid for your purchases? No such luck, right?''

"You mean a fire sale?" Judith asked with a droll smile. "Coz, you're drifting to the right."

"Oh, good grief! First you tell me how to park, now you're teaching me to drive! Why do you and Bill and my mother and the kids think I don't know how to drive after over thirty years on the road?" Renie ran an arterial, causing two cars to come to a screeching halt and several horns to erupt in frantic honking. "Do you know that I got a commendation this year from our insurance company because I have such a good safety record?"

"Luck," Judith said under her breath. Fortunately, the comment was drowned out by a man in a truck who was yelling that Renie was going the wrong way on a one-way street. "Coz . . ." Judith began as terror enveloped her.

But Renie had swung around a corner. "Okay, so I forgot which way the damned street went. As my father once said when he got stopped for going north on a southbound street, 'I know it's one-way. That's what I was doing—going one way.'" Renie shrugged.

Judith closed her eyes. She remembered Uncle Cliff's erratic driving only too well. While Renie had inherited some of her father's more admirable qualities, his road skills—or lack thereof—also resided in the genes.

Miraculously, the cousins arrived downtown in one piece. They spent the next three hours trooping from Donner & Blitzen to Nordquist's to The Belle Epoch. By the time their feet and their money had given out, each had acquired most of the items on their respective lists. At precisely four o'clock, they were in the car again, breathing heavily.

"The stores look pretty," Renie said, somehow managing to reverse out of their parking place without hitting either of the adjacent vehicles. "I like Nordquist's historical Santa Clauses, especially the Russian one."

"The Belle Epoch is so homey," Judith said. "Every year, they convert the turn-of-the-century Thanksgiving window into Christmas. It's a wonderful transition."

"True," Renie agreed, as the big blue Chev snaked up the curving exit lane. "But Donner & Blitzen is always the best. All those silver stars and gorgeous angels make you feel like you're halfway to heaven."

Judith smiled. "The store smells good, too. I wonder if they use a special Christmas spray."

"We'll have to figure out when the kids can get together to come down and have their pictures taken with Santa at Donner & Blitzen. I swear, they'll be forty years old and still have to sit on Santa's lap for the annual photo session." So wrapped up in holiday tradition was Renie that she made the wrong turn and found herself exiting in the opposite direction from Heraldsgate Hill. "Damn," she breathed as they waited for an opening in the steady late afternoon traffic. "Now we'll have to drive two miles out of our way just to get home."

Judith darted Renie a quick look. "We'll be going right through the hospital district," she said, hoping to sound innocent.

"I know," Renie replied. "That's the only way we can get on a one-way street that takes us back to Heraldsgate Hill. Do you think I'm stupid as well as reckless?"

"No-o-o," said Judith. "But as long as we're in the vicinity, maybe we should check on George."

Renie applied the brake too hard, throwing both cousins forward in their seat belts. "Hold it! Are you trying to finagle yourself into this Goodrich thing? What's the point? George killed Enid; George tried to kill himself. Open and shut. Get over it."

Judith sighed. "I know. You're right. But I care about George. I'd like to find out if he's dead or alive. They won't tell us over the phone, so if we drop in, we might be able to talk to Glenda or Art. And if George has died, we'll find out right now instead of waiting to hear about it. Come on, coz, Bayview is only four blocks away. Arlene would never forgive me for passing up this opportunity."

Renie groaned but turned right instead of left. "I should have known when you tried to pump Gary Meyers. Okay, okay," she went on, seeing the arguments forming on her cousin's lips. "It's not easy to turn your back on a murder. It's impossible when it happens two doors down from your house. But you *could* wait until Joe gets home from work. He'll know, won't he?"

"Maybe," Judith allowed. "It depends on whether he and Woody are all wrapped up in the Shazri case."

Parking at Bayview Hospital proved fairly easy, but finding George Goodrich was another matter. The public hospital was an enormous maze with additions, annexes, and employees for whom English was definitely not their native tongue. After twenty minutes, Judith and Renie found themselves outside of the Intensive Care Unit. They also found themselves face-to-face with Sancha Rael.

"Mr. Goodrich's condition has stabilized," Rael informed them in detached tones. "I can't tell you any more than that, and shouldn't have given out the information in the first place. But," she added, smirking at Judith, "you *are* Joe Flynn's wife. I'm perfectly willing to grant him . . . favors."

Judith pretended she hadn't heard Rael's last remark. "So Mr. Goodrich is going to pull through?" She also tried to pretend that there wasn't an edge to her own voice.

Rael nodded in a casual manner that somehow was also elegant. "They got to him in time to get the stuff out of his system. He took sleeping pills. Dalmane."

Putting aside her annoyance with Rael, Judith tried to remember what she knew about Dalmane. It was Renie, however, who spoke up first.

"That's not real heavy-duty, is it? I think my mother took it after she broke her hip. She had trouble sleeping."

Rael seemed indifferent to Renie's comment. "Whatever. The old guy's pulled through, so we can charge him."

Judith pounced. "You've got sufficient evidence?"

But Rael was too savvy to fall into the trap. "We know how to do our job," she said with a tight little smile. "You must hear that from pillow talk with your husband."

Judith fought off the desire to make a snappy comeback. Renie, however, didn't show such restraint:

"Hey, Judith and Joe don't do pillow talk. They just make

mad, passionate love. Constantly." Renie shook her head.
"It's pathetic, really, at their age. I worry about them."

Rael glared at Renie, then abruptly turned and headed back
into the ICU. Renie snickered. "Maybe she's not so nice after
all. What's her point in ragging you?"

Feeling vaguely disturbed, Judith shrugged and sighed.
"Who knows? Maybe she does have a thing for Joe. Or maybe
she's just unpleasant."

The cousins gazed around the reception area, where staffers
were putting up cheerful Christmas cutouts: Santa waving
from his sleigh, a happy snowman with a stovepipe hat and a
carrot for a nose, a trio of wide-eyed angel babies floating on
a cloud. Judith wondered if the loved ones who waited ever
noticed the decor. Certainly the three people who sat in arm-
chairs lined up against the wall didn't seem very jovial. She
was about to suggest leaving when Glenda and Art came
through the double doors that led from the outside. They both
seemed startled to see Judith and Renie.

"We just happened to be in the vicinity," Judith said, wondering why the small fib felt like such a big lie. "We wondered how your father was doing. I hated to go home without
having news for the rest of the neighbors. I'm sure they've
been worrying, too."

Glenda didn't meet Judith's gaze. "He's coming along,"
she murmured. "It's such a relief. I guess."

Art frowned at the floor. "You got to feel as if he wanted
to go, too. I mean, what has Pappy to look forward to now?"

"Prison?" Renie said, then clapped a hand to her head. "I
didn't mean it like that! He won't go to prison anyway. But
after living with your mother, even prison would seem like
a . . ."

None too discreetly, Judith nudged Renie. "A rest," Judith
interrupted. "A rest *home*. My cousin means your father will
probably go to a place . . . like that."

"A mental institution," Glenda said miserably. "You don't
need to spare our feelings. The worst of it is, Pappy isn't
crazy."

"But he had to be," Art put in. "What do they call it? Temporary insanity—that's it."

Glenda was now nodding vigorously. "It might have been like a blackout. Does he really have to be locked up for the rest of his life? It doesn't seem fair."

Art put a hand on his sister's shoulder. "Don't get riled up. He doesn't care what happens. That's why he tried to kill himself."

Glenda seemed near tears. "But what about *us*? Do we have to spend the rest of *our* lives visiting him every Sunday in some loony bin? My God, after all these years of waiting on Mama hand and foot!"

"Now just a minute, sis!" Art gave Glenda a sharp shake. "It wasn't you who called every morning and went over there almost every day. I've done more than my share of looking after them!"

Anger held Glenda's tears in check. "That's because you're out of work! You don't have anything better to do! I've still got a job!"

The nurse at the desk was looking alarmed. She rose and called to Glenda. "Ms. Goodrich, you may see your father now." A smile for Art followed. "You can go in next, Mr. Goodrich."

With obvious reluctance, Glenda quit the field. She squared her shoulders before following the nurse into the ICU. Judith and Renie exchanged quick glances as Art paced the floor and muttered to himself.

"Why don't we get a cup of coffee?" Judith finally suggested to break the awkward silence.

Art didn't respond at first. Judith started to repeat the question, but Art gave an impatient shake of his head.

"Glenda and I just had coffee. In fact, I've had so much coffee today, I'll never sleep tonight. I should take the rest of those sleeping pills home with me."

The reference to "home" made Judith think of JoAnne and the boys. "Where's the rest of the family?" she asked, trying to steer Art to a chair.

Wearily, Art sat down. The cousins settled in on each side

of him. "They were here for a while and then they left. There wasn't anything they could do. Greg and Dave don't like hospitals."

"And Leigh?" Judith tried to keep her voice casual, hoping to calm Art.

The attempt failed badly. Art's pudgy face reddened; his ears actually looked hot. "Leigh! Do you think Glenda'd let her anywhere near this place? For all I know, Leigh's hightailed it back to New York!"

Judith was mystified. "Why? I thought she was staying over until New Year's."

Rubbing at his high forehead, Art shot Judith a look that was half embarrassed, half pitying. "Not after last night, she isn't."

Judith remembered the screams and Jeanne Ericson's report of a row at the Goodrich house. "What happened last night?"

But Art shook his head. "Never mind. It doesn't matter now. In fact," he went on, raising his head and resting it against the wall behind the chair, "it's small potatoes by comparison. I guess."

Judith decided not to press Art about his niece. Instead, she asked who had found his parents. She was almost certain it had been Art, and the sudden drain of color from his face proved the point before he spoke a single word.

"Every morning, even when I was working"—he paused to glare at the door where his sister had so recently passed— "I call my folks around eight o'clock. They always go to bed by nine-thirty, so they wake up early. If they don't answer, I'm right over there. Or JoAnne is. But that hasn't happened more than twice—until this morning." Again, Art hung his head. "I called first about eight-fifteen. No answer. I called a couple more times, thinking maybe the phone was out of order, like it was before. Around quarter to nine, I decided to check on them. It's only ten minutes from our house above the railroad yard."

Judith knew the neighborhood well. It was on the west slope of Heraldsgate Hill, which commanded a view of the roundhouse, the train tracks, grain elevators, and a large docking area that was usually filled with new cars awaiting transport. While there were glimpses of the bay and the mountains, the environs' more commercial nature made the price of real estate considerably less than in other parts of the Hill. Although Art and JoAnne were probably less than two miles from the cul-de-sac on the south slope, the streets that zigzagged to the senior Goodrich house took time to traverse.

"I stopped at the MasterFaster Mart on top of the Hill to cash in a scratch ticket," Art continued, briefly looking sheepish. "It was only a dollar, but . . ." He raised his beefy hands in a helpless gesture. "Anyway, it was a little after nine when I got to the folks' place. I couldn't raise them, so I got the key from the phony rock and let myself in."

Renie wrinkled her nose in puzzlement. "Phony rock? What do you mean?"

Again, Art looked sheepish, his gaze fixed on the jovial Santa cutout. "Mama didn't like us having keys of our own. But we—Glenda and I—insisted we should have some way to open the door in case of an emergency. So Pappy got one of those phony rocks that you put in the garden and hide an extra key inside. I'd never had to use it before."

Judith nodded encouragement. "I've seen them. Cousin Sue has one she keeps by the goat pen."

Art paid no heed to Cousin Sue or her goats. "So I went in and called out and didn't get any answer. I thought maybe Pappy had had to take Mama to the doctor. I mean, I couldn't see what could happen to both of them, right?" Art gazed first at Judith, then at Renie, as if the cousins could deny the terrible truth.

They couldn't, of course. Art swallowed hard. "I went into the bedroom. And . . . there . . . they . . . were." He covered his face with his hands. "I thought they were both dead. There was so much blood . . . I went into the kitchen and called 911. I was so shook up that I let everybody in through the front door. I didn't realize Pappy was still alive until after the firemen came . . ." Art broke down and sobbed.

The three people who were also waiting tried not to stare. Judith and Renie looked at each other across Art's bowed back. The receptionist and the nurse gazed off into space.

The Santa cutout was still waving.

SIX

AT LAST, JUDITH put a hand on Art's shoulder. She didn't say anything, but waited for him to regain control. He finally did, taking out a crumpled blue-and-white handkerchief, and blowing his nose.

"Sorry. It was just awful."

"Of course it was," Judith said, her voice filled with sympathy. A sudden thought occurred to her. "If your father was unconscious, how do you know he . . . ah . . . attacked your mother?"

Art sat up straight, taking another swipe at his nose. "The medics made him throw up. He came around just long enough to . . . admit what he'd done."

"Oh." Judith sat back in her chair. "Have you talked to him since?"

Art nodded. "Just once, about an hour ago, after they said he was going to pull through."

"What did he say?" Judith asked, still full of sympathy.

Art gave a nervous shrug. "Not much. I mean, he was all spaced out."

Glenda reappeared. The visit with her father apparently had dissipated her anger. She gave her brother a feeble smile.

"They're going to move Pappy to a ward. Will you come?"

Art stuffed the handkerchief back in his pants pocket. "Sure. How's he doing?"

Glenda started to say something, seemingly reconsidered, and shook her head. "He's muddled." She laughed lamely, then leaned down to whisper to her brother. "He says he didn't do it. In fact, he insists he's never owned a hatchet."

Art's head shot up. "What?"

"A hatchet?" Judith echoed, unable to suppress the comment. "Was that the weapon?"

Glenda and Art both regarded her with what Judith interpreted as resentment. "It seems so," Glenda said, then quickly turned back to her brother. The tenuous smile played again at her pale lips. "I said Pappy's muddled. The nurse told me that's natural. The sleeping pills make people a little strange when they come to."

"Oh." Art seemed appeased. "That figures." He struggled to get out of the chair. "We'd better go. Where are they putting him?"

It seemed that Art and Glenda had forgotten about the cousins. Brother and sister exited, their heads together in deep conversation. Renie gave Judith a wry look.

"I take it this is our cue to beat a hasty retreat?"

But Judith was chewing on her lower lip. "A retreat, yes. Hasty, no. I'm perturbed."

Renie swung round in the chair, wagging a finger. "Now wait a minute—have you got one of your harebrained ideas?"

The onlookers were once again watching surreptitiously. Apparently, they were expecting another family feud.

Judith and Renie disappointed them. "Not harebrained," Judith replied reasonably as she got to her feet. "Let's go."

They went, but once in the corridor, Judith studied the hospital directory and floor plan. "We're here," she said, pointing to a red dot. "ICU is over there." She indicated the area behind the reception room. "There's an elevator marked 'Service.' " Her finger stopped at a spot in the corridor just off the Intensive Care section. "If George is being hauled to one of the wards, it must be the sixth floor. Everything else is for surgery, cardiac, oncology, pediatrics, and maternity."

Renie had to run to keep up with her cousin's long-legged stride. "Okay, so you're an expert on reading hospital floor plans. I'm impressed. But when I said 'harebrained,' I meant it. What the hell are we doing now?"

The immediate answer was obvious. The doors to one of the eight public elevators glided open. Judith got in. So did a vexed Renie. Along with an orderly, a mother, and two fidgety children, they ascended to the sixth floor.

Judith paused in the corridor to get her bearings. Renie started to carp, but Judith waved her into silence. A moment later, the cousins had slipped inside a swinging door that led down another hallway and around a corner.

"There," said Judith in satisfaction, as she pointed to a service elevator. "They'll bring George up in that. Glenda and Art are probably already in the room. They would have used one of the public elevators like we just did."

"What makes you think George isn't in the room, too?" Renie demanded.

"Keep it down," Judith murmured. "Because they had to get him ready. You know, IVs and transfer and all that stuff. You've been in the hospital with your stupid kidney stones. You know how long it takes for the staff to do anything."

"True," Renie allowed, remembering to lower her voice. "But I'd like to know why we're here instead of in my car going home to fix dinner for our loving families. Frankly, I'm starving."

"You're always starving. Humor me," Judith urged as the doors to the service elevator began to open. "Act confident. Important. Officious." Judith poised herself, ready for the emergence of George.

But instead, two staff members pushed heated carts filled with covered trays. They glanced curiously at the cousins but said nothing. Judging from the unpronounceable names on their I.D. tags, Judith and Renie wouldn't have understood them if they had spoken.

"That smells good," Renie mumbled. "I wonder what they're serving?"

"Weasel," Judith retorted. "Didn't you say hospital meals were inedible?"

"I didn't say they were inedible," Renie responded, still gazing wistfully after the food carts. "I said they weren't very good. There's a difference, especially when you're hungry."

The cousins fell silent, though Judith kept her eye on the floor indicator that marked the elevator's progress. Sure enough, the car was rising again. It stopped on six.

At first, Judith wasn't sure that the patient on the gurney was George Goodrich. The bare, flaccid arms, the pale, drawn face, the sparse, matted hair, and the absence of glasses were all in contrast to George's usual neat, well-groomed appearance. But the elongated features and the thin nose were still recognizable.

"George!" Judith's greeting was effusive. "I'm so relieved! We've been waiting for ages. How are you feeling?"

The two orderlies who were bringing George into the ward stared at Judith and then at each other. "Missus . . ." said one of them who appeared to be Cambodian.

Judith gave him a friendly wave. "Never mind. I'm George's old friend." The orderlies kept moving, and Judith trotted along at the head of the gurney. "I can't wait to tell everybody at home that you're much better," she said, vaguely aware of Renie shuffling behind her. "The whole neighborhood has been upset."

"Señora," said the other orderly. *"Por favor, no es posible . . ."*

"Look!" Judith cried, pointing to George, whose eyes seemed glazed. "He's smiling!" He wasn't. "George," she went on, her voice now more urgent, "what happened this morning?"

George closed his eyes. Both orderlies were growing impatient as they approached the door that led into the ward. Judith lowered her head and her voice as she repeated the question.

"Missus . . ." pleaded the Cambodian.

"Señora . . ." begged the Hispanic.

George's eyes flickered open. For just a fleeting moment,

he seemed to acknowledge Judith. His head lifted almost imperceptibly from the pillow.

"I . . . didn't . . . I wouldn't . . . I couldn't . . ." He fell back, exhausted.

"What?" Judith frowned as a grim-faced nurse marched into her path. The gurney moved on. *"Who?"* she called after the little group which was fast disappearing into a room on her left.

George turned his head just a fraction. A single word slipped between his lips. Judith couldn't be sure, but she thought it was "key." Then George was out of sight.

The nurse was scowling at Judith. "Where did *you* come from?" she demanded, making it sound as if the expected answer might be a dark and dismal swamp.

Judith tried to look innocent. "We're just neighbors. *Good* neighbors," she added hastily. "Close."

The nurse arched thin, black brows. " 'We'? Are there more of you?"

Puzzled, Judith turned. Renie was no longer right behind her. Judith gazed down to the other end of the corridor. One of the food carts was standing about twenty yards away. Renie was next to it.

Ignoring the nurse's last query, Judith rushed away. This time she was determined not to cause trouble but to prevent it. She caught Renie just as her cousin was about to sample a dish that did indeed look a lot like weasel.

Joe Flynn was swearing, sweating, and swinging from the ceiling. Or doing a good imitation, since he had refused to use the stepladder in order to hang the pine garlands. When Judith hurried into the living room shortly before eight o'clock that evening, she found her husband with one foot on a side chair and the other braced against a bookcase.

"You're going to kill yourself," Judith warned. "I almost fell out of the pine tree last Sunday. Let me get the ladder."

"What's one more death around this goofy neighborhood?" Joe growled as he swung a hammer to pound in a slightly awry nail. "Damned if I don't have enough homicides at work. I come home, and instead of my robe and slippers, there's a—ooops!''

The nail flipped out of the molding and fell onto the floor. Joe swore again. Judith searched about in the coffee can for another nail, then handed it to her husband.

"You weren't that upset when you got here," she noted. Indeed, Joe had already learned of Enid Goodrich's death before he left headquarters.

"That," Joe said through gritted teeth as he successfully hammered in the new nail, "was before you asked me to swing like a chimpanzee in order to put up these damned decorations. It was also before you decided George didn't do it." Panting a bit, Joe asked Judith to hand him the pine garland. "No wonder Renie was annoyed with you. Can't you leave well enough alone?"

Judith ignored the irritation in Joe's voice. She knew it had less to do with her than it did with the garland that refused to stay put on the nail.

"It isn't well enough if George didn't do it," Judith replied placidly. She had already explained her feelings to both Joe and Renie. Her cousin had only half listened, being intent on coping with rush-hour traffic. Joe had seemed more sympathetic. But then he'd had the advantage of hearing his wife's theory over a soothing scotch-on-the-rocks.

Now, however, he appeared to have changed his mind. Or perhaps he was merely trying to distract himself from balancing atop two phone directories piled on the bay window's cushioned seat.

"I told you," Judith was saying in a calm voice that masked her worry for Joe's safety. "George isn't a killer. I don't care how aggravating Enid was—he doesn't strike me as the sort who'd resort to murder."

"That's bunk," Joe retorted, managing to strike the last nail evenly. "One thing I've learned from my job is that everybody—absolutely *everybody*—is capable of murder, given certain conditions."

Judith took the hammer from Joe in exchange for another

length of garland. "Then why didn't George kill Enid years ago? And why does he deny doing it?"

Joe got down carefully from the window seat. "Hey, he confessed, didn't he? Patches Morgan is sharp, even if he does think he's part pirate. Did he bring his parrot?"

Judith's voice took on a dark note. "He brought Sancha Rael."

"Rael, huh? She's new but promising." Joe stepped back, reluctantly admiring his handiwork. "It looks good, especially with those strands of gold pearls running through it." In apparent contrition, Joe kissed his wife's temple. "What next, having me crawl down the chimney to see if Santa can fit?"

Judith smiled fondly at her husband. "I can do the rest of the house over the next couple of days. Except the tree—we should buy it this weekend so we can let it stand in water outside for a few days."

Joe replaced the side chair next to the card table that usually held a jigsaw puzzle in progress. "Why bother? We never did that when I was married to Herself."

References to Joe's first wife occasionally still rankled. "What did she do, pickle the tree along with the rest of her?" Repentance immediately enveloped Judith. She put her hands on Joe's shoulders. "Sorry. Sometimes I'm kind of mean."

Tucking his shirt inside his pants, Joe tipped his head to one side. "Jude-girl—has it ever occurred to you that you don't need to do every little thing for Christmas that your family has done since 1901? Fifteen boxes of decorations, five of them just for the tree, church activities, presents, cards, letters, books, recordings, baking, cooking, and now the cul-de-sac. Instead of cutting down on your workload, you add to it. You've got a *job,* for God's sake! Not to mention a husband, a son, a mother, and about four hundred relatives who expect you to put on an annual extravaganza. Give yourself a break."

"But I like it," Judith protested, then realized that Joe might not. Maybe it wasn't just that he didn't share her enthusiasm for the holidays but that he resented the time and energy she expended on preparations. "I enjoy doing things for other people," she said, sounding defensive. "Why else would I run a B&B?"

Joe looked as if he were trying to understand. But his words conveyed a firm if gentle warning. "All this hustle and bustle wears you down. You get cranky. Face it, Jude-girl, you're not twenty years old anymore. And you're only human."

"We still should put the tree in water outside." Judith wasn't giving in easily. She went over to a big carton that sat on the floor by the window seat, then began unwrapping candles of various shapes, including reindeer, bells, snowmen, igloos, and a steepled church. "The Ericsons do it. So do the Rankerses and Bill and Renie. You take a second cut after you get it home, about two inches. Don't you remember from last year?"

If Joe did, he wouldn't admit it. "I sure as hell don't remember that those candles looked as if the mice had eaten them. What happened?"

"The mice ate them." Judith held a white reindeer in her hand. Both its antlers were missing. "Some of these belonged to my grandparents. One year they stored them in the attic instead of the basement. I don't know why. But the mice got into them, and a few actually melted because the attic got so warm in the summer. That's why this lamppost tilts." With a nostalgic smile, Judith displayed a crooked lamp standard made of green, red, white, and yellow wax. "This is older than I am."

Joe tried to look impressed. "Cute," he said. "I think I'll go upstairs and watch TV. This Shazri case is a drag. I hate it when you know who the perp is but the evidence is shaky. Woody and I feel like we're walking on eggs."

Judith looked up from the carton. "That's another thing— there were needles all over the living room floor. Nobody ever walks on that carpet. It's even got a runner."

"What?" Halfway to the entry hall, Joe had turned around.

"The Goodrich house," Judith said, running a hand through the pile of tissue paper to make sure she hadn't missed anything. "Why would there be fir needles on the living room rug? Nobody was allowed in that room except extra-special company, which they hadn't had in years.''

Joe suppressed a yawn. "The firemen. The medics. The cops. Morgan and Rael.''

"It wasn't any of them," Judith asserted as she placed an Eskimo couple on each side of their igloo. "Art was so rattled that he let the emergency personnel come in the front way. The fir needles were from the noble that Jeanne and Ted Ericson had lying in the joint driveway behind the house.''

Joe took a couple of steps back into the living room. "What are you trying to say?''

Judith had gone over to the fireplace, where she was arranging the candles on the mantle. "That maybe somebody else came in the house this morning. Whoever it was entered the usual way, through the back. He or she tracked the needles into the living room and the bedroom. Ted didn't bring the tree home until after eight.'' She lifted her shoulders and gave Joe a quizzical look.

"Maybe it was George. He went outside, then came back in and went into the living room.'' Joe's round face was ingenuous. "Simple, huh?''

But Judith didn't agree. "George never went in the living room. It wasn't permitted. Of course, if Enid was already dead . . .'' She rubbed at the back of her head. "No, then there would have been blood on the carpet. Art told us there was blood all over both his parents.'' Judith winced at the thought.

"Give it up, Jude-girl.'' Joe's voice had grown tired.

"This afternoon George said he didn't kill Enid,'' Judith said doggedly. "He also tried to say something else. It sounded like 'key.' They kept a key in one of those phony rocks outside. Maybe somebody took it and came in and . . .''

Joe threw up his hands. "I'm going to watch something that makes sense, like *America's Favorite Home Videos*. I should make one of my wife, going around the neighborhood with a magnifying glass, looking for cigarette butts and scraps of paper with mysterious phone numbers. Scratch the sable coat—I'm getting you a deerstalker for Christmas.'' Joe headed upstairs.

Judith sighed, then returned to her task. She had almost finished when she heard a knock on the French doors. As she crossed the length of the long living room, she could make out the figure behind the rectangular panes: It was a tall, blond male in a down jacket. His hands were shoved inside his pockets, and in the deep December shadows of the porch, he looked vaguely sinister. Suddenly anxious, Judith stood rooted on her side of the double doors. Then she recognized Dooley.

"Dooley!" she cried, yanking open the right-hand door and beaming. "You've grown another foot! Are you home for Christmas?"

Aloysius Gonzaga Dooley lurched into the room, grinning widely. "I sure am. We start our semester in August. I'm off until January. Hey, Mrs. McMonigle, what's this about Mrs. Badbitch?"

In his previous incarnation as the neighborhood paperboy, Dooley had been fascinated by crime. For a couple of years, he had been a member of the police auxiliary. But as he grew up, his interests had widened. This past year he had enrolled at a small private college on the other side of the state. Judith hadn't seen Dooley since early spring, before she and Joe had gone on their trip to England.

"Want some pop?" Judith asked after insisting that Dooley sit down on one of the matching sofas. "Or beer," she added, remembering that her guest was no longer a mere boy.

"Pop's fine," Dooley said, stretching out his long legs under the coffee table. "Mom's agog. What's happening?"

After fetching a soda for Dooley and herself, Judith recounted the terrible tragedy in the cul-de-sac. "I tried to call your mother earlier today, but she wasn't home," Judith finally said after she had wrapped up her account. "I didn't want to leave such a gruesome message on the answering machine."

Dooley nodded. "She was probably picking me up at the airport. Wow, this is unreal! That old lady was totally mean. She was always complaining that I threw the paper into her flowers or missed the porch or some dumb thing. She reported me a bunch of times to the local manager, but he knew what she was like. I used to watch her and Mr. Goodrich through my telescope when they were out in the backyard. She was always nagging the poor guy. That's how I learned to read lips. Sort of.'' Dooley tried to look modest.

"Do you still have the telescope?" Judith remembered it well, particularly from a certain misadventure involving Gertrude in the altogether.

Dooley chuckled. Maybe he was remembering Gertrude, too. "Oh, yeah. My brother, O.P., uses it a lot. He's almost twelve."

O.P. was Oliver Plunkett Dooley, and, like his brother, he had taken an alias to avoid ridicule as well as comparison to the saints for whom he had been named. While the Dooleys had lived behind Hillside Manor and the Ericsons for almost thirty years, Judith still didn't know exactly how many children the family had or what their real names were. As soon as a couple of them grew up, new babies seemed to appear. The assumption was that they were grandchildren, but their constant presence at the Dooley house indicated they might as well have been replacements.

"Well, darn," Dooley said, leaning his sharp chin on his hand. "It doesn't sound like there's any mystery this time."

"Don't tell me you'd want to help solve it if there was," Judith said, unable to keep from sounding sly.

Dooley shrugged. "Why not? It's good exercise for the brain. Oh, I'm not going to go into law enforcement or anything like that. I'd rather study philosophy and teach at the college level." He suddenly looked older and just a trifle dignified. "But I wouldn't mind matching wits with a killer. Especially one right here in the neighborhood. Everybody's involved, right?" As if tugged by a magnet, Dooley's eyes strayed across the room to the front door. Beyond it lay the Stein house, and the Steins' enchanting daughter, Brianna.

"Brianna's not home from college yet," Judith said, unable to hold back. "I think the school she's attending in California is on the quarter system."

Dooley flushed ever so slightly. "Could be," he said, then

took a sip of pop and assumed a worldly air. "But the local Methodist university isn't."

Judith's eyes widened. Naturally, the Porter house was next to the Steins'. "Gabrielle Porter? Dooley, you're fickle!"

Dooley grinned. "Brianna's dating some studly guy she met in California. He's all bleached out and tanned and buff. Mrs. Stein showed Mom a picture. Besides, Gaby's quite excellent. Remember how she used to be all pigtails and big teeth and skinny legs? That changed."

Gaby Porter had indeed changed. The little girl known as Lean Bean was now an eighteen-year-old semi-goddess. Fleetingly, Judith thought of Brianna, of Gabrielle, of Leigh. All three were products of the neighborhood, directly or otherwise. Judith hadn't yet seen the grown-up supermodel Leigh, but it was obvious that the cul-de-sac had produced natural wonders besides splendid trees and lush flowers. Judith felt a pang of envy for the trio's youth and beauty.

But Dooley was feeling curious. "So what makes you think Mr. Goodrich is innocent?" he asked, exhibiting more understanding for Judith's intuition than Joe had.

"Because he says so," Judith replied. "Yes, I realize that people who come out of a Dalmane-induced state are often confused, even deluded. But tell me, Dooley, can you see Mr. Goodrich taking a hatchet to Mrs. Goodrich?"

Dooley was mature enough to reflect on the concept before answering. "Well . . . maybe. But he's a really nice guy. O.P. was saying that when he sees Mr. Goodrich through the telescope talking to that Mrs. Swanson his whole face gets full of sunshine. At least," Dooley added with a shrug, "that's how O.P. puts it. He's still a kid."

"Really." Judith's voice was soft. "That's interesting."

Dooley, however, was concentrating on the murder itself. "If Mr. Goodrich didn't do it, how come he took those pills?"

Judith frowned. "I don't know. Somebody might have given them to him. In coffee, let's say. There were two empty mugs in the kitchen sink."

Dooley drew his long legs up to his chin. "How many would it take?"

"I don't know. Enid had all sorts of pills in the cupboard. I assume Dalmane was one of them."

Dooley rocked back and forth on the sofa. "Whoever did it—assuming it wasn't George—would have to come in, drug him, and then kill Enid, right?"

Judith considered. "Probably. But as I told you, I think he said something about a key. Maybe whoever it was used the key in the fake rock to get in."

"Could they hide in the house?" Dooley traced something in the air. "I'm trying to remember what I could see inside with my telescope. It's been a while."

"They could hide in the living room," Judith said dryly. "Nobody ever went in there. Plus, there are two other bedrooms. I've never seen them, but I know they're there. One's in the basement. That was Art's. Glenda's was on the main floor."

Dooley polished off his pop. "This is cool." He suddenly looked apologetic. "I don't mean that in a good way, Mrs. McMonigle. But it's . . . interesting." Unwinding his long legs, he stood up.

"I think so," Judith said. "And by the way, it's Mrs. Flynn now."

"Oh!" This time, Dooley flushed all the way to the roots of his blond hair. "I keep forgetting! You married Lieutenant Flynn. He's cool, too."

Judith nodded. "Yes, he is. Most of the time."

"I'll be working on this," Dooley said, heading for the French doors. "It'll keep my mind active while I'm on break."

"Good," Judith replied, noting that the rain had finally stopped. "Say hi to the rest of your family."

"I'll do that." Dooley ambled off toward the fence that separated Hillside Manor from his parents' property. With a dazzling leap, he was up and away and out of sight.

Judith smiled to herself. She had failed to convince Renie and Joe that George Goodrich was innocent. Dooley had proved more reasonable. She had cause to feel smug. An ally had been secured. At least until Gabrielle Porter finished finals.

SEVEN

RENIE WAS EXUBERANT. She stood in the cool night air and all but jumped up and down. "It's great, coz! Your village is absolutely wonderful! I feel like I'm right there in a nineteenth-century New England town. If only I were a midget."

Judith couldn't help but be pleased by her cousin's admiration. It was almost nine o'clock on Thursday, the second day of December. Renie had stopped by on her way from a Christmas decoration meeting at church. She not only praised the miniature town but lavished kind words on the rest of the cul-de-sac.

"It looks so festive," she declared, her eyes darting from the Rankers' Holy Family to the Porters' rooftop Santa to the Steins' tasteful bulbs, and then to the other side of the street with Mrs. Swanson's delicate fairy lights and the Ericsons' charming carolers. If the darkened Goodrich house bothered her, Renie didn't say so.

"How do your guests like it?" she asked, moving to the Rankers' lawn for a closer view of the Nativity scene.

"This is the first night everything's been set up," Judith replied. "It will be even better when the indoor lights are on and the trees are decorated. I've only got four guests tonight anyway. Weekday business will pick up around the thirteenth."

Renie was pointing to the laurel hedge that separated the Rankers' property from Hillside Manor. "Look—I like the way they've got the camels' heads poking out of the shrubbery. But where are the Wise Men?"

"In the hedge," Judith replied. "They're shorter, so you can't see them. Yet." She still had qualms about Arlene's concept. "There aren't any carpet cleaners, though. The hardware store doesn't carry them."

Renie turned a quizzical face to Judith. "Huh?"

Judith laughed. "I forgot, you weren't at our neighborhood meeting. Arlene said she wanted the Nativity scene to include the carpet-cleaners. It turned out that she meant the Wise Men's attendants. Sometimes they're depicted carrying Oriental rugs. You know, 'We three kings of Orient are.' "

"Are rug salesmen?" Renie shrugged. "Maybe they were. That might be how they got so rich. Bill and I priced new carpeting this fall and the estimates were sky-high." She turned to gaze the length of the cul-de-sac. "What are you going to do about the sign that Ted had made?"

Judith grimaced. "Well . . . the police put somebody on duty at the Goodrich house for the first twenty-four hours, but he left this evening before dinner. Nobody else has been around, so I thought . . . ah . . . maybe . . . er . . ."

Renie went right to the point. "Why not? Enid's dead, and I'll bet George won't come back."

Judith gave her cousin a grateful smile. "I didn't want to sound crass. And of course I'll have to ask the other neighbors what they think. Joe says they might let George out on bail, but if they do, I'd guess that he'll stay with either Glenda or Art."

"What else has Joe heard downtown?" Renie inquired, now back at the edge of the New England village.

"Not much. He hasn't had time. If he calls home today, I'm going to beg him to find out about the hatchet." Judith straightened one of the villagers who apparently had been blown askew by the wind that was coming off the bay. "Fingerprints, too. Or signs of anyone else being on the premises."

"So you're still trying to exonerate George." Renie sighed,

then turned solemn. "The hatchet bothers me. It's pretty grue-some. Maybe it wasn't a hatchet. Maybe it was a meat cleaver." The thought didn't seem to cheer Renie.

Judith was staring up at the sky. A few clouds were passing overhead, but she could see a scattering of stars. All around them, the big old trees sighed and groaned. Despite the recent tragedy, the cul-de-sac seemed peaceful.

Or did, until a van careened around the corner, turned with a screech, and pulled up in front of the Ericson house. Startled, the cousins stared as three people got out and hurried to the Goodrich house.

"Who's that?" Renie asked, shivering as the wind began to blow harder.

"I can't see," Judith said. "It's too dark. It looks as if they're heading for the Goodriches'. Unfortunately, a couple of my guests are parked in front of George and Enid's house. But that van doesn't belong to either Glenda or Art."

The squeal of tires had brought Arlene Rankers and Gabe Porter outside. They were both questioning the cousins when the lights went on in the Goodrich house.

"I've seen that Ford E-250 before," said Gabe, who was an expert on automobiles. "It must belong to one of the grand-sons."

Arlene set her chin. "We can't be sure. Let's go over and see what's going on. It might be looters."

"I don't think so," said Gabe, thoughtfully stroking his trim mustache. "Didn't you say they went around back? That sounds like family."

Judith was about to agree when someone emerged through the front door, carrying a chair. Arlene set out at a run. The cousins and Gabe Porter dutifully followed, but at a slower pace.

"I don't like getting mixed up in this," Gabe murmured. "If that's the grandsons, one of them works with me at United Foods."

"Oh?" Judith regarded Gabe with interest. "I didn't know that. Which one?"

"I'm not sure of his first name," Gabe admitted. "He

hasn't been there long, but he's the one who's losing his hair."

"That would be Greg," Judith said. "I think."

Just as Arlene reached the communal driveway, someone else came out of the house, carrying two lamps. Judith was now able to recognize Dave, who was wearing a windbreaker and a baseball cap turned backward.

Arlene already had confronted Greg, who was putting the chair in the back of the paneled van. "Where are you taking these things?" she demanded.

Greg peered out from under the hood of his duffel coat. "Why do you care? It's our stuff."

Arlene stamped her foot. "No, it's not. It belongs to your grandfather. You put those things back right this minute!"

Greg's brother had joined him, juggling lamps and looking annoyed. Hurriedly, he slammed the van's rear doors shut. "What's happening? Who are you?" Greg glanced from Arlene to Gabe to Renie to Judith. "Wait—weren't you at the house yesterday?" The question was directed at Judith.

"We're all neighbors," Judith replied, "except my cousin. But she was with me yesterday when we came to help . . ."

"Guys!" The sharp female voice cut through the chilly air. "Give me a hand with this armchair. I can't get the stupid plastic off of it."

Under the porch light, Judith could see a tall young woman with tendrils of honey-colored hair swirling around her head and face. Taking two steps closer, she saw the strong yet feminine features and the wide-set blue eyes. The hair didn't really swirl, Judith realized; rather, it had been cultivated to frame the beautiful face.

Nervously, Greg looked up from his position at the rear of the van. "You don't need an armchair, Leigh. It'll cost you to ship it back east."

"I can afford it." Leigh's voice held a note of arrogance. "I always liked it because it's so ugly and we were never allowed to sit in it. I'm going to remove the stuffing and plant ivy in it and set it out on my roof garden."

"That's dumb," Dave said, putting the lamps in a cardboard box. "I like that armchair. I'll take it and the couch, too. My apartment's got about two sticks of furniture.''

"*Our* apartment, man," Greg put in. "We want the bedroom set, too."

"Like hell," snapped Leigh. "I covet that dresser and the bureau. They're antiques. You can have the twin beds."

Arlene hadn't recovered from having her authority ignored. She now stood on the porch between Greg and Leigh. "You're all out of order. Who gave you permission to strip this house?"

Arlene was above average in height, but Leigh was almost six feet tall. Her shiny silver boots had high heels, so that when she spoke, the words were directed at the top of Arlene's head. "Who'll stop us? This is family stuff. Butt out, Mrs. Do-Gooder." With a flip of her artistic tendrils, Leigh went back inside the house. Her cousins followed.

"Barbarians!" shouted Arlene as the front door slammed in her face.

Gabe was shaking his head. "I don't like this. You're right, Arlene. It may not be looting, but it sure is greed. What if George comes back? These grandkids will have cleaned the place out."

Judith turned to Renie. But Renie had wandered over to the van and was bending down, looking in the gutter. She saw Judith and came back to the sidewalk.

"Did George say 'key'?" Renie asked in pretended innocence. Opening her hand, she displayed what looked like a house key. "I found it in the gutter in front of the Ericsons', under some leaves."

Judith stared at the key. There were traces of dirt, but otherwise it was shiny. "I wonder," she mused, fingering her chin. She turned to Gabe. "You don't have a flashlight, do you?"

"On me?" Gabe grinned. "No, but I can get one from the garage real quick."

"Get a plastic bag, too." As Gabe headed across the cul-de-sac at a semi-jog, Judith turned to Renie. "Don't move. Just stand there and hold that key exactly the way you've got it now."

"Jeez," Renie grumbled, "what do I look like, one of your village characters?"

"What about those awful grandchildren?" Arlene raged. "Are we going to let them pillage the Goodrich house?"

"We sure aren't. We're going to call the police." Judith threw Arlene and Renie a smug look, then hurried down the sidewalk. "I'm getting Joe."

Joe didn't want to play cop. He was in the third floor family quarters, sitting in the den with his feet up and watching a vintage Bogart movie.

"Send Bogie," he told his wife. "Better yet, send Peter Lorre. I'm off duty and I don't want to put my shoes on."

"Come on, Joe," Judith pleaded. "Those Goodrich kids are pillaging the place. They can't be allowed to get away with outright theft."

Joe clicked the TV volume up a notch higher. "I'm Homicide, not Larceny. Wait until they kill somebody."

Judith turned grim. "Maybe one of them already did."

"What?" Joe tore his gaze away from the screen. "Hey, don't start that again!"

"I'm not," Judith replied calmly. "Renie found a key in the street by the Ericsons'. It may fit the Goodriches' back door. Come on, Joe, give those kids a scare. If nothing else, it'll show them they can't take what isn't theirs."

For several moments, Joe kept his eyes glued on Bogart, Lorre, and Mary Astor. Their predicament over a ceramic bird didn't seem half as interesting to Judith as what was going on in the cul-de-sac.

"Joe . . ." She was verging on a whine.

The movie cut to a commercial. Grumbling, Joe slipped his feet into his loafers. "They aren't kids. I've seen Art's sons. They have to be in their late twenties."

"They probably are," Judith agreed. "Which means they ought to know better. Hurry, Joe. It won't take them long to fill that van."

Judith was right. The Goodrich house was dark again when she and Joe reached the cul-de-sac. The van's lights were on, however, and a stream of exhaust could be seen on the cold night air.

"They're leaving!" Judith cried, now running into the street. "Stop!" she yelled. "Stop or we'll . . ."

It was the van that stopped, just shy of the corner. Arlene also had given chase, but was now teetering indecisively in front of Mrs. Swanson's house. Gabe Porter was coming from his garage, carrying a flashlight. Renie stood quietly at the edge of the Goodrich and Ericson driveway, her right hand extended as she kept the key in its palm. The van's rear end suddenly tilted to the right.

"They've overloaded it," Judith said as she stopped next to Renie.

"Maybe." Renie seemed unusually passive, which Judith recognized as a dangerous sign.

Joe was now moving carefully but purposefully up to the driver's side of the van. Judith started to follow him but stopped and stared at Renie.

"What did you do?" she asked, as the meaning of her cousin's demeanor sunk in.

Renie gave Judith a tight little smile. "You didn't really think I was digging around in the gutter searching for clues, did you? I just happened to find the key after I punctured the right rear tire."

Judith broke into a wide grin. "Coz! You scamp! How'd you do it?"

Renie nodded in the direction of the curb. "With the steak knife I found lying under the rest of the leaves. I was going to use my nail scissors, but they weren't tough enough. I left the knife because I didn't want Arlene to blab it all over the neighborhood." Renie gave Judith a meaningful look.

Judith's grin had faded fast. "A knife?" she breathed. "Was Enid killed with a knife?"

Greg had gotten out of the van and apparently was trying to explain the situation to Joe. Arlene had edged closer but wasn't as yet interfering. Joe gestured toward the Goodrich house; Greg turned in that direction, then gave a jerky nod. A female voice yelled something unintelligible from the van.

Dave got out on the passenger's side and was immediately collared by Arlene.

"What now?" Gabe Porter murmured.

The instantaneous response was the appearance of Mrs. Swanson on her porch, Ted Ericson coming through his gate, and the Steins charging down their front steps. Leigh jumped out of the van, then charged Arlene. Arlene kicked Leigh in the shin, just above the top of her shiny silver boot. Dave ducked for cover in Mrs. Swanson's yard. Joe backed up a few paces until he was in the middle of the cul-de-sac.

"It's all right, everybody," he shouted. "We've got a flat tire here, nothing more. If we all simmer down, there won't be any more trouble."

Judith marveled at the authority in her husband's usually mellow voice. After an exchange of muttered threats, Arlene and Leigh moved away from each other. Dave looked up from under Mrs. Swanson's silver spruce. The Steins stopped at the curb in front of their house. Ted Ericson paused, then closed his gate and presumably went back inside. Mrs. Swanson, however, remained on her porch.

Joe walked over to Arlene, took her firmly by the arm, and led her back to the driveway where Judith, Renie, and Gabe were standing.

"Greg says they won't haul any more stuff out. I couldn't see into the rear of the van, but he says they've got a couple of chairs, some lamps, an end table, the TV, a small radio, and a vacuum cleaner. It *is* family, and nobody's filed a complaint." Joe straightened the corduroy collar on the barn jacket he'd grabbed going out the door. "They'll have to replace the tire before they can get out of here. Let's all go inside and forget we ever saw them."

"But . . ." In dismay, Judith glanced at Renie.

Renie gave a helpless shrug. Gabe discreetly slipped her the plastic sandwich bag, then tucked the flashlight under his arm.

"I guess that means me," he said with a forced chuckle.

"I guess so," said Judith, also sounding forced. "Come on, coz," she said to Renie. "I'll walk you to your car."

Gabe was escorting Arlene in the direction of their neigh-

boring houses. Arlene didn't bother to lower her voice as she
bent Gabe's ear: ". . . Never thought much of Leigh, even
when she was little . . . Imagine, her being a model! Why, she
used to have terrible posture . . . Always sulking and whining
. . . Once, when our Kevin made her eat a bug, she . . ." Arlene's voice finally grew faint as she reached the perimeter of
her property where plastic shepherds watched by night.

At the other end of the cul-de-sac, the three Goodrich offspring were arguing, albeit quietly. It appeared to Judith that
the latest dispute involved who would go and who would stay
with the van. The matter was settled when all three of them
trudged off in the direction of Heraldsgate Avenue and the
local BP service station.

But it was Mrs. Swanson who deterred Joe and the cousins.
Her voice was very soft as she called out to Joe.

Dutifully, Joe trudged back down the street. Judith and
Renie followed, but at a discreet distance.

"Please, Mr. Flynn, I am very worried." Mrs. Swanson had
come down to the walk and was looking pitifully small in her
heavy winter coat. "This is such a terrible thing with Mr. and
Mrs. Goodrich. But I am also disturbed by these vehicles
which come and go but don't belong here. Why is this? Where
do they come from?"

Joe filled his voice with reassurance. "That van belongs to
the Goodrich grandsons. They've had a flat tire."

"Yes, yes," Mrs. Swanson replied, betraying a touch of
impatience. "I recognize it, as well as the young people. I
speak rather of the trucks."

As Judith drew closer to her husband, she could see his
puzzled expression. "What trucks?" Joe asked.

Mrs. Swanson clasped and unclasped her hands. "An older
truck, for one. For the past week, it has been parked across
the street by the Álvarez house. But Mr. and Mrs. Álvarez are
not at home. Each year, they visit their son and his family in
San Diego from Thanksgiving to late January."

Joe, Judith, and Renie all gazed in the direction of the corner
house across from the cul-de-sac. Judith knew Mr. and Mrs.
Álvarez only slightly, from spotting them at church.

"I saw that orange pickup a couple of times, too," Judith said. "So did Renie." She turned to her cousin. "Last Sunday?"

Renie nodded. "It had Oregon plates."

"I think I saw it at least once after that," Judith added. "I drove a pickup the other day. I borrowed it from Kevin, one of the Rankers' sons."

Mrs. Swanson nodded once. "I know that truck. It's a deep green. I see Kevin driving it often. It's the ones I do not know that disturb me."

Joe was again offering Mrs. Swanson reassurance. "Don't worry about it. Whoever owns it is probably visiting somebody down the street and wants to keep their hosts' parking clear. You know the problem on Heraldsgate Hill—all the new apartments and condos, and so many of the houses are old and have only one garage. But most families own at least two cars. They have to park on the street."

Mrs. Swanson still wore a troubled expression. "We have had too much happen that is bad lately. I will never forget all those emergency vehicles yesterday morning. I was uneasy from the start, when the first red truck stopped on the other side of my house." She made a small gesture, again pointing to the main thoroughfare. "It awoke me. Usually, I rise early, but I'd had trouble getting to sleep. I thought the red truck was the fire department. But it wasn't. They came later, almost two hours."

Judith frowned at Mrs. Swanson. "What kind of truck?" Her curiosity was aroused. There was no reason for a commercial truck to stop in the residential neighborhood. If Mrs. Swanson was accurate about the time, it would have been seven-thirty in the morning, too early for service technicians or deliverymen.

"I couldn't see," Mrs. Swanson said, "except that it was red and big. I did not have on my eyeglasses, and the shrubs outside the bedroom window impair my view."

Joe took Mrs. Swanson by the arm. "I don't blame you for being upset. But this time of year, there are a lot of unusual comings and goings. Maybe whoever was driving the red truck stopped on a quiet corner to drink a cup of coffee. I take it you haven't seen the big red truck since yesterday morning?"

"No," Mrs. Swanson replied, letting Joe escort her onto the porch. "Only one time. It stayed for ten, maybe fifteen minutes. Perhaps you are right—someone was drinking coffee." The idea seemed to cheer Mrs. Swanson. "Thank you, Mr. Flynn. I should not be afraid with you as my neighbor." With a charming smile, Mrs. Swanson glided into the house.

Joe joined the cousins, rubbing his hands together. "B-r-r-r," he said. "It's going to freeze tonight. Come on, Jude-girl, let's go in. I've got a fire going in the den."

"Too bad you don't have a fireplace," Renie remarked. "Ha-ha."

Joe grinned at Renie's teasing. The third floor fireplace had not been in the original remodeling plans for the attic. But during the previous summer, Joe had lobbied for the luxury of a hearth in his home quarters. Judith's opposition had been minimal, though the cost had been large. She knew that it wasn't easy for Joe to live in a house that was partially overrun by strangers. The fireplace had seemed like a small concession to her husband's comfort.

"I'll be along in just a minute," Judith said. "I'm seeing Renie off."

Briefly, Joe eyed his wife with suspicion, but the chilling wind was cutting through his barn jacket. He shrugged, then trotted down the driveway to the back door. Judith and Renie lingered in front of the Ericson house.

"Show me that knife," Judith said as soon as her husband was out of earshot.

Renie led Judith to the curb on the Ericsons' side of the driveway. "I know I shouldn't have touched it," Renie said, "but I had to use something to puncture that tire."

The knife lay exposed, though just as Judith reached for the tip of the blade, it was covered by dried leaves that swirled around the street. "It looks like a steak knife," Judith said. "Have you got that sack with the key?"

"Here," said Renie, handing over the plastic bag that Gabe Porter had given her. "Will the knife fit?"

"Barely," Judith replied. "I wish I'd thought to bring a flashlight when I went to get Joe. But I was counting on using Gabe's. Come on," she said, standing up and turning into the shared driveway. "Let's see if we can find that phony rock."

"In the dark?" Renie's tone was dubious.

But when the cousins reached the Goodrich backyard, they saw that the spotlight on the Ericsons' deck had been turned on. No doubt it was a safety precaution, Judith thought, caused by the problems next door at the Goodrich house.

Still, it was difficult to find the fake rock. Judith's hands were growing numb with cold as she concentrated on the strip of garden next to the house. Renie, meanwhile, poked about in the small plot next to the garbage can and the recycling bins. At first, Judith thought the sudden yelp from Renie was evoked by discovery. When Renie started swearing and clutching her index finger, Judith realized it was a cry of pain.

"What's wrong?" she said in a low voice as she hurried to Renie's side. "Don't yell—you'll scare Mrs. Swanson."

"Screw Mrs. Swanson," Renie retorted in a cross voice. "I cut myself. Some damned fool dropped a piece of glass next to the garbage can."

As Renie rummaged in her purse for a Band-Aid, Judith dropped down on her haunches. Sure enough, there was a two-inch sliver of glass. Gingerly, she picked it up and lifted the garbage can lid. She recalled finding another shard earlier in the day.

"The rest of the glass is in here. Whoever broke it and threw it out must have dropped a piece. Are you okay, coz?"

"I'm wonderful," Renie snarled, as she wrapped the Band-Aid around her finger. "Honest to God, the things I do for—ooops!"

Having taken a backward step, Renie's foot encountered an unexpected object that caused her to lose her balance. She grabbed the recycling bin just in time to save herself from a fall.

"Gee, coz," Judith said, with real concern in her voice, "you're having kind of a rough time. Maybe you should go home."

But Renie was now looking down at the offending object. "Well, well," she said, pain and anger fading. "This rock looks a little too smooth to be the real thing."

Judith looked, too. Then she picked up the dark gray ersatz rock and turned it over. Sure enough, the bottom was flat, with a small tab that slipped open to reveal a hiding place for a key.

Except that there was no key. The cousins stared at each other. Judith reached into her pocket and brought out the plastic Baggie. She extracted a Kleenex from another pocket, then removed the key that Renie had found in the street.

"Shall we?" she said, holding the key in the tissue.

"We shall," Renie replied, only a trifle reluctantly.

The cousins mounted the back steps. Judith inserted the key. The lock turned. The cousins stared at each other again.

"Do you still think I'm nuts?" Judith whispered.

"Sure," Renie answered promptly. "But I'm beginning to think you're also right about George. Maybe he didn't do it after all."

If not triumphant, Judith's smile was self-righteous. "I'm glad to have you on the team, coz. Now that we know who didn't do it, we have to figure out who did."

Renie groaned.

EIGHT

BY FRIDAY MORNING, Judith wasn't feeling so sanguine. Since it had been almost eleven o'clock when she finally reached the family quarters Thursday night, she'd found Joe half asleep. Early mornings were not a good time for the Flynns to exchange confidences: Judith had to make breakfast for her guests, play the cheerful hostess, and get Gertrude set for the day. While Judith rose at six, it was usually nine o'clock before she sat down at the kitchen table to enjoy a quiet cup of coffee. By then, Joe had been at work for almost an hour.

Thus, she discovered herself in a quandary about the key and the knife that Renie had found in the gutter. She supposed that she should turn both items over to Patches Morgan immediately. But she wanted to confer with Joe first.

"I'll wait until he comes home tonight," she said to Renie over the phone.

"Unhhh," Renie replied. It was nine-fifteen, and Renie might be out of bed, but she was rarely fully conscious before ten.

"Somebody used that key to the Goodrich back door, and then dropped it," Judith said, content to bounce her thoughts off the drowsy Renie. "The question is, why?"

"Zzzrghhh," said Renie.

"Who knew about the hidden key except Glenda and

Art and maybe JoAnne? And why was it needed?'' Judith poured herself another mug of coffee.

"Nmphhh," said Renie.

"When? That's another point. What caused the person who used the key *not* to put it back where it belonged? And that steak knife—how did it end up in the street, too? Enid was killed with a hatchet, not a knife. Joe finally verified that much for me. But there are too many unanswered questions, coz. Glenda said her father insisted he didn't own a hatchet. Somehow, that bothers me. Last Sunday George or Enid mentioned a hatchet, but I can't exactly recall the context. I was too busy being irked by Enid. I'm going to phone Art this morning and see what's going on with his dad.''

"Grsky," said Renie.

"What? Wayne Gretzky? Coz, I can't understand a word you're saying. Is there something wrong with your phone?"

There was a pause at the other end, then an enormous, wrenching sigh. Obviously, Renie was trying to rally. "George's key," she said in reasonably clear tones. "How did those grandchildren get into the house last night?"

"Oh!" Strangely, the question had eluded Judith. Too much had occurred in the cul-de-sac during the evening. "Of course! They went in the back way but came out the front. They might have gotten George's keys. He probably had them in his pocket when he was hauled off to the hospital. Enid's would still be at home.''

Renie was making slurping noises at the other end, apparently infusing herself with massive doses of caffeine. "Enid's purse," Renie blurted. "Where is it?"

Judith didn't know. "It might still be at the house. Glenda or Art could have taken it for safekeeping.''

"Maybe the hospital staff turned George's personal belongings over to his family," Renie said, sounding almost like herself. "Maybe Leigh got the keys from Glenda. Or one of the boys got it from Art or JoAnne. The question then becomes, Did the grandkids know about the back-door key hidden in the rock? If they did, why didn't they use it? Was it because one of them already knew it wasn't there?" Renie let out a little cry of agony. "Oh, good Lord, I don't believe I'm being rational and it's not yet nine-thirty! What will become of my reputation for morning stupor?"

Judith ignored Renie's attempt at self-congratulation or self-pity or whatever facet of self she was trying to convey. "You're absolutely right. I don't know the answer, but what it does mean," Judith went on, allowing her natural aptitude for logic to function, "is that something happened at the Goodrich house *before* Enid was killed. We know there was a quarrel, but we don't know what it was about. We know that Glenda and Gary Meyers broke up the night before the murder. We know that Leigh has caused some kind of rift within the family. What this looks like is a buildup to a climax that featured somebody taking a hatchet to Enid and maybe trying to poison George." Judith stopped for breath.

"Maybe?" Renie echoed. "Why maybe?"

"Well . . ." Judith paced in a small circle by the kitchen sink. "Why didn't the killer use the hatchet on George, too? Or was George given the sleeping pills so that he would be unconscious when the killer struck? That makes more sense—it's possible that the murderer never intended to do in George. Whoever it was misjudged the dosage. I wish we'd had the nerve to go inside the Goodrich house last night and do some serious snooping."

"You know we didn't dare turn on the lights for fear of upsetting Mrs. Swanson," Renie countered.

"It's daylight now," Judith noted, gazing out the window where a heavy frost still glistened under ominous gray clouds.

"I've got work to do," Renie said. "December isn't just Christmas for me, it's also annual report season."

"You never get creative until noon," Judith pointed out. "As long as we've got the key, we might as well make use of it."

Renie let out another big sigh. "Okay, but give me an hour or two. I've got to stop at the post office to get stamps for my Christmas cards and mail a package off to Aunt Ellen and Uncle Win in Nebraska. The line may take forever."

Judith yielded, though with a pang of guilt. She had addressed only a dozen of her sixty cards and had not yet readied any out-of-town parcels for mailing. Furthermore, she had forgotten to get her mother's approval on the purchase of Mike's Christmas gift. Judith was going out the back door just as Phyliss Rackley was coming in.

"Satan's at work on the Metro buses," Phyliss announced in a dark tone. "Our church took out one of those ads they have inside the buses. It's to remind people what Christmas is all about, and it said 'Jesus Is Lord'. Some pagan made the 'o' in 'Lord' into an 'a.' Blasphemous, I call it." Phyliss bristled with indignation.

"It's . . . silly," Judith conceded, thinking that Jesus undoubtedly had a better sense of humor than Phyliss. "Can you do the inside windows today? I've got a call in for Moonshine Cleaners to do the outside."

Phyliss mulled over the request. "It depends. My rheumatism is acting up something fierce."

Coaxing was never effective with Phyliss, so Judith dropped the subject. Still feeling guilt-ridden, she put off going to see her mother and got out the Christmas cards instead. Upon finishing another dozen, she grabbed her jacket and headed for the toolshed. The clouds were lifting and the frost was disappearing. The forecast called for overcast with a 30 percent chance of rain, high of fifty-two, low during the night of thirty-four. The threat of snow was still remote.

Gertrude was sitting in her favorite chair with the usual clutter in front of her on a rickety card table. Jumble puzzles, snapshots, medicine bottles, circulars, and candy boxes were piled high, within easy reach. Gertrude was playing solitaire and listening to a call-in radio program.

"Spiders," she said, not looking up from the layout of cards. "Somebody found a spider in their bananas, one of those tarantella things."

"Tarantula," Judith said absently. "Mother, are you willing to buy Mike a backpack for Christmas?"

Gertrude put a red eight on a black nine. "A backpack? What does he need a backpack for? He's not Santa Claus. Tell him to wait until the day after Christmas. Maybe Santa can give him his old one." She moved up the ace of diamonds, then plastered it with the deuce. "How much?" she asked in her raspy voice when Judith failed to respond.

"A good one runs about sixty dollars." Judith gulped and waited for her mother's reaction.

"Sixty dollars?" Several cards flew into the air, some landing on the table, others drifting to the floor. "I could buy a new *back* for sixty dollars! And couldn't I use one? New legs, too. Sixty dollars for a backpack to carry around old underwear? What's wrong with a *suitcase*? You've still got your father's old one in the basement. Let Mike use that when he goes gallivanting."

"It's for hiking," Judith explained, bending down to pick up the fallen cards. "He carries a lot of things in it, like water and food and . . ."

"Fripperies," Gertrude put in. "Why does he need to hike when he works in the woods all the time as a forest ranger? Why can't he go see a picture show or visit the zoo on his days off? A show would cost him less than a dollar and the zoo is free."

It was pointless to remind Gertrude that the price of a movie had risen or that there was now a charge for the zoo. If her mother knew that the dollar wouldn't buy what it did in 1930, she would never admit it.

"How about a cooler then?" Judith asked hopefully. "I could buy one of those for you to give him for around twenty dollars on sale."

Frustrated by trying to figure out where the fallen cards belonged, Gertrude swept up the current game. "What do you mean, a cooler? In my day, a cooler was an icebox. We had one in this house until we got a refrigerator after the First World War. A Frigidaire it was, with a fan on top. You're right; it cost around twenty bucks. I'll do it." Gertrude placed the deck in her card shuffler and turned the crank.

"Good," Judith said, hoping that her mother wouldn't ask a lot of embarrassing questions when Mike opened his portable cooler chest at Christmas. "I'll get it this afternoon." She would also buy the backpack.

"Say," Gertrude said, carefully laying out a new hand, "what was all that commotion last night around nine? I would have come out, but it was too cold."

Perching on the arm of Gertrude's small sofa, Judith told her mother about the intrusion of the Goodrich grandchildren. Gertrude was appropriately appalled.

"Their grandmother must be turning in her grave," Gertrude said, reaching for a chocolate-covered peanut that resided in a glass dish. "She had manners; I'll give her that. Say, kiddo, what's for lunch?"

Since lunch was over an hour away, Judith hadn't thought about it. "Chicken salad sandwiches, pears, and butterscotch pudding," she said off the top of her head.

Gertrude nodded as she began building up her aces. "Sounds fine, except for the butterscotch. Make mine chocolate—that dark kind. The pale stuff gives me the willies."

Judith agreed, though it meant whipping up a fresh batch of pudding. Leaving her mother to the solitaire game and the radio talk show, she returned to the house. Judith had purposely withheld the part about finding the key and steak knife. She didn't want Gertrude to think that the killer might not be safely incarcerated. Her mother, like Mrs. Swanson, was too old and vulnerable to live in a state of fear. Gertrude pretended to be tough, but underneath Judith knew she was afraid of many things. Maybe pale pudding reminded her mother of frailty.

Returning to the kitchen, Judith found a box of deep chocolate pudding mix in the cupboard. As she poured and mixed, she thought about her mother's reaction to the Goodrich children's avarice. "Vipers," she'd called them. "Spoiled brats." "Selfish."

Gertrude was right, of course. All three grandchildren had behaved without the slightest show of compassion, either for their murdered grandmother or their suffering grandfather. But Gertrude had said something else that now pricked at Judith's brain. Pouring pudding mixture into glass bowls, she tried to recall the exact words. She couldn't. Gertrude always said so many things, usually critical. Ironically, she was often as accurate as she was harsh.

Just as Judith put the fresh pudding into the refrigerator, Renie arrived. Instead of her usual disreputable winter sweats, Renie was attired in a smart taupe double-breasted suit with a black mock turtleneck underneath.

"I've got a meeting downtown at one o'clock with the gas company," she explained. "I may do some more Christmas shopping after I get done."

Judith offered Renie the last serving of butterscotch pudding. But for once, her cousin declined. An inelegant eater, Renie frankly admitted she didn't want to tempt fate and get her suit dirty. She would, however, accept a cup of coffee.

While Renie sipped, Judith dialed Art and JoAnne Goodrich's number. JoAnne answered, sounding breathless. "I just got out of the shower," she said in apology. "My shift at Falstaff's is eight to five, so I don't get up until around ten."

It occurred to Judith that JoAnne Goodrich was shortchanging herself on sleep. But the question she had for Art's wife was more pressing: "How is George?"

"He's better," JoAnne replied, suddenly sounding on guard. "They expect to let him out of the hospital tomorrow. We'll hold the services for Enid Tuesday at the Congregational Church, ten o'clock."

"Will George be able to attend?" Judith inquired, hoping that the tactful question might provide some illumination on his legal status.

"Yes, I think so," JoAnne answered slowly. "Art figures the police will remand him to our custody. I just wish he weren't so confused."

"How do you mean?" Judith asked, signaling for Renie to go into the living room and pick up the extension.

"Oh—he keeps saying that he didn't kill Enid. He talks about somebody else being in the house, but he doesn't know who it was. Or," JoAnne continued, even more uncertainly, as a faint click indicated that Renie was listening in, "he won't say who it was. Plus, he insists he didn't take those sleeping pills. As I said, poor George is still all mixed up. It must take some time for the effect of the pills to wear off.''

"That's possible," Judith allowed. "Did your father-in-law ever take sleeping pills?"

"Never." Now JoAnne sounded emphatic. "He wouldn't have because he needed to be alert in case Enid woke up and asked for something."

Judith realized that was probably, sadly, true. The poor man hadn't even been able to rest his weary head. "So they'll have to arraign him?"

"I guess so." JoAnne emitted an eloquent sigh. "He'll plead insanity, I imagine. He should. Poor Gramps must be nutty as a fruitcake."

"Have you contacted a lawyer?" Judith asked, sensing that would be Renie's next question.

"Glenda's attorney recommended someone." JoAnne didn't sound enthused. "Lawyers cost the world. We'll probably have to sell Enid and Gramps's house just to pay the legal fees. It doesn't seem fair."

"No, it doesn't," Judith agreed. She didn't add that it would be fair enough if George hadn't killed Enid. "Say hello to George for us. By the way, what did your boys and Leigh do with the furniture they took out of the house last night?"

The sudden silence at the other end of the line indicated shock or embarrassment or both. At last, JoAnne spoke: "I'm sorry, I don't know what you're talking about. Furniture, did you say?"

It was Judith who now felt faintly embarrassed. "Yes, just a few things. Chairs, lamps, the TV—they put them in that van your boys drive. It . . . ah . . . um . . . had a flat, but they must have fixed it. The van was gone this morning."

"I wouldn't know," JoAnne said primly. "I was probably at work when they came to the house. As I said, I just got up a short time ago. I haven't talked to Greg or Dave today. Now that they share an apartment, Art and I try to back off. Children should be independent. You can't hover or let them lean on you. At least that's what Art tells me." The shift in Jo-Anne's tone indicated that she and her husband weren't in complete agreement when it came to parenting.

"Oh." Judith cast about for a pertinent phrase. "I was just wondering if they'd come back to the house today. We're keeping an eye on it, since it's empty."

"The boys are working," JoAnne said, sounding more at ease. "I suppose we'll have to get some of Gramps's things tomorrow."

Judith was about to sign off when a question popped into her mind. "What do the boys do, JoAnne? Gabe Porter said one of them worked with him at United Foods."

"That's Greg," JoAnne answered. "He's in shipping. Dave got on at Pacific Meat Packing, doing something with computers. Gramps got him the job. But they're only doing fill-in right now. They're both commercial fishermen in Alaska during the season."

Judith was faintly impressed. Commercial fishing might be seasonal, but it was often lucrative. It was also demanding and sometimes dangerous.

"I admire them for that," Judith said sincerely. Indeed, she was surprised that Greg and Dave possessed such initiative and spunk. "Was this past season a good one?"

The tension returned to JoAnne's voice. "Not really. That's why they have to work this winter. The catch was way down. Greg and Dave blame the Japanese for encroaching."

It was a familiar story. Judith sympathized briefly, and finally rang off.

"Let's go," she said to Renie as they met in the entry hall. "We'll use the front door."

The cousins were almost to the Goodrich house when a voice called for them to wait up. Dooley came running down the sidewalk, his blond hair flying around his head.

"O.P.'s still in school, so I was using the telescope," he said, catching his breath. "I saw you two come out of the B&B. Hi, Mrs. Jones. What's happening?"

Renie shrugged. "Just the usual breaking and entering. How are you doing, Dooley? I seem to remember you used to be a teenaged klutz."

Dooley grinned. "Maybe I still am. A teenager, that is. But I work out. Coordination cures klutz."

"You look great," Renie said as they progressed along the driveway. "I'm all for physical fitness as long as it doesn't require any effort more strenuous than opening a can of Pepsi."

Judith still kept the back-door key wrapped in tissue. Upon entering the house, she explained the latest developments to Dooley. "All these things make me believe that George is innocent," she said as they stood in the pristine kitchen. All three of them exchanged nervous looks. Dooley in particular seemed to be ill at ease. "The problem is, I don't know who else had a motive for killing Enid."

Renie was cautiously opening cupboards. "Who'd need one? Enid was a motive all by herself."

Judith didn't argue. "What bothers me is that I can't see Art or Glenda taking a hatchet to their mother. It's unnatural for children to kill a parent."

Renie's expression was droll. "Unnatural to do it or unnatural to *want* to? I felt like strangling mine last Sunday. I brought all the fruitcake ingredients to her, but she'd forgotten that the recipe called for booze. The liquor store wasn't open, so I had to go home to get some. We were out of everything except Bill's favorite brandy. After he had a mental collapse, I went back to Mom's apartment, and she didn't have any aluminum foil to wrap the fruitcakes in, so I had to go to Falstaff's. Then she got on the phone with Mrs. Parker and talked for half an hour while I cooled my heels. I didn't get home until almost six, and Bill and the kids were writhing on the kitchen floor, clutching at the refrigerator." As Renie gave her recital, she checked the medicine bottles that took up most of a single shelf. "No Dalmane here. I suppose the police took it with them."

"Probably," Judith agreed, still feeling a bit anxious as she led the way out of the kitchen. "Let's take another look at that desk."

If the living room had never conveyed a sense of hospitality, it now seemed bereft. Not only were the side chairs, the lamps, and the end table missing, but Leigh had left the plastic-covered armchair at an angle by the front door. The framed photograph of Enid lay facedown on the carpet, and a faintly dusty dried floral arrangement was on its side near the hearth.

"Mother's right," Judith said, her forehead furrowed. "Enid must be turning over in her grave."

"She isn't there yet," Renie noted, setting the floral arrangement on the mantle. "Wait till Tuesday."

Judith snapped her fingers. "That's it! Let me see that picture of Enid."

"Humor her," Renie advised as Dooley handed Judith the photograph. "If insanity is contagious, it may be going around the neighborhood."

Judith paid no attention to her cousin. Rather, she studied the photo, then laid it on the sofa. "I wonder," she said softly.

"You wonder what?" Renie followed Judith over to the breakfront with its built-in desk.

"It's something Mother mentioned this morning," Judith said, tugging at the walnut panel. "I thought it was odd at the time, but I couldn't figure out exactly—ooof!" The desk fell open unexpectedly, banging Judith on the wrist.

"Here, Mrs. McMonigle," said Dooley, his tone uncharacteristically tense, "let me grab some of the stuff in those cubbyholes."

"She's Flynn," Renie corrected, also taking a handful of what looked like household bills.

Dooley grew sheepish. "Right. Sorry. This looks like business stuff. Income taxes, maybe?" He handed a sheaf to Judith.

The desk's contents proved unilluminating. Judith, who had endured her own share of IRS problems while married to Dan, closed her eyes to the ominous government forms. Instead, she concentrated on the more mundane, less threatening domestic records. A passbook showed savings of just under seven thousand dollars; the checking account had a balance of two hundred and fifty-eight dollars and thirty-six cents. George's term insurance policy had been taken out in 1947, with a face value of ten thousand dollars. Enid apparently had no policy, except for a Purple Cross plan she shared with George to cover their burial arrangements. The accumulation of a lifetime didn't strike Judith as a motive for murder, at least not by the inflated standard of the late twentieth century. While she envied the Goodriches' comparatively low utility rates, there was nothing else that piqued her interest. Neither Enid nor George appeared to have corresponded with anyone on a personal basis. The cubbyholes were strictly business, though Judith was mildly puzzled by the largest storage section, which was empty. The space looked as if it could hold a telephone directory.

"The phone's in the hall between the bedrooms and the bath, isn't it?" Judith remarked somewhat absently.

Warily, Dooley went to check. "Yeah, it's on a little stand. The phone books are underneath. Here's an address book, but it's only got about ten numbers. I was hoping they might be clues. You know, like looking up under 'M' for 'Murderer.' "

Both cousins chuckled their appreciation, either of Dooley's wit or his ingenuity. Their laughter eased the sense of tension, but the cousins jumped when Dooley let out a yelp. Judith and Renie hurried into the hallway. The young man had turned red, and his eyes were huge. "Sorry," he said, running an agitated hand through his hair. 'I've never been at a homicide scene so soon after . . .'' He gulped. "The bedroom's kind of gross."

"Yes, it is," Judith said solemnly. "Murder is gross." She steeled herself before entering the room. Renie kept back, but Dooley followed.

The red stains had turned to brown. For the first time, Judith realized that most of the blood was on Enid's bedclothes. Maybe she had been asleep when her killer struck. Judith hoped so.

Gritting her teeth, she slowly prowled around the room. The TV was gone, of course, and she marveled at the audacity of the grandchildren. How could they invade this chamber of horrors to swipe a television set? Were they so callous? Or stupid? Or had they hated their grandmother so much that her manner of passing made no dent?

Dooley was studying the collection of medicines on Enid's nightstand. "No Dalmane here either," he said.

Judith stood next to George's bed. While it wasn't in disarray like Enid's, it did appear that he had slept in it. How soundly, Judith wondered? She glanced at his matching nightstand. There stood the clock-radio, the antacid, and the spectacles case. The only difference from when Judith had seen the room the previous Sunday was that George's glasses now reposed in the case.

Turning away, she caught herself. "The glass," she said under her breath. "There was a glass, a pretty one, like Waterford crystal."

"I saw those in the cupboard," Renie said from the hall. "They look Czech to me."

Judith never quarreled with Renie's eye for artistry. "Whatever. But there was definitely a glass on the nightstand last Sunday evening. I'll bet George used it for his antacid."

"Maybe," Renie suggested, still lurking outside of the room, "it got broken during the murder. That might be the glass that cut me."

"Maybe," Judith said distractedly as she moved the window shade just enough to peek outside. "All clear," she breathed. "I sure wouldn't want anybody catching us nosing around."

Judith proceeded to investigate the clothes closet. Enid's purse sat on a bottom shelf, half hidden behind a long cotton robe. In the Grover family, snooping in other women's purses had been a crime almost as great as theft or adultery. Judith winced as she opened the brass clasp.

A coin purse contained four dollars and some change. Enid hadn't carried a wallet, but kept her identification in a faux leather case. There were no charge cards. The rest of the handbag contained a comb, a packet of tissues, a mirror, a lipstick, an emery board, two safety pins—but no keys.

"Somebody took them," Judith said. "I suppose that's natural."

Thoughtfully, Dooley nodded. "The family would have to get in and out to do stuff. Like for the funeral. Do you suppose Mrs. Goodrich had more than four dollars in there?"

Judith understood the question. "A couple of twenties would have been tempting to Greg or Dave. Maybe even Art, at this point. Oh, well. This doesn't tell us much."

Still anxious, Judith posted Renie by the living room window, where she had a better view of the cul-de-sac.

The remaining closet contents proved uninteresting. "We can look at the broken glass in the can on our way out," Judith said, opening and closing bureau drawers. She waited for Dooley, who had gone through the dressing table and was now lifting the lid of the cedar chest. The smell of mothballs filled the air.

"Some kind of fur piece," Dooley said, holding out a fox boa. The glass eyes glittered at Judith. "Lace tablecloths. Blankets. An old quilt. Ah!" Digging in the bottom of the chest, he exhibited minor excitement. "Photographs, formal ones in folders. Want to see?"

"Sure," Judith replied, taking at least a dozen off-white, gray, and brown folders from Dooley. "Good work."

"Good grief," called Renie, who scurried into the hallway on her high heels. Judith and Dooley waited. Renie returned. This time, she dared to poke her head into the bedroom. "It's the cops. Patches Whoever and the Homicide Vamp. They're coming in the front, but I shoved that armchair by the door to hold them off. Let's go!"

Hastily, Judith and Dooley dumped everything but the photos in the cedar chest. They were going out the back door just as they heard Patches Morgan and Sancha Rael enter the living room.

Renie's speed was hampered by her heels, but Dooley was already down the drive and around the corner. Judith couldn't resist a quick stop at the garbage can: Sure enough, a closer inspection of the broken glass revealed not only an elegant etched pattern but some chalky white residue. Clutching the photographs, Judith galloped after Renie.

By the time the cousins reached Hillside Manor, Dooley had

jumped over the fence. "Lunch!" he shouted after landing on the other side.

"What a concept," Renie murmured. "Of course I'd like to join you. But I can't. I'd dirty myself." One hand swept the length of her wool suit. "I had a big breakfast."

"I'm sure you did," Judith said dryly. "I'll eat after you leave, but it's going on noon, so I'd better get Mother fed. Phyliss must be washing the upstairs windows. I wonder what the police are looking for now?"

The cousins were back in the kitchen, where Renie sat down at the table and Judith began mixing chicken salad. "I don't know. Maybe they were looking for what we were looking for. Whatever that might be. They missed the key and the knife."

"I don't know how hard they looked," Judith said, wiping her hands on a dish towel. "Those items weren't on the Goodrich property. With George volunteering a confession from the start, the police might not have been as thorough."

"They should have noticed that the desk had been pried open," Renie pointed out, unable to resist plucking a piece of chicken out of the salad.

"Probably. But what does that tell them? Or us?" Judith was thoughtful as she diced celery. "If George now denies killing Enid, the police might be taking him seriously. They'll think twice about the desk."

Renie was going through the photographs. "Baby pictures," she said. "Art and Glenda, I imagine. A family photo from circa the fifties. Look, Enid let them sit on the couch."

Judith spread chicken salad on white bread, then went over to the table. Glenda's plaid skirt, dark sweater, and single strand of pearls evoked familiar memories for Judith. So did Art's crew cut and the padded shoulders of his sport coat. George seemed vaguely uncomfortable in a suit and tie. Or maybe he was uncomfortable sitting next to Enid, who looked every inch the autocratic matron in her shirtwaist dress and carefully coiffed page boy.

"They look like the all-American family," Judith remarked.

"They were," Renie retorted. "Screwed-up, hostile, and full of frustration. Isn't that typical?"

"I'm afraid so," Judith said. "I'd prefer to call it being human."

"Still," Renie went on as she handed Judith more recent baby pictures of what appeared to be the grandchildren, "Bill says that in the fifties, the family was a much more stable unit. Dad worked, Mom stayed home with the kids, divorce wasn't all that common. Values were more . . ."

"Your mother worked," Judith pointed out. "So did mine, part-time. At least three marriages in this neighborhood ended in divorce."

Renie wrinkled her pug nose. "I think Bill was talking about the Midwest, where he was raised. The point he makes is that in contemporary society, moral standards have been eroded by a lack of . . ."

"Speaking of marriages, here's Glenda," said Judith, again interrupting her cousin's parrotlike recital of Bill's opinions. "Did you ever meet her ex-husband?"

Renie studied the photograph of bride and groom. Glenda wore long white lace with a fingertip veil on her bouffant hairdo. The lean, unprepossessing man who stood next to her was attired in a white dinner jacket. Renie shook her head.

"No, I don't recognize him. But in those days—the early sixties, right?—I was only here for family gatherings or to pick you up if we were going some place together. Until this week, I don't think I've seen Art or Glenda in over thirty years."

Judith had retrieved the wedding photo and was frowning in concentration. "What was his name? Ron? Rob? No, it was Ross. His last name was odd, but I don't remember it."

Renie was opening the last folder. "Here's George and Enid's wedding picture. They almost look happy."

The traditional pose suggested a young couple in love. Maybe they were—then. Enid was wearing a big picture hat and a very short dress. George was in uniform. Judith's jaw dropped.

"I was right," she breathed, then dashed over to the

counter. "Come on, let's deliver Mother's lunch. I've got an important question to ask her."

Dutifully, Renie followed her cousin out through the back door. When they entered the small apartment, Gertrude was watching the noon news.

"Nothing about George making Enid into cutlets," she said in disgust. "What's wrong with these TV stations? Who cares about a bunch of people shooting each other in Acacia? They can't even speak English. Why don't they go to school and learn how to talk? No wonder they don't know what they're fighting about."

"It's Croatia, Mother," Judith said, resisting the temptation to lecture Gertrude on the former Yugoslavia's long-simmering ethnic and religious rivalries.

"Dummies," Gertrude muttered, turning off the TV. She looked up as Renie bestowed a kiss on her aunt's wrinkled cheek. "Hi, there, Toots. Where are you going in that getup? Queen Elizabeth isn't in town, unless the local newshounds forgot to mention that, too."

Renie grinned, picked Sweetums up from the couch, deposited him on the floor, and sat down. Judith served her mother's lunch on the card table.

Gertrude eyed the sandwich with suspicion. "I don't see any hearty chunks of chicken hanging out of the bread. What did you do, shoot a pigeon?"

"It's all there, Mother," Judith said with a small sigh as she joined Renie on the couch. "Let's not get sidetracked. You've been holding out on me." Judith looked at Gertrude with reproachful eyes. "Why didn't you tell me George had been married before?"

NINE

GERTRUDE WAS UNMOVED by the question. She adjusted her dentures, then sank her teeth into the sandwich. Much chewing and swallowing ensued. "Why should I?" she asked, fixing Judith with an indifferent expression. "You never asked."

Renie leaned forward on the couch. "What's this? George had another wife?"

Gertrude nailed a pear. "Myra, that was her name." She gave herself a little shake, as if surprised that her memory had served so well. "Nice woman, Myra—but dim. Plain as a pikestaff, too. Like I said this morning, she had good manners, if nothing else."

Renie poked Judith. "When did you figure this out? Is that what you were babbling about at the Goodriches'?"

Judith nodded. "That's right. I quoted Mother as saying that Enid must be turning in her grave after the grandkids swiped the furnishings. I realized that Enid wasn't in her grave—yet. Besides," she added, again looking at Gertrude, "you said the grandmother had nice manners. Enid definitely did not."

Gertrude remained unperturbed. "So what? It was a long time ago, when you were a baby. Myra got the pip or something, and died young. I suppose she had cancer, but people didn't blab about their troubles so much in those days. Then the war came along, and George enlisted in the army. He was a widower with two little kids, so they assigned him to a local post. Somewhere along the way, he met Enid. They got married right after V-J Day. You were four at the time and not real interested in any neighbors unless they could play in your sandbox. To tell the truth, Myra was always such a mousy thing that I kind of forgot about her. After all, George and Enid were married for almost fifty years.''

Judith was nodding again. ''That was the other thing—the picture of Enid in the living room was taken when she was about sixteen or seventeen. But the outfit she wore was right out of the late thirties. That would make her too young to be Art and Glenda's mother. They're a few years older than I am, which means they were born before World War Two.''

Sweetums was batting a paw at Renie's suede pumps. Renie hissed at the cat; the cat hissed back. With her mouth full of pudding, Gertrude motioned at Judith, then at Sweetums.

''Feeum,'' said Gertrude in an impatient mumble.

''I know it's Sweetums,'' Judith responded, wondering if her mother's mind was wandering more than she realized.

Gertrude swallowed. ''I said, 'Feed him,' you dope. The poor little critter wants his lunch, too.''

Obediently, Judith went into the tiny kitchen, which contained a hot plate, a toaster oven, a sink, and a small refrigerator. Gertrude didn't know it, but she was getting a microwave for Christmas. Taking out a can of Kitty Gourmet Extra Salmon, Judith felt Sweetums weave between her ankles. Then she felt him rake her leg. Judith swore. Sweetums sat down, curled his tail around his furry body, and blinked at Judith.

''The wretch is stowing it away,'' Judith said as she reentered the sitting room. ''Who put the sparrow in his food dish?''

Gertrude scowled. ''He did. Brought it in this morning and played catch with it for almost half an hour. What's the matter—does he want gravy on it?''

Judith tried not to gag. Renie was at the door, obviously

eager to leave for her appointment. "See you, Aunt Gertrude," she said. Then, after waiting for Judith to join her outside, Renie added, "You crazy old coot."

"She's not crazy—yet," Judith countered, walking Renie to her car. "But she does forget things. I'm wondering if she didn't forget about the first Mrs. Goodrich until I asked her just now."

"Could be." The clouds had not only lifted but had cleared off to the south. Renie dug into her purse and got out her sunglasses. Like most native Pacific Northwesterners, the merest hint of sun sent her hiding behind smoked lenses. "Does it matter? Enid and George were married forever, and as far as Glenda and Art are concerned, she was the only mother they really knew."

"I'm not so sure about that," Judith said, shielding her own eyes with her hand. "Art would have been about six when Myra died, and Glenda would have been four. They might remember her. But that's not the point."

"Oh?" Renie was sliding behind the wheel of the big blue Chev. "What, then?"

"Enid wasn't their mother. She wasn't the grandchildren's grandmother, either. If it's unnatural for a child—or grandchild—to kill a parent, then we have to adjust our thinking. We're talking about a stepmother. If you believe half of what you read in the fairy tales, everybody wants to kill them."

Renie turned the ignition key. "This isn't a fairy tale."

Judith's half-smile was ironic. She waved Renie off down the drive, then wandered out to take a look at her New England village in the winter sunshine. The sight pleased her anew. Indeed, the entire cul-de-sac looked festive even in the harsh light of day. It was, she thought, like something out of a fairy tale.

And two doors down was the Goodrich house, where the wicked witch had resided.

Or, as it turned out, the cruel stepmother. Sometimes fairy tales weren't fit for children.

But the murder site was hardly deserted. It appeared to Judith that the police were still inside. It also appeared that they were about to be disturbed by the arrival of the Ford Econoline van. Judith was joined on the curb by Rochelle Porter.

"Now what?" Rochelle asked in her strong, smooth contralto. "I kept out of it last night, though I could hardly wait for Gabe to come home and tell me what was going on."

To the surprise of both Judith and Rochelle, the driver turned out to be Leigh. She got out and started for the house, a willowy figure in black leggings, thigh-high black boots, and a green leather jacket.

"That's the fashion model?" Rochelle asked in a whisper. "My goodness, hasn't she grown?" There was a sardonic note in her deep voice.

"Let's wait," Judith suggested. "The police are inside. See that unmarked city car?"

"I've seen everything around here lately," Rochelle responded with a frown. "The other morning when I went to work there was a beer truck parked around the corner. What next, drug dealers?"

Judith regarded Rochelle with interest. "Was it red? What time?"

Rochelle's pleasant face was contorted with the effort to remember. "Oh—let me think—I was substitute teaching that day way out south, so I had to leave early. It must have been around seven-fifteen."

The time meshed with Mrs. Swanson's account. "Was it a Cascade Beer truck?" Judith asked.

But Rochelle didn't recall. "Aren't most beer trucks red?" she asked.

Judith didn't answer. She was watching Leigh argue with Patches Morgan on the steps of the Goodrich house. Judith felt a small glow of satisfaction. Apparently, so did Rochelle Porter.

"Brats," she said. "Tuesday night, I had to run up to Falstaff's because we were out of milk. One of those Goodrich boys—the one who works with Gabe—was bothering his mother while she was trying to check out customers. I couldn't believe how disrespectful he was. And she just stood there and let him get away with it."

It was clear that the Porter children hadn't gotten away with much. Nor, Judith thought, would any classroom of students over which Rochelle reigned, even temporarily.

And Leigh wasn't getting away with the rest of the household goods, as far as Judith could tell. Patches Morgan had now marched her back to the paneled van. She went unwillingly, and not without a verbal struggle.

"Come on," Judith said to Rochelle. "Let's see what she's up to this time."

Rochelle, however, demurred. She had a rare day off and was heading downtown to Christmas shop. With a friendly wave, she returned to her driveway and got into one of the various cars that Gabe had fixed in his spare time.

Judith reached the van just as Leigh was fussing with the gears. "Yoo-hoo," she called in what she hoped was an engaging manner. "Have you come to pick up things for your grandfather?"

Leigh glared out the window. "For my grandfather? Why does he need anything? He's crazy."

Anger wiped away Judith's beguiling smile. "You don't know that," she said, not bothering to hide her temper. "I'm glad the police won't let you ransack the house. You and your cousins ought to be ashamed."

Leigh's classic features twisted in fury; then she suddenly became almost obsequious. Judith had the impression that this was how the young woman acted in front of a camera, switching moods to suit changing poses.

"Isn't there a cop who lives around here someplace? Do you know who it is?" Leigh inquired, one hand poised on her cheek in apparent perplexity.

"I know him," Judith answered curtly. "Why?"

Leigh now assumed a wistful air. "If he knew how these other cops were treating family members, he'd do something. Do you have any idea how much those pieces of furniture mean to me?"

Judith started to respond, but Leigh kept talking. "It's not easy being a model and having to travel all the time. You don't have a real home. You're never with anyone who cares about you, just a bunch of people who suck up to you because they need your face to sell something. I wanted that furniture to make me feel as if I had a place of my own, with roots and connections.'' The sadness in her green eyes was almost convincing.

Frustrated, Judith sighed. She didn't know whether or not to believe Leigh. ''Look, it's none of my business, but couldn't you wait until your grandfather gets settled? I heard you didn't plan on returning to New York until after New Year's. There's plenty of time to get whatever it is you want shipped back east.''

Leigh's face set in its more familiar hard line. ''No, there isn't. My plans have changed. I'm going back to New York right away.''

Now it was Judith's turn to attempt subterfuge. ''Oh? What about Christmas? Won't your mother and the rest of the family be disappointed?''

Leigh gripped the steering wheel with both hands. ''My mother would like to ship me back right now. The others won't care if I'm not around. When did anybody in this family give a damn about anybody else—except Grandma?''

The ambiguous statement gave Judith a chance to feign ignorance. ''You mean your grandmother cared about you but the rest don't?''

Leigh flung her head back in exasperation. ''Good Lord, no! Grandma didn't care about anybody but Grandma! I meant that everybody else had to wait on her hand and foot.''

''Then why do you care about her furniture?'' Judith moved a bit closer into the shadow of the van. Only a few wispy clouds remained, and the afternoon sun was reflecting off the windshield.

''I care about me,'' Leigh said bluntly. ''Somebody has to.'' A defensive note crept into her voice. ''Oh, my mother pretended to care, but when it counted, she showed her true colors. I look back now and see that she always put herself first. That's why she couldn't stay married to my father. Sure, he had faults, but so did she, like being possessive and jealous. That's why she got so . . .'' Abruptly, Leigh clamped her mouth shut, then looked at Judith with a rueful expression. "Sorry. I feel like a runaway train."

Naturally, Judith wished that Leigh hadn't applied the brakes. "Your father," Judith said quickly, as Leigh started to roll up the window. "What happened to him?"

"Happened?" Leigh frowned. "Nothing. He married somebody else and moved away. It was a long time ago, when I was a kid."

"You haven't seen him over the years?" Judith was now right next to the van. Leigh couldn't drive off without knocking her down.

"Not since I was ten." The green eyes grew suspicious. "Why are you asking?"

Judith had glanced beyond Leigh to the rear of the van. It was empty. But the sunlight was shining straight into the paneled interior. Rust-colored streaks covered the walls. They looked startlingly like the darkening crimson stains in the Goodrich bedroom. Judith suppressed a shudder. Her imagination was overheating. No doubt the streaks were a paint job gone wrong.

With an effort, Judith shrugged and resumed her engaging smile. "I never really knew your father. In fact, I can't remember his name. Do you go by it?"

"Sure," Leigh replied. "His name is Ross Cisrak. Just because my mother wanted to go back to her maiden name doesn't mean I had to change mine. Besides, Leigh Cisrak is more memorable than Leigh Goodrich. It has a foreign sound. That's good, especially when I work in Europe."

Judith tried to recall Ross Cisrak. She couldn't, except in the vaguest sort of way. "I only saw him come to your grandparents' house a couple of times. I think it was when you were a baby."

"He writes to me," Leigh said in a manner that suggested she hadn't heard Judith. "At least he has lately. I think he gets a kick out of the fact that I show up on TV and in magazines. It makes him feel as if he succeeded at something. My mother always told him he was a failure."

"What does he do?" Judith asked as Leigh started the van.

"Whatever he feels like," Leigh said. She rolled the window up halfway, then lifted her chin and spoke through the opening. "If you see that cop, tell him to put some pressure on his hard-assed coworkers. They're trying to screw me over. Greg and Dave are already pissed because I borrowed their precious van. You'd think it was a freaking Rolls-Royce." Not bothering to close the window completely, Leigh put the van into reverse and backed out of the cul-de-sac.

Judith turned around to look at the Goodrich house. It was precisely one o'clock. She should check on Phyliss's progress with the housework. She ought to listen for messages concerning upcoming reservations. She needed to go over her list of buffet items for the wedding reception she was catering at the church hall Saturday night. She had to start wrapping presents and finish decorating the interior of the house and make sure she'd covered everyone on her gift list and address the rest of those cards and buy the backpack and the cooler for Mike . . .

It was only the third day of December, Judith reminded herself. There was no need for panic. She marched up to the Goodrich front door and knocked.

It appeared that Patches Morgan and Sancha Rael were about to leave. Rael eyed Judith speculatively, but Morgan exuded hearty, if wary, warmth.

"Yo-ho-ho, Ms. Flynn!" he said in his deep, exuberant voice. "And what might you be needing on this fine December day?"

"I'm worried about something JoAnne Goodrich told me this morning," Judith said with feigned candor. "She implied that George isn't guilty."

"Well, now!" Morgan made as if to put an arm around Judith, apparently thought better of it, and paced the plastic runner with his hands clasped behind his back. "What makes Ms. Goodrich say such a thing, I wonder? Eh?"

"It's what George says," Judith responded. "Ever since he came to, he's been insisting that he didn't kill his wife. Have you talked to him?"

Morgan smoothed his luxuriant mustache and fixed his good

left eye on Judith. "That I have." He waited for Judith to react. She waited for him to elaborate. The detective fingered the wide lapels of his crimson-lined raincoat. Today, he wore a muted plaid suit with a bright blue shirt and a dark green tie. Judith couldn't help but marvel at his sartorial audacity. "Well now?" he prompted, the left eye twinkling.

"Well," Judith replied, "isn't it possible that George really is innocent? I don't mean to meddle, but I've known him forever, and he certainly doesn't strike me as a killer."

"Now Ms. Flynn," Morgan said in a kindly tone, "you being Joe's wife and all, it's natural that you might want to help us solve this crime. But Detective Rael and I are doing just fine." He lowered his deep voice to a confidential level. "Yes, we've heard Mr. Goodrich deny killing Mrs. Goodrich. We hear a lot of things in this job, as I'm sure your very wonderful husband can tell you. Don't think we aren't considering all the angles. That's why we're here." The left eye winked.

Judith evinced surprise. "Really? You're taking Mr. Goodrich seriously?"

Sancha Rael had sidled up to her superior. "Look," she said with a condescending smile for Judith, "we have to take *everything* seriously. You're married to a cop—you should know that."

"Aye, matey," Morgan said to Rael, "you're absolutely right. We leave no stone unturned."

Judith gulped. The phrase reminded her of the phony rock in the garden. "Actually, you did," Judith said a bit anxiously, delving into her pocket. "Leave a stone unturned, that is. We found this key in the gutter and also this steak knife. I'm sure the key was kept in a fake rock. It fits the back door."

Morgan's mustache seemed to bristle. He took the plastic bag and its contents from Judith. His good left eye regarded her with disapproval.

Rael, however, was clearly outraged. "You've been concealing evidence? How could you, Ms. Flynn, when your husband works for the department?"

For once, Judith didn't try to dissemble. "My cousin found

the items last night by accident. We checked to see if the key fit, but we didn't go into the house. Then.'' Judith rushed on: ''I didn't want to bother Joe. He and Woody Price have enough on their plate with the Shazri case. I'm handing over these items now, which is the first opportunity I've had. Do you want to hear my theory or not?''

''Your *theory*?'' shrieked Rael, throwing up her hands. ''How about the story of your life?''

''Now, now,'' Morgan soothed. ''Ms. Flynn means well, I'm sure. By the Great Hornspoon, what might that theory be, Ms. Flynn?''

''It's sort of vague,'' Judith admitted, trying to ignore Rael, who was stamping around the room in a disgusted manner. ''If George didn't kill Enid, somebody else may have used the key to sneak into the house. I'm not sure who knew where the spare key was hidden, except Art, JoAnne, and Glenda. It's possible that the grandchildren found out about it. Anyway, whoever it was may have been at the house earlier, probably the previous evening. I think he or she put those sleeping pills in George's antacid glass that he kept by his bed. He became unconscious, which allowed the killer to come back and murder Enid. There's a smashed glass in the garbage, which looks as if it contained some milky liquid such as the stuff George took for his ulcers. It was probably broken intentionally by the murderer because he or she didn't intend to harm George but misjudged the dosage. I'm not sure about the steak knife—that may have been the original weapon, but the hatchet must have been handy. It might be smart to compare that knife with the ones in the kitchen. It could be part of a set. The key and the knife were dropped as the killer fled. I think whoever it was had come in through the back, probably after eight o'clock. That's about the time Ted Ericson brought his Christmas tree home. There were Noble fir needles tracked virtually all over the house, including the living room rug. The murderer must have stepped on them in the driveway.'' Judith stopped to catch her breath.

Patches Morgan's bluff features displayed open admiration. ''Oh-ho! Call me a rogue, call me a knave, but I hadn't come to any such conclusion! What a theory you have, Ms. Flynn! You've listened well at your husband's knee.''

''Knee, my foot,'' muttered Rael.

''It's just logic,'' Judith said modestly. ''Should we check those knives?'' Fleetingly, she saw the dark red stains inside the grandsons' van. But there had to be a logical explanation. Judith decided against bringing up a side issue. Enid Goodrich hadn't been killed in the back of a Ford Econoline. ''We could search the kitchen,'' she added a bit lamely.

'' 'We'?'' Morgan arched his dark eyebrows. ''Oh, why not? Come along, me hearties, let's have a peek at the utensils.''

Judith half expected Morgan to whip out a cutlass. Following him into the kitchen, she felt Rael skulking behind her. Morgan quickly inspected the walls and counters for any sign of knives. None were visible. He began opening drawers. On the third try, he shouted in triumph.

''A-ha! Here we go! Knives galore!'' He sorted through the items which included serving spoons, meat forks, and spatulas.

Judith immediately recognized at least three steak knives as mates to the one Renie had found by the curb. She didn't say so but waited for Morgan to come to the same conclusion.

''Yo-ho-ho!'' he cried, holding up two of the knives. ''Shiver me timbers, these are one and the same!''

''Swell,'' Rael said in a sullen voice.

''Ah . . .'' Judith gave Morgan her most innocent smile. ''I suppose you checked for prints?''

''That's what we've been doing,'' Morgan replied jovially. ''Among other things. There seem to be a great many prints. I thought the victim wasn't very hospitable.''

Fleetingly, Judith realized that her own fingerprints were on several surfaces. She didn't let the fact worry her. ''Enid wasn't much of a hostess. But the family did come by regularly. At least Art and Glenda did.''

Apparently, Rael had decided to put her pique aside for the sake of professionalism. ''It seems there's been a lot of traffic in and out of here since the murder. Somebody forced open that desk in the living room. Furniture's been carted away, and the drawers have been ransacked.''

"Ransacked?'' Judith bridled a bit at the word. She and Dooley had tried not to leave disorder in their wake. But, of course, they'd had to flee in a hurry. ''Oh,'' she said airily, ''those grandchildren wanted some souvenirs, I guess. They couldn't wait a decent interval.''

Morgan gave a short nod. ''That Ms. Cisrak put up quite a case for her share of mementoes. We told her to desist. She can leave town without them. This is no time to be hauling off the family heirlooms.''

"Good,'' Judith said. ''I'm glad you let her know she couldn't get away with wholesale looting. That sounds harsh, but she and her cousins have behaved very callously.'' Judith watched Morgan closely to see how he responded to criticism of the Goodrich grandchildren.

He didn't, at least not as far as Judith could tell. ''Don't you worry about those freebooters,'' Morgan said with a wag of his finger. ''We're going to send a patrol car by here at regular intervals for the next few days.''

"That's reassuring,'' Judith replied. ''Do you think you'll have solved the case by then? That is, do you have some leads?''

Again, Morgan winked with his left eye. ''Now, now, Ms. Flynn, that would be telling. You know your husband wouldn't show his hand. I marvel at how close to the vest he and Price are playing this Shazri thing. Not a word about the evidence they're stockpiling against the assassins. But, of course, there's a political angle.''

Judith smiled blandly. She hoped that Morgan and Rael would take her silence for wifely discretion. It wouldn't do to tell Morgan that when it came to evidence in the Shazri case, Joe and Woody didn't have a clue.

Phyliss had indeed washed the inside windows. Judith actually made it to the outfitters in the north end of the city where she bought Mike's backpack and cooler. She even managed to wrap a few gifts, stacking them, as usual, on the third floor landing next to her weeping fig. Later, after the tree was up, they'd be carried downstairs to the living room.

Feeling virtuous, she poured herself a measure of scotch before Joe got home. Not only had she made progress in her holiday preparations, she had handed over the pieces of evidence to Patches Morgan. Judith was sitting in the living room sipping her drink and reading the evening paper when Joe arrived. He was absolutely livid.

"Our perp got whacked," he announced, yanking at his tie and throwing his blazer onto the back of the beige sofa. "They found him in a Dumpster by the ferry dock."

Judith stared. "Does that mean he didn't do it? Or that he did, and somebody wanted revenge?"

Joe circled the space between the matching sofas and the bay window. "Hell, I don't know what it means, except Woody and I have to start from scratch. Why don't Middle Eastern dissidents stay in the Middle East? Or why don't they keep their mouths shut when they move onto our turf? Shazri and his wife were experts at manipulating the media, but so what? All it did was get them killed."

Judith got up to fix a drink for her husband. "They owned a carpet company, didn't they?"

Joe gave a slight shake of his head, then collapsed onto the sofa. "It was his brother. He's lived here for years. He took Shazri into the business after they fled their native land. The brother's not political, but he's the one who fingered the hit man. The guy had worked as a driver for the company a while ago. And now he's lying in the morgue with six bullets in his chest. Damn! Woody and I will have to pull some weekend duty. The media is going to have a field day with this one."

Judith handed Joe his drink. "Oh, Joe—I thought we were going to buy the tree this weekend."

Joe took a grateful sip of scotch and gave Judith a rueful look. "Sorry. Take Renie along. She's got a designer's eye."

"Maybe I will." Judith tried to dampen her disappointment. "Except she and Bill and the kids are going to get their own tree. You know how that goes—they always end up in a five-way fight, and nobody's speaking by the time they get the tree home.''

"They get over it," Joe said complacently. He was scanning the front page of the newspaper. "The latest wrinkle in the Shazri case hasn't made it into this edition." Along with the scotch, the fact seemed to cheer him.

Judith glanced at the grandfather clock. It was going on six. The guests' appetizers were made, but she hadn't yet prepared the punch. Halfway to the kitchen, she heard a timid knock at the front door. Friday's lodgers had already checked in and taken possession of their keys. Puzzled, Judith crossed the entry hall, remembering to turn on the New England village lights en route.

Miko Swanson stood on the porch, huddled in her winter coat. She gazed up anxiously at Judith. "Oh, Mrs. Flynn," she said in her small, precise voice, "I am so sorry to trouble you. But there are questions I must ask, and the telephone is not the means."

"Come in," Judith urged. "If you don't mind, we'll go in the kitchen. I'm getting ready for my guests."

"Oh!" Mrs. Swanson all but reeled in the entry hall. "I should not have bothered you at this hour! But, of course, it is dinnertime. Eating alone makes one forget."

Judith smiled kindly at her visitor. "It's no trouble. My husband just got home and needs to unwind. My mother is another matter," she added somewhat darkly.

"Your mother," Mrs. Swanson echoed wistfully. "She and I should be friends. We are both widows and must have much in common. May I call on her someday?"

"Why not?" Judith marveled that the idea hadn't occurred to her sooner. Or to Gertrude or Mrs. Swanson. It was amazing how distant neighbors could be even when they lived practically on top of each other.

Mrs. Swanson declined Judith's offer to take her coat. "I shall not stay long," she said, easing her small body into one of the kitchen chairs. "But I must ask a question. Please don't find me impertinent."

"Of course not. Would you care for a drink?" Judith asked as a matter of courtesy.

Mrs. Swanson's fine dark eyebrows lifted. "How kind! Yes, that would be most helpful. A gin martini, please, very dry. One olive is plentiful."

Judith concealed her surprise at the unexpected request. As she prepared the cocktail, she asked Mrs. Swanson what was troubling her.

"Today I see the police return," Mrs. Swanson answered, taking a dainty sip from her glass. "That seems strange. Why should they come back unless something unexpected had happened? So when they leave, I go outside to ask what is taking place. The gentleman with the eye patch is very discreet. But he is the same age, or thereabouts, as my son, Jimmy, who lives in Portland. I know when these fellows are trying to evade questions. Jimmy could never deceive me. So I wheedle and make guesses, and finally it becomes clear that this detective is no longer convinced that Mr. Goodrich killed Mrs. Goodrich. I am so glad. I knew he couldn't have done such a terrible thing."

Judith, who had been mixing punch while she listened to the recital, smiled at her guest's obvious relief. "I agree. It never struck me as something George would do, either. Especially not the part about the hatchet."

Mrs. Swanson stiffened and put a hand to her throat. "That hatchet! I am so distressed!"

Judith nodded as she opened a bottle of sparkling cider. "That's what I mean—it's such a violent sort of murder."

"No, no," Mrs. Swanson said quickly. "Horrible as it is, that isn't what I refer to." She pursed her lips and stared unhappily into the martini glass. "You see, I am very much afraid. Do you think the police know that the hatchet belongs to me?"

TEN

THERE WAS NO such thing as the perfect Douglas fir, at least not in the parking lot of Our Lady, Star of the Sea Catholic Church. Judith frowned and Renie grumbled.

"They had some great trees last Sunday," Renie said. "I suppose they got picked over. Why do people buy them so early?"

"Too many so-called designer trees," Judith muttered, more to herself than to Renie, who wasn't listening anyway. "Themes are fine for stores, but real people should decorate with memories."

"All this shearing—that's okay for vapid types who have about ten ornaments," Renie griped. "But we've got hundreds. Bill and I want a tree with branches that come out to here." She gestured into infinity.

"Maybe they'll get another delivery today," Judith said, looking around for somebody who might be in charge. Since the lot was manned by fellow parishioners and the customers were also SOTS, Judith couldn't figure out who was who. "I don't see a single tree that's over seven feet tall. We've got a nine-foot ceiling."

"Three tops," Renie declared in disgust. "Almost every Douglas fir that's bigger than a house plant has three tops. Why can't tree farms grow trees with a single top? It's stupid."

At last, Judith spotted Mr. Scalia taking money from Mrs. Flaherty. Both were longtime parishioners. Judith approached Mr. Scalia and asked if they were expecting a new shipment later in the day.

They weren't. The next delivery wasn't due until Monday morning. Judith thanked Mr. Scalia and wandered back to Renie, who was curling her lip at what she obviously considered an inferior specimen.

"We're out of luck," Judith said. "Shall we try Falstaff's or Nottingham's?"

Renie shook her head. "Falstaff's doesn't have much selection, and Nottingham's is too expensive. There's a Boy Scout lot a block down from Moonbeam's. As long as Bill has abandoned me, let's take a look."

Bill had not actually abandoned his wife but had left her at church to help Judith select a tree. The Joneses had decided to postpone making their selection until mid-week. Their three children were scattered on this rainy Sunday morning, and the family wanted to wait until they were all together. Otherwise, the five of them couldn't engage in their annual Christmas hostilities.

As the cousins drove along the top of Heraldsgate Hill, the windshield wipers were working at a rapid pace. During the night, the temperature had risen and the rain clouds had moved in. There was some concern about flooding in rural parts of the county.

"Remember how we used to cut our own trees when we were kids?" Renie said, looking wistful. "Our dads and Grandpa Grover would drive us way out into the woods to someplace that's probably a strip mall now, and we'd have to hide because usually somebody owned the property and would shoot us if we got caught. It was kind of exciting. Those trees were always perfect."

"Those trees were horrible," Judith declared. "My father almost always had to put in a new top. I remember one year your father cut up two trees and taped them together. The top half turned yellow in about forty-eight hours."

Renie was looking thoughtful. "Maybe my memory's shot.

I'm muddled, like George. What have you heard since Mrs. Swanson confessed to you about her donated hatchet?''

"Nothing," Judith admitted, slowly prowling the first row of trees and trying not to step in any major mud puddles. "I finally remembered George mentioning he'd borrowed the hatchet to chop up some firewood. But that doesn't mean he chopped up Enid, too. As far as I know, there hasn't been anybody at the house since the police threw Leigh out on Friday. The patrol car comes by about once every hour or so. Oh—Ted put the sign up in the Goodriches' yard. None of us felt it could hurt anything.''

Off to one side, a half-dozen larger trees were propped up against a cyclone fence. Judith's boots squelched under her as she moved closer for a better look.

"This is more like it," she called to Renie who had lingered to check out a pile of cedar wreaths. "At least eight feet, unsheared, and the top isn't bad, either. Help me shake it out.''

Together, the cousins managed to haul the big Douglas fir away from the fence. "Is it even?" Judith asked.

"How do I know?" Renie replied in a muffled voice. "I'm not looking at it; I'm in it.''

Sure enough, the tree's long branches enveloped Renie. Judith tried to step back as raindrops rolled off her jacket's hood. "I think it's a keeper. It smells wonderful, too." In her enthusiasm, Judith let go of the trunk. The big fir plunged backward, taking Renie with it.

"Yikes!" Renie shouted, falling into the fence. "I'm killed!''

"Oh, dear!" Trying not to laugh, Judith rushed to her cousin's side. "Coz—are you okay?''

"I'm not if I'm dead," Renie snapped, shaking herself and sending off a spray of water like a wet pup. "How much?''

"These aren't marked," Judith replied, looking around for assistance. It appeared in the form of O.P. Dooley, wearing a yellow slicker over his Boy Scout uniform. Judith smiled brightly at the boy. "I've found the perfect tree," she said. "How much, O.P.?''

O.P. bore a striking resemblance to his older brother, par-

ticularly the fair hair and mobile mouth. But the younger
Dooley was shorter by almost a head, with a handful of freck-
les across his nose and cheeks. Despite the uniform with its
official sash and badges, O.P. looked very young and faintly
miserable with the rain pelting his slight form.

"That one's ninety dollars," O.P. said solemnly.

"Ninety dollars?" Judith reeled in disbelief. "Egad! The
big ones are only eighty at Nottingham's, and they're in the
business! O.P., this is the Boy Scouts!"

O.P.'s chin betrayed only the slightest quiver. "It's our big
fund-raiser, Mrs. McMonigle. We make enough to keep our
troop going."

"Going where? The French Riviera? And it's Mrs. *Flynn*.
It's been Mrs. *Flynn* for almost three years." Judith caught
herself and gave O.P. a sheepish look. "Hey, I'm sorry. It's
just that it's raining cats and dogs, my husband has to work
this weekend, it's hard to find the right tree for our big living
room, and I . . . well, sometimes I get frazzled before Christmas."

"We help poor kids, too," O.P. said with dignity. "You
know, troops that can't raise much money. Scouting keeps
kids out of gangs." He brushed a raindrop from his cheek, or
perhaps it was a tear.

Judith sighed. "I'll take it. We'll have to put it on top of
the car. It's too big for the trunk."

Renie was stroking the branches of the big fir's neighbor.
It was a bit shorter but almost as full. "To heck with it," she
said. "I'll buy this one. My husband and I'll pick it up this
afternoon. How much?"

"Eighty-five," O.P. replied promptly. "I'll tag it for you."

An older boy Judith didn't recognize came to cart off the
giant fir. "Don't forget to make a two-inch cut," Judith called,
then turned back to O.P. "I guess it's worth it. It may be the
nicest tree we've ever had." It was, Judith silently added, certainly the most costly.

Now very serious, O.P. nodded. "It's a super tree. Say, Mrs.
Mc . . . ah, Mrs. Flynn, do you think my brother and me could
talk to Mr. Flynn sometime?"

"Sure," Judith replied, as Renie approached, carrying a pine-and-cedar wreath. "What about?"

O.P. rubbed at his left eye, then brushed an accumulation of rain from his worried face. "It's Aloysius. He says I got to talk to Mr. Flynn about the guy I saw the other day."

"What guy?" Judith asked, feeling her boots sink into the muddy ground.

"I don't know him," O.P. said, blushing a bit. "But I saw him through my telescope before I went to school Wednesday morning. It was still pretty dark out. He went to Mr. and Mrs. Goodrich's house. You know, the back way."

Judith, Renie, and O.P. had begun strolling in the direction of the trailer that served as office and shelter for the scouts. Three people already were lined up, waiting to pay for their selected greenery. Judith didn't get in line. She was too intrigued by O.P.'s information.

"What time Wednesday morning?" she asked, trying to keep the excitement out of her voice.

O.P. scratched at his cheek. "Around seven-thirty, I guess. I leave for school at eight, but breakfast wasn't ready, so I stayed in my room and was playing around with the telescope. I'm too old for TV 'toons."

Two children, both boys who were not much younger than O.P., tugged at his slicker. Apparently, they wanted him to help their parents choose a tree. Reluctantly, O.P. excused himself.

"O.P.!" Judith called after him. "Come over to our house when you get through here, okay? Bring Dooley."

A wave of one slicker-covered arm signaled agreement, or so Judith hoped. Mentally, she kicked herself for not talking to O.P. sooner. But during the years that his older brother had shown no interest in detection, Judith had forgotten about the telescope.

"Who could have come by so early?" Judith muttered as she and Renie finally fell into what was now a six-person queue. "If we take Art at his word, it wasn't him. O.P. might recognize Art anyway. The grandsons, too. Who's left?"

Renie was counting cash out of her wallet. "O.P.'s sure it was a man?"

"He seemed to be." Briefly, Judith's attention was diverted by the sight of the lad who'd hauled her tree away. He was using a chain saw to make the required two-inch cut on the thick trunk. "The red truck," Judith said, under her breath. "Rochelle and Mrs. Swanson saw it. I asked Rochelle if it was a Cascade Beer truck. She didn't know. But aren't they red?"

"Sure," Renie said, digging for exact change. "Red with white writing. Bad choice, from a design standpoint. Black on red would be better for beer. Or reverse it, red on black. Very classy."

"Shut up," Judith ordered. "I'm thinking Gary Meyers."

"I know you are," Renie said blithely. " 'Spurned Suitor Whacks Girlfriend's Mom.' Isn't that the headline you're envisioning?"

The short, chubby man in front of the cousins turned around and gave them a sharp look. Judith recognized him as one of the butchers from Falstaff's. Apparently, he didn't think his store had a very wide selection of trees, either. He also seemed to think Judith and Renie might be a little strange.

"What are you talking about?" he demanded in the gruff voice that usually conveyed an underlying jocular note. Then his face brightened as he apparently recognized two of his regular customers. "That murder on the south side of the Hill?"

Embarrassed, Judith nodded. She remembered that the butcher's name was Harold. "It happened two doors down."

Harold also nodded. "That's right, you own the B&B in the cul-de-sac. Terrible thing. Mr. Goodrich shops at our store. Used to, anyway. I haven't seen him lately. Maybe I made him mad."

"Oh?" Judith forgot her embarrassment. "How so?"

Harold dropped his chin onto his chest. He had almost no neck, and the earflaps on his hunting cap stuck straight out. "Well . . . I gave him a bad time about some shortages in our deliveries from Pacific Meat. He said he didn't actually work there anymore. Maybe I was too hard on the old guy. Shortages seem to be a way of life these days. It's this younger generation, not paying attention to their work. No pride. Gimme, gimme, gimme.'' Harold moved up in line to pay for his tree.

By unspoken mutual consent, the cousins stopped talking about the homicide. Judith saw her fir now leaning against the trailer. Renie was studying the wire frame on her wreath. Harold paid his money, nodded at the cousins, and went off to claim his purchase.

It took almost ten minutes to secure the big fir on top of the Japanese compact. Judith drove home very carefully. Together, the cousins wrestled the tree to the ground. By the time they had dragged it to the side of the house, both Judith and Renie were not only wet but dirty, tired, and out of breath. They were about to seek sanctuary in the kitchen when Gertrude called to them from the toolshed.

''Hey, dingbats—where's *my* tree?''

Judith's shoulders slumped. ''You said you didn't have room for a tree. I thought you were going to use that little ceramic one that Aunt Ellen sent. It's really cute.''

''It's really ceramic,'' Gertrude snapped. ''I had a tree in this packing crate I call a home last year. We put it on the card table.''

Wearily, Judith approached the toolshed. She didn't feel like shouting through the rain. ''You said you didn't want it on the card table again. You had no place for your solitaire.''

''So we'll set it in the middle of the floor.'' Gertrude banged her walker for emphasis. ''I don't like phony stuff. You can put Aunt Ellen's ceramic tree in your bathroom. If you don't like that idea, you can put it up your . . .''

''Mother, I'll get you a tree tomorrow. Renie and I are exhausted. That tree weighs a ton.'' Feebly, Judith gestured at the Douglas fir.

''Hunh.'' Gertrude narrowed her eyes at the fir. ''Now why would you get a redwood? Why do you need anything that big? I'll bet that cost you fifteen bucks! I don't want you paying more than two-fifty for mine!'' With a swish of her housecoat, Gertrude clumped back inside the toolshed.

Renie had remained standing on the porch steps. "My mother doesn't want a tree. But of course she really does. She says it's too much trouble for me. But if I don't get one, she'll be 'low in her mind,' as she puts it, until New Year's. She insists that if I do get one for her, I can't decorate it because she doesn't want to be a burden. But if I don't, she'll put on her martyr's crown and all I'll hear for the next three weeks are deep, heart-wrenching sighs. Is it too early to start drinking?"

"Yes," Judith replied, leading the way into the house. "Except that it's the second Sunday of Advent, which means . . . something or other, like let's have a drink anyway."

Judith poured a small bourbon for Renie, a smaller scotch for herself. The cousins adjourned to the living room where the early-morning fire Judith had built for her guests was now out. Staring at the empty grate, Judith forced herself into action. Moments later, kindling was crackling and paper was burning. An English chorale was singing medieval carols on the CD player. The old house creaked in the wind, and the rain rattled the windowpanes.

"I don't think Gary took a hatchet to Enid," Judith said at last, picking up the thread of their conversation where they'd dropped it at the Boy Scout lot. "Even if she was the cause of the breakup between him and Glenda, that's too extreme. But I'd certainly like to know why Gary—assuming it was him—called on the Goodriches at seven-thirty Wednesday morning. More to the point, I'd like to know what he found when he got there."

Renie was rubbing at the back of her neck. It appeared that she hadn't quite fully recovered from her various bouts with the Douglas fir. "Such as Enid's body and George in a deep sleep?"

Judith nodded. "Exactly." The bloodstained bedroom danced before her eyes. So did the interior of Dave and Greg's van. On a whim, Judith described the rust-colored streaks to Renie.

Renie rolled her eyes. "You're getting carried away. Greg and Dave may be about as smart as your average termites, but they wouldn't drive around in a bloodstained van. And even if they did, what has it got to do with Enid's murder?''

Judith fingered her lower lip. ''That's the part that makes no sense. Logic is lacking, and it bothers me. We've got a spare knife and an extra set of what might be blood streaks. I hate it when things don't fit.''

''You don't know if that's blood inside the van,'' Renie chided, more gently than usual. ''You said 'rust-colored.' So maybe it's rust or paint or some kind of chemical. Drop it, coz.''

Judith did. She forced her mind back on its original track. ''Even though I don't believe Gary killed Enid, I keep thinking he's the key. I wonder how we can arrange to meet him again?''

''Lunch,'' Renie said promptly. ''It sounds as if he usually eats at Buster's Cafe. I'm always ready for lunch. In fact,'' she went on, glancing at the grandfather clock, ''I'm overdue. It's twelve-thirty. I hate to drink and run, but I've got a zillion things to do this afternoon, including the collection of our own monster evergreen.''

Judith didn't try to persuade Renie to linger. There was much to be done at Hillside Manor, too. She began by addressing another dozen cards, then wrapped four more presents, and finished decorating the second and third floors. Each task was interrupted at least three times by telephone requests for reservations. The B&B would be partially closed from December twenty-second to the twenty-ninth. Judith needed two of the guest rooms for Caitlin and Kristin. It was none of Judith's business if Mike and Kristin wanted to sleep together, but under Hillside Manor's roof, they would occupy separate quarters. Besides, Mike had only a twin bed in his old room. Judith had been tempted to convert the space into an office with a computer and a fax machine. But sentiment held her back. Mike came home at least four times a year, and until he was more permanently settled, Judith was loath to cut the cord.

By four o'clock, she was worn out. Reviving herself with a cup of hot tea, she went outdoors in the fading light to take a second cut off the fir. It was no mean feat, since she had to grapple with the tree by herself. Unfortunately, she couldn't manage to right the tree again, let alone hoist it into a bucket of water. She was standing in the rain, wondering when Joe would get home, when Dooley and O.P. bounded over the back fence. To Judith's elation, they volunteered to set the tree in the bucket.

"I feel bad," Dooley confessed after Judith had ushered the two boys into the kitchen and offered them pop. "I should have asked O.P. right away if he'd seen anything at the Goodriches'. But I didn't get home until that afternoon, after the murder had happened. O.P. should have told me sooner about what he saw." Dooley gave his brother a chiding look.

"It didn't seem like a big deal," O.P. mumbled. "I mean, what's so great about people going in and out of Mrs. Badbitch's back door? They do it all the time, especially that one guy and the lady."

Judith assumed O.P. referred to Art and Glenda. "So how was Tuesday night different?" she inquired.

O.P. took a deep breath and furrowed his forehead in concentration. Judith assumed he had already been coached by Dooley to render a full and accurate account. "There was all this yelling," O.P. began, "just before dinner. I looked through the telescope. Nothing. I waited, and the yelling stopped. Then that guy . . ." Hesitating, he turned to Dooley. "Is that Art?" Dooley nodded. "Art comes running out the front door and up to his car. It looked like he dropped something, but I couldn't be sure because it was dark. He got in and drove off. Then the lady left through the back door, kind of running, too. She jumped in her car and took off. Mom called that dinner was ready, so I went downstairs." O.P. gave a little shrug.

Judith thought back to Tuesday evening. Art had arrived while she and Renie were still in the front yard, probably around four. Glenda had stopped by Hillside Manor at six. Sweetums had gotten into the crab dip shortly thereafter, causing the first scream. The second had occurred at least ten minutes later, probably around six-fifteen.

"What time did you go down to eat?" Judith asked.

It was Dooley who answered. "Six-thirty on the dot. I was starved. They only had peanuts on the plane."

Judith mulled over the information that the Dooley boys had given her thus far. "Art left through the front door. How very odd. But Glenda went out the usual way a few minutes later. Okay, what next?"

O.P. looked sheepish. "I don't know. With Dooley home, we sort of horsed around and talked and stuff. But finally Dad told me I had to finish my homework, so I went upstairs. I did my math and some of my Native American paper, but I got tired. So I took a look through the telescope before I got ready for bed. It was around nine. I have to be in bed by nine on school nights." O.P. made a face. "Anyway, there was a van in front of Mrs. Badbitch's house and a guy going around to the back. I've seen him a couple of times before. Usually, he's with another dude about his age."

"The grandsons," Dooley put in helpfully.

"Yeah, right, whatever," said O.P. "So he went in and that was that. I got ready for bed and did a little more on my Native American paper. Did you know the white man gave the Native Americans blankets full of smallpox germs?"

"I'm afraid so," Judith said with a rueful expression.

"Maybe they didn't know much about germs in the olden days," O.P. said hopefully. "Anyway, I took one last look before I went to sleep—I do that almost every night, just to check on everything—and the van was gone, but an old beater was parked out front. I didn't see anybody, so I went to bed. That's it."

"Was the young man with the van bald?" Judith asked.

O.P. shook his head. "I couldn't tell. He was wearing a hood."

"That would be Greg," Judith said, recalling the older Goodrich grandson's duffle coat. "Okay, very good. More pop? Cookies?"

The Dooleys declined the pop but accepted the cookies. Judith had tried a new sugar cookie recipe the previous day, using Santa- and star-shaped cutters. Her icing decorations were inartistic, but tasted good.

"Now what about Wednesday morning?" she asked, waiting for O.P. to finish his second Santa.

O.P. grew doleful. "Nothing, except what I told you at the lot. I saw this guy I don't know go to the back door."

"He went in?" Judith asked.

O.P. started to nod, then grimaced. "I'm not sure. Once somebody gets on the porch, there's a kind of wall so you can't see the door. Anyways, I had to eat breakfast."

Judith recalled the latticework partition that sheltered the Goodrich back porch. "Was he wearing a red jacket?"

"I'm not sure. It was pretty dark, like I told you." O.P. was gazing at the cookie jar.

Judith lifted the lid, offering another round to both boys. "This may sound strange, O.P., but did this man stop on his way to the porch? Like, by the garbage cans?"

O.P. bit off the point of a star. Again, his forehead wrinkled. "Gee—no, I don't think so. He acted kind of jumpy, though."

"Do you remember seeing a red truck parked around the corner by the side of Mrs. Swanson's house?"

"Yeah, I thought it was a Coca-Cola truck."

Judith sat back in her chair. "Your memory for detail is excellent," she said with a smile. "It's wonderful to be observant. And aware. Most people aren't, you know."

O.P. didn't seem particularly pleased by the praise. "But I missed all the good stuff. The police, the firemen, the medics. I was in school."

Gently, Dooley shook his brother by the arm. "Hey, O.P., so what? School's cool, at least when you get to college."

"Get real," O.P. shot back. "School's dumb. I want to be a pilot."

Dooley seemed to realize this wasn't the place for a sibling argument. "Hey, Mrs. Flynn," he said, emphasizing Judith's last name, "when does Mr. Flynn get home? Shouldn't he hear about all this?"

Judith noted that the hands on the schoolhouse clock pointed to almost five. "Well," she said rather uncertainly, "it's not his case. But I can pass it on to him so he can tell Morgan and Rael. They ought to be interested, especially the part about . . . the man who came in the morning." Judith purposely avoided mentioning Gary Meyers by name.

Dooley stood up, then put his hands on his brother's thin shoulders. "You see? You've done your duty, O.P. God and country—that's what scouting's all about, right?"

The phone rang before O.P. could reply. Judith grabbed the receiver with one hand, motioning at the cookie jar with the other. But the brothers Dooley had decided to take their leave. Thanking Judith, they headed for the back door.

Judith couldn't make out the voice on the phone. "Excuse me," she said in an unnaturally loud voice. "Would you repeat that?"

The voice came through the second time around. It was husky and faintly slurred. "Yes," said the person on the other end as Judith tapped her foot. She was accustomed to hesitant would-be guests, wrong numbers, and the occasional crank caller. Judith waited, trying to be patient. "Yes," the voice resumed, gathering strength. "Is this Mrs. Flynn?"

"It is," Judith replied, as the wind whipped up outside and pummeled the kitchen window with rain. "How can I help you?"

"You can't," said the voice with a jagged laugh. "I'm Mrs. Flynn, too. The *first* Mrs. Flynn. This is Vivian, calling from Florida. I wanted to let you know I'm coming to see you and Joe and Caitlin for Christmas."

Judith dropped the phone.

ELEVEN

"SCREW FORENSICS," JOE growled as he came in the back door shortly after six o'clock. "Screw all those nitpicking nerds who sit around the lab all day on their fat butts and squint through microscopes. Now they tell me the guy who got whacked couldn't have fired the gun that killed the Shazris. Okay, I can buy that, but why did it take them two days to figure it out? My weekend just fell into a big, black hole." Joe slammed his fist into the wall by the refrigerator.

Judith swallowed hard. She hoped that her assembled guests in the living room hadn't heard her husband's rantings. She hoped he would recover quickly from his work-related pique. She hoped she had the nerve to tell him about his ex-wife's Christmas plans. She began to hope that she could find Joe's big, black hole and crawl into it.

"I got a tree today," Judith said in an unusually meek voice. "Did you see it out back?"

"What?" Joe was removing his shoulder holster. "A tree? No, I didn't see it. It's raining too damned hard. You know what really drives me nuts? We bring these foreign goons in for questioning and suddenly they can't speak English. Not one frigging word. Woody and I spent four hours today trying to get a couple of these bozos with rap sheets as long as your arm to admit they'd ever seen the inside of a station house. Then we let them call their lawyers and damned if they can't be reached. Out on the golf course, I'll bet, with some poor paralegal holding an umbrella over their heads. I hate voice mail, I hate e-mail, I think I hate the U.S. mail!'' Joe paused long enough in his tirade to glance at the kitchen counter by the phone. "Did we get anything today?"

"No," Judith replied, still meek. "It's Sunday, remember?"

"Oh. Right." Joe began to simmer down. "I guess I'll have a drink. What's for dinner?"

"Lamb chops," Judith replied, not daring to look up from the cornmeal muffins she'd just finished mixing. "I already warned Mother we'd be eating a bit late. I had no idea what time you'd be home."

Pouring out a hefty measure of scotch, Joe snorted. "Neither did I. By the way, Woody and Sondra are looking forward to dinner here next Saturday. If we're not working until midnight, of course."

Involuntarily, Judith glanced at the calendar that hung next to the phone. "Renie and Bill can come, too." Her eyes were drawn back to the month of December. This was the fifth, and Judith had to put the wooden shoes on the front porch for the sixth, St. Nicholas's Day. But it was the twenty-third that loomed larger than the other numbers. That was the day Vivian Flynn planned to arrive in town. She would land at the airport in the early evening; Caitlin was due in from Switzerland that morning at eleven-thirty. Judith hadn't yet written down Herself's arrival time. She was still hoping it was all a hallucination.

"Joe," she began, after putting the muffins in the oven, "I've got some strange news."

Joe was at the kitchen table, sorting through the bulky Sunday paper. "Oh, what?"

A very wet Sweetums strolled into the kitchen, obviously having deigned to use his cat's door. Ordinarily, he preferred flinging himself against the screen and screeching. Sidling up to Judith, he rubbed his dripping fur on her slacks.

Judith cleared her throat. "I got a phone call this afternoon from . . ." Sweetums had entwined himself between Judith's legs as she moved to the table. Tripping over the cat, she caught herself on a chair. Judith swore. "Dammit, Sweetums, you do that on purpose! Get out of here, you mangy little creep!"

Looking offended, Sweetums wandered off down the hallway. Judith watched to see if he'd go back outside. He didn't. With a flick of his plumelike tail, he headed up the back stairs.

"Oh, no you don't!" Judith gave chase. The cat wasn't allowed on the second floor, where the guest rooms were located.

By the time Judith had lured Sweetums out from under a wicker settee in the upstairs hall, Joe was halfway through his drink. His round face had recovered its usually amiable mien, and Judith was reluctant to upset him. Feeling like a coward, she told him instead of the Dooley brothers' sightings at the Goodrich house.

Joe shrugged off the report. "Hey, remember I was at the Goodrich house after all this alleged screaming and fighting and running out of doors. What time was it? Seven-thirty, eight? I didn't see Enid, but George seemed the same—nervous, but no more than usual."

While Judith respected her husband's powers of perception, she still wasn't convinced that O.P.'s account was meaningless. "You weren't gone more than ten minutes. Didn't you notice *anything* odd?"

Joe made a face. "I told you, I didn't get any further than the back porch. George was all apologies, but he said Enid was feeling puny. So when didn't she enjoy poor health? Forget it, Jude-girl. It's sad, but stuff like this happens. Enid pulled George's chain once too often. God knows I can't stand the stink of abusive men, but some of those guys are driven to violence because they have no other way of coping. Way back when, George must have let Enid get the upper hand. He probably didn't even know it was happening. When it finally dawned on him that she had him under her heel, he was too downtrodden to counter. I figure George's self-esteem went out the window forty years ago."

Judith checked the muffins, which were just beginning to

brown. "He had a good job. It takes brains to be an account-
ant. They must have thought a great deal of him at Pacific
Meats. Look how they still had him—oh!" She stopped
abruptly, a finger at her lips. "That's odd."

Joe folded the front section of the newspaper and put it
aside. "What?"

Judith had begun to dish up her mother's dinner. "George
still did some of the meat packing company's accounts at
home, especially at year's end. But I never saw any sign of
his work when we were . . . um . . . looking around the house.
Of course, we didn't go in the back bedroom. Maybe he used
it as an office."

Joe, however, shook his head. "Are you kidding? I don't
think Enid let him out of her sight even to do his job. I've
always been amazed that she'd allow him to work in the garden."

Removing the muffins from the oven, Judith nodded. "Hir-
ing someone would cost money. Enid was cheap. I'm surprised she used to have a cleaning woman. But I suppose that
was mostly before George retired. It must be terrible to live
in each other's pocket and yet not be close. I doubt that George
and Enid shared any real intimacy. Or trust." *Just as we won't
if I keep putting off the news about Herself*, Judith thought
with a guilty twinge. The tip of a wedge started out very small.
"I'll be right back." She gave Joe an unusually warm smile
as she carried Gertrude's meal out of the kitchen.

Half an hour later, the Flynns were finishing their own dinner. This was usually the time of day when Judith unloaded
domestic problems on her husband. Tonight, however, it was
obvious that Joe was very tired. He had worked seven straight
days, with no end in sight. At several intervals during dinner,
he had yawned. As they drank their coffee, Judith noted that
the yawns had turned from expressions of fatigue to signs of
relaxation. She couldn't bear to bring up Herself's bombshell.

Thus, when Joe left for work the next morning, he still
didn't know that his ex-wife was coming for Christmas. Judith
had offered her a room in Hillside Manor, though she fully
expected that Vivian would stay in a hotel. But to Judith's

horror, Herself had accepted. Now faced with the problem of a full house, Judith wondered if Herself would agree to share a bedroom with Caitlin. Mother and daughter should be able to get along for the five nights that Vivian would be with them. But the pair had not always been on good terms. That was one of the reasons Caitlin had taken the job in Switzerland: Joe's daughter wanted to put as many miles as she could between herself and Herself.

"What the hell am I going to do?" Judith asked of a bemused Renie as the cousins drove down to the bottom of the hill in an attempt to find Gary Meyers.

"Dress her up as Santa so Joe won't know who it is?" Renie took the steep hill known as the Counterbalance with an alarming disregard for gravity. "Put her in Santa's bag and let her jump out from under the tree? She's usually in the bag anyway."

"Very funny," Judith muttered as the big Chev came to a stop at the bottom of the hill. "You don't have to worry about having her around."

"Oh, yes, I do," Renie countered as the traffic light changed to green. It was still raining, though not as hard as Sunday's downpour. "She'll be there Christmas Eve when the whole family gathers at your house. Then we'll have to invite her to our place for Christmas dinner. I can't wait to tell Bill. He'll want to meet her. All he knows about her are the stories of the skirts slit up to there and the necklines plunging down to here."

"You're forgetting the false eyelashes, the wigs, and who knows how many plastic parts," Judith said bitterly. "Right after we were married, she sent Joe a bill for her latest face-lift."

Before Renie could comment on Herself's gall, she spotted a big red Cascade Beer truck parked in a loading zone half a block from Buster's Cafe. "I'll bet that's Gary," she said.

Finding a parking place proved even more difficult on this sixth day of December. The shopping district at the bottom of Heraldsgate Hill was attracting a great many gift buyers. Renie had to drive around the block five times before a space opened

up across the street from Buster's. By the time the cousins got
to the cafe, Gary was paying his bill and gnawing on a toothpick.

"Gary!" Judith cried, as if he were her long-lost prodigal
son. "How nice! Say, why don't we buy you a piece of pie?
That's the least we can do for interrupting your lunch the other
day."

Startled, Gary removed the toothpick. "I had pie. Thanks,
but I got to finish my route. I'm due back with the truck by
two."

"But . . ." Judith scoured her brain for another idea. "You
can't, not just yet. The most fantastic thing has happened."

"Yeah, well, maybe so, but I'm parked in a thirty-
minute . . ."

"It's about *you*," Judith said, suddenly turning both grim
and truthful. "In fact, I can't believe it." Indeed, she couldn't
believe her own ears. Did she actually dare accuse Gary Meyers of being at the Goodrich house within the time frame of
the murder?

Now Gary was looking alarmed. His gaze flickered around
the cafe, as if he expected to be accosted from another direction. "About me? Like what?"

A booth next to the door had just been vacated by a careworn young couple who looked as if they had too many regrets
for their tender years. Judith all but dragged Gary over to the
table. Renie grabbed a menu.

Now that Judith had Gary wedged between herself and the
wall, she felt slightly embarrassed. "How about a cup of coffee? Or a Coke? Maybe a root beer float?"

Renie's eyes lighted up. "A root beer float? Wow, I haven't
had one of those in months! I'm going to order a float for
dessert. I hope they have hard ice cream." She disappeared
behind the plastic menu.

"Really," Gary said, sounding a trifle anguished, "I can't
stick around. They mark your tires and give you a ticket if
you're thirty seconds over."

Trying to overcome her embarrassment, Judith nodded.
"Okay, I'll make it quick. Somebody saw you go into the

Goodrich house Monday morning around seven-thirty. Have you told the police that you were there?''

Gary turned pale. ''Ohmigod!'' He hung his head, then scratched at his bearded chin with both hands. ''How . . . ? Who . . . ?'' He swerved on the vinyl seat, and his expression was unexpectedly fierce. ''That's a goddamned lie! Why are you asking me this junk? Let me out of here!'' Gary bounced into Judith. She had no choice but to let him get up from the booth.

''Gary,'' Judith began as he struggled to upright himself in the aisle between the counter and the booths, ''you were seen. So was your truck, parked around the corner from the cul-de-sac. You ought to be honest with the police and tell them what . . .''

But Gary was gone.

Phyliss Rackley arrived Tuesday morning wearing a long black coat and a black hat with a pair of what looked like black crows sitting on the brim. ''I wouldn't miss a funeral for the world,'' she declared. ''I wish Congregationalists had more vim.''

Judith was somewhat aghast. She hadn't expected Phyliss to attend Enid Goodrich's funeral. But, of course, Phyliss had once worked for Enid, which gave her credentials.

''Do you want to ride with Renie and me?'' Judith offered weakly.

''Very kind, thank you,'' Phyliss said, taking off her coat but keeping the hat in place. ''I'll change the beds and do the laundry before we go.''

''Say, Phyliss,'' Judith called to the cleaning woman, who was about to head up to the second floor, ''when did you work for the Goodriches?''

The hat tilted as Phyliss considered. ''Actually,'' she replied, making the word sound like ''akshilly,'' ''I quit the old bag—rest her tortured soul—just before I took you on. It was late winter, with my rheumatism making my joints ache like Satan sat on 'em. So what's that? Five years?''

''Almost six,'' Judith answered. ''Was she really difficult?''

Phyliss clapped a hand to her forehead, almost knocking off the hat. "Oh, she was that! And more! Always arguing about money, trying to shortchange me. Fussy, too. The living room—I had to clean it twice a week, no matter that it wasn't ever used. No vacuum cleaner allowed. Just a carpet sweeper, which was silly because how do you carpet sweep a plastic runner? You don't, that's how. The spare room, too—now whoever went in *there*? Nothing but a catchall. Then there was them salt and pepper shakers—every shape and size you could imagine—just collecting dust. Do you know how often I had to wipe down Martha Washington? George wasn't so bad—he didn't wear a hoop skirt. George Washington, I mean. He was salt, Martha was pepper. George Goodrich had fancies of his own—wouldn't let me change his bed. Said he liked it a certain way. Well, if I was him, I'd have liked it in another county. Living with Enid must have been enough to drive any man crazy as a bear in a beehive."

Judith reflected briefly on Phyliss's outpouring. "Did they replace you?"

Phyliss smirked. "They tried. The last I heard—three, maybe four years ago—they gave up. Nobody could put up with Enid. Hazel Pinckney was the last one, just about the time I had my gallstones out. No, that was two years ago. You remember? I brought the gallstones over to show you in a mason jar."

Unfortunately, Judith did recall the viewing. She turned away from Phyliss, hiding a grimace. The cleaning woman, however, wasn't finished: "Hazel got the sack, and it wasn't from Enid, either. It was George. Goodrich, not Washington." Phyliss chuckled at what she apparently perceived as her own rich wit. "Anyhoo, Hazel just happened to overhear George and that Japanese Jezebel billing and cooing over the backyard fence. Now, I don't hold with adulterous ways, even when the wife's a holy terror, and I don't blame Hazel for being scandalized. But what can you expect from a family that gambles?"

Judith put both hands to her head. She felt confused. "Wait a minute—*who* gambles? George? Enid?"

"Those grandsons," Phyliss replied primly. "Always running off to them Indian casinos. Talk about dens of iniquity! They serve liquor, too. For all I know, they let you dance."

"Sweet revenge," Judith murmured. "What about George and Mrs. Swanson? Surely you don't mean they were"— Judith chose her words carefully—"romantically involved?"

From under the wide brim of her hat, Phyliss cocked an eye at Judith. "Now, now, I wouldn't repeat common gossip. You know better. But just because people aren't as young as they used to be doesn't mean they don't have what you might call carnal desires. My cousin Orville back in Indiana was eighty-six when he got some poor innocent Miss Teenaged Tippecanoe County in trouble. Satan works in mysterious ways, and Orville was one of 'em. The real problem with Orville was that he never did like wearing pants, not even when he was a tot."

Judith didn't think she could stand hearing any more about Cousin Orville. Or, at nine in the morning, about Mr. Goodrich and Mrs. Swanson. She had several phone calls to make, parcels to ready for mailing to Joe's spread-out kinfolk, and a hurried toilette before she attended Enid's funeral.

Somehow, Judith was ready when Renie honked at nine-forty. Renie, however, wasn't ready for Phyliss. She gaped as the cleaning woman climbed into the back of the Chevrolet. Judith motioned for her cousin to keep her mouth shut.

Renie almost did. "Talked to Joe?" she inquired innocently as they drove across the top of Heraldsgate Hill.

"No," Judith replied, staring straight ahead into the incessant rain. "He was still tired when he got home last night. He plans to take off early today, though."

"Hmmm." Renie could barely refrain from simpering. "How's George?" she finally asked, apparently deciding that the set of Judith's jaw indicated a change of subject.

"I haven't heard a thing," Judith answered truthfully. "If he's at the funeral, we'll know he's been remanded to Art or Glenda's custody. Nobody's been around the house since Friday."

The Congregational Church was located a block from the

public library. The building was old and nondescript, though Judith recalled that in the spring, the landscaping was lush and lovely. She had been in the church only once before, when a classmate had married for the second time some fifteen years earlier. Dan McMonigle had become irate when he discovered that there was no liquor in the punch. He had stormed out upon learning that he'd eaten the last of the curried chicken. Judith tried to forget that he'd also eaten the smoked turkey. All of it. Her memories of Dan tended to become remote with time, which was just as well.

"Tonight," she whispered.

"What?" said Renie.

"Tonight. I'll tell Joe tonight." It wasn't fair *not* to tell him about Herself. He'd be upset, but he'd get over it. Joe wasn't Dan. There would be no chair pitched through the living room window, no marathon drinking bout, no endless barrage of verbal abuse. Sometimes Judith forgot that all men weren't alike.

Enid Goodrich hadn't drawn a large crowd of mourners. Glenda, Art, and JoAnne sat in the front pew. At first Judith didn't see George. Then she realized that he was between Glenda and Art, hunched over, with his head down. The curve of his back was barely visible.

The only other mourners were Mrs. Swanson, Naomi Stein, Corinne Dooley, the Rankers, and a half-dozen middle-aged people Judith didn't recognize. She presumed they were friends of Art and Glenda. The Porters, the Ericsons, and Hamish Stein apparently didn't want to take time from work to attend the service. Judith didn't blame them.

"No Leigh," Renie whispered after they had seated themselves in the fourth row. "Did she go back to New York?"

Judith shook her head, then turned as she heard someone else enter the church. It was Patches Morgan and Sancha Rael. Joe often attended the funerals of homicide victims. He had told Judith that observing the survivors often gave valuable insights into their behavior and thus helped form attitudes about possible suspects.

Morgan saw Judith with his good right eye and nodded. He

and Rael sat down across the aisle. Just as Judith realized that neither Greg nor Dave was on hand, the organ began to play "Now Thank We All Our God." The hymn struck Judith as inappropriate. On second thought, she decided that maybe it wasn't. On her left, Phyliss sighed and closed her eyes in appreciation. The casket rolled down the aisle. Greg and Dave Goodrich were two of the six pallbearers. The other four were somewhat older men Judith didn't know. She had the feeling they had been recruited from the ranks of the funeral parlor or perhaps the church.

The minister, however, was a familiar face. Judith couldn't remember his name, but she had seen him around the Hill for the past several years. He was a tall, lean man of sixty with a kindly face. If he'd known Enid Goodrich, he didn't let it show.

Or maybe he had, Judith mused as the minister expanded on St. Matthew's text of the five foolish and five sensible virgins. By the time he had finished, it was difficult to tell into which classification Enid Goodrich had fallen. Indeed, it was hard for Judith to picture Enid as a dewy-eyed virgin. On the other hand, it was impossible to envision her in the throes of passion. Perhaps it was best not to think of Enid at all.

There was no viewing, since the casket was mercifully closed. Briefly, Judith imagined what damage must have been inflicted on the dead woman. The thought disturbed her. Nobody, not even Enid, deserved to die such a miserable death.

A final melancholy hymn resounded from the organ. Phyliss wept. No one else did, not even George, who kept his head down but managed to turn and watch the casket's progress out of the church. Cremation would follow, so there would be no procession to the cemetery. Instead, the minister had announced a reception in the church hall. The small group trudged down a flight of carpeted stairs.

"I made finger sandwiches and punch," Arlene said to Judith. "Someone had to volunteer."

"You should have told me," Judith said. "I could have pitched in."

"This wasn't part of our catering job," Arlene replied. "I

called Glenda last night, and no one had made any arrangements for food. What could I do but offer to help?'' Arlene shrugged off her typical selflessness.

The twenty people who gathered in the large assembly room seemed lost, like survivors of a sunken ship huddling in a single lifeboat. George Goodrich was still flanked by his son and daughter. Judith was vaguely shocked by his appearance. His best suit seemed to hang on him, as if he'd lost a good deal of weight in the past few days. His sparse hair was lifeless, his eyes were vague behind the glasses, and his cheeks were sunken. As Glenda handed him a cup of punch, his hands shook.

Judith approached him warily. But before she could extend her hand, Phyliss intervened. The cleaning woman enfolded George in her arms and knocked off his glasses with her hat.

''Mr. Goodrich! Think of fluffy clouds and golden harps! Think of feathery wings flapping over your head at night! Think of Enid sitting down with our Lord for a cheerful chinwag! Think of . . .''

Glenda had reached down to retrieve her father's glasses. ''Think of poor Pappy,'' she said in an uncharacteristically testy voice. ''He's been through a really bad time.''

With a spiteful look for Glenda, Phyliss let go of George. ''He needs loving arms, soothing words. No wonder he looks like he's been dragged through a knothole!''

''I need a chair,'' George said weakly. His gaze came into focus and landed on Judith. ''If you would be so kind . . .''

Surprised, Judith readily took George by the arm. She led him away from the table to a folding chair near the rear exit. Renie, meanwhile, had neatly sidestepped in front of Phyliss and Glenda. Armed with finger sandwiches, Renie was distracting both women with what appeared to be a dramatic monologue.

''What are you going to do now, George?'' Judith inquired softly as she sat down next to George on another folding chair.

Adjusting his glasses, George sighed. ''I don't know, really. I'm staying with Art and JoAnne now, in what used to be the boys' room. But I'd rather go home.''

"Of course you would," Judith said, then wondered if she'd feel the same way. But she wasn't George; she didn't yet know the truth about what had happened the previous Wednesday morning. Vaguely, she was aware of Patches Morgan watching her and George with his good right eye.

"You see," George was saying as his voice gained strength, "nobody lets me know what's happening. There was supposed to be something yesterday—a hearing of some kind, maybe— but it didn't happen. I don't know why Art and Glenda are so secretive."

"They're protecting you," Judith said quietly. "They love you, George. You've been very ill. And," she added, almost as an afterthought, "you've lost your wife."

The lines in George's forehead grew deeper. "Yes. I still can't believe it. Nothing seems real, not since your husband came by our house—when? A week ago?"

Judith reflected. Time passed so quickly in December. "That's right. It was a week ago tonight that Joe came over to ask about the sign." She grew silent while George sat motionless, his cup of coffee on the floor by his carefully polished shoes. "Do you remember anything about what happened Wednesday morning?" Judith finally asked, almost in a whisper.

A faint, rueful smile touched George's lips. "It's all like a dream. A nightmare, I guess. I remember going to bed, around nine-thirty, like we always do. The only other thing I recall is someone being in the house. It was much later, and I don't think it was completely dark outside. The next thing I knew, I was sick and there were a lot of people in the bedroom. Art was there. And Enid . . ." He turned away, a hand over his face.

"At the hospital," Judith broke in, "you said something to me about a key. What did you mean?"

George uncovered his stricken face. "A key? I said that?" He looked blank. "I don't remember. Were you at the hospital?"

Judith didn't answer. Had George said "key"? Or was it "Leigh" or "tree" or "he" or "she"? In all honesty, she couldn't be certain. George had been virtually incoherent.

"Gary Meyers isn't here," Judith said, deciding to evade the issue for the present. She watched George carefully to see if Gary's name evoked any kind of reaction.

It did. "Gary! I shouldn't think he'd be here! Glenda would have a fit."

"Oh? I know they broke up, but I didn't realize there were hard feelings." Judith's expression was politely inquiring.

George finally reached down to retrieve his coffee. His hand was less shaky as he raised the cup to his lips. "The man's a cad. At least that's what we called them in the old days." George's mouth shut down in a tight line of disapproval.

Even if Judith had found a tactful way of probing further, she wouldn't have had the chance: Mrs. Swanson was tiptoeing up to them, a bittersweet smile on her face. At first glimpse, George's eyes lighted up. "Sunshine," O.P. had said in describing the interaction between the Japanese widow and the beleaguered husband. Judith saw it, and bit her lip.

"Mr. Goodrich," said Mrs. Swanson in her soft, sweet voice, "my thoughts are always with you."

George took the small, dainty hand that was offered to him. "Mrs. Swanson, you are very kind. I miss seeing you more than . . ." He broke off and turned away.

Judith stood up. "Take my chair, Mrs. Swanson," she offered. "I should be going."

Demurely, Mrs. Swanson thanked Judith, who hurried over to Renie and Phyliss. Out of the corner of her eye, Judith saw George and Mrs. Swanson, their heads very close together. She wondered about them. Had George missed the widow more than he missed Enid? Or had he missed Mrs. Swanson more than anything? Either way, it was the same.

Getting Phyliss out of the church was only slightly harder than prying Renie loose from the sandwiches. As they went outside, Phyliss exuded a great sigh of satisfaction.

"There's nothing like a funeral," she said as the trio walked to the street. "It makes you realize how close you are to the Lord."

"You're pretty close to the curb, Phyliss," Renie snapped. "Look out, here comes a truck."

The truck was coming rather fast, at least for traveling on a rainy residential street. In fact, it sped up as it approached the cousins and Phyliss. All three women involuntarily stepped back as water flew from a puddle in the pavement.

"Damn!" Renie grumbled, brushing at her expensive black raincoat. "That jerk got me wet!"

"Don't curse," Phyliss warned. "What's a raincoat for if you can't get it wet?"

"There's a difference between dirty water and rain," Renie replied. "I paid four hundred dollars for this coat."

"Vanity," Phyliss declared as she and Renie started across the street to the car. "Don't you know what the Bible says about vanity?"

"Vanity, my butt," Renie retorted. "It's an investment. I bought this six years ago and it . . ."

Judith didn't hear the rest of the argument. She was still standing on the curb. The truck that had sprayed dirty rain water was orange and battered, and bore Oregon license plates. Judith had not been able to get a good look at the driver, although she had sensed that it was a man.

She was certain it was the same pickup truck she had seen parked the previous week across from Mrs. Swanson's house.

TWELVE

"I WISH," JUDITH said fervently as she and Renie once again headed down to the bottom of Heraldsgate Hill, "we could get back inside the Goodrich house. I shouldn't have given that key to Patches Morgan."

"What's to see, coz?" asked Renie as they passed a Metro bus driven by a man in a Santa suit. "That place is creepy with all the blood and gore. What's to do, for that matter? If George denies he killed Enid, isn't it up to the cops to make a case against him? If they can't, then they'll start trying to find the real killer. Maybe that's what they're doing now."

Judith thought back to the presence of Morgan and Rael at the funeral. "That's possible," she admitted. "The strange thing about this case is that there's only one real motive—Enid herself. It can't be money, because this is a community property state and nobody gets anything unless George dies, too."

"Maybe," Renie said as she barged into the left-hand lane of the one-way street, "George was supposed to die."

"Then why not take the hatchet to both of them? Or poison Enid? She took enough medication to mask just about anything." Judith gave an impatient shake of her head. "That's one of the things that isn't logical about this case. If the killer wanted one of the Goodriches to be un-

conscious while he—or she—whacked the other one, then
why not give Enid the Dalmane? It was her prescription,
wasn't it?''

''Was it?'' Renie remarked, as she turned the corner to head
for the Heraldsgate Hill postal station. Having dropped Phyliss
off at Hillside Manor, Renie had offered to drive Judith to the
post office. From there, the cousins would head downtown to
finish their shopping.

''You're right,'' Judith said. ''We don't know for sure if
the Dalmane was for Enid. We never saw the bottle because
the police had taken it away. It could have belonged to anybody. Maybe the bottle itself was never there.''

The line of cars waiting to get into the post office parking
lot was eight deep. Renie drummed her fingers on the steering
wheel. ''I should buy more stamps. I'd like to mail all my
cards by Friday.''

''I'd still like to get into that house,'' Judith murmured.
''We never saw the back room or the basement.''

''I mailed my foreign cards yesterday,'' Renie noted, moving up a notch in line. ''Postage is so damned expensive.
Every time I drop somebody from the list, I seem to add two
more. It costs money to have friends.''

''Of course, Phyliss said the back room was a catchall,''
Judith said, lost in thought and growing mesmerized by the
swish of the windshield wipers. ''I suppose the room hasn't
been used since Glenda moved out. That was years ago,
though I think that after the divorce she and Leigh stayed
with . . .'' Judith snapped her fingers. ''That's it! Phyliss and
I will volunteer to clean the bedroom!''

Faintly startled, Renie let her foot off the brake. The Chev
nudged the bumper of a white Jeep. The driver turned and
glared. Renie offered a toothy grin and a helpless shrug.

''You're going to clean the bedroom?'' Renie asked. ''Ugh!
Coz, that sounds grisly.''

''It's a dirty job, but . . .''

''Yeah, yeah, I know.'' Renie inched forward in the wake
of the Jeep. ''Well, go ahead. But I wouldn't do it for a million
bucks.''

Judith said nothing. She would do it for free. If the police would let her.

Joe remained a problem, in more ways than one. By four P.M the cousins had completed their shopping. Except for Joe. Judith already had purchased a couple of shirts, a leather belt, a pair of casual slacks, and two of his favorite videos. But that special something was still elusive. Joe was a snappy dresser, though his tastes were relatively conservative: double-breasted blazers, dark slacks, a pin-stripe suit, cotton shirts with button-down collars, classic loafers, and the occasional drop-dead tie. His hobbies were books, movies, music, and cooking. Hillside Manor was well-stocked with all those things, including kitchen appliances. Judith was stumped.

She was also feeling remorse: Two days had passed since Herself's phone call. Judith still hadn't given the news to Joe. On a whim, she called the Manhattan Grill and requested a seven-thirty dinner reservation for two. It was there that Judith and Joe had become engaged almost four years earlier. Actually, it was their second engagement, but, as Judith thought wryly, who was counting?

"What's the occasion?" Joe asked when he arrived home shortly before six. "Did I miss your birthday?"

"Of course not," Judith said with her most enchanting smile. "That was in October, and you gave me a Wacky Vac."

Joe arched an eyebrow. "And perfume and earrings and a silver negligee that matches your hair and makes me crazy." He nipped Judith's ear. "So what's going on tonight?"

Picking up the appetizer tray for her guests, Judith evaded her husband in more ways than one. "Just . . . us. This time of year gets so hectic that I thought it would be fun to have an evening all to ourselves. I don't mind knocking myself out for everybody else during the holidays, but we can use some time off. You've been working too hard."

Joe didn't argue. There was still no breakthrough in the Shazri case. He and Woody were extremely frustrated. Judith listened to his complaints as she went between the kitchen and the living room, playing hostess to her guests. Hillside Manor was full on this Tuesday night, mostly with visitors who had come to the city for a marathon day of shopping. It was only after Judith had taken dinner out to Gertrude that she made her suggestion about cleaning the Goodrich house.

"Do you think Morgan and Rael would go for it?" she asked, trying to keep the eagerness from her voice. "It's got to be done, and I know Phyliss would be willing. She used to work there."

As he looked up from the evening paper, Joe's expression was exasperated. "I don't know what your fixation is about the Goodrich murder. George has had second thoughts, that's all. It happens."

"Were his prints on the hatchet?"

"I told you, the handle had been wiped clean. That doesn't mean a thing."

"I think George and Mrs. Swanson are in love."

"Good for them. That gives George an even better motive." Joe started to open the local news section of the paper, then glanced at the clock. "Hey, we'd better change. It's going on seven."

Judith decided not to press the issue. An hour later, they were at a linen-covered table in the Manhattan Grill. The brass fittings and soft leather were enhanced by evergreen garlands and big wreaths tied with golden bows. Judith permitted herself to be enchanted through the first round of drinks.

They had placed their orders by the time the second round arrived. Judith took an unusually large sip of scotch. "Herself is coming for Christmas," she blurted. "It's not my fault."

It appeared that Joe hadn't heard Judith. As usual, the restaurant was teeming with customers. They seemed to be in a festive mood, and their laughter reverberated off the mirrored walls and oak paneling.

"I could eat a whole cow," Joe said, puffing at his cigar. "What did you cook for your mother tonight?"

"Liver and onions." Judith tipped her head to one side. "Joe? It was Sunday, when you were working overtime, and I got a phone call around . . ."

Joe was watching a pair of beauteous young women in short skirts exiting a booth. "I know." He took another puff on his cigar. "Why do girls giggle so much? Is it because they're nervous? Or because they think it's cute? It is, but once they hit twenty-five, they stop."

Mouth open, Judith stared at Joe. "I've no idea. What do you mean, *you know*?"

The magic green eyes once again rested on Judith's face. "Vivian called me at work last week. I was wondering if she'd have the nerve to go through with it. My guess was that she wouldn't."

Judith's shoulders sagged. "Joe! Here I've been stewing and fretting and hating myself for not telling you. Why didn't you say something?"

Joe waited until the Caesar salads had been delivered. "Why upset you if she changed her mind?" He paused just long enough to let the thought sink in. "Well? When does the bomb land?"

"The twenty-third, the same day as Caitlin. Oh, Joe, what will your daughter think about all this? Should we tell her?"

"I already did." Joe forked up an anchovy. "I called her Friday, just in case. Caitlin can handle it. She's remarkably mature. Growing up with an alcoholic mother will either make or break you. It made Caitlin, and she's not entirely ungrateful."

Judith let out a rippling sigh. "I've been so upset. I should have known everything would be okay."

Joe's green eyes glinted. "I didn't say *that*. Hey, I'm sorry as hell that Vivian's going to impose on you. But she *is* Caitlin's mother, and we were family for a long time. Don't let it spoil your Christmas. We're all grown-ups."

Briefly, Judith felt that old stab of envy. Herself had been Mrs. Joseph Flynn for almost a quarter of a century. Judith couldn't quite get over her resentment. She still felt cut off from a large part of Joe's life. In many ways, those twenty-three years had been a wasteland for Judith. But it was Advent, with Christmas fast approaching, and Judith knew that she should rid herself of such ugly feelings.

"I just wish sometimes that I didn't feel like a stranger," she said in a hushed voice.

Joe frowned. "You aren't. You never were. You were always there, even in the roughest times. Especially then." He lowered his gaze, concentrating on his salad.

"Oh, Joe!" Judith reached across the table and placed her hand on his.

Joe grinned. "Hell, Jude-girl, there isn't anything you don't know about me. All the fights with my brothers, the downside of breaking in as a rookie cop, the vicious cycle of trying to deal with Vivian—all my hopes and dreams were always tied up in you. The only thing you couldn't give me was my fantasy of being a pilot in World War Two. I'd have loved shooting the crap out of the Luftwaffe."

Judith's black eyes were wide. "You never told me that."

"I didn't? I thought I had, years ago, when we booked a room at the Ebbtide Inn and fished from the window, or took a picnic lunch out on a rented tugboat."

Judith's mind flew back to the halcyon days of their first courtship. Those times had been exciting, romantic, even outrageous. But in middle age, she preferred a quieter pace: watching old movies on TV, playing gin rummy, having dinner in a fine restaurant like the Manhattan Grill. She sighed with contentment.

"I feel so relieved," she said with a wide smile. "It was silly of me not to tell you about Herself's phone call. It was even sillier to get so upset."

Joe made a dismissive gesture. "Basically, this is my problem. I'm used to holiday horrors. I'll make sure it doesn't spoil your annual Christmas fantasy."

The irony in Joe's tone didn't sit well with Judith. But this romantic interlude wasn't the time to say so. Instead, she shrugged. "Okay. Now I can concentrate on Christmas with a free mind."

The waiter removed their salad plates. Joe looked up from his half-finished scotch. "Can you?" His tone was sardonic.

Judith didn't answer.

* * *

In the Roman Catholic Church's liturgical calendar, December eighth was the feast of the Immaculate Conception. Thus, Judith and Renie found themselves at the eight-thirty A.M. Mass, which was celebrated by Father Francis Xavier Hoyle amid the entire student body from Our Lady, Star of the Sea Parochial School. Two pupils from each grade read petitions, or rather mumbled, stuttered, shouted, and in one distressing case, fell off the lectern. By the time Mass was over, Judith and Renie were both feeling somewhat less than spiritually uplifted.

Arlene Rankers, however, was energized. "That little Grazini boy—isn't he adorable? I *love* the way he lisps!"

" 'Thar of the Thea'?" Renie mocked, as they exited through the north vestibule. " 'Bleth our letthonth'? What the hell does that mean, Arlene?" It wasn't quite ten o'clock, and Renie was only now becoming fully conscious, though still in a cranky mood.

Arlene evinced annoyance. "You know perfectly well what it means, Serena. I remember when your Tony read the Epistle in fourth grade and his pants fell down."

"They did not!" Renie countered. "He walked out of his shoes. Your Kevin was the one who stepped on Frances Cabrini Dooley's hem and ripped her skirt off! I always figured he did it on purpose."

Arlene's blue eyes flashed. "Nonsense! One of the Duffy boys tripped him! What about the time your Tom was an altar server and put his cassock on backwards?"

"At least he didn't drop the chalice like your Tim," Renie shot back.

It appeared to Judith as if Renie and Arlene were about to square off in the church parking lot. It wouldn't be the first time the two women had almost gone beyond verbal blows. They liked each other a lot, but both were volatile as well as feisty.

Just as Judith tapped Renie's arm, Carl put a hand on Arlene's shoulder. "I like the part where we left the church," he said at his most pleasant. "Which is what we're going to do now. Come on, Arlene, let's go home and move the camels."

Arlene fired a parting shot: "Your Anne made out with one of the Kramers behind the Big Toy on the playground!"

"Your Mugs played doctor with a Paine kid!" yelled Renie. "That was second grade, and man, was he ugly!" Brushing Judith off, Renie nodded. "Okay, okay, I'm done. Mugs wasn't so pretty at that age, either."

"Your children and the Rankers' kids have grown into good-looking, responsible adults," Judith said in a reasonable voice. "Why do you and Arlene have to rake up all that old grade-school stuff?"

Renie checked her watch. "Because it's only five to ten and I'm still crabby. Let's have coffee at Moonbeam's. Then I'll be my usual charming self."

Judith sighed, peering up into the relentless rain. "We can't. We're supposed to get our mothers' trees. Come on. Let's see what they've got in our very own parish. We know there are small ones, because that's all we could find on Sunday."

The cousins did indeed find two suitable trees that would fit into Gertrude's toolshed and Aunt Deb's apartment. Naturally, they cost considerably more than the two-fifty maximum Gertrude had given her daughter. Renie had been allotted a slightly more generous five-dollar figure, and ended up paying four times as much. By the time the cousins had put the trees in their respective trunks, Renie still wanted coffee.

On a drizzly Wednesday morning, Moonbeam's was predictably crowded. Judith and Renie waited more than five minutes in line but were lucky to find two stools just being vacated by the window that looked out onto Heraldsgate Avenue.

Judith was telling Renie about her dinner with Joe when JoAnne Goodrich came through the door. She appeared frazzled and seemed daunted by the long line.

"She's up early," Renie remarked in a low voice. "Maybe she didn't work last night."

A faint memory clicked in Judith's brain. "She worked last Tuesday night. I know, because Rochelle Porter saw Greg hassling his mother while she was checking customers.'' Judith kept her gaze fixed on JoAnne, who apparently hadn't noticed the cousins at their counter perch.

Renie sipped her mocha, oblivious to the whipped cream that adorned her upper lip. ''I should stop at Falstaff's on my way home. I promised Bill babyback pork ribs for tonight, but they were out yesterday. Harold, the butcher, was having a fit because he said they only got half their order Tuesday morning.''

Briefly, Judith gazed at Renie. ''Really? I should figure out what we'll have Saturday night when you and Bill and the Prices come for dinner. How about a standing rib roast?''

Renie licked her lips, inadvertently wiping away half of the whipped cream. ''Sounds great. But you'd better order ahead. Harold claims they're getting screwed over by their meat supplier.''

Judith frowned into her latte. ''How can that be? Falstaff's does a huge business. You wouldn't think their wholesalers would dare cheat them. The store ought to . . .'' She stopped abruptly.

''What?'' Renie asked. ''Change wholesalers? Raise their own cows? Let live pigs wander up and down the aisles?''

But Judith gave a sharp shake of her head. ''Skip it. Here comes JoAnne.''

Art Goodrich's wife had ordered her coffee to go. She spotted the cousins as she headed for the exit. They weren't easy to miss, since Judith was waving wildly.

''How's everybody doing since the funeral?'' Judith inquired, lowering her voice along with her arm.

JoAnne rubbed her temple with her free hand. New lines seemed to have crept around her eyes in the past week. ''Oh—okay, I guess. It's hard having Gramps live with us. I wish the police would let him go home.''

''Have they scheduled the arraignment yet?'' Though Judith's voice was barely above a whisper, several customers were casting curious glances in JoAnne's direction. Heraldsgate Hill was in the heart of a big city, but its relative isolation lent it the air of a small town. People often knew, or at least recognized, each other.

"No," JoAnne gulped, apparently aware of the prying eyes. "Really, I should go. I had last night off because of the funeral yesterday, but tonight I have to . . ."

Judith had gotten to her feet, escorting JoAnne to the door. "If there's anything I can do, just ask," she said with sincerity. "I know what it's like to have an elderly parent under the same roof. Or almost. Old folks can be a real trial, even more so sometimes than kids." The two women were now out on the sidewalk under the coffeehouse's canopy. Judith could glimpse a vexed Renie through the window. "It's a relief to have our boys raised, isn't it?"

"It's a relief not to have them living at home," JoAnne replied, grimacing slightly. "Greg and Dave have had their apartment for almost two years, but rents are so high on the Hill. It wouldn't surprise Art and me if they had to move home eventually."

The conversation had almost taken the turn that Judith wanted. She allowed herself a small detour. "But they've both got good jobs, don't they? Plus their Alaskan fishing season."

JoAnne's face seemed to crumple around the edges. "I don't know what kids do with their money these days. Art and I've always been so careful about spending. Since Art lost his job, the boys don't have us to fall back on. I'm hoping it'll make them see they have to cut down."

A fleeting remark made by one of the Goodrich sons struck Judith. "What do they spend it on? I recall them saying they didn't have much furniture. And that van isn't new. Do they share it?"

Once again, JoAnne seemed anxious to be off. Her glance darted around the intersection, to Holiday's Pharmacy, Begelman's Bakery, and the state-owned liquor store. "Sometimes. Dave wants to trade in his beater for a Jeep of some kind. Greg wants a motorcycle. That's the problem—there's always something." The lines around JoAnne's eyes deepened.

"Oh, isn't that the truth?" Judith put a hand on JoAnne's arm, as much to detain her as to offer comfort. "And their timing is usually off! They're like two-year-olds, pestering you when you're on the phone or in the bathtub! They never seem to outgrow that nasty habit. Rochelle Porter told me how you had to deal with Greg the other night while you were checking. Believe me, I felt for you!''

There was no sign that Judith's overblown sympathy raised JoAnne's suspicions. ''It was so embarrassing,'' she said in her usual abject manner. ''And all because Greg left his wallet at Mama and Pappy's house. These kids are so careless. Forgetful, too. Really, Greg's almost thirty. Do they ever grow up?''

Helplessly, Judith shook her head. ''I wouldn'. know. Mike's only twenty-six. In fact, he must be the same age as Dave.''

''Dave's a year older.'' JoAnne was looking rueful. ''I wish now I hadn't told him where to find that key.''

Judith tensed. She felt as if she had missed something. But JoAnne had spoken more to herself than to Judith. Now she was starting around the corner, presumably to where her car was parked.

Braving the rain, Judith was right beside her. ''Why did he need the key?'' She made her voice sound innocently confused. ''I mean, his grandparents were home, weren't they?''

JoAnne had reached the Goodrich Toyota, which was pulled into a slot by the laundromat. ''Oh, yes,'' she answered distractedly. ''But they were in bed. At least Greg had the good sense not to disturb them. That's why he needed the key. And of course he didn't want to drive without his license. It was in his wallet. I shouldn't blame him, I guess. He and Dave already have too many traffic tickets.'' The thought must have triggered a reaction in JoAnne. She looked up at the sign on the utility pole indicating that parking was limited to an hour. A tiny smile tugged at her lips. ''I've plenty of time left. To park, I mean. Good-bye, Judith.'' JoAnne got into the car with a vague sense of triumph. Any victory, however small, seemed to satisfy JoAnne Goodrich these days. Feeling sad, Judith returned to Moonbeam's.

Renie was drinking a second mocha. Judith's latte had

grown cold. "Well?" Renie inquired, apparently mollified by her caffeine intake. "Did you nail that poor woman to the telephone pole?"

Judith held her head. "Sometimes I hate myself. I deep-six good manners for the sake of tact, and it all comes out wrong. Does that make sense?"

"No." Renie shook an extra packet of sugar into her mocha. "Life doesn't make sense. So what else is new?"

Judith thought about it for a while. "I guess that's why we went to church this morning."

Renie nodded. "Get another latte. Between Father Hoyle and Moonbeam's, we might make it to New Year's." Sipping at her mocha, Renie acquired another white mustache. "Then again, we might not."

Judith didn't argue.

THIRTEEN

JUDITH BRACED HERSELF for the confrontation over her mother's Christmas tree. It would be too tall, too short, too wide, too thin, too ugly. Judith would be a dope, an idiot, a moron, and an inconsiderate daughter. She knew in advance how Gertrude would receive the jaunty little fir from the SOTs' lot.

Or so she thought. But Naomi Stein was the first to inform Judith otherwise. Racing over to Judith's Nissan, Naomi pointed to the unmarked city car that was parked in front of the Goodrich house.

"They're questioning the neighbors," Naomi said in a breathless voice. "First, Mrs. Swanson, then the Rankerses, and finally, me. Nobody else is home—except your mother."

"My mother?" Judith gaped at Naomi, then jumped out of the car to look down the driveway. She saw nothing unusual, except Sweetums, who was stalking an unseen prey in the shrubbery.

"They're questioning her now," Naomi added, backpedaling to her own property. "Don't worry, Judith. I'm sure she'll be treated with respect."

That wasn't what concerned Judith. With a halfhearted wave for Naomi, she all but ran to the toolshed. There wasn't time to think about the awful things Gertrude could say to the police, especially about Joe Flynn. Judith yanked the door open.

Patches Morgan was standing by the tiny window that looked out onto the backyard and the Dooleys' house. With arms folded, Sancha Rael leaned against a side chair that had originally belonged to Judith and Dan. Gertrude was sitting on her sofa, smoking fiercely, and wearing a tiger-print housecoat under a lime-and-black cardigan. She glared as her daughter came into the small sitting room.

"Well! Just in time, you stool pigeon! What are you trying to do, get me sent up the river?"

Judith's mouth dropped open. "What? Of course not! What's happening?"

With his good left eye, Morgan winked at Judith. "Now, now, me hearties, this is just routine. But," he continued, growing serious, "it seems that certain threats against Mrs. Goodrich were made by Mrs. Grover. You don't deny that, do you, ma'am?" His expression was deceptively benign as he turned back to Gertrude.

Gertrude hid behind a haze of blue smoke. "I make a lot of threats," she mumbled. "It's my way. I can't remember them all."

Judith stepped between Gertrude and Morgan. "Excuse me—who told you that my mother threatened Enid?"

Morgan's good eye avoided Judith. "Now, I can't be revealing my sources, eh? You know that anything we might regard as a threat has to be investigated when there's a homicide involved."

"It was years ago," Judith said, then bit her tongue. "I mean, it must have been—*I* don't remember it. Either," she added lamely, with a commiserating glance for Gertrude.

Sancha Rael stepped forward, a smirk on her beautiful face. "This threat involved a family pet. It had something to do with"—she grimaced slightly—"sauerkraut."

Gertrude stubbed her cigarette out. She shot Morgan and Rael a defiant look. "I forget. I'm old. Senile, too. Maybe I've got Alzheimer's. Who are all you dopey people anyway?" Her small eyes rested on Judith. "You, for instance—I've never seen you before in my life. Are you the maid? You know, the French girl who comes in with a short black skirt and a white doily on her head and dusts with one of those feather things."

Judith didn't know whether to grin or groan. She did neither. "Look," she said to Morgan, "this is silly. I can't believe you're wasting the city's time interrogating my mother. Does she look like the sort of person who'd take a hatchet to somebody?"

Morgan eyed Gertrude closely. "In truth, she does," he said. "Where were you Wednesday morning, December first, between seven and eight-thirty A.M.?"

The menacing expression on Gertrude's face did nothing to dispel the unfortunate image she'd given Patches Morgan. "Here—where else would I be? Do you think my lame-brained daughter ever takes me any place? As for that worthless son-in-law of mine, he'd like to put this cardboard box of an apartment on wheels and send me right down Heraldsgate Hill into the bay. The only time they'll let me out of this dump is when I go sticks up."

Judith was now getting angry. "Mother, you know that's not true! You play bridge, you go to bingo, you get out to dinner with Auntie Vance and Uncle Vince . . ."

Gertrude's face went blank. "Bridge? Bingo? Who are Auntie Vance and Uncle Vince? Where am I? What happened?" She began to hum, a tuneless rendition of "Mademoiselle from Armentieres."

In exasperation, Judith threw up her hands. "Do you mind?" she said to Morgan. "Leave her alone. She's . . . difficult."

Gertrude took out her dentures. She smiled, a fearsome sight.

Morgan surrendered. "We can come back," he said under his breath, motioning to Rael. "Let's talk to Ms. Flynn inside the big house."

"The big house?" Gertrude echoed in a singsong voice after replacing her teeth. "Am I going to the big house? Oh, my! I'll have to wear a striped suit and one of those funny hats shaped like a custard cup and a ball and chain and . . ."

Judith softly closed the door on her mother's irksome rantings. "I'm sorry," Judith said tersely. "As I told you, she can be difficult."

"So your husband informed us," Morgan replied. "If you don't mind, we'd like to ask you a few questions, too."

"Sure, why not?" Wearily, Judith led the way to the back door.

The schoolhouse clock told Judith that it was almost eleven-thirty. She could hear Phyliss Rackley upstairs. With any luck, the cleaning woman wouldn't come down until after the police had left.

Judith seated Morgan and Rael in the living room. She didn't offer coffee, since she wanted to keep their visit short. But even as she sat down in Grandma Grover's rocker, the reason for the detectives' call struck Judith.

"Wait a minute," she said, her face animated. "You're carrying on with this investigation because you really don't believe George is guilty, right? Plus, the arraignment's been postponed or maybe canceled." She waited for a reaction. Neither Morgan nor Rael responded immediately. "Well?" Judith prodded.

Rael seemed to be admiring the big gilded holly wreath over the mantel. Morgan had picked up a glass ball that contained three singing angels. He shook it, causing snow to fall inside.

"Nice," he remarked without enthusiasm, setting the ball down on the coffee table. Accidentally, he triggered the music box mechanism. "Hark, the Herald Angels Sing" pealed gently through the living room. Morgan cleared his throat. "Yes, very nice. You understand I can't tell you exactly what lines of investigation we're following, Ms. Flynn." The detective was now very much the professional. The carol was tinkling at a speedier pace. "What we'd like to learn from you is your whereabouts last Wednesday morning. Purely routine, of course."

"Of course." The glass ball's music was going faster and faster, and at a higher pitch. Judith's mind went back to a week ago. Carefully, she recounted her activities, as well as she could remember. "So you see," she concluded, as the music reached a frenzy, "I didn't hear the sirens because of the vacuum cleaner. The first thing I knew about the tragedy was when my neighbor, Arlene Rankers, came over to tell me something had happened at the Goodrich house." Judith jumped out of the rocker, grasped the ball, and shut off the screeching carol.

Morgan looked relieved as the music box went dumb. "You're certain you didn't see or hear anything unusual?"

"That's right." Judith tried to remember what she'd already told the detectives. And what she hadn't: The commotion at the Goodrich house Tuesday night. The mysterious orange pickup. The odd stains in Greg and Dave's van. Greg, taking the spare key from its hiding place. Gary Meyers, calling on the Goodriches Wednesday morning. What O.P. had seen through his brother's telescope. "Have you talked to the Dooleys?" she finally asked.

Morgan frowned. "Who?"

Judith explained that while the Dooleys didn't live in the cul-de-sac, they had a good vantage point behind Hillside Manor and the Ericson house. It would be better if Morgan and Rael heard O.P.'s account firsthand. Maybe Mrs. Swanson had already mentioned the Cascade Beer truck. Ted and Jeanne Ericson had heard the row on Tuesday night; no doubt they would be questioned later, when they got home from work.

Morgan had gotten to his feet. "Your husband told me how he went over to the Goodrich house Tuesday night. It isn't often that a member of our own crew has such firsthand knowledge of the victim and the family." The detective's face was expressionless.

It hadn't occurred to Judith that Morgan and Rael would interrogate Joe. "My husband didn't see Mrs. Goodrich Tuesday night. She was ailing. We'd been at loggerheads with her over the Christmas decorations in the cul-de-sac," Judith said, wondering if she and Joe were actual suspects. A shiver of apprehension crept up her spine. "Joe probably mentioned that," she added a little too casually.

Morgan nodded. "Your husband gave us a very fine personality profile of the victim. He's been extremely helpful. He's also been able to tell us about the rest of the neighbors in the cul-de-sac. Having such a reliable source right in the department is unusual.'' The detective's face remained impassive, but Rael snickered as she joined her colleague.

Judith's eyes widened. "Joe didn't tell me," she blurted. "About being questioned." A surge of anger replaced the previous fear. "You have to remember that he doesn't know these people as well as I do." She regarded both detectives with a dark expression.

A hint of color spread across Morgan's broad face. "He did his best. And your husband is a very fair man."

Fair, my butt, Judith thought. Joe had ratted on Gertrude. Given her mother's attitude toward her son-in-law, Judith could hardly blame Joe. But she was still angry.

Judith and the detectives had reached the front door when Phyliss came panting down the stairs. She took one look at Morgan and Rael, then let out a shriek.

"Jehovah's Witnesses!" she cried, and fled back upstairs.

Judith didn't bother to correct her.

Judith wasn't up to another shopping expedition, not downtown, not the nearest mall, not even the top or bottom of Heraldsgate Hill. But she was frustrated. Her gifts for Joe were so pedestrian. She wished she could think of something exciting to give him.

"How about a fat lip?" Renie suggested on the phone that afternoon. "Do you really think he told Morgan and Rael about your mother threatening Enid?"

"Who else?" Judith demanded. "Mother said it happened a couple of years ago. I honestly don't recall, but if she's right, then it was after Joe and I were married. He must have remembered, and decided to wreak a little revenge on his mother-in-law. It would be mean if it worked. But, of course, Mother was outrageous."

"Of course." Renie was matter-of-fact. "How'd she like her tree?"

Judith sighed. Sometimes it was hard to decide if she should be mad at Joe or her mother—or both. "She said it was scrawny and dry. She called me a knothead, which just happened to be one of the things I didn't think of while I was anticipating her tirade."

"My mother cried. She said her tree was beautiful, and I shouldn't have bothered." Renie emitted a low groan. "Then she told me not to decorate it, she could maneuver her wheelchair around and do it herself. Of course it would bother her arthritis and her bad knee and her back and her ankles and her eyebrows or whatever else she's got left. So I decorated the damned thing then and there. I just got home."

Judith couldn't help but be touched by Aunt Deb's sentimental streak. It was not unlike her own, and a far cry from Gertrude's view of life. "So was she thrilled?"

"She cried again." Renie sighed. "Then she said it was too soon to put up a tree and why didn't I leave it out in back of the apartment in a bucket of water like my dad used to do. It'll turn yellow before Christmas and all the needles will fall off and she'll have to crawl around with her chin on the rug, trying to vacuum. She swears that when I was a kid, she and my dad never put the tree up until Christmas Eve. That's true, but damn all, this is the nineties!" Renie's voice had risen to an aggravated crescendo.

"You can't win," Judith said, trying to be philosophical. "Mothers, husbands, kids—we're always in the wrong."

There was a pause, as the cousins mulled over their situation in life. "Herself," Renie said at last. "Are you going to buy her a present?"

Judith let out a squawk. "Are you kidding? What would I get? A noose?"

"We-ll . . ." Renie was trying to sound reasonable. "You know how it is on Christmas Eve—we make sure everyone there gets at least a couple of token presents."

Wincing, Judith thought of the many occasions when their shirttail relations and hangers-on had showed up at the last minute, empty-handed but eager-eyed. Their sometimes unexpected arrivals triggered last-minute rustling in closets, cupboards, basement, and attic for suitable, if generic, gifts.

"I'll lay in a supply of coffee from Moonbeam's and some Fandango truffles from Donner & Blitzen," Judith said. "Which reminds me, I've got to grocery shop. I'll order the rib roast for Saturday."

"Yum," Renie said appreciatively. "Yorkshire pudding?"

"Sure." Judith was now smiling into the phone. Her cousin's honest appetite was far more endearing than the presumptive greed of other people. At least certain people, such as Herself and the shirttail relations. In her own way, Renie was as generous as Judith. Or were they both put-upon? Judith had gotten so she couldn't tell the difference.

Falstaff's was busy in the noon hour. Judith had to wait at the meat counter behind three other people who were already putting in their orders for Christmas dinner. Two turkeys and one goose later, Judith was face-to-face with Harold, the butcher. She ordered a standing rib roast for seven and tried not to calculate the cost at five ninety-nine a pound.

"I'll pick it up around eleven on Saturday," she told Harold. "Do you think I should order my turkey now? A lot of customers seem to be jumping the gun."

Harold's genial smile fled. "You'd better, too, Mrs. Flynn. It's going to be first come, first served at Christmas." He leaned across the counter and lowered his voice. "We came up a dozen turkeys short at Thanksgiving. You wouldn't want to be left out in the cold."

Trying not to let her sleeve fall into the specialty meats display, Judith also leaned closer. "I don't get it—is there a turkey shortage?"

Harold gave a sharp shake of his head. "Not that I know of. It's the problem I mentioned with our main supplier, Pacific Meats. Those people can't count anymore. I've asked our manager to check it out, but he's so busy this time of year that I don't think he's gotten around to it."

Behind Harold, one of the other butchers was cutting a side of pork into spare ribs. Noting the stains on his apron and the matching set on Harold's, Judith began to get a strange idea.

"Do you buy direct?" she asked.

Harold had straightened up, his gaze shifting to the next

person in line. But his manner remained affable as he answered Judith: "Not exactly. We get everything through our main wholesaler, United Foods. They actually own the store, you know."

Judith did know. The big grocery supply house owned at least two other stores outright and also sold to chains and independents throughout the region. The strange idea began to grow, and in the process, became less strange.

"Thanks, Harold," Judith said, shoving her cart out of the way. On a whim, she picked up a jar of oysters for dinner. Then she proceeded to the baking aisle, where she selected ingredients for Gertrude's penuche and divinity. Judith also bought a big jar of whipped marshmallow cream for her own special fudge.

Four aisles and fifteen minutes later, she was standing in line at the checkout counter behind a young mother with two squirming children. Judith remembered those days of hauling Mike to the store. She wondered if he'd like the two sweaters she'd bought him for Christmas. Or the CD player. Or the slacks or the hiking boots or the camping equipment. She was still wondering when a timorous voice spoke up behind her.

"Hello," said Mrs. Swanson. "You must be baking." Her gloved hand indicated Judith's cart, which was filled to overflowing.

Judith nodded. "My mother and I try to get an early start. We'll probably make our candies Sunday."

Edging her own cart closer, Mrs. Swanson dropped her voice to a whisper. "The police called on me this morning. It made me very nervous, though I don't know why. Except for the hatchet, of course."

With a grimace, Judith's eyes darted around the store's front end. No one seemed to be paying attention to her and Mrs. Swanson. The mother with the two children was now being checked through, and a tall, disheveled man of about fifty at the next register was counting out food stamps.

"Do the police know the hatchet belonged to you?" Judith whispered back.

"I told them so," Mrs. Swanson said with a small shudder.

"To lie would be dishonest. I have nothing to hide."

Judith was about to agree when she noted that Mrs. Swanson's black eyes abruptly shied away. Faintly disconcerted, Judith heard the checker call to her. She began to help unload her items onto the counter.

"Did they stay long?" Judith asked over her shoulder.

"Not so long," Mrs. Swanson answered. "They asked what I had done and heard and seen that morning."

Judith said nothing but waited expectantly for Mrs. Swanson to elaborate. The other woman merely inclined her head toward the big window that looked out onto the parking lot. Following her gaze, Judith saw a Cascade Beer truck parked by the loading dock.

"You told them?" Judith said in hushed tones.

Mrs. Swanson seemed shaken. "I told them of a red truck. Only now do I recognize it as that type. Should I telephone the eyepatch man?"

Judith considered. "If you're sure, yes."

Mrs. Swanson nodded. "Then I will do so. Thank you, Mrs. Flynn."

With a reassuring smile, Judith turned back to the checker, a young man named Randy. Efficiently scanning items, he engaged in friendly patter.

"Looks like you're going to be busy, Mrs. Flynn. Fudge, I'll bet. Oysters for tonight? These yearlings are great. Nice broccoli for this time of year, up from California. Walnuts, huh? For the fudge, right?"

Judith shook her head. "For the divinity. My mother always puts walnuts instead of pecans in hers. I leave nuts out of my fudge because my cousin can't eat them."

"Gee, that's too bad." Randy looked genuinely dismayed. "That'd be Mrs. Jones, I'll bet. I waited on her a week or so ago when she got the stuff for her mother's fruitcake. No nuts, she said, because she was allergic. Can you imagine fruitcake without nuts?"

"I've had to," Judith replied with a smile. "That's how my Aunt Deb makes it. Believe me, it's still delicious."

Randy, however, looked dubious. "I don't think I'd like it

that way. I'd miss the nuts. You know the saying—'nutty as a fruitcake.' That'll be ninety-eight dollars and fifty-six cents, Mrs. Flynn."

After writing a check, Judith bade farewell to Randy and Mrs. Swanson. Following the courtesy clerk out into the parking lot, Judith glimpsed Gary Meyers starting up the Cascade Beer truck. He was too involved in angling the vehicle out of the loading area to notice Judith.

The six bags of groceries were quickly placed in Judith's trunk. She had just thanked the courtesy clerk when she saw the disheveled man who had paid with food stamps. He was carrying two paper sacks with the Falstaff logo and heading for an orange pickup truck with Oregon plates.

Taken by surprise, Judith couldn't think of any excuse for accosting the man with the pickup. But she had the presence of mind to memorize his license number as he drove out of the lot. As soon as she got into her car, she wrote the number down on a piece of paper.

"No," she said fifteen minutes later to Joe Flynn over the phone, "I have no idea if he has anything to do with the Goodriches. But what's the big deal about running the license number through Oregon's Department of Motor Vehicles?"

The sigh that Joe let out seemed to curdle the phone line. "One, we're not in Oregon," he said, sounding impatient. "Two, this isn't my case. Three, I'm extremely busy, in case you haven't noticed. Four, you're reaching. Five, I'm hanging up now."

"Six," Judith said quickly, "you love me."

Joe hung up anyway. Annoyed, Judith unloaded the groceries. Ten minutes later, she was carrying Gertrude's candy ingredients out to the toolshed.

"You expect me to make candy in this orange crate?" Gertrude demanded. "What next, I play tennis in my so-called sitting room? I'm lucky I got room to sit!"

Judith suppressed a sigh. "I thought you'd like to see what I bought. We didn't plan to actually make the candy until this weekend."

Grumbling, Gertrude began to sort through the plastic bag. "Dark corn syrup, okay. Light brown sugar, right. Sour cream—it'd better not spoil. Walnuts . . . *shelled* walnuts? What is this, some kind of *joke*?"

Judith knew that her mother preferred whole walnuts in the shell. She also knew that Falstaff's hadn't carried them for at least ten years. Her mother knew that, too. Judith had been prepared for resistance but had hoped that maybe this year, Gertrude might forego the annual argument.

"Listen, pinhead," Gertrude rasped, batting at one of the two cellophane-covered walnut packages, "*real* candymakers start from scratch. In *my* day, we went out in the woods and picked the walnuts off the ground."

"You never . . ." Judith began.

"Your Uncle Cliff knew exactly where to find them, over across the lake off a dirt road that . . ."

"Those were hazelnuts . . ."

"Free, except for the gas, which was six cents a gallon, and I always paid my share . . ."

"There's a tenplex movie house where the hazelnut orchard was and before that, a bowling alley . . ."

"It was *walnuts*!" Gertrude stamped her foot, unfortunately, on Sweetums's tail. The cat howled, leaped in the air, and clawed Judith's ankle.

Judith also howled. "Damn! That cat's ornery! And so are you!" She glared first at her mother, then at Sweetums. They both glared back. "Why do you insist on walnuts in the shell? It's such a trial for you to crack them." Trying to control her anger, Judith rested a hand on her mother's card table.

"I like cracking them." Gertrude's mouth set in a grim line. "I pretend they're people I know." She made a swinging gesture with her hands. "Whomp!" She swung again. "Thwang!" She brought her clenched fists down a third time. "Smack-o!" The small eyes peered up at Judith. "Guess who? Hint, hint. You can start with your husband."

Judith didn't really blame Gertrude for being mad at Joe—*if* her mother suspected that he'd told Morgan and Rael about the silly threat to Enid Goodrich. On the other hand, Gertrude always felt like bashing in Joe's head. Rubbing at her temples, Judith tried to calm down.

"I'll take this stuff back into the kitchen," she said quietly. "The recipes are in my file box."

"Who needs 'em?" Gertrude huffed. "You think I can't remember how to make penuche and divinity? I'm not that addled. Yet," she added on a note of uncertainty.

Judith's defenses collapsed completely. "Of course you're not," she declared, reaching down to hug her mother. "You make wonderful candy. I'll do the fudge."

Gertrude was now leaning back in her chair, looking thoughtful. "Mexican wedding rings. I used to do those, too. What do you think?"

Judith shrugged. "That's up to you. I'll be going to the store at least once more before Sunday."

"We'll see." Gertrude had turned away; her wrinkled face was in shadow. "It was your grandmother's recipe. You remember?"

"Of course." Judith's voice was soft. She remembered so much about her grandparents, especially at holiday time. Not only did she recall the treasured personal memories but those that had been handed down from the previous generation. One oft-told tale was how her grandmother and her great-aunt had never approved of the Christmas trees that her grandfather and great-uncle cut down in the forest that adjoined the farm where the family had lived in the early part of the century. The two sisters would hitch up a swaybacked, flatulent animal named Bob-Horse and go off into the woods to find more suitable evergreens. They would return triumphant in their long skirts and petticoats, while Bob-Horse left a noxious trail behind him.

But her favorite story was of the mysterious figure who showed up every year on St. Nicholas Day in a flowing beard and long white robes on a steed far more majestic than Bob-Horse. He would ride through the trees to the edge of the fallow field, pause, wave, and disappear into the mist. Grandma and Grandpa Grover and Great-Uncle and Great-Aunt Malone swore they didn't know who he was. But later in the day, the Grover and Malone offspring would find small cloth bags of candy hidden in the barn.

"I still miss them," Judith said, feeling a catch in her voice.

Gertrude didn't respond at once. "Them," she said at last, and it sounded like an indictment. "Grandma and Grandpa. Cliff. Your father. Those two went too soon. They pegged out early on Deb and me. No wonder Deb talks so much. No wonder I talk so mean." She put her fist against her mouth but still didn't look at Judith. "Go away, kiddo."

Judith didn't move. "I don't want to leave you alone."

The small eyes finally veered in Judith's direction. They were far too bright. But Gertrude's voice was firm, and surprisingly strong: "Don't fuss yourself. I'm not alone."

Judith left.

FOURTEEN

GABE PORTER USUALLY got home from work before five-thirty. As Judith prepared her guests' hors d'oeuvres, she occasionally went in the front parlor to look out into the cul-de-sac. It was already dark and still drizzling. The shadowy outline of bare tree branches was etched on the bay window, an illusion that always pleased Judith. It made her feel as if nature had crept inside the house to hide from winter.

At five-forty, Gabe Porter pulled into his driveway. Judith dashed out the front door, calling his name. Gabe turned slowly, a big shopping bag in one hand.

"I got Rochelle a bathrobe for Christmas," he said, jiggling the bag. "I hope it's the right size."

Judith asked Gabe if he'd mind coming inside for just a minute. He hesitated, then shrugged. "I'm already late, but that's because I stopped to buy the bathrobe. Sure, what's happening?"

Judith waited until they were in the kitchen to explain. "Don't think I'm crazy, or be offended, but I'm working on a theory concerning Enid's murder. It involves motive. Would you like a beer?"

Gabe grinned. "I come home late and with beer on my breath? I don't think so, Judith. Have you ever seen Rochelle when she gets mad? She can be one wild woman."

Judith grinned back at Gabe. "Okay. But tell me—how hard would it be for one of your United Foods employees to steal meat that was intended for a grocery store?"

Gabe's reaction was studied. "Oh—that depends. I imagine there's a little pilfering every now and then, especially with produce. It's hard to keep track of. How much meat? We usually ship in bulk."

Judith had sat down across the kitchen table from Gabe. "I don't really know. Here's what I'm guessing."

Carefully, she explained about the reddish brown stains in the back of Greg and Dave's closed van. Then she relayed Harold's complaint regarding shortages at Falstaff's. "Greg Goodrich works with you at United Foods in shipping. Dave got on at Pacific Meats, where his grandfather still helps with the books. I don't know what Dave does there—it's something to do with computers. You probably think I'm a suspicious, nosy person, but I wonder if the two grandsons have a meat scam going."

Gabe took off his glasses and rubbed at his eyes. "Collusion, huh? Having one of them at each site would sure make it easier. I run the produce section for the big chains, so I haven't heard anything about problems with meat deliveries. But it could be done, at least on a small scale."

"What would they do with the meat?" Judith asked. "That's the part that stumps me."

Gabe's expression was rueful. "There are lots of people who can't afford meat. Immigrants, the elderly, the unemployed. United Foods has a program where we give our overstock to the food banks. Usually it's canned goods, but sometimes produce and bakery items. Dairy, too—anything perishable. Never meat, though. As our meat manager says, we cut it too close to the bone." Gabe chuckled at the inhouse joke.

Judith, however, was nodding thoughtfully. "So if Greg and Dave were stealing sides of beef or pork or whatever, they could take them into one of the poorer neighborhoods, sell cut-rate, and still make money."

"Sure." Gabe put his glasses back on. "They wouldn't get

rich, because they can't be dealing in volume or somebody would have noticed by now.''

"Harold has noticed," Judith pointed out.

"Yes—but did we say Greg and Dave were smart?" Gabe's smile was awry. "Truth to tell, I don't know either of them. I see Greg at work just enough to recognize him. But judging from that stunt they pulled the other night with their cousin, Leigh, I'd guess they're a pair of dumbbells. If they're stealing from us—or Pacific Meats, or both—they'll be caught. In fact, I'm going to talk to our meat manager first thing tomorrow morning." With a grunt, Gabe lifted his big frame from the chair.

"It's only a theory," Judith said, faintly alarmed.

"It's only a suggestion," Gabe replied. "On my part, that is." But his brown eyes were hard. At the swinging door into the dining room, he paused. "Hold on—are you saying that this theory of yours has something to do with Enid getting killed?"

Grimacing, Judith heard the back door open. Joe was home. "Sort of," she said hurriedly, anxious to keep her latest sleuthing efforts from her husband. "It could provide a motive. I'll explain later. Lovely bathrobe, Gabe. See you."

Joe had entered the kitchen, wiping raindrops from his high forehead. "Gabe came calling in his bathrobe? Should I be jealous?" He brushed Judith's lips with a kiss.

Flustered, Judith laughed weakly. "It's Rochelle's bathrobe."

Joe raised his eyebrows. "Gabe's wearing his wife's clothes? What's happening to this neighborhood?"

Hearing the tread of her guests on the stairs, Judith whisked the hors d'oeuvres tray off the counter. "I'll explain later. Dinner won't be ready for another fifteen minutes."

Returning to the kitchen, Judith checked the pork chop she'd fried for her mother. Gertrude hated oysters. Spearing broccoli from a steamer and removing a baked potato from the oven, she readied her mother's plate. Five minutes later, she was back at the stove, putting crumb-covered oysters into a sizzling skillet.

Joe was at the kitchen table, drinking a beer and reading the paper. Judith asked him about the Shazri case. He and Woody were making progress, Joe replied, apparently absorbed in the sports page. Judith waited for her husband to inquire about Gabe's presence, but Joe said nothing further. Feeling foolish, Judith decided not to mention her meat scam idea. She was about to dish up the oysters when the phone rang. The caller was from Utah, wanting to book two nights in February. Judith wrestled with her reservations calendar, her ledger, and her calculator while trying to turn off the stove. She dropped the calculator and almost knocked the skillet onto the floor.

"I need a computer," she grumbled after she'd finally taken the reservation and rescued the oysters. "I could put it on the far counter by the door to the pantry. If I wait until we redo Mike's room, it'll be the twenty-first century."

Joe set the newspaper aside. "The five-day forecast calls for temperatures down in the low thirties. I'd better wrap the outside pipes Saturday. Assuming I can take the day off."

Judith looked up from her broccoli. "You have to. Renie and Bill and the Prices are coming to dinner."

"Woody and I can still eat," Joe said. "Or did you want me to cook?"

"No, it's just that you're always so beat when you work weekends. Besides, I thought you were going to put the tree up Saturday."

Joe didn't respond. He seemed absorbed in his dinner, particularly the oysters, which were a great favorite of his. Out in the living room, they could hear the polite conversation of guests who were strangers to each other. They spoke stiltedly over the faint strains of carols from the CD player.

"We could do the tree Sunday," Judith finally said. "The candy can wait until Monday or Tuesday."

Joe made an indifferent gesture. "Like I said, it depends on what's happening with the investigation."

"The tree's a big job. It takes most of the day. Maybe Sunday's best."

"I thought you wanted to show it off to Woody and Sondra."

"Maybe they could drop in for drinks later during the holidays. They could bring the children. I haven't seen them in ages."

"At three and eighteen months, they'll trash everything. Both the Price kids are full of hell."

"I don't believe that. Woody and Sondra are excellent parents." Judith swallowed her last oyster and regarded her husband with a wary eye. "You're trying to distract me. From what, may I ask?"

Joe broke into a grin. "From asking questions. Don't you want to know what I found out from the Oregon DMV?"

"Oh!" Judith slapped a hand against her cheek. "But I thought you weren't going to check."

"I wasn't. I didn't. But I passed on the license number to Sancha Rael. She's always very cooperative."

The muscles along Judith's jawline tightened. "How nice." But curiosity overcame annoyance. "Well? What did the beauteous Ms. Rael learn?"

Joe's green eyes glittered. "That orange pickup was recently resold by some guy in Enterprise, Oregon. The new registered owner actually lives in Idaho. His name is Ross Cisrak."

Judith couldn't contain her excitement at discovering that the battered pickup that had been sighted around Heraldsgate Hill belonged to Glenda Goodrich's ex-husband and Leigh Cisrak's father. But Joe didn't share her elation. Without rancor, he told his wife that he'd closed the door on crime for the day when he left the squad room at five-twenty. Thus, Judith was forced to phone Renie.

"Ross Cisrak," Renie repeated. "So why has he been hanging around the cul-de-sac? Why not Glenda's place?"

"Maybe he has," Judith replied, stretching out on the bed in the cheerful white-and-yellow room she shared with Joe on the third floor. "I saw him at Falstaff's today, and he looks pretty down-at-the-heels. He used food stamps to pay for his groceries. Maybe he came here to ask for money.''

''Ask who? Glenda?'' Renie sounded dubious.

''Not Glenda. Leigh. She's the only one in the family who makes a decent living. Plus, she seemed fond of her father, even though she hasn't seen him for years.''

'' 'Hasn't' or 'hadn't'?'' Renie asked.

Judith understood the distinction. ''When I talked to her the other day after Morgan threw her out of the Goodrich house she spoke as if she hadn't seen him since she was a kid. For all I know, she returned to New York. Leigh wasn't at the funeral.''

''Was Ross?''

Judith thought back to the half-dozen people she hadn't recognized. None of them had looked particularly shabby; if memory served, none of them resembled Ross. Yet his pickup had passed by the church as she and Renie and Phyliss were leaving.

''Maybe he's trying to reconcile with Glenda,'' Judith said. ''In any event, Morgan and Rael know about him now. They'll probably track him down and bring him in for questioning.'' The thought caused her to roll over on the bed and peer down into the cul-de-sac. It had stopped raining, and the moon was out, augmented by a wintry white glow. Sure enough, the unmarked city car used by the homicide detectives was parked in front of the Stein house. ''The cops are here now, probably talking to Ham and the Ericsons and the Porters. They were all at work this morning.''

''Didn't you tell me that Leigh said her father remarried?'' Renie's question was accompanied by the sound of tinkling ice. Judith could picture her cousin embarking on one of her marathon Pepsi-drinking bouts.

''That was years ago,'' Judith replied. ''He could have married, divorced, married again—who knows? Somehow I got the impression that he was something of a drifter.''

''He drifted to Heraldsgate Hill,'' Renie noted, making a faint glugging sound.

Judith moved on to her idea about the meat scam, which didn't sound so preposterous when she related it to Renie.

"Those two idiots might try something like that," Renie agreed. "But how is that a motive for murdering Enid? It would be George who might unearth something in the books. Assuming Dave was juggling them with the computer. Ergo, George, not Enid, should be the victim."

"True," Judith admitted, "except you have to take the personalities into account. Joe says you can often figure out who killed someone by studying the victim's character. If George had discovered discrepancies, would he turn his grandsons in? I don't think so. He'd warn them. They're his flesh and blood. But Enid wasn't their real grandmother, and she was hard as nails. She wouldn't have thought twice before giving them up to their employers or even the police."

Save for a slurping sound, Renie grew silent. When she spoke again, she posed a question: "Why did they need the money? Greg and Dave fished in the summer, they held jobs in the winter. What did they spend it on?"

"Everything," Judith answered. "According to Glenda, they were always in debt. You know how young people are these days."

"Don't I, though," Renie breathed. "But our kids are classy spendthrifts. Unless I'm missing something, the Goodrich grandsons don't have much to show for their ill-got gain."

The thought had only occurred briefly to Judith. Now she considered Renie's statement carefully. "You're right— maybe it's drugs."

"Alas," Renie lamented, "that's often the case. It could be women."

"Somehow, I doubt it with those two," Judith differed. "They seem socially inept. Phyliss had a rumor about gambling. It was secondhand, and she's not always reliable."

"Gambling? Where?" Renie hiccoughed gently. "Nevada?"

"Native American casinos. They're all over the place around here now."

"Happily, yes. Bill and I've visited a few of them. No slot machines, though. Not yet." Another sound of splashing Pepsi rippled over the phone line. "What happens if gamblers don't pay their debts to the local casinos? Do they send out a war party?''

''They probably send the cops,'' Judith said, then remembered to tell her cousin about running into Mrs. Swanson. ''She said she'd let Morgan know about the Cascade Beer truck. Call me crazy, but I still think Gary Meyers is the key to this whole thing.''

''You're crazy,'' Renie said obligingly. ''I thought you were sure that Gary didn't kill Enid.''

''I didn't say he did,'' Judith replied, somewhat enigmatically.

Renie yawned in Judith's ear. ''You're being coy. As usual. I'm going to watch Bill watch an old Nazi movie, get my second wind, and have a crack at the concept for the gas company's annual report. Right now I'm in the mood to create a cover design with a family overcome by deadly carbon monoxide fumes. How's that for the Christmas spirit?''

''Appropriate,'' Judith retorted. ''At least in this neighborhood. G'night.''

Looking back down into the cul-de-sac, Judith saw Morgan and Rael trudging from the Stein house. No doubt they were headed for the Ericsons'. Perhaps they'd called on the Porters first. She wondered if they'd follow her suggestion and talk to O.P. Dooley.

The homicide detectives had disappeared from view. Through the window, Judith could see the Rankers's Nativity scene. Mary and Joseph hovered over Baby Jesus, while the cow and the donkey sat complacently behind them. Carl had suspended an angel from the maple tree, and two shepherds were clustered with their sheep in front of the crib. A gold star shone from the branches of a rhododendron.

Next door, she saw the illuminated Santa with his reindeer prancing across the Porters' roof. Santa's bag was stuffed with toys as he prepared to make his descent down the chimney.

Finally, Judith admired the display of blue-and-white lights strung amid the shrubbery and the bare branches of the ornamental cherry trees, and across the facade of the Stein house. From this vantage point, she could only imagine Mrs. Swanson's delicate fairy lights, the Ericsons' merry carolers, and her own New England village. Still, Judith couldn't help but smile. The neighborhood was typical of the human race, with its diversity, its generosity, its willingness to compromise. There was evil, too, represented by the darkened Goodrich house with its unwanted sign in the front yard. Yet the existence of the sign struck Judith as a small triumph. Her gaze returned to the Nativity scene. She kept smiling.

Phyliss Rackley was torn. On the one hand, she had vowed never to set foot in the Goodrich house again. On the other, she was morbidly curious about the murder scene.

"What are they going to pay us?" she demanded of Judith on that foggy, cold Friday morning. "Are you sure the police approve?"

"I spoke with Detective Morgan yesterday afternoon," Judith assured her cleaning woman. "He said that they had gathered all the evidence they needed. We can go ahead and clean the place at thirty dollars an hour. We'll split it right down the middle, Phyliss. It shouldn't take long. The bedroom is the only real mess." Judith winced in spite of herself.

The fee was considerably higher than what Judith paid Phyliss. The cleaning woman's eyes sparkled. "I suppose it's the Christian thing to do. Nobody ever accused me of shirking a duty."

"Good," Judith said from her position at the kitchen sink where she was watering the five poinsettias she'd bought that morning at Nottingham Florists. "We'll go over there after we finish up here. Morgan is dropping off a key later this morning."

Judith was arranging the potted plants on the staircase landing when the phone rang. Glenda Goodrich sounded very nervous.

"The police just called," she said in a fretful whisper. "I'm at work, and I'm not supposed to make personal calls. They're very strict here. I have to work until five o'clock Christmas Eve, and we didn't get the day after Thanksgiving off, either."

Glenda seemed to catch herself and spoke more rapidly: "Is it true that you're going to clean Mama's house?"

Judith said it was. Glenda expelled what might have been a sigh of relief. "I think we should put it up for sale. But Art and JoAnne want to move Pappy back home. That doesn't make sense."

Getting involved in a family controversy was definitely not on Judith's agenda. "Take your time," she counseled. "By the way, did Leigh go back to New York?"

"Yes." The word was sharp and final. "I must go. Thanks, Judith." Glenda hung up.

Judith frowned into the receiver. She'd wanted to ask Glenda about Ross Cisrak. On a whim, she punched in the number for New York City Directory Assistance. A minute later, she was listening to the phone ring somewhere in Manhattan.

By the seventh ring, Judith was ready to hang up. But a breathless voice answered, and Judith recognized Leigh Cisrak. Surprised, Judith almost forgot her excuse for calling.

"Leigh!" she cried in friendly astonishment. "This is Judith Flynn, the neighbor at the end of the cul-de-sac on Heraldsgate Hill. I was wondering if . . ."

"Excuse me," Leigh interrupted in a brisk tone. "I just came in the door. I went to the agency to see if they had any last-minute . . ." She stopped, apparently fumbling with the phone and whatever other encumbrances were hampering her style. "Judith Flynn? I'm sorry, I don't know . . ."

"I own the B&B two doors down from your grandparents' house. We talked the other day when you were trying to get your . . . ah . . . keepsakes." Judith grimaced into the receiver.

"Oh." Leigh sounded both disappointed and disapproving. "Yes, I remember. What do you want?"

"It's about your father," Judith said, still trying to sound friendly. "Did he ever catch up with you while you were in town?"

The sudden silence indicated shock or surprise or reticence. Judith wondered which. Then Leigh spoke, and her attitude was clear: "*My father*? You talked to my father? When? Where? Ohmigod!"

"I saw him at Falstaff's Market," Judith said, feeling as if the truth were a lie. "And outside the church after your grandmother's funeral." She deliberately omitted the sightings across from the cul-de-sac.

The response was slow to come but ultimately explosive. "I hate my mother! She's a total bitch! It's all her fault! Where's my father now?"

"I don't know," Judith answered honestly. "I last saw him two days ago. That was Wednesday, at Falstaff's."

"Find him," Leigh ordered. "Have him call me. *He'll* understand."

Puzzled, Judith frowned. "Understand what?"

Leigh's manner went through one of its chameleonlike changes. She actually simpered. "It's only stupid, selfish women like my mother and grandmother who don't get it. That type is all wound up in outdated morality. You follow your feelings. So what if they change from day to day, hour to hour? That's part of being alive. Why shouldn't I sleep with Gary Meyers? It made both of us feel good. Why is that so wrong?" Leigh scarcely missed a beat. "When you find my dad, make sure he calls me."

The phone went dead.

FIFTEEN

JUDITH WAS TRYING to reach Patches Morgan when he showed up on her front porch. Naturally, the detective was surprised by Judith's effusive greeting.

"Thank goodness! You're just the person I need!" She ushered him into the living room and offered coffee.

Morgan declined. "Bless me, I came to give you the key to the Goodrich house," he said, regarding Judith with frank curiosity. "What's wrong? You seem all at sea."

Judith unloaded about Ross Cisrak. "I'm not suggesting that he's a serious suspect," she concluded as Morgan gazed out of his good right eye, "but he was in the vicinity before the murder. He's stayed on since. His daughter desperately wants to talk to him. If I were you, I'd start with Glenda Goodrich."

"You're not me," Morgan said flatly. His usual bonhomie had disappeared. "We'll put out an APB. As for Ms. Glenda Goodrich, if she knows where he is, then she'll put him in touch with their daughter."

"It's not that simple," Judith asserted. "Glenda and Leigh have had a serious falling out. Leigh slept with her mother's boyfriend, Gary Meyers, which reminds me—did Mrs. Swanson tell you about the Cascade Beer truck?"

Now Morgan was looking downright mystified. "Beer truck?" His forehead creased under the swatch of silvered black hair. "Oh, yes, Mrs. Swanson left a message about a beer truck. But I don't see what that has to—"

"Gary Meyers was driving it," Judith interrupted. "He went to the Goodrich house the morning of the murder, around seven-fifteen, seven-thirty. I don't know whether or not he got in, but he was there. Did you question O.P. Dooley?"

"O.P.?" Morgan seemed a bit unsettled. "I thought you said P. C. The tyke can scarcely talk yet."

Peter Claver Dooley was a grandson, not quite two. "No, no," Judith corrected. "O.P., for Oliver Plunkett. He's twelve, and very bright. The Dooleys named all their children after saints, and the tradition has been handed down to the grandchildren, but some of them use only the initials."

Patches Morgan wasn't interested in what or how the Dooleys called their offspring. "If what you're saying is true, this could make a serious case against Gary Meyers." The good right eye was fixed on Judith's face.

In the wake of the phone call to Leigh Cisrak, Judith was forced to reconsider Gary as a suspect. But again, Enid as victim didn't make sense. In a classic triangle, it was one of the trio who was doomed to die. Judith offered no comment.

Rising from the sofa, Morgan brushed at his flowing black raincoat, which had acquired several cat hairs, courtesy of Sweetums. "If I were you, Ms. Flynn," Morgan said in a strained voice, "I'd stop trying to figure this out on your own. Hasn't your good husband told you that his shipmates are pretty fair sailors?"

"Oh, definitely!" Judith enthused. "It's just that . . . well, living in the same neighborhood with the victim, it's natural to hear gossip and pick up stray facts that might otherwise . . . go unnoticed." Judith flinched at her own words.

"Everything comes to us, all in good time." Morgan was striding to the entry hall, the black raincoat sailing around his legs. "Good luck with the housecleaning. We'll pick up your vouchers when we collect the key."

Judith's farewell was barely audible. At least she hadn't given Morgan her theory about the grandsons' possible meat scam. No doubt he would have laughed outright. Positioning herself against the door, she watched the detective's progress to his car. Sancha Rael was in the passenger seat. The two drove out of the cul-de-sac, swallowed up by the fog before they reached the corner. Perhaps they were heading for the Dooley house. Judith frowned. O.P. was in school. Still, Dooley himself could relay his brother's information.

Half an hour passed before Judith's curiosity got the best of her. Phyliss was ironing in the basement, while running a load of laundry. Clasping the key to the Goodrich house, Judith sneaked out through the front door. She had reached the driveway between the Ericson and Goodrich properties when Renie emerged out of the fog in her blue Chev.

"Where are you going?" Renie asked after she'd rolled down the window.

Judith put a finger to her lips. "I'm skulking. Want to join me?"

Renie swung the car around so that she could park in front of the Ericsons'. "Let me think—you'd be avoiding . . . ? Arlene? Your mother? Phyliss? The cops?"

"All of the above," Judith replied as they trooped along the driveway. "How come you're here?"

Renie gave her cousin a feeble smile. "Aunt Ellen's Christmas box arrived this morning from Beatrice. This year, she sent it to our house. I'm distributing the presents."

"But it's only the tenth of December," Judith pointed out as she inserted the key into the lock on the Goodrich back door.

"Right, but you know how thrifty Aunt Ellen is. She wrapped her gifts in plain tissue for ten years after nobody else did. Then she used grocery sacks, newspaper, and old campaign banners for the losing gubernatorial candidate in Nebraska. This year, it's plastic produce bags, held together with those twisty-ties from garbage sacks. Aunt Ellen made some of the twisties into rosettes, which are kind of nice, but the bags are falling apart. I wanted to get everything delivered before the whole batch came undone and we couldn't figure out who was getting what. Plus, the tags are kind of hard to read. She used the little plastic things from loaves of bread."

Judith, who had been standing transfixed with her hand on the doorknob, blinked three times in a row. "Dare we guess what the presents are this year?"

"You don't have to guess," Renie responded. "You can see through the produce bags. Heaven forbid Aunt Ellen would waste money on *boxes*. Your present is a wreath made out of thirty-five-millimeter film, no doubt left over from when she worked for that portrait photographer. Mine's a wall plaque covered in bottle caps." Renie maintained a straight face.

So did Judith, nodding as she opened the Goodrich back door. "Otherwise, Aunt Ellen's a darling. Please don't tell me what she sent our mothers."

Renie suppressed a snicker. Then all merriment fled as the cousins approached the bedroom.

"*I'm* not going in there," Renie declared, clinging to the hall doorway. "After you and Phyliss clean it, maybe, but not now."

"You don't have to," Judith said. "I want to see the spare room and the basement. They don't need to be cleaned, and I don't want Phyliss snooping any more than she has to. That's why I'm here without her."

But the spare room held no secrets. As catchalls went, Glenda Goodrich's former bedroom was quite orderly. The bureau, which smelled of mothballs, contained a few items of clothing dating from a quarter of a century earlier. The closet held rainboots, a straw hat, a couple of tie-dyed dresses, extra bedding, and more mothballs. The single bed was made up, though it didn't look comfortable. It did, however, look rumpled, which struck Judith as odd, given the general orderliness of the Goodrich house.

"I wonder," Judith murmured, casting an inquiring glance in Renie's direction.

"What?" Renie followed her cousin's gaze to the bed. "Come on, coz, you aren't thinking about George and Mrs. . . ."

"No!" Judith exclaimed, then realized she hadn't yet told Renie about the telephone conversation with Leigh. When she was done, Renie made a face.

"Leigh and Gary, making mad, passionate love with Enid across the hall? Dubious, coz. How about poor George coming in here to lie down and escape from his nagging wife?"

The idea made sense. "Maybe," Judith agreed. "Let's visit the basement."

The basement revealed no more than the spare room. In one corner, an area was covered with a worn rug. Another single bed, probably the mate to Glenda's, was stripped down to its mattress pad. There was a desk, a chair, and a table lamp. The only personal note was a poster of an early Boring jet passenger plane.

"Art's room," Judith said. "It reminds me of a monk's cell. Except I've never seen one."

The storage items in the rest of the basement seemed ordinary—the washer and dryer, a clothes tree, a couple of coiled garden hoses, empty boxes that had once held appliances, a snow shovel, two aging pairs of roller skates, and a small box marked "Xmas Dec."

"I guess the Goodriches never were much for holiday festivities," Judith remarked, heading back to the wooden stairs.

"They weren't much for anything," Renie said as they returned to the kitchen. "What now? Haven't you looked everywhere else?"

In fact, Judith had. She made a frustrated sound. "I keep thinking I must have missed something. What could it be?"

Renie lifted one shoulder. "What would you expect to find? Typically, I mean. Clothes, furniture, dishes, linens, books, medicine—take mental inventory."

In a cursory way, Judith already had. "The police would have taken away anything that could be construed as evidence," she said, more to herself than to Renie. "But evidence is a funny thing."

"Hilarious." Renie was looking skeptical. "That hatchet really makes me laugh. So does the Dalmane and maybe some bloodstained clothing and a bunch of gory photographs."

"That isn't what I mean." Judith was frowning as she surveyed the living room. "Evidence is often something very ordinary that gets overlooked. Sometimes, it's what *isn't* there. Such as George's books for Pacific Meats.''

Renie raised her eyebrows. ''True. You think Dave swiped them in order to cover up his T-bone theft?''

Judith gave a short nod. ''That's possible. We certainly haven't found any ledgers.'' She pointed to the walnut desk. ''There's an empty space inside. An account book would fit perfectly.''

''There's something else missing,'' Renie said after a short silence. Her eyes had been roaming around the room, taking in what was left of the solid, if inexpensive and aging, furniture. ''Money. You found that passbook with what—seven, eight grand? That's not much for a couple like the Goodriches. This house must have been paid off forty years ago. They weren't lavish spenders, and Enid certainly wouldn't have been generous with their kids or grandkids. Did they ever travel?''

Judith considered. ''Not that I know of. Maybe their money was spent on doctors for Enid.''

''No. They probably had some kind of health care plan through George's job, plus Medicare. And Enid didn't actually go to the hospital much, did she?''

Again, Judith thought back to the Goodriches' known history. ''I guess not. Arlene is always full of news about anybody being hospitalized.'' Frustrated, Judith rubbed at the back of her neck. ''So where's the money? If there's a safety deposit box, there must be a key. If there are stocks and bonds and CDs, there should have been records in the desk. If they'd put their savings in . . . ah!'' Judith snapped her fingers. ''The IRS! Where are they when you actually need them?''

''Everywhere,'' Renie replied gloomily.

Judith was already opening the breakfront desk. ''There were tax statements in here. I ignored them because they make me crazy. And poor.'' Eagerly, she sorted through the Goodriches' business records. Sure enough, a xeroxed copy of their most recent IRS filing was at the bottom of the pile, where Judith had left it.

''Well?'' Renie inquired, coming to stand next to Judith. ''Are they fabulously rich?''

George and Enid had filed a short form. They certainly weren't rich; the Goodriches had been entitled to a six-hundred-dollar refund. The list of assets corresponded with the other financial information Judith had found previously in the desk.

''Shoot,'' breathed Judith. ''No assets, other than this house and their savings. That doesn't seem right.''

''George isn't the type to hoodwink the IRS,'' Renie pointed out.

''So what did they do with their money?'' Judith demanded.

''Who knows?'' Renie said, leaning against the fireplace mantel. ''Maybe George was secretly helping Art and Glenda or the grandsons.''

A knock at the front door startled both cousins. Judith peered through the bottle glass but was once again thwarted. She could distinguish only a form.

Arlene Rankers wore an indignant expression. ''It's not fair,'' she announced, marching into the living room. ''Why do you two get to come in here and browse around while I stand out in the fog trying to move Melchior?''

''How did you know we were here?'' Judith asked suspiciously.

Arlene was eyeing the open desk. ''I went to your house, but Phyliss didn't know you were gone. Your mother hadn't seen you since breakfast. Your car was still in the garage. The fog's starting to lift, and I saw Serena's Chevrolet parked at the curb.'' The thorough reconnaissance was typical of Arlene's intelligence methods.

The logic of it all made Judith smile. ''Okay, Arlene, help us figure out what the Goodriches did with their money.'' She gestured at the desk. ''No clues there. What do you think?''

Briefly, Arlene looked puzzled. Then she brightened and beamed with triumph. ''Eggs! They spent it on eggs!''

Renie wrinkled her pug nose. ''What kind of eggs? Fabergé?''

Arlene threw up her hands. ''Heavens no! *Nest* eggs!

George referred to sitting on his investments. Hatching them, as it were.''

Judith and Renie exchanged bewildered glances. ''The hen-house must be a Swiss bank,'' Renie finally said. ''There's no sign of nest eggs here.''

Arlene's blue eyes hardened. ''Are you doubting my word, Serena?''

Swiftly, Judith intervened. She also changed the subject, since they seemed to be getting nowhere with the Goodriches' financial status. ''Arlene, you keep so well-informed about what happens in the neighborhood. Think back to the week before the murder. What, if anything, was going on at the Goodrich house?''

Sinking into the armchair that Leigh had abandoned, Arlene knitted her brow in concentration. ''Nothing startling. Enid and George went to Glenda's for Thanksgiving. When they drove off, we were out in the front yard trying to coax Mugs's husband out of the car. They'd had a fight about gravy. Last year, I didn't put giblets in it and . . .''

''That would be Thursday,'' Judith interrupted. ''What about Friday?''

''Friday? You mean the day after Thanksgiving?'' Arlene considered. ''George went to the dentist. No, that was the previous week. He did his regular grocery shopping in the morning, just about the time Carl was working on the downspouts. We had that big wind in mid-November, and the leaves got . . .''

Judith forced a smile. ''You're talking about Friday morning?''

Arlene nodded, somewhat impatiently. ''Of course. If you'd let me finish . . . Anyway, the downspout fell off, and Carl had to go to Earnest Hardware. That was after lunch. He left just as George was taking Enid to the doctor. While Carl was gone, I scrubbed down the dining room because we'd had a little accident during dinner. Sort of a small fire, actually. When Carl came back, Glenda's car was parked at her folks' house. Gary Meyers was with her. I saw him leave.''

Arlene paused for breath while Judith tried to keep the comings and goings straight. Despite the digressions, the narrative thread was fairly clear. But something Arlene had said gave Judith mental qualms.

"Art stopped by Saturday afternoon while I was taking down my Thanksgiving decorations," Arlene said, shifting on the plastic-covered armchair. "JoAnne was there Sunday—I saw her on our way back from Mass. Art came around again at noon on Monday, and Leigh was there in the evening. She'd borrowed her mother's car. Tuesday—well, you know what happened Tuesday."

Judith was impressed by Arlene's ability to keep tabs on the cul-de-sac. She only wished that her neighbor had been eyeballing the vicinity early Wednesday morning. "No other sightings?" Judith asked hopefully.

Arlene's expression was apologetic. "We still go to bed early, even now that Carl is retired. We get up early, too, but unfortunately, the only house we can see from the dinette is yours. It's very dull."

Renie, who had been standing by the fireplace fiddling with the artificial flower arrangement, nodded with understanding. "I never see what's going on in our neighborhood. Our street's too steep and all the trees have grown up so that it's practically like living in the woods."

"You have to create opportunities, Serena," Arlene said in encouragement. "For example, the other day I happened to be standing on my toilet, and I saw Naomi Stein come home with a huge Nordquist's box. I'll bet she's buying Ham an overcoat for Christmas. Or would that be Hannukah?"

"It would for the Steins," Judith said with a smile. Over the years, Arlene was prone to stand on her toilet, though she never explained why—but everyone knew it was so she could get a better view.

"That was Monday," Arlene continued, apparently still offering Renie advice. "Last Friday—or was it Thursday?—there I was, on top of the garage. I saw Corinne Dooley, making her bed at two in the afternoon! Granted she has a lot of children, but wouldn't you think she'd get right at that in the morning?"

"Maybe that's why," Renie ventured.

"Why she has so many children?" Arlene was frowning at Renie. "Yes, you have a point . . ."

"No," Renie broke in, "I meant why she's so busy . . ."

"Then a week or so ago," Arlene blithely went on, "I was hanging out of the attic window . . ." She stopped herself with a wave of one hand. "No, it was the day you borrowed Kevin's truck, Judith. I was watching for you to come back in one piece. Anyway, an attic is a wonderful vantage point. Remember that, Serena. A really sweeping view."

Renie was looking bemused. "So what did you see? Someone sweeping?"

"Exactly!" Arlene's voice was fraught with enthusiasm. "Rochelle Porter, out on her back porch. She'd gotten home early from work. Or else she hadn't been called to sub that day. Oh—I saw Mrs. Swanson, talking over the fence to George. She doesn't come out much during the cold weather. Being from Japan, I suppose she's used to a tropical climate."

Judith considered correcting Arlene, both about the Japanese weather and the half century Mrs. Swanson had spent in the Pacific Northwest. But Arlene was still talking: "That's when she gave him the hatchet, of course."

Renie blinked; Judith gaped. Arlene started to get out of the armchair.

She was immediately tackled by both cousins.

"Honestly!" cried Arlene, "you don't need to twist my arm so *hard*, Serena!"

Abashed, Renie let go. Judith, however, blocked Arlene's passage. "You've never mentioned the hatchet before," she said in reproach. "At least not to me. Did you tell the police?"

Arlene's face was blank. "Tell them what? They know about the hatchet. You said so yourself."

Judith had to concede the point. "But you should have . . ." She stopped, aware that the argument went against the grain of her own belief in George's innocence. "Let's be precise. What did you see George and Mrs. Swanson doing?"

With a hand to her forehead, Arlene wandered to the hearth.

"I wasn't concentrating on *them*. The Ericsons had gotten a delivery from UPS that morning. They weren't home, of course, so the box was still on the front porch. You can't see their porch from the street because of the high fence. I think it was for their computer. Goodness, in all the other excitement, I forgot to ask Jeanne about it."

"George?" Judith coaxed. "Mrs. Swanson?"

Arlene was growing exasperated. "I told you, I wasn't paying much attention. They were at the fence, with the hatchet. That's it."

Judith reflected briefly. "That was Tuesday afternoon, the day before the murder?"

"Yes, yes." Arlene now sounded cross. "As I said, it was the day you borrowed Kevin's truck. Really, I should get home. Or you should." Arlene's gaze wandered off in the direction of the bedroom.

Judith knew that Arlene wouldn't be satisfied until she'd had a look at the rest of the house. "You're right. Don't forget, we're serving the Lutheran Church's St. Lucy's Day buffet Monday night." Judith didn't know if she and Arlene had been asked to cater the annual celebration of light in the spirit of ecumenism or because the Lutherans were sick of lutefisk. "I'm coming back with Phyliss this afternoon. You might as well leave the back door open."

Arlene's blue eyes widened in feigned innocence. "You mean . . . But I was . . . You're *leaving*?"

Judith nodded. "Immediately. It's all yours." She led the way for Renie.

"Is that a good idea?" Renie asked when the cousins were back on the sidewalk.

Judith shrugged. "Where's the harm? We've already been all over the place, along with Dooley. So have the family members. And the cops, of course. Phyliss will launch her frontal attack when she shows up to clean. Let Arlene have her fun. We did."

"If you can call it that," Renie muttered.

It was nearly noon, and the fog had almost dispersed. The

air felt damp and chilly, with overcast gray skies. Renie lingered by her Chev.

"I should go home and get to work. Let me dig Aunt Ellen's box out of the trunk."

Judith waited at the curb, her mind far from Aunt Ellen and Uncle Win in Nebraska. Indeed, her thoughts were in the gutter.

"Greg dropped that key," she declared, gesturing across the driveway to the parking strip in front of the Ericson house. "For some reason, he couldn't park where you are now. Tuesday night, he took the key out of the phony rock after JoAnne told him where to find it. Enid and George were in bed. Greg let himself in, then dropped the key on his way out. Why?"

"He's dippy," Renie replied, handing a carton to Judith. "It's not heavy. You know Aunt Ellen—she doesn't like paying postage, either."

Judith cringed at the pile of plastic-shrouded presents. "She means well. I think."

"She does," Renie said, sounding unusually mellow. "What time do you want us tomorrow?"

Judith was roused from her mental gymnastics. "Huh? Oh—five-thirty, I guess. I'll call you." She jiggled the carton experimentally. At least she couldn't hear any sounds of broken parts, unlike in other years. "Hey!" she called suddenly as Renie opened the car door. "If you were Arlene, what would you have just seen?"

Renie made a face. "What are you talking about?"

Judith jiggled the box again. "When you gave me this. Think about it—frozen in time, a glimpse."

Renie ducked into the Chev. "Bye, coz." Her voice was muffled.

"You wouldn't have been able to tell if I was taking or giving," Judith shouted. "In a cursory look, *I* might have been handing this to *you*."

Without a backward glance, Renie drove away.

SIXTEEN

THE AFTERNOON DIDN'T go as smoothly as Judith had hoped. She and Phyliss spent four hours scrubbing down the walls of the Goodrich bedroom, washing the blood-stained bedding, and trying to clean various other items that offered mute evidence of the gruesome crime. Both women agreed they would have to come back, probably on Monday. The beds had to be made up, they should straighten the living room, and the bath was in need of a good cleaning. Phyliss was game. After her initial screeching reaction to the murder site, she had been remarkably subdued.

The following day, Saturday, Joe was able to stay home. But he didn't put up the tree. Instead, he wrapped the outside pipes, tinkered with his MG, and cleaned the furnace filters. Busy with dinner preparations, Judith didn't nag. They could do the tree on Sunday. As she had said, the candy and cookies could wait.

In the late afternoon, Dooley and O.P. stopped by. Judith was readying the rib roast for the oven. The boys had nothing new to report, a fact that seemed to grieve them both.

"There's a lot of coming and going in your street," O.P. said very seriously, accepting a reindeer-shaped sugar cookie from the batch Judith had baked that morning. "But it's mostly the police and delivery trucks and people coming to the B&B."

"I know," Judith said, rubbing a mixture of salt, pepper, and garlic onto the big roast. "Say, did you notice a beat-up orange pickup parked around the neighborhood in the last few weeks, O.P.? You haven't mentioned it."

O.P. munched the front legs off his reindeer. "Maybe—did it have tools in the back? I think I saw it across the street about two weeks ago."

Dooley swung his long legs out from under the table. "I saw it a couple of days after I got home. But it wasn't near the cul-de-sac. It was sitting a couple of blocks away, by the park."

The nearby park was a panoramic viewpoint that overlooked downtown, the bay, and the mountains. Nobody connected to the Goodriches lived in the vicinity. Judith wondered why Ross Cisrak seemed to be roaming aimlessly around Heraldsgate Hill.

She also wondered why Dooley was on his feet. He was eating a frosted star and looking out through the kitchen window. "Great Nativity set," he remarked. "Gee, I forgot, you can't see much past the Rankers', can you?"

"Try the dining room," Judith said dryly.

With long, swift strides, Dooley did.

"Girls," sneered O.P.

"Gaby Porter's due home today, I take it." Judith tapped the cookie jar.

O.P. extracted a fat Santa. "Yeah. That's dumb. Being possessed by a girl, I mean."

"*Obsessed,*" Judith correctly gently. O.P. shrugged. The sound of a car door slamming could be heard faintly in the kitchen; the sound of the front door slamming could be heard loudly in the kitchen.

Judith looked at O.P. and grinned. O.P. made a disgusted face. "Dumb," he repeated, and ate another cookie.

The dinner party was a big success. The Joneses and the Prices got on well, which wasn't surprising since Renie had a special fondness for Woody. The two of them shared a love of opera and spent much of the evening exchanging opinions about current international stars and recent local productions. Sondra was a movie buff, which suited Bill admirably. Then there were sports, in which everyone had an interest, except perhaps Sondra, whose eyes seemed to glaze at the mention of anything involving a ball and men wearing strange costumes in public.

What wasn't mentioned was crime—not the Goodrich murder, not the Shazri case, not so much as a minor mugging at the bottom of Heraldsgate Hill. Awash with warm feelings, roast beef, Yorkshire pudding, and Galliano on the rocks, Judith put the neighborhood tragedy aside. Indeed, she was downright sleepy when the Prices announced they had to rescue their baby-sitter. Standing in the middle of the New England village, Judith, Joe, Renie and Bill waved them off. Then the Joneses started for their Chev. Bill was never one to linger over farewells.

But to Judith's surprise, he did an about-face at the edge of the lawn. "Joe—I didn't want to say anything in front of Woody, but I've got two tickets to the NBA game tomorrow. It's at noon, because it's nationally televised. They're excellent seats, center court, eight rows up. Would you like to go?"

Joe waved the stub of his cigar. "Wow! That's a big game, even this early in the season! Sure, I'd love to! How'd you get the tickets?"

Bill shrugged modestly. "I had to commit someone yesterday. He's a season-ticket holder. His wife and her analyst can't make this one. I wish I had an extra so I could have asked Woody. He seems like a fine man."

"He is." Joe was grinning from ear to ear. "What time?"

"Eleven? Right after Mass, anyway. We'll get out on time. Father Hoyle has season tickets, too." With a wave, Bill got in the car.

"Wow," Joe repeated, but this time more softly. He started back toward the house, flipping his cigar butt in the direction of the old mill.

"Pick that up!" Judith's voice cut through the cold night air. In fact, it startled her as much as it did Joe. Anxiously, she glanced up at the second floor windows. All of her guests were settled in. Hopefully, she hadn't disturbed them.

Joe couldn't find the cigar butt in the dark. Judith stomped over to the area where he'd thrown it, picked it up, and waved it in front of his face.

"Here, you selfish creep," she hissed. "Put it in the fireplace or the trash or up your ... whatever." Angrily, she marched into the house.

Joe started to follow her, then stopped. For some moments, he paced the front yard, oblivious to the cold. The lights in the village went out. The first hint of frost was sparkling in the moonlight. Joe wandered over to the Rankers' property. He looked at the Holy Family.

On the stroke of midnight, Joe went inside.

At breakfast, Judith was still angry. She had pretended to be asleep when Joe had finally come to bed around twelve-thirty. But in fact, she had lain awake a long time, at least until two. Now it was nine o'clock in the morning, and she'd been up since six. She was tired, cross, and mad at the world. Her ire was primarily directed at Joe, but she saved some for Bill. And Renie. She could hardly wait to confront her cousin at church. What was Renie thinking of in allowing her husband to sabotage Judith's plans for putting up the tree?

Judith and Joe had been consuming their meal in a silence as frosty as the ground outside. It was Joe who finally spoke, not mildly, as Judith had expected, but with an edge to his voice.

"I'll bring the damned tree inside and set it up now." He rose from his chair without looking at Judith.

"Don't bother." Judith stared furiously into her coffee mug.

Joe ignored her. Five minutes later, she heard him grunting and groaning in the living room. Obviously, he'd carried the tree in through the French doors. Judith waited. More grunts and groans ensued, as did considerable cursing. Judith endured the first crash, but upon the second, she went into the living room. The card table had been upended; jigsaw puzzle pieces were scattered across the carpet. The piano bench lay on its side, along with a book of Christmas carols. Joe and the giant fir looked as if they were locked in mortal combat. Judith left the room.

Shortly before ten, Joe came into the kitchen. Judith was switching on the dishwasher. She refused to turn in Joe's direction.

"The tree's in the stand," he announced, the gruffness in his voice undermined by a gasping for air.

Judith didn't respond. Five minutes later, she was still tight-lipped when they reached the parking lot at Our Lady, Star of the Sea. Joe got out of the car, banging the MG's door behind him.

"Wait!" Judith jumped from the MG. At the church door, Joe turned. "Joe!" Judith slipped on an icy patch but kept her balance.

Several parishioners, most of whom Judith recognized, stared discreetly. Judith ignored them, hurrying to Joe's side. She tugged at his sleeve.

"I can't go to Mass when I'm so angry," she said in a low voice. "Come on, let's go back to the car and talk this out."

"No." Joe's round face was inscrutable. "We'll talk later."

Judith stamped her foot. "We have to talk now. You're going to the basketball game later."

"So I am." Joe shook off Judith's hand. With an unconvincing smile for the Dooleys, he went inside the church. Glumly, Judith followed.

"It looks like you're my chauffeur again, coz," Renie said brightly, after Joe and Bill had driven off to the basketball game in the Joneses' Chev. "If you give me a ride, I'll give you an eggnog."

"I'll give you a sock in the kisser," Judith snapped. "You traitor! How could you?"

Renie stopped and stared as Judith stalked across the parking lot to the MG. "Hold it!" Renie yelled. "Why are *you* so mad?"

It was all Judith could do to keep from driving off without Renie. She couldn't even muster a smile for her curious fellow parishioners, who looked as if they were beginning to think

that a Philistine had landed in their midst. Judith knew that
her reputation for congeniality was fraying around the edges,
but she couldn't seem to help herself. Gritting her teeth, Judith
waited for Renie to climb into the MG.

"You know why I'm mad," Judith snarled. "Why didn't
you go to the game with Bill? You like basketball. How could
you let him invite Joe?"

Renie had taken out her compact and was reapplying lipstick. Reversing out of the parking space, Judith purposely
braked hard. The lipstick careened off Renie's mouth and
struck her nose.

"Damn," Renie breathed. "I think we'd better wait until
we get to our house to discuss this. You're kind of fractious."
She pulled a Kleenex from her purse and began swiping at the
errant lipstick mark.

Inside the Joneses' living room, another big fir stood un-
adorned in another heavy tree stand. The rest of the house
looked very festive, from the garlanded staircase to the English
village atop the spinet piano. Judith, however, was in no mood
to appreciate Renie's handiwork.

Renie headed directly to the kitchen. "The kids are gone
for the day. They went to a church-sponsored sleigh ride and
then caroling at a nursing home on the east side of the lake.
Do you want your eggnog with or without?"

Renie's concept of eggnog was unorthodox: She drank it
straight, without milk or liquor, and claimed that she lost
weight in the process. Her rationale was that instead of snack-
ing between meals as she usually did, she got filled up on
eggnog. And because she was so busy with annual reports, in
addition to her regular workload, routine family duties, and a
host of holiday-related events, she burned off calories. The
strangest part was that it was true: One year, she had lost
sixteen pounds in six weeks. Renie was the only person Judith
knew who actually ended the holidays weighing less than
when she started.

But at the moment, Renie's eggnog diet was of no interest.
Judith's request for a dollop of rum was made in a surly voice.

Renie obliged, then ushered her cousin back to the living room.

"Okay," said Renie, settling onto the dark green sofa, "here's my rationale—I don't want Bill or the kids around when I decorate the tree. They argue; they bitch; they bunch all the lights together; they put the ornaments in the wrong place; they're lucky they don't knock the damned thing over. It might take me all day, but I'd rather put some carols on the CD player, drink a quart of eggnog, and take my time doing it right. It saves a lot of emotional wear and tear on everybody."

Judith glowered at Renie. "It doesn't save on energy. Aren't you ready to collapse by the time you're done?"

"Sure," Renie answered cheerfully. "But so what? Inside, I feel *good*."

Judith wasn't convinced. "It's not right to let everybody else off the hook."

Renie looked askance at Judith. "Decorating the Christmas tree shouldn't be a punishment, coz. It should be *fun*. It is, for me. But it's a chore for Bill, and the kids only enjoy it during the first ten minutes. The real reason that you're mad is because Joe isn't exactly like you. And Bill isn't exactly like me, either. For whatever reason, they don't bring the same sense of exhilaration—or maybe it's duty—to the holidays. That doesn't mean they don't like Christmas. It just means they aren't us. Which is good, when we think about it rationally. Come on, coz—where's your famous logic?"

Judith sighed. "Maybe you're right. But Joe acted like a real jerk."

"He feels guilty because he doesn't share your joy. Cut him some slack. It's taken me years and years to do the same with Bill. I still haven't got it down pat."

Finishing her eggnog, Judith got to her feet. "I'd better get started on that tree."

"Me, too." Renie walked Judith to the door. "The problem with you—and maybe me—is that we want to give, give, give. What we have to consider is that not everybody wants to get, get, get. It's hard for us to realize that Advent is supposed to be a time for inner reflection. Putting up the tree all by yourself helps. Every ornament isn't just a memory, but a prayer.'' Renie winced, embarrassed by her private revelation.

But Judith understood. She gave Renie a quick hug, and headed across the steep sidewalk to Joe's MG.

Judith had reached the tinsel stage when the front doorbell sounded. It was going on four, and she assumed it was one of her guests. The first two couples had checked in an hour or so earlier.

Glenda Goodrich looked even more haggard than when Judith had last seen her at the funeral. She was huddled inside her down jacket, pale and without makeup. Judith's offer of coffee was accepted, though Glenda seemed so distraught that she almost sat on a box of extra Christmas lights.

''I stopped by Mama's house just now,'' she said, accepting the coffee mug with an unsteady hand. ''You've done a good job cleaning. So far.'' Glenda closed her eyes as she swallowed. ''Do you think it will be ready for the real estate agent by Wednesday?''

Judith was surprised. ''So you're going to sell it? Isn't this a bad time of year?''

''We can list it before Christmas,'' Glenda replied, her eyes darting around the room but not seeming to take in the minor chaos of empty boxes, extension cords, and a trail of silver tinsel that hung from the very top of the tree. ''Then, after New Year's, buyers start looking again. Art and JoAnne have agreed to keep Pappy. At least until . . .'' Her voice died away.

Judith didn't want to ask. But she did anyway. ''Until he's arraigned? Or someone else is arrested?''

A spot of color flared on each of Glenda's cheeks. ''What takes the police so long? Why can't they decide whether Pappy did it or he didn't?''

''Procedure,'' Judith answered calmly. ''They have to jump through all kinds of hoops. Sometimes, another case comes along that takes priority.'' She paused, regarding Glenda with a sympathetic expression. ''Does your father still deny his guilt?''

''Yes.'' Glenda snapped off the word. ''I don't blame him

for saying that. In fact, I think he believes it. He probably blanked out. His memory has been failing lately. He admits it. I guess the rest of us just haven't paid attention to how he's been going downhill.''

"That can happen," Judith allowed, thinking of Gertrude. "It's gradual, especially when you see the person all the time.''

Glenda emitted a jagged little laugh. "He didn't remember much about coming to my place for Thanksgiving. He swore Leigh never came to see him and Mama at all while she was in town. She wouldn't have, either, if Mama hadn't ordered her to come.'' Bitterness dripped from Glenda's voice.

"Oh?'' Judith's dark eyes widened. "Why was that necessary?''

Glenda's lips clamped shut. She eyed Judith warily. Then she gazed off into the far reaches of the living room, above the plate rail, where the pine boughs hung with their golden pearls and gauzy ribbons.

"Leigh has no morals. What's wrong with young people these days?'' Glenda demanded.

"Revenge.'' The word leaped from Judith's lips and astonished both women. "I'm sorry,'' Judith said quickly, putting a hand out as if she could retrieve the reply. "It's none of my business, but your daughter still seems resentful about your breakup with her father. Isn't that why she made a play for Gary Meyers?''

Glenda went white to the lips. "How did you know?'' she asked in a trembling voice.

There was no point in evasion. "George took Enid to the doctor the Friday after Thanksgiving. You had to work that day—you told me so yourself. But your car was at your parents' house, so it was natural to assume you were driving it. Nobody saw Leigh, but Gary was spotted when he left. Leigh borrowed your car, just as she did Monday when your mother asked to see her. I don't know if your folks came home and caught Leigh and Gary, but it's a good guess. Your mother read Leigh the riot act Monday night, and then told you about the rendezvous on Tuesday. That's what all the screaming was about. Naturally, you broke up with Gary and told Leigh she wasn't welcome anymore. Gary came back the next morning to see your parents. Did you know that?''

Glenda looked as if she would faint. Judith jumped off the sofa, snatched up the coffee mug, and hurried out to the kitchen. A moment later, she returned, after adding a measure of brandy.

"Drink this," she said to her guest, who seemed to be in a state of semi-collapse. "I'm sorry to be so blunt, but this is a murder case, after all. Secrets are outlawed."

Slowly, Glenda opened her eyes. Her expression was malevolent. "You're an awful person, Judith. All these years, I'd never have guessed it."

"Think what you like. But I'm right." Judith paused for an answer. She didn't get one. "Well?"

Glenda drank from the brandy-laced mug, then choked, sputtered, and tried to sit up straight. "Yes. But I didn't know about Gary coming by Wednesday morning. I don't believe it."

"He was seen by at least three people." The statement was only a slight exaggeration.

Glenda took another swig. Her temper rose. "This neighborhood! It's always been full of snoops and meddlers!"

"They're people who care about other people. It's better than locking yourself away like your mother did and never giving a flying fig about anybody else." Judith's tone was stern. "If I were you, I'd talk to Gary. The police probably have done that already."

Glenda drained her mug, then shot Judith a venomous look. "I'll do that. I certainly don't want to talk to you again—not ever." Clumsily, she got up from the sofa and stormed out of the house.

If Glenda had looked back, she would have seen Judith smiling. Grimly.

Joe thought the tree looked gorgeous. Judith silently agreed with him, but when she finished just before five o'clock, she was too tired to be enthusiastic—or angry. In fact, she had been worried for the past hour: The game should have ended by three, and the drive from the coliseum at the bottom of the Hill took less than ten minutes, even in heavy traffic.

"Triple overtime," Joe informed Judith. "Plus, they take all those extra commercial time-outs when the games are nationally televised. Is that top a little crooked? I could straighten it."

Judith was too weary to care if the top took a left-hand turn. "I was just going to get Mother so she could take a look. You can stick her up there. I don't give a damn." Staggering to the French doors, Judith felt a blast of cold air. She flipped on the porch light and gasped. "It's snowing!"

"Right," Joe said equably. "That's another reason we were late getting home. Driving up Heraldsgate Hill was kind of tricky. Bill did all right in that big Chev, but a lot of other cars were spinning out."

"Good grief," Judith muttered, closing the French doors. "I had no idea . . . I was so busy putting up the tree. It must have clouded over this afternoon."

"Let's walk up to Athens Pizza after your guests are served," Joe suggested. "Your mother can eat a TV dinner."

Judith started to protest, then stopped. Gertrude actually liked TV dinners. The pizza parlor was only five blocks, albeit uphill. "Okay," Judith said. "I'll start the hors d'oeuvres."

"I'll fix them," Joe volunteered. "I found a recipe in a magazine the other day for sole and calamari with ginger."

Judith gaped. "We don't have any sole or calamari."

"Yes, we do," Joe replied. "Bill and I parked in the lot by the coliseum that's next to TLC Grocery. He picked up a bunch of deli stuff for their dinner so Renie wouldn't have to cook. How about a scotch?"

Feeling weak, Judith toppled onto the sofa. "Sure," she said in a thin voice. "Why not?"

Five minutes later, Judith was reclining with a drink in her hand, the Oberkirchen Children's Choir on the CD player, and 240 multicolored lights glowing on the Christmas tree. In the kitchen, she could hear Joe singing along with the Austrian choir.

Renie was right. Sometimes it was better to receive than to give.

"Don't you dare laugh at me," Judith warned Renie as the cousins joined forces in making spritz cookies, "but this Goodrich case is beginning to make sense."

Renie twisted the cookie press, spewing snowflake-shaped dough onto a pan. The kitchen windows were covered with steam, and the aroma of baking cookies filled the house. Monday afternoon had turned warm, bringing rain, which had almost washed away the scant two inches of snow. But Phyliss Rackley had begged off coming to work: She didn't trust the barometer and was afraid of getting stranded on Heraldsgate Hill. In consequence, Judith had been forced to postpone the Goodrich cleaning project. She was philosophical, however, since the time could be used making spritz and preparing the food for the Lutheran buffet.

"I've got a pretty fair picture of the events that led up to Enid's murder," Judith continued, removing a cookie sheet filled with small decorated wreaths. "Between the known facts and the personalities involved, we can make certain logical assumptions."

"Uh-huh," Renie said, exchanging the snowflake design for a camel. "Is there room in the oven for this batch?"

"No," Judith retorted, a bit impatiently. "Listen, coz. Take each of the suspects. Start with Glenda. Her boyfriend cheated on her with her daughter. Enid finds out and gives Leigh hell, then rats on her to Glenda. Three generations are now mad at each other. But would Glenda or Leigh kill Enid?"

Renie held up another cookie press disk. "Is this a squirrel or a gopher?"

"I don't think so. They'd kill each other first. As for Gary," Judith went on, removing a sheet of small snowmen from the oven, "I'm sticking to my guns. No motive, not after Enid let the cat out of the bag the previous night."

Violating the premise of her eggnog diet, Renie stuffed a chunk of cookie dough in her mouth. "Are you sure this is Auntie Vance's recipe? Did you add salt? She doesn't."

"Consider Art. We only have his word for it that he came *after* Enid was dead. Early Wednesday morning, JoAnne would still have been at work or asleep, depending upon the actual time of the murder. Art would never kill his father, but he might knock him out with sleeping pills. He could have put them in the glass by the bed Tuesday evening. Why murder Enid? I can think of a couple of reasons—Art couldn't stand seeing his father suffer Enid's abuse any longer. That's one. Two is that Art has . . ."

"Silver balls," Renie said. "Where are they? I want to decorate these gophers with them instead of the red-and-green sprinkles."

Snatching up the pan of snowflakes, Judith glared at Renie. "Dammit, coz, are you listening? This is important!"

"So are spritz cookies. They're Bill's favorites." Renie dug out more dough with an index finger, popped it in her mouth, and sighed. "I *am* listening. Excuse the expression, but I think you're beating a dead horse."

"No, I'm not!" Judith insisted. "I've already eliminated three suspects—Glenda, Leigh, and Gary. I'm working my way through Art. I think he wanted money."

"Who doesn't?" Renie sprinkled silver balls with a lavish hand.

"Art's out of work; it's Christmas; he's desperate; he's humiliated. Who pried that desk open? The marks were fresh; the steak knife was at the curb where we saw Art's car on Tuesday."

"The key was there, too," Renie pointed out.

"I know. But I'm sure Greg dropped the key. Nobody saw Art come back that evening. It's a coincidence that the key and the knife should be in the same area, but it happens. Parking is limited in the cul-de-sac. Art was still at the house when Enid told Glenda about Leigh and Gary. We know that because of what O.P. saw and the screams I heard. So where was Art while that exchange was going on? Not in the bedroom, I'll bet. Art wouldn't want any part of a quarrel between his stepmother and his sister. Maybe Enid had already turned down his request for money. What does Art do? He goes into the living room, figuring there's money stashed in the desk. He gets a knife from the kitchen and pries the desk open. Then Enid figures out he's in the forbidden living room—or maybe George finds him—and Art panics. He runs out the front door, drops the knife, and drives away." Judith paused, waiting for Renie's reaction.

"Logical." Renie tipped her head at Judith in approval. "But did Art get the money?"

Judith checked the oven. "I don't know. We certainly didn't find any. If he did, one of my motives for Art is shot down."

"True," Renie agreed, now creating tree-shaped cookies. "It all becomes strictly psychological. Abused husband, abused stepson, son sees himself becoming his father. The mother figure is the destroyer, in complete control. Bill says it's like spiders, where the . . ."

The front doorbell rang. Judith was spared another echo of Bill's opinions. "Guests," she said, going to the door.

Judith was right—up to a point. A pair of widowed sisters from Port Royal who had reservations stood on the porch with their tartan suitcases. But behind them, down on the walk, was Ross Cisrak. He stood in the rain looking uneasy and forlorn.

"I'm Mrs. MacLeish," the taller of the two women announced.

"I'm Mrs. Somersby," the broader of the two women asserted.

"We were here last year," they said together, and then laughed.

"We're sisters," Mrs. MacLeish said, as if to explain the chorused response.

"But not twins," Mrs. Somersby put in.

Judith couldn't help but look beyond the women to the nervous figure of Ross Cisrak. "Welcome to Hillside Manor. Let's get you registered." The women picked up their suitcases and trotted into the entry hall. Judith smiled inquiringly at Ross Cisrak. "And you, sir? May I help you?"

"Maybe." Ross took a tentative step forward. "It's . . . personal. Are you Mrs. Grover?"

"No," Judith replied, gazing uncertainly at the two women

on the other side of the threshhold. She beckoned to Ross. "Not exactly. Come in. I'll join you shortly in the parlor." Judith gestured to the first door off the entry hall.

It was ten minutes before Judith's guests were registered and settled in their room. After a quick word to a curious Renie, Judith finally joined Ross. He was standing in front of the small stone fireplace, staring at the pewter candlesticks that Judith had festooned with holly sprigs.

"Have a chair," Judith offered, sitting down on the small window seat.

"My name's Ross Cisrak." He didn't hold out a hand, but sat in an oak side chair near the hearth. "You probably think I'm nuts."

Ross leaned forward, bony hands gripping his knees. He wore faded jeans and a not-quite-matching denim jacket lined with imitation sheepskin. Up close, Judith saw a slight resemblance to the young man in the wedding photo with Glenda. But twenty-odd years had eroded Ross Cisrak's features. At fifty-plus, he looked as if futility was his best friend.

"You're Leigh's father," Judith answered in her usual friendly manner. "Why would that make you nuts?"

A faint light that might have been hope shone in Ross's gray eyes. "I remembered some Grovers living in this house when Glenda and me were married. You're not . . . ?" The question dwindled away as the light in his eyes went out.

"I am," Judith said. "My maiden name is Grover. Now I'm Mrs. Flynn."

Ross looked relieved. "I hoped somebody from the old neighborhood was still around. I'm trying to find Leigh. I didn't feel right asking any of Glenda's family. They think I'm a creep. You know where Leigh is?"

Judith nodded. "She went back to New York. She wants you to call her there. Do you have her number?"

"No. I got her address, though." The lines deepened in Ross's thin face. "Is she in trouble?"

"Not exactly," Judith replied carefully. "She and her mother had a falling-out."

"Ha!" Ross almost smiled. Judith wondered if he'd forgotten how. "Glenda! She's a nagger, like her ma. I bet she got on Leigh's case."

"Sort of," Judith said vaguely.

Ross hunched over in the chair, inspecting his scuffed cowboy boots. "I shoulda called Leigh. But I was afraid Glenda'd answer. Damn." He raised regretful eyes to Judith. "I really need to get hold of my kid. Her old man's kinda tapped out." Ross's laugh was pathetic.

"Call her in New York," Judith said, with an anxious glance at the Venetian clock on the mantel. It was after three, and Judith still had much to do. "It's six on the East Coast. Use the phone in the living room. One more long distance charge won't make much difference—it's a business expense. By the way, did you talk to the police?"

The question made Ross jump. "The police? What for?"

Judith made a self-deprecating gesture. "My husband's a policeman. I asked his colleagues to find you so that Leigh could get in touch with you. I didn't know where you were staying."

"Oh." Relief washed over Ross's gaunt face. "Thanks, that's nice of you." Somehow, he managed to laugh without smiling. "You had me going there for a minute. I thought the police wanted to ask me about the poison."

Judith stared. "*What* poison?"

Ross grew sheepish. "It wasn't real poison; it was a book. I don't know where it came from, but I found it in the back of my pickup a couple of weeks ago. It seemed kinda weird. Creepy, too."

Judith felt her spine tingle. "Where was your truck parked?"

Shutting his eyes, Ross considered. "I don't know the street names around here. Four, five blocks away—west. I know directions. Most nights, I been sleeping in the pickup. Motels ain't cheap."

"When? Do you remember which day?" Judith's voice had taken on an edge.

But Ross wasn't sure. "I kinda lost track of time after I got to town. I'm used to the country. The city's different. I never did like it much. You know, pressure. Like Glenda, always nagging me about a job. What's so big about a job? It just ties a man down."

It seemed to Judith that Ross had paid a high price for freedom. But she kept to her previous question: "Did you find the book before or after your ex-mother-in-law was killed?"

Ross's startled expression couldn't possibly have been feigned. "Mrs. Goodrich? Killed? You're putting me on!"

Solemnly, Judith shook her head. "She was murdered, the first day of December."

By turns, Ross looked stunned, incredulous, and bemused. "I'll be damned! I never did hear of such a thing! Well, now!"

For the first time, Ross Cisrak smiled.

SEVENTEEN

"SO WHAT DID he do with this so-called poison book?" Renie demanded after Ross had made his call to New York and Judith had enlightened her cousin.

"He tossed it," Judith replied grimly. "It was 'creepy,' as he put it."

"Why do you care?" Renie had finished baking the spritz in Judith's absence. She was now placing her share in a plastic container.

Judith was getting out the ingredients for a chicken casserole. She planned to make enough for the catered buffet and her own dinner. Two other hot dishes were required by the Lutherans, along with condiments. Arlene was preparing the salads and desserts.

"I'm not sure I do care," Judith admitted. "But it's odd. George is poisoned, and a book on poison is discarded four blocks away. Now that's a coincidence that makes me wonder."

Renie, however, wasn't inclined to speculate about the book. "I'm glad he got hold of Leigh. Ross must be pretty stupid. How could anyone who deperately needed money just hang around for over two weeks without making an attempt at contact?"

"He was trusting to luck," Judith said distractedly. She was still mulling over the poison book. "Ross said he was afraid to keep watch by Glenda's because he and his ex aren't on good terms. He figured that eventually Leigh would visit her grandparents. She did, of course, but he missed her—both times. Then, he not only didn't realize she'd left town, but he didn't know Enid was dead.''

Renie put on her purple hooded jacket. "As I said, he's stupid."

"Maybe," Judith allowed. "Mostly, he's unconscious, one of those vague souls who stumble through life, walking into walls and wondering why the impact hurts."

"Let's hope Leigh sends him a plane ticket." Renie picked up the container of cookies and her big black handbag.

"He'd hate New York," Judith said. "Maybe Leigh will send him the money. Hey," she exclaimed, "I never finished telling you about my deductions!"

In the rear entryway, Renie turned to grin at Judith. "Yes, you did. I know the rest, because I know you. Mrs. Swanson is too dainty to kill anyone, the grandsons are too dumb, and JoAnne's too tired to lift a hatchet when she comes off work at five A.M. That leaves George. See you, coz." Renie was out the back door.

Judith was working on her third entrée when she decided to call Gary Meyers. Surely the police had questioned him by now. His guard would have to be down. Unfortunately, the phone book had several listings for people named Gary Meyers. Judith didn't get the right one until the fifth try.

"I know you think I'm a nosy pest," Judith said after identifying herself, "but have you talked to the police?"

Gary had, the previous Friday. "The girl was great," he said over a background of TV noise. "That weird guy with the eye patch let her ask most of the questions."

Sancha Rael had her uses, Judith thought with a touch of annoyance. "So you've nothing to worry about." Her voice conveyed a comfortable statement rather than a prying question.

Gary laughed weakly. "I never did, but who'd believe me? At least that's what I figured until this girl cop talked to me. After all, I was at the house before the murder."

Judith's hand froze on the receiver. "*Before* the murder? What do you mean?"

Gary laughed again, though on the other hand, he might have been choking. "It had to be before. Mrs. Goodrich came to the door."

"She did?" Judith was flabbergasted. "She never did that. She hardly ever got out of bed."

"Well, she did that morning," Gary insisted. "Glenda and I'd had kind of a . . . misunderstanding. I wanted to ask Mr. Goodrich to tell Glenda how bad I felt and that I wanted her back." His voice dropped a notch. "I really care about Glenda. But Mrs. Goodrich told me to go away."

At the moment, Judith wasn't interested in Gary and Glenda's muddled love life. "How odd. About Mrs. Goodrich answering the . . ." Judith interrupted herself. "Where was George?"

"I don't know," Gary replied. "I didn't get to see him. He must have been in bed. Mrs. Goodrich made some crack about him sleeping his life away."

Judith paused, her mind busily fitting pieces together. "That was what—? Around seven-thirty?"

"I guess. I was headed for my delivery stops on the top of the Hill," Gary replied. "I usually hit Athens Pizza first, right around that time."

"How did Mrs. Goodrich seem?"

Gary snorted. "Like she always does. Crabby."

With a couple of perfunctory comments, Judith rang off. Putting the chicken casserole in the oven, she checked her reservations book. To her dismay, she noticed that she had overbooked for Tuesday night. Written in her own hand were six sets of guests for five rooms. Frantically, she grabbed the phone to call the state B&B association for nearby availability.

Ingrid Heffleman sounded surprisingly pleased to hear Judith's voice. "Let me check, Judith. It's a Tuesday night, so there's probably something . . . What did you do, press the wrong key on your computer?"

"I don't have a computer," Judith replied, trying not to sound testy. "If I did, this might not have happened."

"That's true," Ingrid agreed. "You had a similar problem in September, as I recall. And twice in August . . . Ah, here we are, Rogers House, over on the other side of the Hill. They had a cancellation just half an hour ago. They're tied directly into our network, you know." Ingrid's voice was smug.

"Thanks, Ingrid," Judith said with relief. "I'll give you the registration information. If they arrive by cab, I'll pay their way to Rogers House."

"Of course." Ingrid efficiently took down the information. "By the way, Judith, an opening on the state board is coming up in January. Would you be interested in serving a two-year term?"

Judith had been dodging the request for the past three years. But Ingrid had just done another favor for Judith. "Ah . . . Can I think about it?" Judith hedged.

"Certainly," Ingrid answered cheerfully. "And while you're at it, think about a computer. It would save everybody a lot of trouble." A touch of steel rang in Ingrid's voice.

The last thing Judith needed was more things to think about. Luckily, Arlene volunteered to deliver the food for the St. Lucy's buffet. Judith didn't argue. It was too late in the day to start the candy-making and too early to make hors d'oeuvres. She had mailed off her cards that morning, but there were still presents to wrap. In fact, there were still a few to buy, including that special elusive something for Joe.

At five-thirty, Judith was wrapping Gertrude's microwave. She put a big red bow on the bulky red-green-and-white-striped package, then picked up the cordless phone and dialed Renie's number.

"I'm still working, you twit," Renie complained. "You know I don't quit until five-thirty."

"It *is* five-thirty," Judith countered. "And you'd better get dinner together by six to ward off Bill's ulcers. Wait until you hear what Gary Meyers told me."

"Rats," muttered Renie. "Okay, I'll take the phone upstairs to the kitchen and start peeling potatoes."

"Good." Judith cradled the phone against her shoulder, recounting her conversation with Gary. "What do you make of that? Enid told Gary that George was quote, 'sleeping his life away.' ''

''So he was already knocked out from the Dalmane?'' asked Renie, who was making a considerable amount of noise at her end of the line. Judith guessed that her cousin was closing up the design shop for the day.

''It could be,'' Judith said, choosing an elegant gold foil in which to wrap a pair of earrings for Mike's girlfriend, Kristin. ''George must have been out of it, or Enid would never have roused herself to go to the door. That was around seven-thirty. Ted Ericson drove off to get his tree shortly before eight. He noticed nothing unusual. He came back around eight-fifteen, give or take five minutes. Then he left again. Art started calling his folks about that same time. I think we can pinpoint the murder to eight-twenty.''

Renie could be heard thumping up her basement stairs. ''That's closer than the police will ever come,'' she said dubiously. ''What are you basing that on—those fir needles that were tracked into the Goodrich house?''

''Exactly,'' said Judith, searching for a tag to match the small gold package. ''If George was already unconscious, he couldn't have gone outside after Ted brought his tree home. It couldn't have been Enid, because she wouldn't have dirtied her precious carpet. Thus, it had to be the killer, who obviously doped George's antacid the previous night.''

Renie sighed. ''So we're back to Art, Glenda, Greg, and Dave, because we know they were all at the house.'' Cutlery rattled in the background. ''Of course, there's always the possibility that someone else who wasn't spotted came by.''

''I know,'' Judith agreed, fitting Uncle Al's driving gloves into a box. ''O.P. missed a couple of hours while he was eating and visiting with Dooley. Even Arlene can't see everything that goes on in the cul-de-sac. When the Rankerses eat in the dinette, all they can see is us.''

''Whoever it was, they got into the bedroom,'' Renie pointed out over the grating noise of her potato peeler. ''They had to, in order to put the Dalmane in George's glass.''

''True,'' Judith agreed, cutting a sheet of blue wrapping

paper off a long roll. "I'm still fretting over the hatchet. If Arlene's right, that thing changed hands the afternoon before the murder. The question is, did George give it back to Mrs. Swanson, or did he borrow it again?"

"Why would he borrow it a second time?" Renie asked, now to the sound of running tap water. "Didn't you gather that he'd gotten that load of wood a while ago?"

Judith had already considered that question. "Chopping wood is like doing yard work. It got him outside, away from Enid. What other excuse did George have this time of year?"

"Good point. Hey, coz, got to go. Bill's bus was late, and he just came home." Renie hung up.

Adding Uncle Al's gift to the colorful stack of presents, Judith considered taking some of them downstairs to put under the tree. But it was too soon. She didn't want guests accidentally trampling the packages or, worse yet, Sweetums shredding the wrappings.

But it was the hatchet that preyed on Judith's mind as she prepared the guests' hors d'oeuvres, delivered her mother's dinner, and took the call from Joe saying he'd be at least an hour late. Just before six-thirty, Judith put on her jacket and headed out into the rain.

Fleetingly, she noticed that the three Wise Men were now in full view. The Porters had added cutouts of busy elves, fittingly positioned above their double garage. On the other side of the street, Judith could see the tip of the Ericsons' noble fir through the front window. From what she could tell, Ted and Jeanne had used only small white lights.

Just before Judith reached the shared driveway, Jeanne Ericson pulled up in her Volvo. Judith waited for her to get out of the car.

"Hi, Judith!" Jeanne called, coming down the drive. Her trim figure was burdened with shopping bags, briefcase, and purse. "Traffic downtown is getting awful! It took me half an hour to get from my office to the bottom of the Hill."

"Your tree looks pretty," Judith remarked, brushing raindrops from her cheeks. "At least what I can see of it. Ted must have turned it on."

But Jeanne gave a shake of her damp blond hair. "Ted's not home. He has a meeting. The lights are on a timer." Jeanne juggled her various items, then opened the gate that led to the walk. "Come in. I'll show you the tree."

Judith hesitated, then agreed. But when Jeanne got to the wide front porch, she turned in a jerky motion. "Oh!" Jeanne uttered a nervous laugh. "I forgot! I have to make a couple of phone calls right away! Come by tomorrow night, okay?"

Puzzled, Judith retraced her steps back to the sidewalk. "Sure, that's fine." She had gotten as far as the first stair to the porch, which was far enough to notice a large cardboard box sitting by the front door.

Judith didn't believe Jeanne's excuse for a minute. She couldn't help but wonder why one was needed.

Two doors down, Mrs. Swanson seemed pleased to see Judith. "You must take something—tea, sake, gin, scotch?"

"Scotch sounds great," Judith said. "Just a tiny bit."

"Excellent," Mrs. Swanson replied, going to a lacquered liquor cabinet. The Swanson living room was a harmonious blend of East and West. Sitting on a blue sofa with tasteful ivory-and-brown stripes, Judith felt a sense of peace overcome her. Ironically, she also felt as if she were on a fool's errand.

"I mix myself a small martini," Mrs. Swanson said with a self-effacing air. "I never drink alone. After my husband died, I wished to. Often. But I would not permit it."

Judith felt like saying that she had wanted to drink—often—while her first husband was still alive. But instead, she merely smiled and commended her hostess on her self-control.

Mrs. Swanson graciously accepted the compliment. Sipping her martini, the black eyes turned shrewd. "You are troubled, Mrs. Flynn. Why else do you come?"

Judith winced. She wished she could say it was merely a neighborly visit to a lonely widow. "It's about the hatchet," she blurted. "Did Mr. Goodrich ever return it?"

Plucking the olive out of her glass, Mrs. Swanson gazed across the room at a Japanese hanging scroll depicting a waterfall. "Why, yes." She popped the olive in her mouth, chewing slowly. "How odd that I'd forgotten!"

"But . . ." Judith frowned into her scotch. "You told me that the weapon was yours. I assumed Mr. Goodrich still had it."

Mrs. Swanson looked chagrined. "I thought he had. Then I remembered he'd returned it." She shook her head in apparent dismay. "We old people tend to forget."

"Oh," Judith said innocently. "You still have it, then?"

"No, I don't." Mrs. Swanson took another sip from her drink. "The Salvation Army came by the other day. Before Christmas, I always contribute whatever I don't need. Along with clothing and a small cash donation, I gave them some tools. Including the hatchet." She looked straight at Judith. "What good is a hoe to an old woman my age? Or a heavy shovel or metal cutters—or a hatchet?"

"I see." Judith lowered her eyes. The residents of the cul-de-sac seemed to be avoiding the truth. It was impossible not to wonder why.

Somehow, Judith and her mother managed to make their candy without killing each other. There were injuries, however, including Gertrude smashing a plate along with the walnuts, an unnerved Judith spilling melted chocolate bits on the floor and slipping onto her backside, and Sweetums scorching his whiskers when he jumped into the sink to lick the still-hot divinity pan.

But by noon, the candies were finished. Judith fixed her mother's lunch, hurriedly ate a tuna sandwich, and checked with Phyliss Rackley to see if she was ready to head to the Goodrich house. Phyliss was—almost. The cleaning woman needed another ten minutes to retrieve the laundry from the dryer. Judith spent the time going over her bookings to make sure she hadn't made any more mistakes.

"Your cat's in the dryer again," Phyliss said as she came into the kitchen. "I'm spinning his satanic ways out of him. Cats have always been a witch's familiar, you know Terrible animals, cats. Ever see a picture of Our Lord offering a ball of yarn to a cat?''

Judith didn't respond. Assuming that Phyliss was kidding about Sweetums being on spin, Judith led the way to the Goodrich house.

''Well now!'' Phyliss exclaimed in self-righteous triumph as she surveyed the stripped-down twin beds. ''Like always, the Lord works in mysterious ways. The only thing that got Enid out of her bed was the Grim Reaper. As for George, he never let me touch his bed. Now I'm going to do just that— but will he ever lie in it again? That's in the Lord's hands, too.''

''Actually,'' said Judith, who had fetched clean linens from the hall closet, ''it's up to the police and a court of law. If George is innocent, he may want to come home.''

''But I thought those worthless kids of his were going to sell the place,'' Phyliss said, taking a plain white set of sheets from Judith.

''They intend to,'' Judith answered, starting in on Enid's bed, ''but the final say is up to George. He owns the house. Once he pulls himself together, he might want to live here again. I think Glenda and Art are jumping the gun. Especially Glenda. I don't think JoAnne wants George staying at their house forever.''

Sausage curls bobbing, Phyliss tried to get the fitted bottom sheet on George's mattress. ''Art and JoAnne probably hope George will go to jail,'' the cleaning woman said, still wrestling with the bedding. ''It'd be easier and cheaper. In fact, it's as good as bumping off both the old folks. The rest of the family will get what money there is, plus the house. From what I hear, they can all use—Bless me! What's that?''

Phyliss stopped trying to tug the sheet's fourth corner into place. She had dislodged the mattress, and with it, a large rectangular item.

Judith came around from Enid's bed. ''It's a book,'' she said, as Phyliss raised the mattress a scant inch. ''I'll get it.''

In full view, Judith was able to identify George's ledger at once. She flipped through the pages as Phyliss lowered the mattress and finally secured the sheet.

"Dirty ditties?" Phyliss inquired, stuffing a pillow into a case. "Lewd pictures, maybe?" She tried to lean over Judith's shoulder.

"It's the account book for Pacific Meats," Judith said, her initial excitement dwindling. "George must have kept it under his mattress. I wonder why?"

Seeing the long columns of figures, Phyliss lost interest. "Why not? What else did he have to call his own except the bed? Even there, he wasn't safe from Mrs. G.'s nagging."

Judith started to sit down on Enid's bed, thought better of it, and perched on the cedar chest instead. For once, Phyliss was making sense. George—and his work—had been confined to the bedroom. As Judith paged through the ledger, she noted that the last entries were dated December first.

"He must have worked on this during the night," she said in a curious voice. "O.P. said the house was dark at nine-thirty Tuesday, the thirtieth. But sometime after midnight, George got up and made his entries. The question is, when did he drink his antacid?"

"When he needed it," Phyliss asserted, finishing George's bed.

"True," Judith replied in a thoughtful tone. "He told me that he liked to nibble when he worked late. Maybe he ate something that set him off." She began working her way backward, trying to make sense of the numbers. After scanning a few pages, Judith realized it was fruitless. She had no point of reference. But she did notice a half-dozen question marks in the margin. "I wonder," she murmured to herself rather than to Phyliss.

"Don't we all," Phyliss said as she finished Enid's bed for Judith. "Take you Catholics—heathen ideas, if you ask me. What's this business about carpet cleaners? In my church, we don't have such a thing. Where do you find carpet cleaners in the Bible?"

The question wrenched Judith from her speculation about the account book. "You've been talking to Arlene Rankers?"

"You bet." Phyliss tried to pull her housedress down over the uneven lace of her slip. "I know Wise Men and camels but not those carpet cleaners. Do you Catholics worship them or what?"

"Certainly not," Judith replied firmly, though she was forced to smile. "Arlene sometimes . . . gets carried away. Like saying that George has a nest egg, when, in fact, there's no sign of . . ." Inspiration struck, if not precisely in the form of carpet cleaners, at least in the concept of carpets. Judith spun out of the bedroom.

"Give me a hand with this living room rug," she called to Phyliss who had gone into the bathroom, presumably to start cleaning. "I think there's something under it."

Wearing a dubious expression, Phyliss entered the living room. "What would Enid think? We roam all over her precious house, then we start tearing up the carpeting?"

"That's right," Judith said, on her hands and knees. "Let's see if we can lift the part of the rug that's under the plastic runner."

Lifting the two-foot-wide segment proved easier than Judith had expected. Slipping her hand between the carpet and the pad, she felt an envelope, then another, and just beyond her reach, a third. Sitting up, Judith opened the first, which was a standard manila type with a metal clasp. She gave the envelope a little shake.

At least twenty one-hundred-dollar bills fluttered to the floor. Phyliss gasped with amazement; Judith clapped in triumph.

"The nest egg!" Judith cried. "It was here all along, under the carpet! No wonder Enid wouldn't let anybody walk on it!"

"How much?" asked Phyliss, counting the fallen bills.

"Who knows? There are at least two more envelopes under the rug. There could be forty of them between here and the front door. I guess George didn't trust banks. Or maybe it was Enid's idea."

Phyliss waved the bills under Judith's nose. "Twenty-two

hundred dollars, right here! Did they tithe? That's two thousand for them, two hundred for God.''

"They never went to church, as far as I know," Judith answered vaguely. She was still overcome by the discovery. She was also dismayed. The Goodriches had a small fortune under their carpet, but it was doubtful if Enid ever allowed them to spend a penny of it to help anyone, including their own children. "What a waste," she sighed.

"What are you going to do about it?" Phyliss asked, obviously reluctant to let go of the bills.

"Nothing," Judith responded, gently taking the money from Phyliss and putting it back in the manila envelope. "Except tell the police."

"The police?" Phyliss's gooseberry blue eyes widened. "What about George? And those kids of his?"

Replacing the envelope under the rug, Judith got to her feet. "George knows. His kids don't need to—yet." She glanced at the desk. "There was never any money in there, I'll bet. So why did Art . . ." Her voice trailed off as her brain began to whirl. She looked sharply at Phyliss. "What did you say about killing off both old folks when we were in the bedroom?"

Startled, Phyliss jerked her head back, causing two of the sausage curls to stand straight up, like horns. "What did I say? Oh—if George goes to jail, he might as well be dead, as far as his kids are concerned. Is that what you meant?"

Judith nodded. She also knew what Phyliss meant. At last, she felt she understood the killer's intentions.

EIGHTEEN

JUDITH HATED TO admit it, but Gertrude gave her the idea for Joe's special Christmas gift. On Tuesday night, when Judith went out to the toolshed to decorate her mother's tree, Gertrude was watching an old World War II movie.

"Look at our boys," Gertrude urged, poking Sweetums in the rump. "They're going to shoot the stuffing out of those Nazis! Off they go, into the wild blue yonder! Bang, bang, bang! Ack, ack, ack! Down in flames! Three cheers for the army air corps!"

Judith was standing by the door, trying not to get in Gertrude's line of sight with the TV. "Mother, where do you want your tree?"

"Right up Hitler's behind!" Gertrude cried, waving a fist at the screen. "On to Berlin! Get the little devil with his stupid bristle mustache! Yahoo!"

Judith edged into the room. A fir branch blocked the TV set. Gertrude howled. Judith grew impatient.

"Mother, it's after eight. I don't want to be decorating this thing at midnight. Where do you want it? In the corner next to the TV? By your chair?"

"I don't want it in front of our gallant fighting men," Gertrude retorted, leaning so far to the left that she almost squashed Sweetums. "Look, here they come, back to wherever they left from about five minutes ago. See that

237

clean-cut young fella with the big grin? He's going to get shot down in the next ten minutes. He dies every time I see this moving picture.''

In spite of herself, Judith's eyes veered to the TV screen. Sure enough, a handsome actor Judith didn't recognize was striding across an airfield that resembled the Warner Brothers back lot. Judith had to admit that he looked very dashing in his army air corps cap, leather jacket, and long white aviator's scarf.

"Yikes!" Judith cried, almost dropping the tree. "That's it!"

"No, it isn't," Gertrude snapped. "They've still got to pound those Nazi planes into the ground, get three more American boys killed, and figure out that they're a real team and not a bunch of flying cowboys. Oh, and kiss the blond girl who's waiting in a basement somewhere pushing little stick things around on a big map."

Judith wasn't listening. She had propped the tree up against the sofa and was trying to fit it into a small stand. "Between your chair and the TV," she said, trying to keep the excitement out of her voice. "We'll have to move the set a bit, but it'll work."

"I like my TV where it is," Gertrude grumbled, but she didn't put up a serious fight.

Judith began to set up the tree in earnest. Gertrude ignored her efforts, concentrating on the American destruction of the German Luftwaffe. Unfortunately, that was accomplished before Judith finished decorating. It also appeared that the Nazi defeat might have been achieved with less bloodshed than the battle of the toolshed.

"You've got two red lights together," Gertrude complained. "The bottom's all dark. Move 'em."

Judith did.

"The angel on top looks like she's drunk," Gertrude griped. "Fix her."

Judith complied.

"That big blue ball always goes in the middle," Gertrude grumbled. "Put it where that green bell is."

Judith obeyed.

An hour later, Judith was finished. Or so she thought. Gertrude was eyeing the tree with displeasure.

"It looks crummy," she said. "You've bunched everything up. I can't see any of the birds. They're all in back. Where's the Santa at the mailbox? There's money in that mailbox. Every year, I put in a couple of pennies. I'll bet there's sixty cents in there. Did you swipe the mailbox?"

"It's right here." Judith pointed to a stout branch almost at the bottom of the tree. Then she started indicating the half-dozen hand-blown birds with their silver tails. "There's your parrot, here's the cardinal, there's the . . ."

Sweetums leaped off the sofa and nailed the parrot. Judith grabbed the cat by the scruff of the neck and gave him a good shake. Miraculously, the glass ornament rolled onto the floor intact.

"It's nine-thirty," Judith announced. "I'm tired, you're impossible, and Sweetums is . . . a cat." She took a deep breath, observed Gertrude's sour expression, and hurried to the sofa. "I'm sorry. It's ten days until Christmas, I feel faintly frantic, and your tree actually looks wonderful. Admit it, Mother. You're pleased."

"What if I were?" Gertrude rasped. "What does that buy me? New legs? Better eyes? Real teeth?"

Judith sighed. "Of course not. It doesn't buy me anything, either. You can't 'buy' the stuff that counts." She leaned down and rested her cheek against the top of her mother's head. "We didn't 'buy' each other. But that's what we've got. It's okay with me." *Usually*, Judith thought, feeling Gertrude shake a bit.

After a long pause, one of Gertrude's gnarled hands crept up Judith's back. "Yeah, right, why not?" Her old voice was very thin. "It's okay with me, too, kiddo. What else can it be but okay?"

Judith would have been the last to argue.

Somewhere under the window seat in the living room was a J. Paulson catalog. It was buried with all the other mail-order Christmas books and brochures Judith had begun receiving in mid-August. Since Joe was upstairs in the third-floor family quarters, perhaps watching the same movies that entranced his mother-in-law, Judith took the opportunity to rummage through the storage area.

She found what she wanted on page eighty-six: a real leather World War II aviator's jacket, fully lined and complete with brass zippers. The price was three hundred and eighty-five dollars. For another forty-five, she could get the white silk twill scarf. Gritting her teeth, Judith dialed the 1-800 number. Joe would have his fantasy after all.

Except for the Luftwaffe. Even Judith's credit card couldn't buy him that.

Patches Morgan stopped at Hillside Manor the next morning around ten o'clock. He had the voucher for the completed work at the Goodrich house. Judith handed him the key. She also told him about the money under the rug.

Morgan didn't try to hide his astonishment. Staring at Judith from his good left eye, he clapped a hand to his head. "By the Great Hornspoon! What was the old boy doing, hoodwinking the IRS?"

"Oh, no," Judith replied, ushering Morgan into the living room. "He and Enid weren't earning any interest. I'm sure he reported his regular income. It's just that one of the Goodriches—or both—apparently didn't trust banks."

Morgan brushed at his wet raincoat. The rain had turned to sleet overnight as the wind blew down from the north. Settling onto the sofa, Morgan picked up the coffee mug that Judith had offered upon his arrival.

"Well, I'll be keelhauled!" Morgan was still evincing amazement. "How does that stash figure into this case, I wonder? Mr. Goodrich is still proclaiming his innocence." The detective winked with his good left eye. "I'm inclined to go along with him, as you've probably guessed."

"Well . . . yes," Judith said, avoiding the disconcerting single gaze. "If charges haven't been pressed by now, I have to assume you don't believe George killed Enid."

"We've questioned the grandsons, the son, the daughter, the daughter-in-law, even the daughter's boyfriend," Morgan said, now staring at the coffee table where the usual collection of books and magazines had been replaced by an alabaster Madonna and child encircled by holly. "Not to mention the neighbors, including yourself. Alibis, there's the thing. Everybody has one."

Judith blinked. "They do?"

Morgan nodded. "More or less. Those grandsons were both at work by eight o'clock. So was the young Ms. Goodrich, Glenda. We've checked with the phone company—Art Goodrich placed the calls when he said he did. He also insists his wife was home in bed. The granddaughter—Leigh?—had moved into the Cascadia Hotel the previous night. She called room service just before eight Wednesday morning. That leaves the neighbors."

Judith could guess where most of them were. "The Porters and Jeanne Ericson and Ham Stein had gone to work. Ted Ericson was buying a Christmas tree. Naomi Stein was doing errands; ditto Carl Rankers; Arlene was home; so were Mrs. Swanson—and me."

Patches Morgan's grin was off-center. "As well as your dear mother. So where does that leave us?"

Judith admitted that she didn't know. "By the way," she inquired, trying not to sound overly anxious, "did you positively identify the murder weapon as belonging to—who?"

With a hand at the knot of his wide purple-gold-and-black tie, Morgan regarded Judith with interest. "Did I say we identified it as belonging to someone?"

"No," Judith said in an agreeable manner, "that's why I asked. It must have come from somewhere." She lifted one shoulder in an exaggerated shrug.

"Mr. Goodrich had a woodpile. Mrs. Goodrich was killed with a hatchet. Now, what would you deduce, Ms. Flynn?" Morgan smiled slyly.

"Well . . . yes, of course. It's obvious, isn't it?" Judith smiled back. She sensed that her expression was more vapid than sly.

"Nothing's obvious," Morgan answered enigmatically.

It seemed to Judith that she and the detective were getting nowhere. She considered mentioning the poison book, but her hypothesis was too outlandish. George's ledger was another matter. Judith explained how she and Phyliss had found it under the mattress.

"There were entries for December first," she said. "There were also some notations in the margin."

It struck Judith that Morgan's interest was feigned. "So Mr. Goodrich was capable of working in the wee small hours. That would indicate the sleeping pills didn't take effect until later."

"That's right," Judith replied, hoping that the eagerness in her voice would spur Morgan. "I understand that Gary Meyers told you and Detective Rael that Mrs. Goodrich answered the door Wednesday morning around seven-thirty."

Morgan nodded. "Aye, so he did." The policeman waited expectantly.

"Did he also tell you and Rael that Mrs. Goodrich said Mr. Goodrich 'was sleeping his life away'?"

The good left eye roamed the ceiling. "Words to that effect. Are you implying that Mr. Goodrich was already drugged at seven-thirty?"

"I'd have to think so," Judith said. "You may not realize that Enid Goodrich never went to the door."

"Is that so?" Morgan's interest now seemed genuine. "Well, well." He stood up, the black raincoat unfurling like the sails of a ship. "We'll have to tend to that booty under the rug. It looks as if the younger Goodriches won't be able to put the house on the market quite yet."

It looked the same way to Judith.

Two days later, however, Art Goodrich appeared in the cul-de-sac with a dapper young man who was obviously a real estate agent. When the two pulled up in a late-model Lexus, Judith happened to be on the front porch, checking her ever-green swag for signs of dryness. Curbing her curiosity, she went inside to finish her household chores. Twenty minutes later, on the pretext of seeing if the rain had turned to snow, she was back on the porch.

Art was talking to the agent in front of the house. Judith still tried to restrain herself. But a moment later, Arlene was sprinting across the cul-de-sac. Judith couldn't help but follow.

Having gone to get her jacket, Judith was a minute late into the conversation. The agent had retreated inside the house again, but Arlene had collared Art.

"You should have called our daughter," Arlene was saying in a vexed voice. "Cathy's been with Peter Peach Realty for years."

Looking intimidated and defensive at the same time, Art had his back up against the agent's Lexus. "I forgot. Really. I still think of Cathy as a teenager."

"She's thirty-four," Arlene snapped. "Why can't you keep neighborhood business in the *neighborhood*? One thing I'll say for your parents—they were always good neighbors. As long as your mother stayed inside, of course."

With rain running off the end of his nose, Art now looked just plain miserable. "I'm sorry, Arlene. Like I said . . ."

But Arlene had turned away and was heading for the house. "Never mind. I'll talk to this interloper myself. He'd better make it a multiple listing." She glared at Art over her shoulder. "You won't even have a lookiloo this time of year. January fifth, that's when prospective buyers start thinking about moving again. Cathy says so. And she's always right. Except when she's wrong." Arlene stomped up the front stairs.

Art was holding his head. "Everything's a mess. Who'd want to buy a house where somebody was . . . murdered? It's all a nightmare. Now I can't even please the neighbors! Damn!"

"Don't worry about the neighbors," Judith soothed. "Come over to my place, Art. We'll have a cup of coffee while Arlene and your agent duke it out. Okay?"

Art seemed to have no will of his own. Like a lost lamb, he followed Judith to Hillside Manor. It was midafternoon on a dark, chilly Friday. In the kitchen, Judith decided to offer her guest a Tom and Jerry.

Art brightened. "I'm no drinker, but that sounds good. Thanks, Judith." He grew silent, sitting at the table while Judith heated the teakettle, set out mugs, removed the refrigerated Tom and Jerry batter, and got a bottle of rum from the shelf above the counter. "Where's this all going to end?" Art asked with a heavy sigh.

"Logically?" The word flew out of Judith's mouth. Indeed, she herself hadn't looked that far ahead. Waiting for the teakettle to boil, she sat down across the table from Art. "If your father's innocent, his future is up to him. Does he want to stay with you and JoAnne? Would he rather come home? Has he thought about a retirement place?"

Art looked askance at Judith. "He doesn't want to think about anything. Pappy's letting the rest of us make the decisions for him. It's like he doesn't care. The only thing that worries him is that he thinks he's losing his mind."

"But you found his money," Judith said quietly.

The statement jarred Art. "What? Oh—yes!" The hint of a smile played around his mouth. "*You* found it, I hear. That was a shock."

"So what happened to it?" Judith stood up as the teakettle whistled.

"JoAnne insisted we put it in the bank." Art was looking dazed, apparently still overcome by the discovery. "Pappy said Mama thought banks were dishonest. He knows better—but she always had to have her way. So JoAnne opened an account yesterday for Pappy. Did you know there was thirty-six thousand dollars under that rug?"

Judith laughed. "No. But I'm not surprised." She stirred the Tom and Jerry ingredients, then handed Art a steaming mug. "Did your father realize how much was there?"

"I don't think so." Art was looking downcast again. "I don't think he cares. He said Glenda and JoAnne and I could have it as far as he was concerned. Money doesn't mean anything to him."

"It will if he decides to go into a retirement home," Judith pointed out. She had sat down again, cradling her mug in both hands. "Art, what did you find in the desk after you pried it open Tuesday evening?"

If Art had been startled by Judith's question about the money, he now went completely still as the color drained from his face. "How . . . ?" He couldn't go beyond the single syllable.

Judith retained her matter-of-fact air. "It wasn't that hard to figure out—the part about the desk being pried open, I mean. The fresh marks were there, the steak knife that matched your parents' set was in the gutter by where you'd parked your car—and something was missing from the desk. It wasn't money or your father's account book, which were my earlier guesses. So what was it?" Judith's black eyes were fixed on Art's ashen face.

"Oh, Judith!" Art gripped the seat of the chair and swung away, his head down. "It was a book." The words were barely audible. "About poison." Art hesitated, then finally looked at Judith. "I think Pappy wanted to kill himself."

Judith nodded once. "I see. He was that unhappy?"

"Unhappy?" Art seemed to be savoring the word, as if it were an exotic delicacy. "He was never what you call happy. But lately . . . maybe around the time I lost my job . . . he seemed to go downhill. He says now that was when his memory began to slip. My problems affected him, I guess." Art laughed, a harsh, mirthless sound. "They sure never bothered Mama."

"She wouldn't lend you money." The statement was simply put.

Art nodded slowly, then drank from his mug. "She was tightfisted. Oh, hell, that's putting it mildly! She wouldn't have given us a dime if we were starving! And here was Christmas coming up, and I didn't have any money for presents . . . Poor JoAnne works her butt off at Falstaff's, and those boys of ours are always wanting something . . . I felt like such a dud. Isn't a man supposed to provide for his family?" Art seemed close to tears.

"You always have, until lately. That's not your fault." Judith tried to cheer Art with a compassionate smile. "I worked two jobs to support my family when I was married the first time.'' She didn't add that her efforts hadn't seemed to trouble Dan McMonigle. But the truth was, she didn't really know.

A touch of color returned to Art's drawn face. ''Anyway, it seemed to bother Pappy. But he couldn't offer help—Enid would have killed him.'' The irony of his words made Art grimace. ''You know what I mean. I knew there must have been money around the house because Mama hated banks. I thought it might be in the desk—why else lock it up? That Tuesday evening, Mama and Glenda and Pappy were in the bedroom. Mama was carrying on something fierce with Glenda about Leigh and Glenda's boyfriend, Gary. I couldn't stand listening to them, so I was going to leave. But then I thought about that desk and maybe there was money in it and Mama had told me I'd burn in hell before she'd loan me a lead nickel—well, I took the knife and forced the desk open. There wasn't any money, but there was this book right in the middle compartment, and it was all about poisons. I knew then that Pappy was going to commit suicide.'' Art raised a stricken face to Judith. ''I grabbed that book and ran out of the house and got into my car and drove away and pitched that god-damned book out into the street! Do you blame me?''

Judith was caught in midswallow. ''No,'' she said, putting her mug down on the table. ''Of course not. That's what I figured.''

At precisely noon on Saturday, it started to snow. Renie had just arrived at Hillside Manor, carrying a loaf of her mother's fruitcake wrapped in aluminum foil. She took one look out of the kitchen window and screamed.

''I can't drive in snow! I'll be killed! I'm out of here!'' And she was.

Smiling, Judith picked up Aunt Deb's fruitcake. Removing the foil, she sliced off a piece and popped it into her mouth. There were no nuts. It was delicious. Judith suddenly knew who had murdered Enid Goodrich.

*   *   *

Joe Flynn didn't give a hoot about his wife's theory. He was busy in the basement. If Judith wanted to drive to Art and JoAnne's house in the snow, that was up to her. He had things to do. Like with the wiring, he added unconvincingly.

"There's nothing wrong with our wiring," Judith protested from the head of the stairs. "It has to be up to city code because this is a B&B."

Joe didn't answer. Frustrated, Judith went out on the back porch. There was still rain mixed with the snow; the thermometer registered thirty-three degrees. Judith's Nissan had studded tires, but there were several steep streets between the B&B and the neighborhood above the railroad yard. Heraldsgate Avenue was the most treacherous thoroughfare of all. When it snowed on Heraldsgate Hill, residents who didn't have four-wheel drive were virtually marooned from the rest of the city. Judith was thwarted.

She was also upset. Maybe calling on the younger Goodriches was foolish. Perhaps she should talk to Glenda first. Or Mrs. Swanson. Judith went back indoors, still mulling things over as she made gingerbread cookies. When the last batch was done an hour later, the ground was covered in white.

Judith put on her jacket and went outside. The aroma of gingerbread followed her to the front porch. Noting that the New England village was dusted with snow, she went back to switch on the lights. The cluster of buildings and figures seemed to spring to life. Judith couldn't help but smile.

Exactly one week before Christmas, the cul-de-sac looked beautiful. And quiet. Even though it was a Saturday, no one seemed to be stirring. Perhaps some of the inhabitants were shopping. Judith felt the snow melt against her face as she walked toward Mrs. Swanson's house.

Nearing the driveway between the Goodrich and Ericson properties, Judith saw Ted's handsome sign with its season's greeting. On the parking strip was another sign, put up by the real estate agent. Judith slowed her step, feeling sad.

Amid the other neighbors' festive facades, the Goodrich house looked particularly poignant. The darkened windows seemed to stare out hopelessly at Judith. She picked up the pace; Mrs. Swanson's fairy lights drew her like a beacon on troubled seas.

At first, she didn't hear her name being called. Indeed, it was the footsteps padding softly in the snow that made her turn around. George Goodrich, wearing rubber boots, a heavy wool jacket, and a crumpled fisherman's hat was standing by the walkway to his house.

"George!" Judith cried in astonishment. "What are you doing out in this weather? Did you come all the way from Art and JoAnne's?"

George looked a little sheepish. "I did. It was so pretty out, I thought I'd take a walk. I ended up here." As Judith approached him, he nodded at the real estate sign. "Isn't that something? A month ago, who would've thought it?"

Up close, Judith tried to see if the idea disturbed George. But his wrinkled face was unreadable. In fact, it was virtually blank.

"Is that what you want?" Judith asked, pointing to the sign.

George gave a minimal shrug. "It's the right thing to do, isn't it?"

"I can't answer that." She took George by the arm. "Why don't you come over to our house and have something hot to drink? Two miles is a long walk."

George's tired eyes strayed to Hillside Manor. The snow was coming down so hard that only the amber lights of the village could be seen from the sidewalk.

"No, thank you, Judith." His attempt at a smile was pathetic. But as he turned toward his own house, he brightened almost imperceptibly. "Would you like to come in . . . here?"

Judith noted that he avoided referring to the house as his. No doubt he already felt dispossessed. But in retrospect, Judith realized that nothing had seemed to belong to George. It was Enid's house, Enid's garden, Enid's living room, Enid's furniture. George had lived at the same address for almost sixty years, but Judith guessed that after he married Enid, the house never felt like home.

"Sure," Judith said, still holding George's arm. "It's getting really cold. I'll come in for a few minutes." She paused as George led the way around to the back. "Have you been inside since . . . we cleaned?"

"I just was." He started up the porch steps, treading carefully. "Thank you for taking care of things, Judith. It was awfully kind."

Judith began to say that she and Phyliss had been paid for their efforts. Maybe George knew as much. If not, Judith would let him think they had done it out of kindness. It occurred to her that she would have, if she hadn't felt it necessary to secure police sanction.

George went straight to one of the kitchen cupboards. "I'm not sure what's on hand. Coffee, tea, maybe some juice in the refrigerator . . ."

"Don't bother," Judith said, sitting at the kitchen table. "Have a seat, George. You must be tired."

Woodenly, George obeyed. Judith was reminded of his son, also acting as if he'd lost his will.

"I am tired," he admitted. "I suppose I was foolish, walking clear over here in this snow. Now I'll have to figure out how to get back." Ironically, George didn't seem perturbed by the problem.

Judith, however, was perturbed by George. For a long moment, they sat in silence. The north wind was blowing hard and the snow was piling up outside on the kitchen windowsill. Judith watched the swirling flakes, then turned to George. He was watching Fred Astaire and Ginger Rogers, their small ceramic figures caught forever in an attitude of grace.

"George," Judith began, the unsteadiness of her voice surprising her, "why now?"

George had removed his fisherman's hat when he entered the house. He picked it off the table and wrung it in his hands. "Now?"

Judith nodded. "Over the years, there must have been a hundred occasions when Enid drove you to the breaking point. What finally put you over the edge? *Why now?*"

The question didn't seem to shock George. He placed the crumpled hat on one knee and picked up Ginger Rogers. "Enid wasn't the one who was supposed to die," he said, his voice surprisingly strong. "I was. I'd thought about it for a long time, especially after Art got laid off. But it wasn't right."

Judith nodded again, more slowly. "That's why you bought a book on poison?"

George raised his white eyebrows. "You knew about that? Did you take it?"

"No, of course not. Art did. He was afraid for you."

"Ah!" George seemed both relieved and somehow pleased. "I wondered. It was gone when I looked for it that morning." With almost reverent fingers, he turned Ginger Rogers upside down.

"What was wrong about killing yourself, George?" Judith asked quietly. "The morality of it?"

"Oh, certainly. Suicide's a terrible thing. It's so selfish. But that wasn't all. I may not be much of a man, but I always tried to serve as a buffer." He righted Ginger, set her on the table, and moved Fred to stand in front of her. "If I died and Enid lived on she would only have made life even more miserable for the rest of the family." Apologetically, George gazed at Judith. "Am I making sense?"

"You always did." Judith smiled feebly. "That's why I had trouble believing that your mind was going. You couldn't have worked on those accounts if you were muddled or forgetful."

A hint of pride shone in George's eyes. "I kept my hand in. They trusted me at Pacific Meats, for almost fifty years. I wish I could say the same for my grandson."

"Dave?" Judith had seen George's sense of pride replaced by chagrin. But this wasn't the time or place to discuss Dave and Greg's scam. It was sufficient to acknowledge that George apparently had caught some discrepancies. "I still wonder what set you off, George. After Enid died, everybody marveled that you hadn't . . . acted sooner."

Another silence filled the kitchen. At last, George stood up and walked to the window. "You and your husband asked us to put up those decorations. It was a nice idea, I thought. But Enid didn't agree—as usual. She turned you down. That bothered me—I always tried to be a good neighbor. Oh, I did my best to make her change her mind, but she was impossible. She always was.''

He stopped speaking, then turned to beckon Judith. ''Look out here. You can't see much with all this snow, I'm afraid.''

Judith joined George at the window. He was right: She couldn't see any further than the driveway. Their footprints were already obliterated.

''I'd worked late that night, trying to go over the November figures, which they'd just sent me Tuesday afternoon. It was the thirtieth, you see. I don't think I went to sleep until after four. Usually, I'm up by seven, to fix Enid's breakfast and dispense her medicine by eight. But I must have been awfully tired. Tuesday night had been very upsetting, what with Enid and Glenda fighting, and both Art and Greg asking for money. As a matter of fact, I dropped off right after nine-thirty, when we usually went to bed. But then Greg came back and let himself in—I suppose his mother told him where to find the extra key—and the noise disturbed Enid. I don't know what he wanted—looking for money, I suppose. Anyway, Enid scared him off. That woke me, and then I laid awake for a long time until I decided I might as well use the time to do the books.'' He stopped, staring out into the world of white.

''So I slept in.'' The statement sounded like the toll of doom. Which, Judith realized, it was. ''In the morning, somebody came to the door—Enid later told me it was Gary Meyers. But she couldn't rouse me then, so she went to answer it. Except for Art, it's unusual to have anyone call that early. After she got rid of Gary, she made sure I woke up. Enid was furious. I needn't go into it. I dressed and got her medicine and was going to start breakfast when I saw Ted Ericson pull into the driveway.'' George pointed through the window. ''He took a tree out of his car. Now Ted's no handyman, and I knew he didn't have any tools to speak of, so I thought I'd offer him Mrs. Swanson's hatchet to take a two-inch cut off the trunk. I'd borrowed the hatchet again the day before to split some kindling. I put on my jacket and gloves before I went outside to get the hatchet. By then, Ted was driving away. I hurried down the driveway to stop him, but he didn't see me.'' George's voice began to drag. ''Even in the morning, the rest of the cul-de-sac looked so pretty. All of a sudden, I had this strange feeling, the one you get when you're a little kid and you still believe in Santa Claus and being happy and everything in the world is wonderful . . . I'd forgotten what that was like.

''And then I saw the Ericsons' tree. It was beautiful. It was fresh and green and fragrant. It was the perfect Noble fir.''

George lifted his chin, the haunted eyes still gazing into the snow-covered driveway. ''I went back into the house. With the hatchet.''

He turned away from Judith and walked into the living room.

NINETEEN

ONE OF JUDITH'S favorite Christmas traditions was lunching with Renie at Papaya Pete's. The holiday decor never quite worked among the tiki gods and coral reefs, but the food was always wonderful. The cousins sipped their beverages of choice as Bing Crosby sang on a background tape about Christmas in Hawaii.

"Admit it, coz," Renie chided over her bourbon. "You were wrong. Excuse the expression, but you were dead wrong."

Judith winced. "Okay, okay. Still, I finally got it right. I never took into account George's . . . wiliness. But he had to have some survival skills or he would have killed Enid forty years ago."

It was Wednesday, the twenty-second of December. The snow had fallen through Sunday, but a warming trend had set in Monday afternoon. Rain had returned. By Tuesday, the snow was almost gone, though there was more in the forecast for the Christmas weekend. Judith had mixed emotions about the weather: Mike and Kristin were due at four in the afternoon. They would have no trouble driving from the eastern part of the state, where Mike was meeting his longtime girlfriend on his way from Idaho. But the following day, Herself was scheduled to land at the airport. Judith would have wished for a blizzard—except that Caitlin was also coming in from Switzerland.

"So George confessed," Renie remarked, digging into the rich dark bread that had been brought along with the drinks. "Why, I wonder."

Judith's expression was rueful. "He didn't want to cause trouble. I haven't had a chance to tell you, but I got a Christmas card from him in the mail just before we left for lunch. It was a beautiful card, showing a lovely home all decorated for Christmas, and it said, 'neighbor to neighbor' on the front. I should have brought it with me. Inside, George had written, 'Thank you, Judith, for understanding. Wherever I go, I'll finally be free.'" Judith's eyes misted over.

"Jeez." Renie gulped at her bourbon. "Where *will* he go?"

Regaining control, Judith shrugged. "At his age, maybe a mental hospital. But, of course, he's as sane as we are."

Renie cocked her head to one side. "Is he? Why did he take the Dalmane, confess, and then deny he did it? That sounds daffy to me."

"Not really. George panicked. Imagine the scene." She saw Renie blanch. "Okay, don't imagine it. He'd killed his wife in a horrible manner. Then he ran into the living room to get the poison book—that's how those needles got tracked all over the house. Apparently, George only got blood on his shirt, so there were no traces anywhere outside the bedroom. Once he reached the living room, he discovered the book was gone. Without it, George couldn't be sure of the dosage. He didn't intend to kill himself. But he had to guess how many pills would merely knock him out. So he swigged down some sleeping pills with his antacid, then took the glass outside, broke it, and threw it in the garbage."

Renie didn't respond until after the waiter had delivered their salads. "Why break the glass?"

Judith set her scotch aside and picked up a fork. "It was typically George. His first thought was for the rest of the family. They'd suffer badly if their father was a murderer. He wanted to make it look as if a third party had tried to kill both of them and wanted to get rid of some of the evidence. In fact, what George did was set up a frame—for himself.''

Renie stared. "You mean he made it look as if somebody else had set him up to do exactly what he actually did? But who?"

Judith made a helpless gesture with her free hand. "I don't know. I don't think he knew. Anybody, as long as it wasn't family. Or Mrs. Swanson. A robber, maybe, though robbers don't usually poison their victims. But George wasn't thinking clearly at this point. Everything happened very fast, in that brief span of time after Ted went back up to the top of the Hill and before Art started calling his parents."

Renie was applying extra salt and pepper to her fresh Bibb lettuce. "So why did he confess?"

"George hadn't considered his reaction to Dalmane," Judith said with a wry expression. "It can cause hallucinations, but mostly it triggers confusion. In George's case, it made him blurt out the truth. Think of the shock to his system. He'd obviously taken more than he meant to. When his brain began to clear, he had to retract his confession and play the part he'd concocted earlier."

Stuffing salad in her mouth, Renie shook her head. "Wild. And he almost got away with it because everybody thought he was nuts."

Judith smiled at Renie. "I thought so, too—at first. That was the problem—I didn't want to believe George was the killer, yet the more I considered the man himself, the more I realized he wasn't nutty at all. He was like your mother's fruitcake—it's still fruitcake, but there aren't any nuts."

Renie rolled her eyes. "*You're* nuts. What did he mean when he said 'key' at the hospital? Are you sure he wasn't saying 'kiwi' just to throw everybody off the track?"

"George's brain was still a little foggy," Judith replied, unperturbed by Renie's incredulity. "I honestly don't know what he said. Maybe it was 'tree.' The Ericsons' tree set him off that morning. But 'key' stuck in my mind anyway. I kept saying that Gary Meyers was the key to the mystery, which he was. He saw Enid alive at seven-thirty. No one else was seen coming to their house after that. Oh, it was possible, but unlikely, given that everybody else had an alibi. Except Mrs. Swanson.''

"Who wouldn't smack a bug," Renie put in. "What about those grandsons and their larcenous ways?''

Judith used a piece of bread to soak up the last drops of tangy salad dressing. "Gabe Porter alerted United Foods' meat manager. No doubt they're passing the word on to Pacific Meats. George had already questioned some of the November entries. Greg may have come back to the house that night to get money, but I think Dave wanted the ledger. He knew his grandfather would find the discrepancies. Of course, Dave never got in the house, because his brother had taken the key and dropped it after Enid frightened him away.''

The salad plates were removed. In keeping with tradition, the cousins ordered a second round of drinks.

"Why did those two need so much money?" Renie asked, though she knew that Judith hadn't figured it out. "I'm guessing it was gambling. It suits their so-called mentality—always looking for the big score, never accepting that their luck can't change.''

"Could be," Judith allowed. "As a family, the Goodriches are a disaster. Maybe Glenda will take Gary back. Art and JoAnne probably will get some of the money from George to tide them over. Leigh always stuck up for her father, and now she's stuck with him.''

"Art may find another job," Renie pointed out. "That would be the best thing for him.''

"True." Judith smiled at the waiter as he brought their fresh drinks. "Remember how I thought Art might have killed Enid because she had destroyed George? I realize that works both ways—George saw Art turning into himself—that is, his father. Art was becoming downtrodden, defeated, ineffectual. I'm convinced that preyed on George's mind.''

Apparently, Renie agreed. At least she didn't argue as the cousins sipped their drinks in companionable silence. The restaurant was busy. It looked as if several large tables were hosting office parties. Barbra Streisand's voice on the background tape was almost drowned out by the cheerful din.

"Speaking of screwed-up relatives," Renie said at last, "how are you and Joe coping with Herself's imminent arrival?"

Judith gazed up at a cluster of glass balls held in place by fishnet. "Okay, I think. I keep trying not to dwell on it. It's easy, because there's so much else to do. I just wish she weren't coming—for Joe's sake. Let's face it: He doesn't have the Christmas spirit. Not like you and I do, anyway."

Renie shrugged off Judith's words. "I told you, that's okay. Nobody gets graded on Christmas spirit. Sometimes I think Bill's greatest Christmas gift is that he lets me do all the crazy things I go through every December. That's real generosity."

Judith looked up from her drink. "You have a point. And I can't begrudge Herself visiting us. Joe—and Bill—have to put up with our goofy relatives for all the holidays."

"So do we." Renie grimaced. "But you're right. Some of the best presents don't come in boxes."

Judith lifted her glass. "Amen. Here's to you, coz. You've been a favorite gift for over fifty years."

Renie touched Judith's glass with hers. "Ditto, coz. Merry Christmas. Where's our food?"

Renie was never one for sentiment. But Judith didn't doubt her cousin's feelings. Both women took a long sip, and smiled.

It had stopped raining by the time Judith returned home at two-thirty. Since a UPS truck was parked in the middle of the cul-de-sac, Renie let Judith out at the corner. The big blue Chev had just driven off when Mrs. Swanson called to Judith from her front porch.

"I feel very sad," Mrs. Swanson said as Judith joined her on the walkway. "Poor Mr. Goodrich. I'd so hoped it wasn't true."

Judith smiled kindly at the older woman. "He doesn't seem to mind as much as you'd think," she said. The words were inadequate, but there wasn't much else to say.

"Wherever he goes, I'll visit him," Mrs. Swanson declared. "I shall certainly miss having him next door. Despite the terrible thing he did, I believe Mr. Goodrich is a fine, decent man.''

Judith agreed. ''You've been a good friend to him,'' she added.

A tiny smile touched Mrs. Swanson's lips. ''I hope so. I even lied for him. Can you forgive me?''

Judith, who had been known to tell a few fibs in her time, laughed lightly. ''About the hatchet? Don't worry—I admire your loyalty. I'm sure George does, too.''

''Yes. Perhaps.'' Mrs. Swanson shivered. It was getting colder, and she wore only a lambswool sweater over her housedress. ''I'd like to see a young family move in next door. A *happy* family,'' she added, ''like my son's. I leave for Portland tonight to visit them for Christmas.''

''How nice,'' Judith said with enthusiasm, as the UPS truck drove off. ''We'll keep an eye on your house for you.''

Mrs. Swanson's smile bloomed fully. ''Thank you, my dear. It does make me nervous when there are two vacant houses in a row for several days. Except,'' she continued, turning toward the Goodrich residence, ''who did that?''

''Did what?'' Puzzled, Judith also turned.

Ted Ericson's holiday sign was still in place, as was the one put up by the realtor. But the dogwood tree and the shrubs twinkled with green-and-gold lights. So did the front porch and the eaves. Judith gasped.

''I've no idea,'' she said in amazement. ''It looks . . . lovely. Did you see anybody around? Art or JoAnne or Glenda, maybe?''

''No. I've been packing. I only noticed the lights a few minutes ago. That's how I happened to be on the porch when you came by.'' Mrs. Swanson looked as mystified as Judith felt.

''Whoever did it has nice taste,'' Judith said. ''It makes the whole cul-de-sac come alive.'' Noting that Mrs. Swanson was now shivering in earnest, she put a hand on the older woman's arm. ''Get inside. It may snow again. Have a wonderful trip, and a merry Christmas.''

After Mrs. Swanson went up her front steps, Judith walked

down the sidewalk to admire the Goodrich decor up close.

"Cool, huh?" said Dooley, who had seemingly materialized from out of nowhere but probably had vaulted the fence and come down Hillside Manor's driveway. "Did you do that?"

Judith shook her head. "I've no idea who did it. I'm stumped."

Dooley admired the lights, then gave Judith a sidelong, almost diffident glance. "We were wrong, huh? About Mr. Goodrich, I mean. But then you were right. You're pretty sharp at figuring this stuff out, Mrs. Flynn."

"Sometimes," Judith allowed. Her gaze shifted to the Ericson house. "I can't figure everything out, though." She recalled Jeanne's odd change of mind about the invitation to view their tree. "People are often unfathomable."

"I guess. But this is the time of year that they act odd. Secrets and stuff. You know. Everybody likes to be a little kid again." Dooley had taken on an air of kindly condescension.

"That's true," Judith said. "I think it's nice."

"I guess." Dooley shrugged, then turned to gaze in the direction of the Porter house. "Maybe I'll see if Gaby's home." He yawned in an exaggerated manner. "See you, Mrs. Flynn." His long legs were suddenly in gear as he all but flew across the cul-de-sac.

Smiling at the romance of youth, Judith approached Hillside Manor. Joe's MG was parked in the driveway. It was a Wednesday afternoon, and Joe was almost never home early on weekdays. Fearing that he might have fallen ill, she hurried into the house through the front door.

Joe was sitting at the kitchen table, drinking a glass of sparkling cider and reading a Western novel.

"Oh!" she exclaimed. "You're all right! How come you're home?"

Joe raised his head to accept Judith's kiss. "Woody and I closed the Shazri case this morning. We got the rest of the day off. I must have come home right after you and Renie went to lunch."

Judith collapsed into a chair across the table from Joe. "Wonderful! Congratulations! Whodunit?"

Joe grinned. "It's the damnedest thing—Woody and I'd begun to think it was the brother. At least that he was the one who hired the hit man. But after we sifted through the evidence about a hundred times, we realized there was someone else involved. In fact, *I* realized it—thanks to Arlene Rankers."

"Huh?" Judith looked stumped.

"Sure," Joe replied cheerfully. "It was the carpet cleaners."

Joe's explanation was so complicated that Judith took in only about half of it. Now that she was home, the two drinks and the heavy meal had made her brain fuzzy. She listened, she commented, she nodded and smiled. But when her husband was done, she had a different question for him.

"Are Morgan and Rael getting kudos for solving their case?"

Joe smoothed the graying red hair back from his temples. "Well—I suppose. I've been too wrapped up in the Shazri thing to notice. Morgan's a smart cop, and Rael seems like a real comer."

"She's certainly beautiful," Judith remarked, hoping to sound objective.

Joe was at the refrigerator, replenishing his cider. "Want some?" he asked. Judith shook her head. "What about Rael? Oh—right, she's not bad looking. It's Morgan's appearance that puts suspects off. For one thing, he confuses them."

Sensing that Joe's indifferent reaction to Sancha Rael's charms was genuine, Judith smiled. "All that corny pirate talk and those flamboyant clothes? Yes, I can see where he'd unsettle some people."

Joe sat down again at the table. "Not that. You don't rattle hardened killers with flowing crimson ties and a yo-ho-ho. I'm talking about the eye patch."

"The eye patch?" Judith frowned. "How odd. The only thing I wondered was how the department allows Morgan to stay on the job. Having only one eye must be a detriment in his line of work."

Joe choked on his cider. "You're kidding, right?"

Judith's frown deepened. "No. It's kind of a handicap, isn't it?"

Throwing his head back, Joe roared with laughter. "Jude-girl! I can't believe it! I thought you were the most observant person on earth!"

"What are you talking about?" Judith snapped.

Joe rested his elbows on the table and leaned closer to his wife. "The eye patch. Morgan has two perfectly good eyes. The patch is flimflam. That's why suspects under interrogation get rattled. They start to disbelieve themselves, which makes it hard to lie. Didn't you notice that Morgan switches the patch back and forth, from one eye to the other?"

Judith twisted in the chair, squealing with disbelief. "No! Oh, good grief! I feel like an idiot!"

"You had your mind on other things," Joe said calmly. "Like solving a murder and running the B&B and expecting family visitors and getting ready for Christmas."

Still feeling chagrined, Judith got out of the chair. "I'd better change clothes. Mike and Kristin will be here in a little over an hour. I hope. I put all their presents under the tree this morning."

Judith started for the back stairs, but the Christmas tree reminded her of the new decorations in the cul-de-sac. She turned at the kitchen door. "Say—have you seen those lights over at the Goodrich house?" Judith didn't wait for a response. "They're lovely, and they add just the right touch to finish off the cul-de-sac. I could kiss whoever did that!"

Rising from the table, Joe stretched his arms wide and puckered up. Judith let out an incredulous little yip, flew across the kitchen, and fell against her husband. Suddenly, it felt a lot like Christmas.

In a way, it seemed impossible that Judith had never met Herself. Over the years, she had heard the stories of Vivian Flynn's daring dresses, her smoky voice, her three husbands, and her love affair with Jack Daniel's. In Judith's mind, Vivian had become a cliché for every whiskey soprano in thick makeup and a plunging neckline. Judith also knew that her former rival was approximately twelve years older than Joe, but the fact didn't really register. Thus, Judith wasn't prepared for the real woman, who was pushing seventy and used a cane.

But in many ways, Herself lived up to her reputation. The bouffant hair was dyed platinum blond, the figure was still voluptuous, and her style of clothes lived up to her reputation. Vivian had arrived at the airport wearing a mink coat over cashmere slacks and sweater, with a white turban wound around her head and huge sunglasses firmly in place. For Christmas Eve, she had chosen crimson satin, clinging to every curve. Judith frankly marveled at Herself's figure.

So did Renie. "Not bad for a lush, huh?" said Renie as the cousins dished up the buffet offerings in the kitchen. "Bill's tie is on fire. Where'd she get that mink coat?"

"Not where—how," Judith replied, tossing a green salad.

"At her age?" Renie looked dubious, then reconsidered. "Okay, she wouldn't need to be mobile or sober. How are she and Caitlin getting along?"

"Not bad." Judith lined up three separate bowls of salad dressing. "Caitlin's very sweet. No," Judith contradicted herself, "not *sweet*. Honest and sensible and genuine. Smart, too. I like her very much."

The cousins trotted out their various dishes to the dining room and placed them on the long oval table. In the living room, a hubbub of voices could be heard: Bill and Uncle Al were arguing about the upcoming bowl games; Aunt Deb was relating a recent atrocity committed by her neighbor's poodle to Uncle Vince; Uncle Vince was snoring in the green recliner while Sweetums clawed holes in his cardigan sweater; Mike's girlfriend, Kristin, was explaining to Anne Jones why shopping for clothes was irrelevant and definitely not the spiritual experience that Bill and Renie's daughter claimed; Auntie Vance and Gertrude were wrangling over something that ended when Auntie Vance called Gertrude "goat-breath" and Gertrude dumped the rest of her eggnog on Auntie Vance's shoes. It was a typical Grover holiday gathering.

Almost. Back in the kitchen, Renie grabbed a pair of pot

holders and opened the oven to remove the chicken lasagna she'd made at home. "I love your idea of reinstating the hidden Christmas tree and having Santa come. It takes me back to my youth, which is getting to be quite a trip. What time is Carl Rankers due to play Santa?"

"Seven-fifteen," Judith replied. A glance at the schoolhouse clock told her it was now shortly after six. "We have plenty of time to eat. I gave Carl a list of the family names so he could call on everybody from behind the curtain. Do you think it's too crowded with that half of the living room shut off?"

"It's fine," Renie replied. "There'd be more room for people to sit down if Herself wasn't sprawled out on the sofa like Madame Récamier."

"Did Madame Récamier drink?" Judith asked, then bit her lip. "Sorry. I'm trying to think good thoughts. The best one is that Herself will be gone in five days."

In five minutes, the buffet was ready. Already late with his meal schedule, Bill Jones was first in line, managing to out-maneuver three of the Grover shirttail relations. His sons were pushing their grandmother in her wheelchair. Gertrude used her walker to shove Sweetums directly into their path.

"My cat!" she yelled. "You're going to kill my cat! Watch it, you morons!"

"Run right over the damned thing!" Auntie Vance urged. "I hate cats! They're the dumbest animals God ever made! With one exception." Her sturdy figure turned. "Vince! Wake up! We're eating! You can go back to sleep when you get to Gertrude's potato salad!"

Judith checked the table to make sure that she and Renie hadn't forgotten anything. Then she glanced into the living room. The dark blue flannel sheets were still securely in place, despite the best efforts of Cousin Sue's small grandchildren to dislodge them. Judith was pleased by the effect, with the far end of the room shrouded in mysterious darkness. The floor under and around the tree was literally covered with presents. For Judith, the most mysterious of all were the big blue-and-silver boxes with her own name on them. They had suddenly appeared just before the relatives started arriving. The tags were written in Joe's handwriting.

It had taken Judith a few minutes to solve the nagging little mystery: The UPS delivery Arlene had seen at the Ericsons' the day before the murder; Jeanne's odd reaction to inviting Judith into their house the following week; Joe's Saturday afternoon in the basement, allegedly working on the wiring—everything came together in logical order. Joe had bought her a computer system for Christmas. She was excited, not in the unbridled, greedy way of childhood, but with a deeper feeling, of appreciation for her husband's desire to please her, just as she hoped to fulfill his dreams with the leather flight jacket.

Judith smiled fondly at Cousin Sue's grandchildren. The girl was almost three, dancing around the room with anticipation. The boy wasn't quite a year, on the verge of walking, and though he lacked understanding, he was charged with contagious excitement. Someday, perhaps, Judith would have grandchildren of her own. Her gaze roamed to Mike, tall, broad-shouldered, honed to manhood by his work as a park ranger. He stood at the end of the buffet line with Kristin. She was almost as tall he was, a blond Viking goddess of a young woman who loved the outdoors as much as Mike did. After more than four years together, they seemed to love each other. Maybe an official engagement was nigh. The fond looks they exchanged indicated that it was due, even overdue, in Judith's opinion.

On one of the matching sofas, Herself still reclined. She was looking up at Joe and making gestures with her fingers. Judith tried to behave in a casual manner as she crossed the room to join them.

Herself transferred her seductive smile to Judith. "Joe's going to get me a plate. He says you're the most marvelous cook. I was telling him not to let me gorge. If I eat too much, I'll simply explode out of this dress!" Vivian Flynn laughed in her husky manner, then gave Joe a little pat on the arm. "Run along. You need to get your food, too. A man has to keep up his . . . strength." The false eyelashes fluttered alluringly.

Joe obeyed. Judith perched on the arm of the sofa. As far

as she could tell, Herself was relatively sober. The highball glass on the coffee table was still more than half-filled with bourbon.

"You must find this rain depressing after living in Florida," Judith said, seeking refuge in talking about the weather. "Of course it's supposed to snow tonight and get very cold. I just hope it holds off until everybody drives home safely. The forecast could be wrong—snow's been predicted for the last few days. But this afternoon, my mother said she could feel it in her bones." Judith suddenly stopped, aware that she was running on like a river.

"I like the rain," Herself said. "I lived here for many years, as you may recall." She flicked her tongue over her scarlet upper lip. "Florida is getting too crowded. And there's so much crime. Sunshine isn't important if you don't get outside much." One hand with its long acrylic nails tripped across the back of the sofa.

"I've never been to Florida," Judith said, suddenly at a loss for words.

"Much of it is lovely," Herself said, tucking a stray tendril of platinum hair behind her ear. "I'm right on the beach, but most of the people who live nearby are so *old*. They look old; they act old; they talk all the time about being old. That's very bad for them."

Judith nodded, a bit uncertainly. "I guess that's why they're . . . old."

"Who's old?" Bill Jones asked as he set his plate down on the coffee table and seated himself on the matching sofa.

"Oh—" Judith replied vaguely. "People. In Florida."

Bill nodded. "It's a retirement mecca, not only for Americans but Canadians, too. Most of them come from big eastern cities, such as New York, Washington, Boston, Toronto. It's an interesting mix, psychologically speaking. Throw in the exiled Cubans and Haitians, not to mention the existing natives, which include African Americans, Caucasians, and what's left of the Seminoles, and what you have is a . . ."

" 'For Sale' sign in your front yard," Renie interrupted, sitting beside her husband. "Tell me this, Professor Jones, what kind of psychological profile would you draw on somebody who'd buy the Goodrich house?''

Bill never answered questions impulsively. He thoughtfully chewed on a marinated chicken wing before giving his answer. ''It's not psychology so much as economics. That house is going to be very hard to sell. There's a law requiring the agent to disclose the fact that a capital crime has occurred on the property. Naturally, the price becomes negotiable because the Goodrich family will have to lower it under market value.''

Seeing Joe approaching with Herself's plate, Judith got off the arm of the sofa. ''You mean somebody will get a bargain on Heraldsgate Hill? That doesn't happen very often. Prices up here are sky-high.''

''True,'' Bill agreed, ''but this is one of those rarities. All the same, I wouldn't expect that house to sell for a long time.''

Joe delivered his ex-wife's plate. She gushed; she cooed; she thrust her bust every which way. Joe started back to get his own meal, then stopped and turned to look at Bill.

''You're right,'' Joe said. ''But maybe somebody will buy it as an investment.''

''A rental?'' Judith cringed. ''I hope not. Mrs. Swanson wouldn't like that. I'm not sure I would, either.''

Renie made a face. ''Joe has a point. Who else would be crazy enough to buy that house and live in it?''

Herself raised her highball glass. The deep blue eyes slid from Renie to Joe to Bill and finally to Judith. Her scarlet mouth tilted upward in a provocative smile. ''I would. The 'sold' sign goes up Monday.'' She put the glass to her lips. ''Merry Christmas.''

Murder Is on the Menu at the Hillside Manor Inn

Bed-and-Breakfast Mysteries by

MARY DAHEIM

featuring Judith McMonigle

⮬JILL CHURCHILL⮮
"JANE JEFFREY IS IRRESISTIBLE!"
Alfred Hitchcock's Mystery Magazine

Delightful Mysteries Featuring
Suburban Mom Jane Jeffry

GRIME AND PUNISHMENT
76400-8/$5.99 US/$7.99 CAN

A FAREWELL TO YARNS
76399-0/$5.99 US/$7.99 CAN

A QUICHE BEFORE DYING
76932-8/$5.50 US/$7.50 CAN

THE CLASS MENAGERIE
77380-5/$5.99 US/$7.99 CAN

A KNIFE TO REMEMBER
77381-3/$5.99 US/$7.99 CAN

FROM HERE TO PATERNITY
77715-0/$5.99 US/$7.99 CAN

SILENCE OF THE HAMS
77716-9/$5.99 US/$7.99 CAN

WAR AND PEAS
78706-7/$5.99 US/$7.99 CAN